praise for Joe Gores and his classic
CASES

"This picaresque and surprisingly suspenseful sort-of-mystery seems, for much of its always-enjoyable length, to be entirely episodic...but then Gores ties many of the incidents together in ways that make sense not just metaphorically but concretely....An expertly detailed look at some of what was nastiest in American life in the early '50s."

—*Washington Post Book World*

"Mr. Gores writes some of the hardest, smoothest, most lucid prose in the field."

—*New York Times Book Review*

"A mystery wrapped in a reminiscence...evocative of another age but as immediate as today....Gores is a top-notch writer."

—*Rocky Mountain News*

"Evocative prose....Nasty characters...tied together by an inventive, recurring situation."

—*Chicago Tribune*

"A three-time Edgar winner famous for giving his readers their money's worth, Gores scores again....Flamboyant coming-of-age scenes involving murder, betrayal, and even a dab or two of tenderness."

—*Philadelphia Inquirer*

"Gores writes beautifully, with never a wasted word and with a fine feeling for characterization. He handles violence as a wise man handles nettles."

—*New York Times*

"A thought-provoking, satisfying story."
—*Cleveland Plain Dealer*

"A tough, taut writer who views his subject matter unsparingly and unsentimentally."
—*Washington Post*

"As entertaining as it is thought provoking...far more compelling than most detective stories, for it gives the reader a very real glimpse of the making of the cynical and hardened persona of the detective himself."
—*Rapport*

"The private-eye procedural is Gores's specialty, maybe his invention."
—*San Francisco Chronicle*

"Rich in atmospheric pleasures and sharp sketches...Gores is a master of noir fiction, an exuberant practitioner of staccato prose deepened by occasional moral reflection."
—*Publishers Weekly*

"One of the very few authentic private eyes to enter the field of fiction since Dashiell Hammett."
—Anthony Boucher

"A fast-paced raunchy yarn glowing with nostalgia for the days when the guys were armed, edgy, and dangerous and the molls were beautiful, insatiable, greedy, and equally dangerous in their own way."
—*Library Journal*

"If you want to know in today's terms what a Hammett yarn was like, read Gores."
—*Mystery Magazine*

"A master."

—*Chicago Sun-Times*

"A paean to another time, another place, people with wistful, wishful blondes, hot music, and written with perhaps an unconscious salute to both Hemingway and Hammett."

—*Hartford Courant*

"Not since Hammett and Chandler has anyone written quite as well as Joe Gores."

—Ross Thomas

"CASES is a gracefully textured voyage of a young man....It's an intriguing concept—part autobiography, part real-life work experience, part fiction from another era."

—*Northern California's Complete Literary Guide*

"Awash in vivid detail...a picaresque adventure morphed into a pulpy detective story."

—*Booklist*

"A bold and complicated mixture of forms....A lean, hard-boiled style."

—*London Free Press* (Ontario, Canada)

"If it's excitement you want, CASES has it in megadoses. And though it may not seem that way, Joe Gores has mysteries hidden away here, mysteries that don't become apparent until near the end of CASES, and aren't resolved until its final pages."

—*I Love a Mystery*

BY JOE GORES

NOVELS
A Time of Predators
Interface
Hammett
Come Morning
Wolf Time
Dead Man
Menaced Assassin
Cases

DKA FILE NOVELS
Dead Skip
Final Notice
Gone, No Forwarding
32 Cadillacs
Contract Null & Void
Cons, Scams and Grifts

NONFICTION
Marine Salvage

COLLECTIONS
Mostly Murder

ANTHOLOGIES
Honolulu, Port of Call
Tricks and Treats
(with Bill Pronzini)

SCREENPLAYS
Interface
Hammett
Paper Crimes
Paradise Road
Fallen Angel
Cover Story
(with Kevin Wade)
Come Morning
Run Cunning
Gangbusters
32 Cadillacs

TELEPLAYS
Golden Gate Memorial
(miniseries)
High Risk
(with Brian Garfield)
"Blind Chess" (B.L. Stryker)

EPISODIC TV

Kojak
Eischied
Kate Loves a Mystery
The Gangster Chronicles
Strike Force
Magnum, P.I.

Remington Steele
Scene of the Crime
Eye to Eye
Helltown
T.J. Hooker
Mike Hammer

CASES

JOE GORES

Published by Warner Books

A Time Warner Company

Copyright ©1999 by Joe Gores
All rights reserved.

 Mysterious Press books are published by Warner Books, Inc., 1271 Avenue of the Americas, New York, NY 10020

Visit our Web site at www.twbookmark.com.
For information on Time Warner Trade Publishing's online publishing program, visit www.ipublish.com.

 A Time Warner Company

The Mysterious Press name and logo are registered trademarks of Warner Books, Inc.

Printed in the United States of America
Originally published in hardcover by Warner Books, Inc.
First Trade Printing: August 2001

10 9 8 7 6 5 4 3 2 1

The Library of Congress has cataloged the hardcover edition as follows:
    Gores, Joe
        Cases / Joe Gores.
            p.   cm.
        ISBN 0-89296-593-2
        I. Title.
        PS3557.075C37   1999
        813'.54—dc21   98-22542
                                                                  CIP

ISBN 0-446-67793-0 (pbk.)

Cover design and illustration by Daniel Pelavin

For
DORI

The Wind Beneath My Wings

And in memory of

The sunshine and shadow
of these early years

If they weren't exactly as I remember them
they should have been

In going where you have to go, and doing what you have to do, and seeing what you have to see, you dull and blunt the instrument you write with. But I would rather have it bent and dulled and know I had to put it on the grindstone again and hammer it into shape and put a whetstone to it, and know I had something to write about, than to have it bright and shining and nothing to say.

—Ernest Hemingway

And what have you got,
At the end of the day?
What have you got,
To take away?

A bottle of whiskey,
And a new set of lies,
Blinds on the window,
And a pain behind your eyes.

—Mark Knopfler,
"Private Investigations"

AUTHOR'S NOTE

The central characters of all novels lurk inside their creators' psyches, otherwise they couldn't emerge on the printed page. But Pierce Duncan, the protagonist of *Cases,* is—dare I say it?—a special case.

Dunc stole my grandfather's name and much of my early life. He claimed that, like me, he was raised in Rochester, Minnesota, graduated from Notre Dame in the summer of 1953, and worked his way west through Las Vegas to Los Angeles, where he dug graves, wheelbarrowed cement, and fell in love for the first time.

Eventually, like me, he got to San Francisco and became a private detective with the L.A. Walker Company (he called it Edward D. Cope Investigations) at 1610 Bush Street. He and I both lived in Ma Booger's rooming house at 1117 Geary just up from Tommy's Joynt. Dunc's first week as a P.I. was my first week, most of his investigations were really mine.

Cases began in my office storeroom when I unearthed three forgotten notebooks from the early fifties, plus the case files and field reports from my first months at L.A. Walker. I even found the old snapshot, taken on the day of my arrival in Eagle Rock from Las Vegas, that we have used as our author's photo.

Cases became real through the generosity of others.

First, always and forever, is Dori, wife and lover, the largest soul

I have ever known, who works with me on all of my novels. But with *Cases* it was a virtual collaboration.

Fellow writer Dick Lupoff dug out the week-by-week Hit Parade songs from the ten months covered by the novel. Bill Malloy, editor in chief of Mysterious Press, furnished expertise on the blues, jazz, and bop musicians of the era. Along with my agents, Henry Morrison and Danny Baror, Bill also bought me the time I needed for the novel at no small personal expense.

Tim Gould worked the internet for material to strengthen my memories of the red-light district in Juarez, and of Van de Kamp's pioneering Los Angeles drive-in restaurant. Sportswriter Royce Feour shared his memories of the early prizefighting scene in Las Vegas. Frank Glover of the Sutro Library found me a list of such marvelous old San Francisco phone exchanges as ORdway, TUxedo, and MIssion. Pat Holt triggered many forgotten detective memories with her wonderful book about P.I. Hal Lipset's pioneering San Francisco years, *The Bug in the Martini Olive.*

In *Cases* I have tried to mix fact and fiction so thoroughly that nobody—not even myself—can now untangle them. I have also tried to honestly re-create the language, raw prejudices, hopes, dreams, despairs, sentimentality, violence, and social and marital attitudes of America's early fifties as seen through the eyes of a somewhat naive twenty-one-year-old man.

Portions of *Cases* previously appeared in markedly different form in three long-defunct magazines: *Manhunt*, last of the pulps; *Mike Shayne Mystery Magazine*; and *Rogue*, one of the early slick-paper *Playboy* clones.

<u>ONE</u>

The Summer of '53

Chapter One

It was the summer of '53, he was twenty-one years old and thought himself gloriously drunk in the doorway of an empty box-car clanking through the hot southern night. Sweat gleamed on his face and trickled down between his shoulder blades. He raised his voice in song:

> *"Frankie and Johnny were lovers,*
> *Oh my God how they could love.*
> *Swore to be true to each other,*
> *True as the stars above,*
> > *He was her man*
> > *But he done her wrong."*

In a far corner of the boxcar another voice also was raised, not in song. "Hey, shut the hell up."

He drained the last of the half-pint and threw the empty out into the darkness. After what seemed a long time he heard it shatter somewhere behind them. It didn't take much to get him high, he wasn't really a boozer: first time he ever got drunk had been just two years ago, on a bottle of seventy-nine-cent dessert wine. There had been grape skins in it. For a month afterward he'd gotten sick every time he saw a billboard advertising liquor.

> *"Frankie worked in a crib joint,*
> *Crib joint with only one door,*
> *She gave all her money to Johnny,*
> *Who spent it on a high-price whore.*
> > *He was her man*
> > *But he done her wrong."*

"I said knock it off." Same voice, pissed now. "Goddamn brakeman hear you, it's all our asses."

The train was starting up a grade into some cracker town he didn't know the name of, the engine straining, the *click-click* of the wheels slowing against the joins of the rail sections. The wind blew rich swampland into his face.

> *"Frankie went up and down State Street,*
> *She wasn't there for fun,*
> *Under her red kimono,*
> *She packed—"*

There were sudden scrabbling sounds from the corner of the box-car, the thunder of charging feet. But he grabbed his duffel bag and was out the open doorway, floating, *crunch!*, already running when his heavy hack boots hit the cinder right-of-way beside the tracks, still belting out his song:

> *"—a .44 gun . . ."*

He ran a dozen paces abreast of the moving train, slipping on the ties but keeping his feet. When he got himself stopped, still upright, he could see the pale retreating angry faces in the boxcar doorway. He cupped his hands to yell after them:

> *"She was looking for her man*
> *Who was doing her wrong!"*

Chuckling, he trudged toward the thin cluster of lights half a mile ahead. Too bad he'd had to jump off the train, but running was better than fighting. This way he could get something to eat before trying to catch another rattler. Tonight, for sure, miles to go before he'd sleep. When he had covered half the distance into town, it started to rain.

A big man came from the still-open diner to pick his teeth by the light from the front windows. Yellow highlights gleamed on his black rain slicker as he moved down the street and around the corner and out of sight.

The dishwater-blond waitress, alone behind the counter, reached under it for a movie magazine she placed open between her elbows on the red linoleum top. She leaned swaybacked with her behind stuck out while she read. The counter's wooden edging had been chipped and carved by generations of pocketknives. Most of the stools had rips in their imitation-leather seats.

When the man off the night freight came in and shook water from his army fatigue cap, she straightened quickly, blushing at being caught goofing off. His fatigue jacket was wet-darkened across the shoulders. The walk in the rain had sobered him up. He was not tall, but wide and blocky. He grinned at her.

"Good night for ducks."

She had the sort of soft Georgia accent that made every sentence a question, almost every phrase a sort of invitation.

"Don't figure you look as if it'd melt you none?"

"That's for sure. You still serving?"

"Burgers an' fries? Chili 'n' beans with oyster crackers?"

"I'll have it all. Uh . . . you got tea? Maybe with lots of cream and sugar for it?" He didn't much like tea, but he liked coffee less.

She giggled. "Tea's for little old ladies."

"That's about what I feel like, with the rain and all." He jerked his head toward the three booths under the windows that fronted the street. "Over there?"

"You just pick your spot, Johnny Doughboy."

Must be an army base somewhere around here; he was just as glad she hadn't noticed all his clothes weren't government-issue. In the end booth he opened his duffel bag and took out a dog-eared Gold Medal Original by John D. MacDonald, then sat with the paperback open in his hands, looking out through the window's cheap wavy rain-streaked glass at the deserted length of side street. Two pale lights bounced above the wet-gleaming gravel like buttons on a string.

The main street, at right angles to this, would probably be called Center or Main or Broadway. Unless it was named after Robert E. Lee or Stonewall Jackson. Here in South Georgia, that war was still being fought. That's why he'd chosen the booth: if the big man showed up again, he'd be out the back door. A week of riding the box-cars had made him wary and observant.

When the man didn't appear again, he started to read *The Damned*, was instantly immersed in the lives of the people at a stalled river ferry in a sun-scorched little town south of the border down Mexico way. Be nice to see Mexico for himself.

As he read, two dark shapes dropped off another rattler when it slowed for the same grade outside town. Their heavy shoes also struck the embankment running, but because of the rain sank into the soft grade fill to send out showers of wet cinders. One of them missed his footing in the dark, rolled down the slope until the long wet grass be-side the right-of-way stopped him. He sat up and sniffed the half-acrid smell of dirt newly wet down.

He laughed. "Hey, man, old brakeman never catch us now."

A moving shadow trudged back, slid down the embankment on its heels, lit a cigarette, became a man.

"I'd of whupped that bastard flat, you hadn't stopped me."

The cupped match flame revealed a young, hard face with deep-welled blue eyes and a square, cleft chin. His hair was brown and curled tightly against his skull by the rain.

The Negro, taller, stood up to brush the red loam off his brown cord trousers. "We don't need no more trouble." Slanting rain popped on his leather jacket and slid off, glistening. A dirty plaid cap hid his kinky hair. He was light-skinned enough to be called high yaller. "Come on, let's go into town and get us something to eat. I got two bits and two dimes and two pennies. You got any loot?"

"Half a pack of butts," said the white man. "God, Larkie, could I use a drink. I'm wet and cold clean through."

"No whiskey, Dale. Won't no one serve a white man and a colored man anyway."

"If we weren't tap city—"

"But we is."

They waded through the sodden saw grass and smartweed that choked the ditch. A quail exploded from beneath their feet to squeak away into the darkness. Beyond the tracks was a shallow-rutted road of muddy sand. They turned toward the fitful yellow pocks that marked the town through the falling water. Far ahead, the freight train they'd left dropped its pressure with a sigh. Buckthorn and beaked hazel bushes flanked the road to their left, smelling fresh and sweet in the rain.

The dirt track became a badly maintained gravel street. The rain seemed to drift through the wind-tossed streetlights' dim glow, but it drummed the wooden sidewalk like running feet.

"Diner up ahead," said Dale.

They hesitated in the windows' pale yellow glow to peer in cautiously. There was a lone patron in a window booth, munching a hamburger, immersed in a paperback. He wore an army fatigue jacket and was maybe a couple of years younger than they were. Probably from some local army base, as much a stranger as they. No worries there. A homely waitress was behind the counter, washing fountain glasses in gray soapy water.

"What you think, Dale?"

"I think she's got a kindly face. I think I got to get something into my gut."

Normally Larkie would have waited outside, but it was raining hard now. The door's hinges squeaked. They stopped just inside to drip water on the floor. The girl looked at them uncertainly, then at the man in the window booth, then back at them. She finally came down the counter drying her hands on the towel wrapped around her middle like an apron. Her hair was the color and texture of straw, nearly as straight. She was without makeup and with a slight squint.

"Yes?"

"Look, miss." Larkie's hands moved like instruments to measure her credulity. "We got us forty-seven cents. It's cold and wet out and we just passing through. What that buy us?"

She bit her lip, looking at the man in the booth again. But after his first quick sharp glance, he had not looked up from his book.

"Well—I'll let you have two bowls of chili and two coffees, if you promise to eat fast? It should be fifty cents but I'm about to close up? I'm not supposed to serve—"

She stopped abruptly. Perched at the end of the counter they slurped hot chili and drank steaming coffee as fast as their mouths could stand it, crunching down the whole heaped bowl of oyster crackers she brought.

"Any work around here?" asked Dale. Under the light he was too big-boned for his size; although his hands were thick and powerful, his wrists managed to make them seem small.

"No work in the state, I don't think." She looked around nervously, then leaned across the counter the way she had done to read her movie magazine. Her hair smelled of dime-store shampoo. "Listen, where are you boys from?"

"Up no'th," said Larkie.

She nodded. "You'd better . . . Uh, they're sort of funny about . . . coloreds and whites around here. You'd do better to either split up or else go back up north again. You don't know how it is in this state."

"We're learning," said Dale. "Me and Larkie have—"

"Much obliged for the food, ma'am," said Larkie. He laid his forty-seven cents on the counter. "Wisht we had something extra for you."

The girl blushed. "Oh, that's okay. You take care."

"We most surely will, ma'am." He turned to Dale. "Come on, white boy. Let's blow."

The big man in the black slicker was standing on the boardwalk, absorbed by a dusty display of women's hats in the millinery store two doors down from the diner. He looked like the sort of man who would find women's hats singularly uninteresting. Without seeming to, he blocked their way.

Larkie said, "Uh-oh," as Dale skipped sideways like a monkey, his hand whipping toward his trouser pocket. Larkie shot out a long arm to lock the white boy's wrist with strong fingers. "Easy on," he said.

The big man hadn't moved except to put his right hand under the shiny slicker. His straight brown hair, touched with gray at the temples, was combed severely back from a high forehead. His broad face wore bleak eyes and a gunfighter's mustache.

"You got a head, black boy. Just passing through?"

"You John Law?"

"Yep."

"Just passing through."

The big man shook his head slowly, almost sadly. A drop of rainwater fell from the end of his blunt nose.

"Looks to me like maybe you're waiting around for little Sue Ellen to shut up the diner there. Then who knows? Maybe you plannin' on followin' her home—"

"We wouldn't do nothing like that, Mr. Sheriff."

"Or maybe you waitin' to rob the place." He swung around to point at the man reading inside. "Could be he's your lookout."

"The soldier boy?" said Dale disdainfully. "We never laid eyes on him before."

"He's no soldier boy, he's out of uniform—wrong shoes, wrong pants." Through the window he caught the eye of the man not quite in uniform, gestured for him to come out. "Brakeman off the train told me 'bout you two 'bos. Said to keep an eye on *you*, white boy. Said you think you're handy with a knife."

Dale stepped back, blinking his eyes against the water running down from his tight curls. His face was deeply tanned and he wore a blue navy watch sweater that smelled of wet wool.

"We ain't done nothing in your town, mister." His voice was low and sullen.

"And you ain't about to," said the sheriff as he gestured at the man inside again, this time impatiently.

"Shit," said the almost-soldier boy under his breath.

He splayed his paperback open on the tabletop, raised his eyebrows in exaggerated query as his left hand pointed at his chest in apparent surprise. Why hadn't he got out when he'd had the chance? Because he'd gotten lost in *The Damned*, that's why.

Instead of bumming around the country in boxcars, maybe he should have stayed home in Minnesota, worked at the lumberyard another summer, or behind a desk in his dad's accounting office, gone home at night to his mom's good cooking off nice china.

But that wasn't what you did if you wanted to be a writer.

Meanwhile, his right hand was already digging in his pants pocket. There were a wallet and two twenties and a five in there, along with some silver. Two fingertips drew his Social Security card and driver's license out of the thin worn leather, sandwiched them in the fold of the twenties. Outside, the big man in the slicker gestured again, as if vexed by the delay.

The youth slid partway out of the booth; he had noticed a rip in the seat just wide enough to slip his twenties and identification into and out of sight. With only pocket change, he was a vagrant; but the twenties would be taken anyway, then used to suggest he had pulled a robbery somewhere back up the line. His Uncle Russ, who'd ridden the rods during the Great Depression, had warned him about that.

He carried his duffel bag over the waitress, said, "Could you put this behind the counter and hold it for me until I pick it up?" When she nodded, puzzled, he made her wide-eyed by tossing the folded five down in front of her. "That's for holding the bag, miss. And for me and the other two boys. You keep all of that for yourself. Don't tell your boss about it."

Outside, he joined the three waiting men, putting on his fatigue hat against the rain.

"What's your name, 'bo?" said the sheriff.

As a throwaway line in "The Joint Is Jumpin'," Fats Waller had sung, "Don't give your right name, no, no, no."

"Peter Collinson," he said.

"Army man?"

"Not anymore." Not ever, but why tell the sheriff that?

"What I thought. You're about halfway in uniform but you could have bought your clothes at an army-surplus store. I was just telling your friends here that maybe you three 'bos was planning a little larceny in my town."

"You know I never saw these men before, Sheriff," said Collinson evenly. "You saw me come into town alone."

"Know what I know. Saw what I saw. Riding the rattlers. Bumming meals in white restaurants where nigras ain't allowed. No visible means of support . . . Know what all that means, 'bos?"

Nobody answered him. Nobody had to.

"Vag, that's what it means. Lots of road going through here, the state's poor and it needs cheap labor." He took Larkie's arm in one big paw, said to Dale, "Walk in front of us, 'bo, and keep your hand out of that pocket." He added, almost as an afterthought, "Jail's right comfortable, my wife does the cooking. Won't be but overnight anyway."

They turned the corner and started down the main street. Confederate Boulevard, noted Collinson. That figured.

Larkie pulled his plaid cap down against the rain, said politely, "Nice little town you got here, Sheriff."

"It grows on you, 'bo. It grows on you."

Chapter Two

At 8:27 in the morning, last night's rain was just a fond memory; the big thermometer outside the red brick courthouse showed eighty-nine hot degrees. Six tall windows down the left side, open to catch any morning breeze, still left the crackerbox courtroom sweltering. A languid fan turned below the high ceiling without appreciable result. In the blossom-fragrant magnolia outside, a pair of purple grackles argued their day's agenda.

The courtroom's hardwood floor was worn bare of wax and varnish by decades of miscreants and their captors. There were eight rows of wooden benches for spectators, those on the right deserted except for an unshaven slat-thin almost seven-foot drunk who smelled of whiskey and urine. He was talking to himself in low reasonable tones. Across the aisle, glancing over at him like disapproving relatives at a shotgun wedding, sat the sheriff with his three captives. The boys were now all in handcuffs.

Dale was still arguing.

"Sheriff, why're we here? We didn't *do* anything. We—"

" 'Bos, let me give you a piece of advice. Judge Carberry was planning to be out after bluegills and crappies this morning, but he had to convene court just for you three. He ain't in the mood for much lip."

Beyond the handrail were the deserted prosecution and defense tables. The massive hardwood bench, from which the judge would dispense the town's particular brand of justice, was flanked by American and Confederate flags. Most of the wall behind it was covered with a gold-fringed Georgia state flag.

A uniformed bailiff wandered in from a side door, scratching his crotch with the innocent delight of a hound dog with fleas and saying all in one sentence without pause, "All rise for the Honorable Judge Hiram Carberry court is now in session God guide these proceedings."

Judge Carberry came from chambers to take his place behind the bench, wearing his black robe of office despite the heat. He was in his late fifties and his hair was white-blue like shadows on snow, his face aristocratic, his China-blue eyes just slightly too close-set on either side of a narrow aquiline nose.

Despite there being little in the way of description—"proud-looking" was the only adjective Twain had used—the judge reminded Collinson of Colonel Sherburn in *Huck Finn*, saying disdainfully to the mob that had come to get him, "The idea of you thinking you had pluck enough to lynch a *man*."

"Morning, Sheriff Swinton," said Judge Carberry.

"Your honor," said Swinton.

Everyone had sat down again. The judge was looking at the drunk. "Gideon. You stand on up now."

Gideon stopped talking to himself and stood up to gaze at the judge with watery eyes. "Yessir, y'r honor."

"I thought the last time you were before me, I ordered you to stay out of the Johnny Reb."

"Well, y'r honor, my dog ran in under them swingin' doors an' I went in to—"

"You damn fool, you don't have a dog."

"Oh." Gideon thought about it. "My cat?"

"Don't have a cat, either. But you do have a wife. She'll be worried. You go on home, and you thank God that good woman'll put up with a piece of worthless white trash like you."

Gideon's face screwed up into a pathetic squinch. "She beats on me when she's mad, y'r honor."

"Go on home with you now, you old reprobate."

Seeing only flint in the judge's gaze, Gideon shuffled sadly out of the courtroom like a lanky crane.

"Stand up, 'bos," whispered the sheriff.

The three young men stood up as Judge Carberry turned his gaze on them. The bailiff was sitting in a straight-back chair below the bench, cleaning his fingernails with a pocketknife.

"What do we have here, Sheriff Swinton?"

"Well, your honor, these three men were hanging around town last night in the rain. When I spoke to them, they gave me evasive answers. None of them has any identification, none of them has any money, none of them has any visible means of support. No local ties that I could uncover, your honor."

"You are telling me that they are vagrants."

To Collinson, the two men were like actors in a play so well rehearsed that they knew each other's lines.

"It appears that way, your honor."

"Are they all three together, Sheriff Swinton?"

Swinton indicated Collinson. "He came into town alone, ahead of the other two, but they're of an age."

"I see." The judge turned a seemingly benevolent eye on the three men. He said pleasantly, "Do you gentlemen have anything to say on your own behalf?"

Dale, deluded by the soft tones and kindly look, said, "Your honor, we were just passing through town lookin' for work. We weren't bothering nobody . . ."

"Sheriff?"

"These two, your honor, they went into the diner together."

Carberry leaned forward on the bench like a stooping hawk. "A nigra and a white boy in Imelda Joad's diner together?"

"Yes, your honor."

"And they were served?"

"Chili and coffee. It was Sue Ellen, your honor."

"And the other fellow was already in there and didn't do or say anything to defend the young lady's honor?"

"That's how she stacks up, your honor."

The judge leaned back, shook his head in gentle exasperation. "You get Sue Ellen on up here to my chambers this afternoon, Sheriff. I want to have a talk with that young lady. She's just too softhearted for her own good." He looked down at Collinson. "What about you, son? Any statement you want to make about all of this?"

"None, your honor."

The judge nodded. "Three drifters off the trains." He leaned forward on his elbows, chin on his interlaced hands. "We can't have it, gentlemen. We *won't* have it. Not in my town."

"And a lot of new road going through," said Larkie almost under his breath.

"What was that, boy?" demanded the judge sharply.

"Calling on the Lord, your honor. I'm a good Baptist."

Judge Carberry nodded, picked up his gavel, pointed it at Dale. He had not asked, nor had he been given, any of their names. "You. Six months hard on the road crew." He slammed the gavel down, *bang!* Pointed it at Larkie. "You. Six months hard on the road crew." *Bang!* Pointed it at Collinson. "You. One month hard on the road crew." *Bang!*

"All rise court is dismissed," intoned the bailiff.

The judge disappeared back inside his chambers. Swinton checked his watch, a big old turnip on a fob that he took from his pants pocket. "Two minutes and fifty-eight seconds for you three. Judge Carberry just set hisself a new record."

"Bluegills must be bitin' real good," said Larkie.

"Happens after a good rain," said Collinson with a careless grin. But he could hardly breathe he was so scared.

"Truck's waiting, 'bos," said the sheriff.

*　　*　　*

The compound was four miles off the road behind barbed wire, in the last county in Georgia where road-gang prisoners still wore ankle chains. Their pay was two bits a day and found—beans and rice and a sliver of fatback at a dime a day per man. The convicts lived in a single one-story clapboard building much like an army barracks except it was feces-brown instead of urine-yellow. The unglassed, screened windows had wooden covers that could be hinged upward and held open by brace sticks.

It was set on a low ridge above the floodplain. Behind it, crowded into the dense shagbark hickory and swamp chestnut, was the outhouse; lime was dumped into its two holes once a week for sanitary purposes. There were two showers made by water pipes run up outside the back wall of the barracks and then bent over at an angle. The showerheads were tin cans with holes punched in them.

Inside the barracks, a row of twelve bunks ran down each side, set head to the wall. In the center of the room was a potbellied iron woodstove. Wire stays held its black sooty stovepipe in place. Now, in the summer heat, the stove was cold.

Captain Hent had a two-room cabin all to himself, could cook and shower, had a bed with a mattress and springs and a headboard. Since there was a convict-dug septic tank, he and the four guards in their dormitory had running water and flush toilets. There was a cookshack and a commissary with a huge shiny padlock and heavy-mesh screens across the windows.

That first night, as they got their prison issue of clothing and the leg irons fitted around their ankles, Dale's blue eyes showed white all around like those of a spooked horse.

"I don't know if I can take this," he said urgently.

"You gotta take it," said Larkie. "Ain't no way out short of six months or dyin'."

Dale indicated Collinson. "Only one month for *him.*"

"He kep' his big mouth shut fronta the judge," said Larkie, "and he wasn't running with no nigger." He said to Collinson, "Me 'n' Dale jungled up together 'cause we both figured wasn't neither of us able to whup the other one. Figure the same 'bout you. We all gotta look out for one another, you see that?"

"I see that," said Collinson, thanking God. When the hinged iron had gone around his ankle he'd almost lashed out blindly, like a claustrophobic in a closet.

After two free hours following their evening meal of fatback and wormy beans, the twenty-four convicts were fastened to their beds like dogs in a kennel. The chain, threaded through the staples on their leg irons and passed down each row of cots and padlocked to plates in the walls, saved roll calls and night patrols.

There was supposedly no talking after the kerosene pressure lantern was extinguished, but with three bunks in a row the three of them could whisper together. Collinson wasn't sure he could have handled that first night otherwise. It had all happened so fast. Like going down Plummer's hill in his coaster wagon when he was a kid: once you started moving, you couldn't stop.

Uncle Russ had been smart enough to do his hoboing west by north, not east by south, so he'd had no words of wisdom Collinson could apply to this situation.

But he got used to it. The work was hard, but just that—hard work. He already had a strong back and callused hands from six years at the lumberyard after school and summers, unloading boxcars of lumber, coal, shingles, cement, plaster, and bricks to stay in shape for football and to get money for college.

The road was being cut north through a mixed pine forest of shortleaf, longleaf, loblolly, and slash. Two crews cleared brush and cut trees, a third came along behind them to lay the roadbed.

Simultaneously the road was being pushed south across a corner of the Okefenokee, so the last road crew had to build a levee out into the swamp. This was the toughest work because it meant hauling a lot of red Georgia clay. A 'dozer and trucks could have done it in a month; but since the local pols' graft was safe no matter what, the county would just use an endless rotating supply of men with picks and shovels and wheelbarrows for as many years as it would take.

The three of them ended up on the swamp crew, with Collinson wondering aloud about Pogo, Albert the Alligator, and Faithful Old Dog Tray. Nobody else had any idea of what the hell he was talking about.

There had been no rain since the night of their arrest, seventeen days before, so they had to stamp on their shovels to make them bite at the earth even though it had been pickaxed first. Reddish dust drifted from each shovelful of clods that went into the wheelbarrows. It reminded Collinson of emptying gondola cars of coal at Kruse Lumber back in Rochester: he and another college guy had been able to shovel fifty tons a day. He'd had to ride home on the front fender of his dad's car because he was too filthy to ride inside.

Two men always picked, two more shoveled; the other two, unchained, wheeled the barrows. Each midday they rotated jobs. The backs of their necks were red and sore from the sun, their palms cracked from sweat-slick tool handles.

To pass the time and keep his fear at bay, Collinson told stories about Uncle Russ during *his* hoboing days. The other convicts would stop and listen as if they were learning something Collinson didn't know was in the story.

Uncle Russ in Wyoming, wanting to be a cowboy. When the ranch foreman asked him if he was good with horses, Russ bragged, "Born on 'em," though he'd never been on a horse in his life. So they cinched a stallion too tight and put him on it. Of course it started to buck.

"When Uncle Russ got bucked off, and was high in the air," said Collinson, "he thought, 'God, how I wish I was down on the ground.' When he lit on the ground and broke his collarbone, he thought, 'God, how I wish I was back up in the air again.'"

Then there was that argument in the San Francisco saloon.

"Uncle Russ remembered the old saying about having a chip on your shoulder, so he put a wood chip on his shoulder from the sawdust on the floor, and told the other guy, 'Knock that off.'"

"Did he?" demanded Anderson, a lanky whipcord Texan with flat black hair and pale challenging eyes who was doing five hard years for rape.

"Knocked the chip off his shoulder and broke Uncle Russ's jaw in the bargain," said Collinson.

Anderson laughed really hard at that story.

The ones they liked best were Uncle Russ's Alaskan years in the Army Corps of Engineers during World War II. Two of the three older men were veterans themselves—mostly of PX rip-offs and black-market cigarettes and stockade time. But Uncle Russ had helped build the Alcan Highway against a possible military thrust through Siberia and the Aleutians into Alaska. The kind of stuff men not going anywhere liked to hear about.

"They got so far out across that muskeg that they ran out of fill. But they had to get the highway built. So they just started running trucks, cars, semis full of supplies, drums of oil, anything, into that swamp and letting it all sink, until they had a foundation for the highway."

"They ought to do that here," said Dalton, a short, once-chubby man who suffered the heat more than the others. He'd embezzled from a bank, had stupidly hit a cop with a baseball bat while on the run. "We got no trucks, but they could use our barracks for fill."

Collinson also told them about the Alaskan mosquitoes.

"Those muskeg mosquitoes were so big that six of them could carry a man off screaming."

Huge bulking Blackman Brown stopped his wheelbarrow in rapt wonder. He was a gentle Negro who'd caught his wife in bed with another man, backhanded her across the mouth, and broke her neck. A long knife scar ran diagonally across his face.

"They ever find any of them men again?"

"Just bones with skin draped around them, thin as parchment paper," said an utterly solemn Collinson. "The mosquitoes had sucked every bit of blood and meat right out of them."

"I would of liked to of seen that."

"Goddammit! Get to work! What we paying you for?"

That was Captain Hent, who had left his paperwork back at the compound to ramrod their crew personally. The long-timers had gone very still when he'd shown up, as if it meant more than was apparent. Hent was medium-sized, heavy-bodied, mid-forties, thick without fat, with cold blue eyes and a strong-jawed face always in need of a shave. Low on his right hip rode a .44-caliber revolver in a stained and shiny leather holster; low on his left, a razor-sharp bowie knife in a fringed leather sheath.

Collinson noticed how the long-timers reacted to Hent taking over their crew, but he just kept his silent count. Thirteen more days and a get-up to go. He kept telling himself he could do the time standing on his head, hugging the release day like a child hugging a giant teddy bear.

Then it would be just another adventure to recount.

His own this time, not Uncle Russ's.

Chapter Three

Things went sour on the eighteenth day. Larkie started clowning around while he shoveled, as he had done with the guard in charge before Hent.

"Cap'n," he said.

"What is it, niggerboy?"

Captain Hent was standing beside his chair under the shade of a lone bald cypress with its trunk rising up out of the water like an upside-down trumpet; its flared base was five feet bigger around than the upper trunk. Hent's thick arms were crossed on his chest, his hips were slung forward in a comfortable slouch. His shirt was black with sweat. By his right foot was the water jug, its sides beaded with moisture.

"How about a drink of that there water, Cap'n?"

"You know better than that, niggerboy. Only ten minutes to lunch break."

His voice was like the baying of an old hound gone mean from too many beatings. The only other sounds were the grunts of the men, the rattle of earth in the barrows, the liquid chirping of passing redwings. Each time a man bent to shovel or pick, beads of hot sweat rained from his face onto his hands and wrists. Their bodies were caked and streaked with red clay dust.

"Cap'n."

Hot breeze moved shadow across Hent's face from the Spanish moss festooning the cypress. "What you want, niggerboy?"

"How 'bout giving me my time? I figure on quittin'."

Anderson, the Texas rapist, snickered. The captain's face reddened and his eyes got hot and hungry. He stepped closer to Larkie, unfolding his arms.

"You making fun of me, niggerboy?" he asked softly.

Larkie's eyes widened in surprise. They became almost too wide for real surprise.

"No, Cap'n, I mos' surely ain't. We out here expiatin' for our sins, sure ain't any of us gonna draw no time."

A spiny softshell turtle was half buried in the mud beside the levee, its pointed tubular snout just breaking the surface of the shallow brown water. Captain Hent grabbed Larkie's shovel, made two giant steps down the side of the four-foot embankment, drove the sharpened, pointed blade down to cut the turtle almost in two. Its frantic scrabbling clouded the water with blood.

Hent chuckled and gave Larkie back his shovel. "You want lunch today, niggerboy, you eat that there turtle."

Dale straightened up, a hand to the small of his back.

"Captain, all you got's a gun makes you feel like God almighty. I ever get you alone without one . . ."

Captain Hent brought his whisker-stubbled face inches from Dale's. "Boy, maybe tonight at the compound we'll have us a little shot at that there. No gun. Tonight on your own time."

In the evenings they were unchained inside the barbwire enclosure, could shower, take a dump, shave, sew, or wash their clothing. They could even, if so inclined, sit on the weathered front steps and listen to the birdlike whistle of the tree frogs, *wit-wit-wit* repeated a score of times without pause.

"Makin' up stories in your head?" asked Larkie as he sat down beside Collinson.

"Listening to the tree frogs. They sort of sound like somebody calling his dog."

"Yeah." Larkie hunkered down, his hands clasped between his knees, and lapsed into uncharacteristic silence. Finally he said, "Wisht I hadn't of got funnin' at that old cap'n this afternoon. Dale thinks he faced the man down, but . . ." He turned to look at Collinson. "What you think gonna happen?"

A barred owl sailed wide-winged into the top of a dead tree high above them. He gave his two distinctive hoots, then fell silent, alert for any swamp rabbit or tiny golden mouse spooked by his cry.

"Maybe he'll lose some privileges," said Collinson.

Two guards were striding toward them across the flattened grass of the compound. They paused at the foot of the steps, fleshy men in their late twenties, vets come home seven years earlier to a world perhaps safe for democracy but with no assurance of steady jobs for ex-servicemen.

"Where's your buddy, black boy?"

"Inside. But there ain't no need for you to . . ."

They were already clumping up the steps. They came back out with Dale between them. He looked pale and frightened, but determined. With a burst of maniacal laughter, the owl spread its wings to sail off into the gathering dusk.

Captain Hent's door opened to silhouette him against the light. Slapping the nightstick in his right hand against his left palm, he stepped back so they could go past him into the cabin. Two minutes later the guards came back out, one carrying Captain Hent's holstered .44. The door slammed behind them.

"Oh sweet Jesus," Larkie had moaned at the sight of the gun.

The guards blew the bed-check whistle. The convicts not already inside began gathering. Larkie stood there, irresolute.

"There isn't anything you can do," said Collinson.

That's when the thud of nightstick on flesh started. As the other convicts got into their bunks, not meeting the two boys' eyes, defiant cries joined the blows. The guards strung the chains through the staples on the ankle cuffs.

"What about Dale?" asked Larkie.

A guard answered with a muttered curse. He released the pressure of the kerosene lamp, there was a low hiss as the mantles began to fade. Collinson lay stiff and silent on his bunk, listening to the voracious whine of mosquitoes, the whistle of the tree frogs. No more blows; just a voice now, pleading.

Then a new sound started, carried on the clear night air. Regular, steady, gradually increasing in speed and urgency. Collinson could almost feel Larkie's rigidity in the next bunk.

Captain Hent's bedsprings, squealing . . .

Collinson woke sometime in the night. There was no moon, he could see little. Could hear only night sounds; then the bedsprings started again. When he woke just before dawn, Dale was back on the bunk in a fetal position, silently crying.

For noon they ate balls of cooked rice and rested on the sloping side of the levee for half an hour, away from the others. Collinson had no stories that day.

"He said he was gonna do me again tonight," Dale said suddenly. His voice was almost unrecognizable. He sat between Larkie and Collinson, looking straight ahead across the swamp. "We gotta—"

"Ain't no gottas here, man," said Larkie. " 'Cept we gotta see us plenty of country once we's outta *this* bind. Ain't gonna last forever, even if . . . even if . . ."

He stopped, not able to go on. Dale turned to Collinson.

"When I was a kid we lived in a big white house with a white fence around it and a red pump out in back higher than I was. I'd stick my head under there, hot days, and my daddy would pump cold water on me. I remember things like that, I know I can't take any more of what Hent did to me. You're smart, you been to school. You gotta think of something."

"Okay, I'll try," said Collinson. Maybe try to get to the judge . . .

Maybe do himself some good, too. "But you've got to promise me you won't do anything dumb before then. Okay?"

Captain Hent's whistle ended the noon break. The convicts started painfully to their feet, working tightened muscles.

"Okay," said Dale, "I promise."

Captain Hent sat like a bullfrog in his puddle of shade, drinking water, a half-smile on his face, watching the muscles strain under Dale's blue shirt. At the water break, the men laid down their tools to start for the jug. Hent stopped Dale.

"Bet you wanna kill me, don't you, boy?"

Dale shut his eyes for a moment, his face taut, fighting for control. Finally he opened his eyes and raised his arm to wipe the sweat from his face with the sleeve of his shirt.

Captain Hent's hand swept the big .44 from the holster on his hip with a fluid movement that denoted long hours of practice before a mirror, an elated, transported expression on his face.

He fired from a crouch with his body turned in the approved Police Manual method. The heavy slug took Dale just under his right eye; the back of his head split outward like a melon. He fell on his face. His nose broke against the pink earth.

"Sweet Christ in Heaven!" cried Larkie.

He dropped to his knees beside his dead buddy, breathing like a man just kicked in the groin. Collinson was frozen in place, afraid of being sick; he had never seen anyone die except his granddad, and that had been in the odor of sanctity, doctor in attendance, family around him, wife to hold his hand so he wouldn't be scared as he went gentle into that good night.

"He said he was going to kill me." Captain Hent looked around at the eyes he was sure had not seen, the lips he was sure would not speak. "You all heard that. Then he raised his hand to me. When the investigators come around, you'll tell them what he said and how he raised his hand to me."

Larkie cried, "All he did was go to wipe his face. Just a man gonna wipe his face—"

"He wasn't no man, niggerboy—just a backwards pussy for me to fuck." Captain Hent gave a harsh bark of laughter and turned away. "Okay, all of you. Back to work."

Larkie bent to whisper something against Dale's strong dead throat. Blood from the exit wound in the back of the skull glistened on the callused pink palms of his brown hands, impregnated the denim of his trousers. Captain Hent spoke again.

"You too, niggerboy."

Larkie slid the body off his lap. Dale's left hand struck the dirt as softly as a girl's breath stirring a curtain.

"Here I comes, Cap'n," said Larkie with a desperate gaiety.

By the time Hent let them trundle Dale back to the compound in a wheelbarrow, the dead man's head was covered with big, fat, shiny green flies buzzing loudly like a radio warming up. Black vultures circled overhead in silent frustration.

That night Collinson and Larkie dug the grave; on Saturday morning they put Dale in the ground. Larkie said a few Bible words, then handled that day's barrow work alone, working with maniacal energy. Captain Hent was in high spirits, cracking jokes and giving out extra rations of water. He even let the crew's five remaining men share out Dale's ration of food.

But they were still a sullen and slow-moving lot, quick to take offense with each other. Collinson and Anderson, chained together, kept getting in each other's way. Finally Collinson gave the rapist a shove.

"Why don't you watch how you use that goddamned shovel, you Texas asshole? You almost took off my toes!"

"How about I take off your fucking head?"

Anderson swung the gleaming pointed blade. Collinson ducked under it, pumped fists into Anderson's gut. They went down in a flail of arms and legs.

"Knock it off!" yelled Hent. He reached down to grab Collinson by the collar and jerk him to his feet.

Hulking Blackman Brown's shovel-strengthened fingers scrunched Hent's right hand so the hand could reach neither collar nor holstered .44. Collinson jerked Hent's left arm wide so his scattergun hit the dirt. Anderson's unshackled leg whipped, Hent went down, sprawling on his belly in the dust.

He opened his mouth to shout, though the nearest guard was half a mile away at the quarry, but mild little accountant Dalton shoved a torn shirtsleeve, foul with brine, between his teeth. Clods dug his belly and chest. Dalton's hands ripped the keys from his belt, Larkie's the huge bowie knife from its sheath.

It went just as planned, hard, sharp, quick, physical—almost like a football game, except you couldn't limp off this field, helmet in hand, in the middle of the game.

"Turn him over," said Larkie to Blackman Brown; to Collinson, "hold his arms"; to Anderson, "his feet."

Larkie jerked down the squirming captain's pants to expose his thick white flanks. He grabbed the handful of sex between Hent's thighs and looked into the captain's wildly rolling eyes.

"Gotta borrow these here, Cap'n," he said with diffidence.

The bowie knife flashed. Hent convulsed, whipping his head from side to side, trying to buck Collinson off, trying to scream. Collinson hung grimly on, sick, frightened, confused, but unable to release his frozen grip on Hent's arms. Larkie straightened up, holding his bloody prize above his head; then he threw it far out into the swamp.

"For the turtles," he said.

He stooped, drove the blade into Hent's lower abdomen and ripped it upward to the sternum. Hent thrashed and tried to kick, tried to scream, and tried to tear his arms loose. But most of all he tried to die, which took way too long.

Collinson, eyes shut, kept repeating his silent litany: *It's an adventure. It's all just another adventure. It's an adventure. It's all just . . .*

The corpse, draped in their leg irons, was sunk in the swamp, the bloodstained earth spread over the embankment and covered. Brown took the shotgun, Anderson the .44, Dalton the money, Larkie the big bowie knife. Collinson took the water jug.

They got off the levee, spread out through the woods, each man going his own way to confuse the dogs that would be brought at dawn. They all knew that if they stayed together, any man caught would give up the others to avoid the noose.

Collinson moved silently through cover; he had hunted with his dad since he was a kid. Near nightfall, he waded a half mile through water to throw off the dogs, pine resin heavy in his nostrils, mosquitoes, ticks, and leaches feasting on his sweat-soaked body. But finally he worked his way into the center of a dense briar patch on the edge of town and settled down to wait.

Please don't throw me in that briar patch, Br'er Fox.

He prayed all through the sleepless night, something he hadn't done much of since being sent to the chain gang: *Glory be to the Father, to the Son, and to the Holy Ghost, as it was in the beginning, is now, and ever shall be, world without end. Amen.*

It being Sunday, he felt an intense desire for Mass, but not for confession because he couldn't repent. He hadn't committed murder, but he'd helped, and would again: he'd do almost anything not to be next on those squealing bedsprings . . .

Almost anything. Would he ever be able to do what Larkie had done? He hadn't been able to release Hent's arms—why not? Was there a part of him able to mutilate and murder? Maybe part of being on the road was finding out things like that about yourself . . .

At dawn he lifted a bottle of milk from among others on a back stoop, stole a shirt and trousers from a lineful of early wash flapping in the hot breeze. The gooseberry lay, his Uncle Russ had called it.

He wore only one day's stubble on his face; after shoving his convict clothes down into a trash barrel behind the general store, he slicked his hair back with water from the town square's drinking fountain. What if Sue Ellen was working the morning shift at the diner?

What if Sheriff Swinton was having before-church breakfast? What if the end booth was in use and he had to wait, naked and exposed, until he could get to it?

No on all counts. He sat looking out the window as the fingers of his right hand delved into the rip in the red imitation leather, groped desperately . . . Yes!

In vast relief, "Ham and eggs and grits and toast and coffee, ma'am, thank you very much." They'd remember tea.

He ate fast, his Social Security card and driver's license under his real name once more in his pocket. As he paid at the cash register with one of his precious twenties, he saw his duffel bag still under the counter. He just reached down and scooped it up, nodded his thanks to the iron-haired cold-eyed woman behind the register. Imelda Joad, without a doubt.

"Ma'am, I'd purely 'preciate you thankin' Sue Ellen fer keepin' this here fer me," he twanged in a bogus cracker accent.

She stared hard-eyed after him as he left, but he was counting on her being all too aware of Sue Ellen's kind heart. In the paperback rack at the bus station he found a new copy of *The Damned*, caught the first Greyhound out. Didn't matter which way it went: out of town, out of Georgia, over a state line before the bloodhounds came baying down his back trail.

He had his duffel bag back, no one could trace him through that. They hadn't even taken his fingerprints. Peter Collinson meant "son of nobody." He could go back to his own name. The shackle scars on his ankle would heal; in time, the nightmares would stop.

Somehow he knew he would never be telling any tales about that chain gang.

He quit telling Uncle Russ stories, too.

TWO

Headin' for the Border

Chapter Four

Pierce Duncan, usually called Dunc, had coal-black hair cropped tight to his head, alive brown eyes, a good chin, and the thick neck of a man who has done a lot of weights or a lot of manual labor, or both. He was being carried west in style on the crushed ivory leather backseat of a white Cadillac convertible as long as a hearse. A pair of curved Texas longhorns graced the Caddy's grille. Hot wind blew on his face. This was the life! He needed a little of this after Georgia.

The Caddy whispered through the desert afternoon at a hundred miles an hour. The driver was large, soft, reddish, with a red sunburned face and thinning russet hair blown by the wind. Sunglasses hid his eyes. He steered with a single finger crooked around the wheel. There were freckles on the backs of his sunburned hands. Pink hairs curled on his bare forearms.

"Nice car," called Dunc, trying for casual even though the Caddy, at this speed, skittered as if on glare ice. His words were whipped away by the wind of their passage.

"Eats up the miles," yelled the big man. In the rearview mirror his face wore a wide grin. His voice was surprisingly thin to come from such a large body. "I need a car can get me there fast. I need lots of fast."

"I need to pee," whined the blonde riding beside him. She also wore black glasses and was about thirty, but still with a good figure well displayed by a cotton sunsuit. Her narrow fox face had a sly thin-lipped mouth with half the lipstick eaten off.

"Now, Mae, there's not much of a place to go around here," said the driver mildly. He caught Dunc's eye again in the rearview, winked. "Tracks we're making, we'll hit a town soon."

Maybe literally, thought Dunc. The reddish man went on, as if hearing the unspoken thought.

"Thing is, I gotta go all over the West all the—"

"I'm gonna go all over the seat you don't stop right now."

"Just a few more minutes, honeybun." To Dunc, he said, "So where you heading for?"

"Anywhere."

"Coming from?"

"Nowhere." Surely a Georgia chain gang was nowhere.

Mae said in a snide voice, "Must be grand, get to smart off to people nice enough to give you a ride."

"Wasn't trying to be smart, ma'am," said Dunc quickly. He didn't want to get stranded under a cactus somewhere. "I just graduated from college last month and I'm taking the summer to bum around and see the country."

" 'Ma'am'? How goddamn old does he think I am?"

"I was just being—"

"Arnie, find me one of those cactus things to go behind."

Arnie sighed and took his foot off the gas. The Cadillac began to lose altitude.

"Where'd you go to school?" he asked Dunc.

"Notre Dame."

"Arnie!"

"I'm doing it, honeybun, I'm doing it."

The car stopped on the shoulder. They were maybe fifty miles beyond the intersection where 281 came down from Wichita Falls and Oklahoma City. The blonde opened her door to flounce away through the dry sand with an exaggerated twitching of fanny. She disappeared behind some mesquite bushes. Dunc and Arnie got out to stretch their legs.

"Great football school. But you lost a couple last year."

"We had a killer schedule," said Dunc defensively. "We played just about the top ten teams in the country. And we beat USC—that always makes it a good year. Heap and Lattner—"

But Arnie chuckled. "Wait until next year, huh?" It caught Dunc up short: the man was right. Notre Dame was behind him. "Me, I set up syndicates that finance wildcat oil wells. You put in so much money, you get so many shares. We hit a gusher, everybody's rich. We bring in a dry hole, everybody loses. It's a real crapshoot."

Except for you, thought Dunc. Big new Caddy, Mae in her tight sunsuit. He asked, "You score very often?"

"Now, you quit talking about honeybun, hear?" chortled Arnie. He got serious again. "I've brought in my share. And it's a good life. Meet lots of good old boys. Sometimes I'll outrun a highway patrol car without evening knowing it, they set up roadblocks to stop me. We usually have a good laugh all around when they're givin' me the ticket. Meet lots of good little ladies, too"—another wink, a guffaw—"like Mae there."

His laughter, unlike his voice, fit his body. Anecdotes like that about the highway patrol roadblocks would make prospective investors see Arnie as a real wildcatter.

Mae was coming back across the desert, buttoning up her sunsuit. "Dump him off here, Arnie," she said.

"Now, Mae." The big man caught Dunc's eye and winked yet again. "Man said he wasn't being a smart aleck—"

"He was watching me while I went." She had taken off her sunglasses, was holding them in her hand. Dunc expected her to start smiling, but her slightly bulging eyes were bleak and accusing. "Watching me through the bushes."

"I was right here with Arnie the whole time, honest."

"Were not," she said. "You were watching. I saw you. Tryna see my pussy when I stood up."

Arnie sighed in exasperation.

"Mae, there isn't any call for you to be that way."

"You don't leave this bastard right here, Arnie, I'm gonna get my own motel room tonight on your money." She added in malicious triumph, "An' you won't get *nothin'*."

"Aw *shit!*" said Arnie, and kicked Dunc in the gut, hard, moving real well for a big fleshy man out of shape.

Dunc went down, gagging, managed to roll groggily away from the kick Mae aimed at his face. He kept rolling, trying to wheeze big gulps of air into his lungs, swirled to his feet in as close to a fighting stance as his inexperience allowed, fists cocked to give fucking Arnie something to think about.

Fucking Arnie had already thought of something: he was three yards off with a small flat automatic, maybe a .32, pointed at Dunc's chest. Dunc went still except for trying to breathe.

"Just so we don't get into somethin' stupid out here," said Arnie. "Nothin' personal, boy—but you come between me and my lovin', it's the same as gettin' 'twixt a gator and the water. Can't stand for that. I gotta have my little Mae gal here."

"Oh, Arnie," said Mae in a breathless little-girl voice. "You're so romantic!"

They went back to the Cadillac, Mae wiggling her rounded behind in an exaggerated manner because she knew Dunc would be watching, Arnie covering all her rear-guard action with one big paw and walking a little stiffly from his hard-on. They went to their respective doors, Arnie pausing to toss Dunc's duffel bag out onto the shoulder of the road in a puff of dust.

Dunc, still a little bent over and breathing funny, watched the big car fishtail back onto the highway. As the big man honked in derisive goodbye, Mae threw a triumphant look over her shoulder before dipping her head down toward Arnie's lap.

Dunc walked around in tight circles for a few minutes, cursing them both to hell and trying to get his breath back. He was sure going to have a sore gut tomorrow. But he got his spiral notebook out of his duffel bag and sat down on the canvas case to write out his adventure.

"I bet they put on their little vaudeville act for every male hitch-hiker they pick up," he wrote. "What do they mean, Arnie and Mae? Do they ever wonder what relative value they have to anyone else? To the universe?"

He stopped writing to stare out across the desert. Heat waves suggested a cool blue lake shimmering a couple of miles off. He could almost see palm trees at an oasis with water bubbling out of the sand; hunger, heat, and thirst created Bedouin tents and patient camels and belly dancers in swirling silks with shimmy coins tinkling against their rolling, oil-slick hips.

Reality was Joshua trees—the legions of the old General—long arms uplifting, writing his exploits on the sky.

Dunc wrote: "Well, what the hell relative value do I have to anyone else? There's Arnie with Mae's head in his lap, here's me writing about it in my notebook."

Them what can, does. Them what can't, teaches. Or writes.

With that, he finally started to laugh at himself.

The sun had westered two more hours, and Dunc was thinking about maybe hiking over to check out that oasis, when a '49 flathead-eight Merc that had seen better days squealed to a stop after it had already passed him by. He grabbed up his duffel bag to run a little lopsidedly up the road, hoping the guy wouldn't pull away just as he got there. They did that a lot.

He opened the door and peered in. The driver was a good-looking solidly built man in his early thirties, with clear eyes, wide, even teeth, curly hair, and a small neat mustache.

"Didn't see you 'til I was almost past. Hop in."

Dunc did. The car accelerated. It smoked and smelled and sounded as if the pistons were changing holes every other stroke.

"You're not from around here," stated the driver.

"Minnesota."

"Knew you wasn't from around here."

Dunc settled back against the stained fabric. All four windows were wide open but it was hot in the car, his throat was parched and his lips were dry.

"There's a jug of water on the floor of the backseat."

Dunc found it, drank, waited, drank again. Nothing had ever tasted better than that tepid water. The driver said he'd been in Oklahoma City, waxing cars by hand for fifteen bucks apiece.

"Did two hearses last December, got sixty-seven bucks. Money for Christmas. But too much money isn't good for a man." He gestured at a neat travel bag on the backseat. "Two suits and a squirt bottle of suit cleaner, that's all I need."

He drove with both hands on the wheel, ten and two o'clock, steering with short quick sawing movements as if he were hitting 150 on an oval track with pursuing race cars tight behind.

"I was drinking beer in a bar on the west side one night and a cop who was usually on the east side came in and put a hand on my shoulder. 'I see you on the east side now and then,' he says to me. 'I never see you,' I says to him."

Dunc capped the water jug. "They're bad news, all right."

In Rochester the cops had been benign, only throwing them out of Emerson's Pool Hall once in a while because they were too young to hear that sort of language. But on the road he'd found cops to be only grief.

"Get you down to the station house and ask you over and over until you tell two stories, just for meanness, then they stick you in jail. I mind my own business. In Oklahoma City, I was there a year and a half, you always see me alone. No one's got anything on me, I can look anybody right in the eye."

Dunc shifted in the seat. His gut was starting to stiffen up for sure. The desert flowed by outside the open windows. He found it hard to keep his eyes open—forty-eight hours without sleep . . .

He came up out of dark nightmare with a start. Jesus! He stole a look over at his companion, afraid he might have screamed aloud as he woke. But it must have been just long enough to have the dream he already couldn't remember.

". . . drove a load of vegetables up to Fairbanks last year on the Alaskan Highway. The boss, he drove with me on the way up, but I had to drive it alone on the way down. Got seventy a week and board, he couldn't get no experienced drivers to run that highway for less than a hundred a week."

Dunc had driven the Alcan himself two years before, when he was nineteen. He'd driven and driven and driven, two thousand miles from Minnesota, had thought he'd be in Alaska and was still in Idaho.

"Gotta be careful with women," said the driver. "I had a sort of steady girl, God what a beautiful body—she was a beauty queen up there in Oklahoma City. She was only about twenty. I had to pull it out each time with her, but I told her it was better than her having a baby. Maybe your wife's playing around on you, but I'm never going to tell you. Man gets his name known that way. They've never had my name down yet and if I can help it they never will."

Chapter Five

Somehow they'd gotten his name down, and Dunc was alone in a strange city at 6:15 in the morning—St. Louis, Chicago, maybe New York. Then the familiar bells of St. Olaf's started playing the *Stabat Mater*, and he realized he was walking down Tenth Street in Minneapolis, with a killer stalking him.

He came up behind a limping man who wore blue denims, an old sport jacket that didn't fit, a green shirt, a brown cap, and a lumberyard apron. His face was round, red, vacant. His voice was slow, high-pitched, singsongy. For sure not the killer.

"We get a three-day weekend for Decoration Day this year," the man said. "Three days for the Fourth of July, too, even though it falls on a Saturday—we get the Monday."

They started across Second Avenue together; dust eddied about them in little swirls.

"A man is trying to kill me," said Dunc in desperation.

His companion thrust a key into his hand. "Second apartment house, room at the top of the stairs on the left."

Dunc turned off as the other man limped on down Tenth, looking straight ahead. Neither of them said goodbye. He pounded up the stairs, used the key, ducked into the room.

A girl his own age was sitting on the edge of the bed. She wore a red knit dress that clung beautifully to her curves. Great legs, dimples at the ends of her wide full-lipped mouth, crystal-clear wide-set hazel eyes, and a mass of chestnut hair that framed a round face. Short nose, lovely arched brows.

Dunc looked out between dingy lace curtains. In the ground-floor window across the street was a big Bible, open on a lectern. Bright light shining on it reflected a golden nimbus on the bulky man standing beside the window, so one side of him glowed, the other was in darkness. His felt hat was pulled low over his eyes and his hands were bunched in the pockets of his tan overcoat. Dunc knew each fisted hand held a gun.

The killer started across the street without looking either way. Dunc whirled away from the window, terrified. The chestnut-haired girl on the bed was smiling a Mona Lisa smile.

"Running away won't do you any good." She had a musical voice, even though she was speaking gravely. "You'll have to face this. Here. Now."

He listened at the door. Heavy footsteps on the stairs. He grabbed a chunky brass lamp from the bureau, stood against the wall beside the door. At least he'd go down swinging.

The door was kicked open to rebound off the wall on the side opposite of Dunc. The killer's guns came through first, ranging the room. Dunc was already swinging the lamp. The killer made a strangled sound, his round red face was a mask of blood, bone, shattered teeth. He sagged as Dunc jerked him inside. A second blow wasn't going to be needed.

"Now you can go on," the girl's Mona Lisa smile told him.

"You okay? You were sort of yelling out in your sleep."

Dunc sat up, drenched in sweat, knuckling his eyes. He'd been sprawled over against the door. The Merc was stopped in a narrow rutted one-track dirt road going from the highway into a desert made otherworldly by the rising moon.

"I go north to my folks' place from here. You're welcome to come along, but it's twenty miles off the highway and—"

"No, this'll be swell." Dunc's door creaked in the desert twilight. "I'll get something here in no time."

He reached in the back to haul out his duffel bag. His gut, from Arnie's kick, was stiff and sore.

"Hey, better take the water jug, too. I won't need it 'fore I get home."

The big jug three-quarters full of brackish water was a real gift. Dunc's dream was still vivid in his mind. If he saw the girl in real life, would he know her? Though the killer had worn a different face, he had to have been Captain Hent.

Dunc watched the Mercury crunch away up the narrow track, following its twinned headlights bouncing along the uneven road until their glow was gone and the car's rattling had diminished to silence. Nice guy, but he really covered up in the clinches.

Alone in the moonlight, Dunc spun around in a circle, arms wide, heavy work shoes scuffing the blacktop, then sat down on his duffel bag. It was so bright that he could write up the latest ride in his spiral notebook by moonlight. He was getting it all down, good and bad, the expected and the surprises. From the notebook he would write short stories, maybe someday when he got the guts for it, a novel . . .

He heard a thin distant whine on the desert air. He stood up, stuffing the notebook into the duffel bag in case it might be a ride, but it was going east. The massive semi truck-trailer festooned with colored lights whooshed by him, the warm wind almost knocking him off his feet.

He'd been east. He wanted to go west.

On the Glee Club's Easter tour to California three months before, he'd seen his first ocean, his first palm tree, his first desert, and, in San Francisco just across the Embarcadero from the Ferry Building, his first illegal after-hours joint. He and four others from the club had sung all night for beer before running across the street to catch the Southern Pacific train to Los Angeles without even getting back to the St. Francis to pack.

A little buff and gray animal with a bushy black-tipped tail trotted across the road under the paper-cutout moon. Enormous ears, tiny body. Desert fox, kit fox, trotting with that tongue-lolling grin all foxes wear going about their business, it was gone into the mesquite silent as cloud shadow.

Dunc dug out his windbreaker; the full moon gave plenty of light, but no heat. He had just sat back down when he saw a hairy black dinner plate coming across the road at him. He was frozen in place as a tarantula, nearly a foot across with all its hairy legs outstretched and moving, crossed his boot and was gone.

He let out a long silent breath, had a huge drink of water, took a leak in the nearest mesquite bush, lay down on his back with his duffel bag as a pillow to wait for the sound of a ride. The moon was setting, a million stars crowded the blue-black sky. Trying to pick out constellations, he slipped down and down and down and was gone. Just like that.

Dunc woke from dreamless sleep to a cold, hungry dawn, so hungry he actually thought he could smell bacon frying. But what brought him bolt upright was a horrendous screeching noise.

Nieng-haw! Nieng-haw! Nieng-haw!

He was looking into a pair of beautiful, mild brown eyes, with the most sweeping, romantic lashes he had ever seen. The donkey shoved a muzzle like velvet into his cupped hand. It was little and brown, with a darker mane and tail, was cinched and packed with a blanket roll. On one side was a pickax and a flat metal pan gleaming like polished silver, on the other a .30-30 carbine, the old 1897 Winchester with the octagonal barrel.

A grizzled old man appeared wearing a wide-brimmed hat, faded red shirt with long sleeves, and lace-up boots with canvas trousers bloused into them. Equally faded gold suspenders crisscrossed the shirt, a wide leather belt held up the pants. He patted the donkey's flank with great affection.

"Señorita was afraid you was dead."

"The donkey's name is Señorita?"

The old prospector sang in a cracked voice:

> *"There's a song in the air,*
> *But the fair Señorita*
> *Doesn't seem to care,*
> *For the song in the air."*

He stuck out his hand. "Folks call me Harry."

"Folks call me Dunc."

Señorita exclaimed, "Nieng-haw! Nieng-haw!"

"I come by last night, you looked near enough t'dead as damn t'swearing, so I figgered you'd be hungry enough t'eat a dead turtle when Señorita decided to wake you up."

Dead turtle. Hent and Larkie. A nightmare shudder went through him. But he said, "You figured right, Harry."

The old man led him fifty yards back into the desert to a smoke-less stone-banked mesquite fire with eight thick hand-cut strips of bacon sizzling slowly in a pan set to one side, coffee brewing in a big blue ceramic-ware pot.

Dunc asked casually, "Looking for gold?"

"Mebbe gold. Mebbe silver. I ain't rightly sayin'."

Harry got out silverware, halved the bacon onto two tin plates. They sat down. Señorita kept nuzzling Dunc's right ear as half a dozen eggs popped and blackened in the hot bacon fat.

Dunc gestured at the Winchester cased against the donkey's side. "You use that for hunting, Harry?"

"Just for meat." The old prospector got a faraway look in his eye. "Used to trophy hunt. When I was livin' in Cuba just after the turn of the century, I used that there very rifle to try and get me the biggest damn deer in the whole Sierra Maestra."

He shook on pepper and salt, flipped the eggs out onto the tin plates. His eyes still had their faraway look.

"Teddy Roosevelt had led them Rough Riders up San Juan Hill five, six years before, and Cuba was wide open. There was big coastal towns like Santiago and Havana, and most of the island was sugar-cane, pineapple, banana. But down south in Oriente Province it was wild country, son! Bucks as big as elks back in them mountains. I wanted me one of them big old geezers."

Dunc ate bacon. Señorita gave his ear a velvety kiss.

"No roads in the high country, so I needed a packhorse. But all I could find was a man with a mule in a little village near Alto Cedro. Fat, dirty fellow with a sash around his middle who *loved* that mule—once I wanted to buy it! Wouldn't sell. Rent. Three days at a dollar a day. Dollars, mind, not pesos!"

Dunc shook his head in wonder, busy poking one of his eggs in the eye. They were the best eggs he'd ever eaten.

"That mule had a hunting heart, son; I could have trained him to retrieve game. We pushed up into the mountains, eight thousand feet high and everything steaming from the heat. Then something *huge* crashed off through the brush . . ."

Dunc had finished his eggs and bacon.

"I unslung my carbine and that mule was like a thoroughbred at the gate. He knew—*he knew!* Son, that was a hunting mule! When I tied him to some brush at the edge of the clearing, his eyes pleaded with me to take him along."

"So why didn't you?"

Harry poured half a tin of peaches into each plate. They ate the fruit with their forks, slurping the juice.

"Mules can't make no silent stalk, son. So I went creeping on alone up and down that hillside through that steaming brush. Must of been two hours later I broke out into a clearing. On the far side I could see a pair of unwinking eyes and a patch of sun-dappled hide. Them eyes was so high off the ground, son, I knew he had to be the biggest deer in Cuba! The snick of my hammer going back was thunderous. I shot right between them eyes. There was a fearful thrashing in the brush, and then . . . silence."

Harry grunted his way to his feet, started scouring his plate and silverware with desert sand. Dunc, doing the same, finally burst out, "So did you get him? Did you get your deer?"

Harry had hauled out an old tin of Prince Albert and had started to roll a cigarette.

"Son," he said solemnly, "I shot my mule."

Chapter Six

The first driver Dunc stuck out a thumb at gave him a ride. He was mid-thirties and six-one, built like a fullback. Wavy blondish hair and startling blue eyes somehow askew in a tawny wise-guy face. A chain-smoker, lighting one cigarette off the butt of the other as they went along. Suntan, bright long-sleeved sport shirt. He said his name was Jack Falkoner and that he was from Palo Alto, where Dunc knew Stanford University was. He drove the red MG with a loose, easy abandon. It had California plates and the top down even though the desert air was still dawn-cold.

"My big brother had a car just like this for a couple of years after the war," said Dunc. "Even the same color. But then he traded it in for a Jaguar."

"Must have had a lot of money and liked a lot of speed."

"He liked the speed, all right, but he got behind in the payments and they came and took the Jag away from him and then he didn't have anything at all."

Falkoner feathered smoke through his nostrils, gave a bitter laugh as the slipstream whipped it away.

"I've got another TC being overhauled in Palo Alto right now. Just like this one, except it's black." He squiggled the steering wheel back and forth, zigzagging them down the empty highway. "Only two and a half turns, lock-to-lock."

The low red car ate up the road. Falkoner shrugged.

"But I guess a man can't have sports cars and a wife at the same time. She filed on me two weeks ago. I took off before—"

"She left you over a couple of sports cars?"

"No, she drove the MG real good. I was proud of her."

He pushed smoke through a nose once broken and healed slightly crooked; that, and an inch-long patch of shiny scar tissue over his right eye, made him not only handsome without being pretty, but possibly tougher than his manner suggested.

"But we were only married a month and she was running around on me. Two different guys." His voice was suddenly guttural. "I'll deal with that when I get back." He turned to study Dunc. "You ever been to Ciudad Juárez, in Old Mexico?"

Dunc hadn't, but he remembered how exotic Mexico had seemed in that Robert Mitchum movie *His Kind of Woman.* They picked up Highway 80 at Van Horn, rode it 120 miles to El Paso, which was just across the river from Juárez. They zipped past the vast sprawl of Fort Bliss, the red car turning the heads of the crisp-uniformed MPs manning the gates. Falkoner, driving left-handed, unconsciously massaged his forearm with his right hand.

"Had enough of that crap to last me a lifetime." He jerked up his left sleeve. The forearm was scarred and disfigured, little of it remaining beneath the shiny scar-tissued skin except the bones. "Little gift from the fucking krauts. Army surgeons wanted to cut my arm off, said I'd never be able to use my hand again." He worked his fingers and grinned angrily. "A hell of a lot of weight lifting got the remaining muscles to take the place of those that are missing. So I've got full control. Fuck 'em."

He jerked down the sleeve and drove left-handed while snapping the cuff button shut with his other hand.

"Those bastards hurt me plenty," he added obscurely.

El Paso was a booming oil town with a population squirting ahead almost as fast as the oil was squirting from the ground. The Franklin

Mountains sliced the growing city right down the middle, made the east and west sides almost two separate towns.

Late afternoon shadows were reaching out for them when Falkoner parked the distinctive red sports car in a lot a few blocks from the border. He casually tossed Dunc's duffel bag in the trunk—he called it the boot—with his own luggage.

"A lot of car-theft rings operate out of border towns like Juárez, a car like this draws 'em like flies."

They walked along South El Paso toward the bridge spanning the thick brown swirling waters of the Rio Grande. On the other side was Mexico. Tall wooden derricks were scattered along the river, some still pumping to fill the air with the rotten-egg smell of crude, others with their rusting machinery quiet.

"Don't expect anything of the real Mexico in Juárez," said Falkoner. "Border towns don't belong to any country."

Most of the foot traffic on the International Bridge was going against them, from Juárez to El Paso, most of it Americans, many of them soldiers in khaki uniforms with their cunt caps set at jaunty angles on close-cropped heads.

"This morning it would have been Mexican women going into El Paso to shop; in another hour it'll be Mexican maids going back into Juárez from their jobs in the big *gringo* houses."

Dunc tried to see in the Rio Grande the clear sparkling river of a hundred Saturday morning serials, where the white hats splashed their horses across the Río Bravo in pursuit of the black hats. This was more the muddy Mississippi at flood stage.

"I hear they have bullfights in Juárez."

"Not today. They get their big crowds on the weekends."

Leaving his own country for the first time—Canada didn't really count—had Dunc up, excited, asking stupid questions.

"If the bullring's closed, what'll we do over there?"

"Anything we're big enough to do." Falkoner gave him an evil white grin with a lot of teeth in it; just beyond midspan he paused to spit down into the moving brown waters. "And in Mexico we can do even *more* than we're big enough to do."

The two beer-bellied, dark-skinned, uniformed guards in caps with exaggerated brims didn't even look at them as they walked through the Mexican checkpoint.

"I thought we'd need passports or something."

"White faces bring in them old Yankee dollars."

On this side of the river, South El Paso had become Avenida Juárez. Dunc could see the sprawling oval of the bullring, plastered with fight posters in Spanish. Dunc was in Mexico—*Mexico!* He felt an excitement that was like being scared.

Falkoner was different here, swinging his shoulders when he walked, not caring who else was on the street. He'd brought a lot back from the war besides the mutilated left arm. Like the airmen in Fairbanks, linking arms down the main drag of town, knocking man and woman alike off the wooden sidewalks into the muddy street. Until they met bands of loggers doing the same.

Falkoner turned west off Juárez on Tiaxcala, after a time turned left on Degollado, muttering something like "Calle Mujeres" almost to himself. He suddenly stopped in front of a storefront joint on a narrow dirt street. "Yeah, it's still here. The Red Arrow." To Dunc, the cantina looked no different from any of the others. But Falkoner's eyes were feverish, his face tight and shiny. "I started my war ten years ago right here at Fort Bliss. They didn't have the neon arrow in those days."

There was indeed a red neon arrow on the wall pointing down at the delights hidden behind the double swinging doors, then folding up into a pointed squiggle, then snapping out straight again. It was enough like Alaska that Dunc stopped short.

"Let's make sure there's a back way out first."

"Of course there is," said Falkoner. "I know this place."

But they went to look anyway. The narrow dirt alley's smell of refuse overrode the pervasive hot oil and spices and frying tortillas of Juárez. Half a shattered small-watt lightbulb hung over the Red

Arrow's warped back door. Dunc noted with approval a thirty-inch two-by-four leaning against the wall.

Inside, the Red Arrow was like the saloon in *High Noon*, where everybody turned down Caine's request for help with fighting the outlaws coming to town for revenge. Do not forsake me, oh my darling, on this our wedding day . . .

Falkoner's wife had forsaken him a month after the wedding day. Not Dunc's business. But somehow he wasn't surprised.

The bar was down the left wall, a wooden stairway led up to the second floor. Serapes and high-crowned Mexican sombreros hung above the backbar as decorations. Half a dozen ten-gallon cowboy hats hung off hooks between booths crowded with foursomes.

Falkoner slid onto a stool and held up two fingers. "*Dos cervezas*— cold."

The bartender set out two dripping brown bottles that made instant puddles on the scarred bartop. He reached for the church key hanging from his belt by a leather shoelace, but Falkoner stopped him by flipping off the caps with his Swiss Army knife.

"Never use a glass in Mexico—and open 'em yourself."

They tapped bottles, drank icy beer. The Red Arrow was crowded with cowboys in high-heeled boots and off-shift roughnecks with permanently crude-blackened fingernails. The rest of the men were of assorted ages but all wore parrot-bright sport shirts hanging outside khaki pants, black shoes, and hair cut so short above their ears that their heads looked white.

Some of the girls were dusky-skinned, others obviously Anglo, some almost ugly, some pretty, two almost beautiful. All of them, whatever their configuration or race, were blond and wore low-cut blouses above tight skirts.

Dunc fired down his beer, he'd been really thirsty, nodded at the bartender to set up two more, unopened, on the bar, then jerked his head at the crew-cut men scattered through the crowd.

"Soldiers from Fort Bliss?"

"Yeah. If they came over in uniform the MPs'd get 'em."

Falkoner *bit* the caps off these beers.

On the jukebox, chapel bells were ringing and Little Jimmy Brown was getting married. Falkoner was getting divorced after two months. A couple went upstairs. The chunky Mexican girl's skirt was so short Dunc could see the curve of her buttocks. He felt a stirring in his groin and looked quickly away.

A buddy who'd joined the navy after high school had written him at Notre Dame, "Jesus, you should of seen the bitch I nailed in a cathouse in Yokohama! Jesus, could she fuck!"

That's when Dunc, jealous but superior, had sworn he'd never pay for it. Nor had he. In Fairbanks the old-fashioned parlor houses had been the only decent places to drink. Red plush on the walls, a bar, a couple of couches, rooms upstairs, girls coming through not wearing very much—but even there, he hadn't paid for it. He'd just gone without, as it were.

His second bottle was empty, he was into his third. Hell, who was he kidding? He'd been a virgin until he was a junior in college, had screwed only four girls, once each, none in bed.

The alcohol was hitting his empty stomach. He slid off his stool, leaving the change from his final ten for another round.

"I gotta tap a kidney."

"Yeah, you don't buy beer—you just rent it."

Dunc wove his way into a tin-sided box with a wet concrete floor and a trough along one wall. The reek of urine was sharp as smelling salts. Scrawled above the trough was WHAT ARE YOU LOOKING UP HERE FOR? ARE YOU ASHAMED OF IT? Underneath, a different hand had scrawled, NO, IT SCARES ME.

In the middle of the room was a wooden cubicle without any door; inside was a brown-stained ceramic toilet. As he buttoned up, one of the bar girls went in and hiked up her skirt and stood bent-kneed over the toilet pissing cowily, like the whore in Joyce's *Ulysses*.

Back in the bar there was a fresh beer beside his half-finished one, and his change was gone. An Anglo woman with slightly buck teeth but big breasts barely concealed by a loose white blouse had her hand up the inside of Falkoner's thigh to his crotch. She was making her eyes round as if in amazement.

"*Olé, mucho hombre, no?*"

"*No tengo* the lingo, girlie," said Falkoner. "And I shouldn't have to with somebody as blond as you."

"Blond all the way *down*, sugar." Her fingers were busy. Falkoner's pants were beginning to bulge.

"How much?" he demanded.

"Twenty dollars."

"*What?*"

"Ten dollars."

"I'll give you two."

"I'll take it."

Falkoner slid off his stool, leaving beer, money, cigarettes, and lighter behind. "Keep my place, Dunc."

Chapter Seven

Dunc tried to spread himself across two stools, keeping his elbows wide to protect Falkoner's place. Six drunken soldiers wearing their off-duty uniforms of khakis and bright shirts bellied up to the bar. One, with a sweaty red face and master sergeant written all over him, started to slide his fat butt onto Falkoner's stool despite the beer, cigarettes, money and lighter.

"Hey, sorry, pal," said Dunc, "that's my buddy's place."

The soldier wore his khaki pants down under his paunch, and a black short-sleeved sport shirt with yellow flowers on it. A pack of Camels was partially rolled up in the left sleeve.

"He can tell me this is his stool when he gets back."

"I'm telling you now."

"Well, Jesus, that scares the livin' shit outta me."

He poured beer into his face; sweat gleamed on his jowls, he had to be over forty, had to have his twenty in. What was he doing trying to pick a fight in a Mexican whorehouse? What was Dunc doing letting him pick a fight in a Mexican whorehouse?

"I've got no fight with you, Sarge," he said reasonably.

"Gutless fuck, ain't you?" He turned to his pals. "We got us a PFC here, men."

"What's a PFC, Sarge?"

"A poor fucking civilian."

The sarge finished Falkoner's beer, shook a cigarette out of Falkoner's pack, lit it with Falkoner's lighter, and stuck that in his shirt pocket along with Falkoner's cigarettes. He then put Falkoner's folding money into his pants pocket.

"Now your buddy ain't sitting here no more."

"Well, shit," said Dunc.

He slid his wristwatch into his pocket. His heart was pounding wildly. From his years of football he knew he could take a lot of punishment and could dish it out, but knew he was just barely a good enough brawler to still have all his teeth.

They started for the alley to the incongruous "Song from *Moulin Rouge*" on the jukebox. The squat fat soldier walked with a rolling gait; a beer keg would be easier to knock over.

"Age before beauty," he said with a sly and nasty grin.

So he could jump Dunc from behind. Dunc said nothing. He went through the back door fast, grabbing the two-by-four he'd seen there, spun around swinging for the fence. Tom Nieblas had saved their butts with that trick one night up in Alaska.

The beer keg sergeant was already rushing him from behind, clasped hands swinging to club the back of Dunc's neck, so the makeshift bat hit him in the face with a meaty sound, ripping open his forehead and spreading his nose from cheek to cheek.

Kathwuck!

He flew backward, smashed into the door frame, spun around to crash face-first into the garbage pails. They went over, showering him with filth, landing on top of him. A three-quarter eggshell rolled unevenly across the alley floor.

Dunc dropped the two-by-four and fell to his knees beside the downed warrior. Sluggish blood seeped out from under the sarge's face. Dunc felt suddenly very sober indeed.

Dunc gingerly rolled him over, expecting at the very least to see an eyeball hanging out on his cheek. No. The flattened nose was pouring blood and he made a long harsh sound. A snore. Knocked down by the two-by-four, passed out from the beer.

Dunc dipped trembling fingers into the soldier's shirt pocket, found Falkoner's cigarettes and lighter, then dug his hand into the trouser pocket for the sheaf of folded bills Falkoner had left on the bar.

Feeling sick to his stomach, he went back into the Red Arrow to face the sarge's buddies. But Falkoner was back on his stool and arguing pro football with them.

"Hell, Joe Perry is the greatest running back ever played the game. Three thousand-yard seasons and he isn't done yet. And with Hurricane Hugh in the lineup . . ."

One of the soldiers saw Dunc, blurted out in surprise, "What the fuck?"

"He's sleeping it off in the alley."

A black-haired skinny bespectacled soldier laughed as he scooped up the greenbacks strewn across the bar.

"Told you the sarge was gonna get took!" he crowed. "We'd better get him outta that alley before he gets rolled."

It felt good to slide the cigarettes and lighter onto the bar in front of him, then slap the folded money down beside them.

"He took your stool."

Falkoner laughed, riffled his money, stuffed some of it into Dunc's shirt pocket.

"Hey, that's not—"

"Not mine, either," said Falkoner. "Let's blow this joint."

"I gotta give it back to the sarge." But all they found in the alley were the overturned garbage pails and a patch of blood-soaked dirt. Dunc got into a laughing jag. "I just rolled a guy for the first time in my life, and I didn't even know it!"

It got drunk out. The night was a purple-black bruise, hot and sweaty, chilly, loud and raucous, silent, frantic with neon in the middle of a narrow dusty Mexican street, serene in the desert with a billion uncaring stars overhead. A kaleidoscope of images with only fragments of memory clinging to them like flesh to shards of bone on a slaughterhouse floor.

Another bar, an incongruous shuffleboard in back. Soldiers in uniform playing it, shouting and drinking beer. Somebody grabbing Dunc's arm. "Your buddy over there says he's too drunk to fight but that you're lookin' for trouble."

Dunc shook his head. "I've already had mine, thanks."

The lanky cowboy sighed sadly. "Shit, can't get nobody to give me a fight. Lemme buy you a beer."

In a diner, sloppily eating things he'd never seen before, hadn't even heard of—*tacos* and *chiles rellenos* and *huevos rancheros* and *refritos* and *burritos*, some of them so hot with chili peppers that he was chugging down beer after beer just to keep his ears from smoking as he listened to all the good old boys trying to out-Texas one another.

"Saw your wife the other day, she looked mean as ever."

"Mean? Last week she hit a guy with her Cadillac and knocked him forty feet down the highway, yesterday she sued him for leaving the scene of an accident."

Dunc ran every Texas sally and witticism through his mind, savoring it for his notebook.

"Was playin' golf with Sam the other day, and we hadda wait for two women gassin' by the eighth hole. So I started over to ask 'em to move on, then I seen who they was and come back and said to Sam, 'You gotta go talk to 'em, Sam, one of 'em's my wife and the other one's my mistress.' 'Shit,' says Sam, 'I was just gonna say the same thing to you.'"

Falkoner said musingly, "You want to find Texas, kid, you just go west far enough to smell it, and south far enough to step in it, and you'll be in Texas."

All sound ceased in the eatery. Not a fork rattled against a plate, not a cup scraped on a saucer. The few Mexicans in the place were already edging toward the door.

"Say what, hoss?" demanded the burly, crag-faced cowboy on the stool next to Dunc. There was amazement in his voice.

"I said if you ever wanta give the world an enema, Texas is the place to do it," said Falkoner, and leaned around Dunc to hit the man in the face with the bottle of ketchup.

Dunc saw a fist coming his way, slipped it, got knocked off his stool by someone else, kicked somebody in the stomach, got stomped on, got slammed into a table leg, scuttled for the door on his hands and knees. Scrambled to his feet, narrowly ducked a chair coming out the diner's window in a beautiful crystal parabola of shattered glass, was running down the street, careening from side to side, laughing crazily.

Running beside him, Falkoner panted out, "What . . . do you tell a Texan . . . on his way . . . to the electric chair?"

"Wha . . . what?"

"Don't . . . sit . . . down."

Somewhere else, a nude girl on a table, humping her way on down to Satchmo's "Blueberry Hill" from the jukebox, until she was squatting over a silver dollar balanced on edge, then picking it up without using her hands to wild applause from the all-male clientele. She repeated the action.

"Hey, watch this!"

A drunken giggling soldier was heating one of the dollars with his lighter before he balanced it for her. Someone smashed a chair over his head. It might even have been Dunc.

And still later, a broken-down shack on the edge of the desert with no electricity but a cockpit out in back starkly illuminated by the headlights of a dozen parked cars, mostly Cadillacs, dented and unwashed from hard desert miles, all with their motors running to keep the batteries alive.

Gas fumes made people cough. Male and female voices shrieked in Spanish and English as fighting cocks with shaved thighs and metal spurs fastened to their strong, skinny legs leaped and flapped and feinted and gouged. Half obscured by clouds of dust, *gabaneros*-shirted handlers blew into the beaks of live birds or cradled dead ones in their arms. The air was heavy with cigarette smoke, blood, sweat, the stink of fear and birdshit and testosterone.

Falkoner was leaning farther out across the wooden edge of the ring than Dunc would have thought possible, eyes bulging with excitement, sweat pouring from his face. Veins wriggled down the sides of his neck like snakes, pulsed down the center of his forehead like a forked tree. He was waving bills and shouting to get his bet covered for the next fight.

It was short and quick: within seconds, to mingled *olés* and curses from the crowd, one of the birds was dead in an explosion of blood and brown and white feathers.

For the second time that night, Dunc was almost sick to his stomach. Not from watching the blood and death. It was just that he wished it was the fucking handlers in there, being forced to leap into the air to rowel each other with steel spurs strapped to their shins while drunks screamed at them.

"Jesus, did you see it?" exclaimed Falkoner. "Did you see that fucking kill?" He turned away, pocketing his winnings. "I gotta fuck me a woman right now. *Any* woman. Right now."

Chapter Eight

Dunc's first coherent morning memory was of throwing up into the Rio Grande from the middle of the bridge. He shambled back into the States wondering: which one did I puke into, Mexico or Texas? He sort of hoped both.

Maybe his thoughts weren't so coherent, after all.

His knuckles were skinned, his nostrils crusted with dried blood, one eye was puffed up—he'd be lucky if he didn't get a shiner. His side was sore, his ribs ached, his gut felt as if it had been drop-kicked, and the small of his back was so stiff it might have been stepped on. Hey, it probably had been.

He had huge amounts of great stuff for his notebook—except he'd been too drunk to remember it. Lock himself in a room with a head of lettuce and a bottle of water for a week; he could be like Proust and have remembrances of things past.

Trouble was, his notebook was in the boot of Falkoner's MG. And he couldn't remember when he'd last seen Falkoner.

A parking lot, a few blocks from the border. But El Paso's dawn streets all looked the same. And if Falkoner wasn't there, how could he get his duffel bag out of the trunk? Buy a cheap screwdriver, jimmy the boot of the MG and . . .

Yes, definitely not too coherent yet.

And buy a screwdriver with what? His watch was gone and his

pants pockets were all turned out. Thank God he'd left his ID in his duffel bag. Then he remembered Sarge's money. By some miracle his breast pocket hadn't been torn off his shirt and whoever had rolled him had missed such a stupid place to leave your stash. It was still there: seventeen bucks. Fat city.

But an hour later when he shambled into the lot where they had parked the MG, it was gone. With his duffel bag, his ID . . .

Later, somehow, some way, sometime, he was going to have to get to Palo Alto and find Falkoner and get his notebook and ID back. But right now all he wanted was out of El Paso, out of Texas. Hung over. He drank about a gallon of water at a public fountain, almost threw up again.

At a five-and-dime near the railroad marshaling yards on the western edge of El Paso he bought a ballpoint and a spiral notebook and a small tin of aspirin, washed down four of them with a cherry Coke. In a gas station men's room Dunc washed his shirt and put it on wet, brushed his teeth with his finger and soap from the dispenser; he'd forgotten to buy toothbrush and toothpaste. He got to the highway and stuck out a thumb.

Fifteen minutes later he was on his way to Lus Cruces, New Mexico, on Highway 80, in a rattly pickup full of Mexican migrant workers who shared their tortillas with him and dropped him at the bypass where 180 headed west for Tucson. He had no Spanish, but thought they said they were going north to Albuquerque.

All together it took him seven rides and thirteen hours to cover 275-odd miles of scorching, mostly empty desert to Tucson, a land of multicolored rock and sand and buttes and coulees, sparse mesquite and paloverdes and saguaro.

His final ride was with two Negroes in a dirty bashed-up black 1939 Chevy. He sat in the back, the springs poking at him through knife-slashed seat cushions, the erupted stuffing looking like dried custard.

"You comin' from where?" asked the rider.

"El Paso."

"I been there," he said solemnly. He wore a faded maroon sport shirt, had a little stubble of beard on his chin, rolled his eyes a lot, and was big: big of frame, arms, hands. He kept his arm on the back of the seat. "And 'fore that?"

Pick a town, Dunc thought. "Shreveport."

"Been there, too. Where 'fore that?"

"Baton Rouge." This could go on forever.

"Baton Rouge? Been there, too."

"How far you guys going?"

"Just outside Tucson. Man tole us 'bout some work at a tire-retreader there. Ain't worked in six months." Then quickly, as if that might have sounded like an implied threat, "But we let you off anywhere you want. Right, Jeremiah?"

"That sho be right, Zeke," said Jeremiah solemnly. He was small, thin, stooped, thick-lipped, and receding of chin, and he talked just like the old radio show *Amos 'n' Andy.* "That be right, sho nuff. Yassah. Lets him off anywheres he wants."

The car swayed and drifted as if the tires were half-flat or the steering gone or the tie-rods missing, or all three. A puff of black smoke rolled through the firewall.

"You smell somethin' burnin'?" demanded a panicked Jeremiah.

"I don't smell nuthin," said a placid Zeke.

Dunc fought mightily against slipping over the edge of sleep, afraid of one of his nightmares. He was jerked awake by Jeremiah's low gravelly voice going up the scale dramatically.

"Ah knowed it, Ah jes knowed it!"

A tractor had pulled into the highway in front of them. The Chevy's tires shrieked as the car tried to go in four different directions at once because each brake shoe grabbed its drum at a different time.

"Lots of luck," said Dunc conversationally, but Jeremiah got slowed down in time. Dunc let himself relax back against the gouging seat springs. No worries about falling asleep now.

"Ah knowed he'd pull out theah, fo he did it." Jeremiah carefully passed the tractor. "Jes knowed it fum the way he cum 'cross that field." Another puff of black smoke. In instant panic, "You smell somethin' burnin'?"

Soothingly, "I don't smell nuthin."

They dropped Dunc at a roadside truck stop outside Tucson. A dozen truck-trailer rigs sprawled on the concrete apron like basking dinosaurs, their running lights twinkling in the dusk like colored fireflies.

Inside, a junk-crowded gift shop offered rubber sidewinder rattlesnakes, rabbit's-foot key chains lucky for everyone except the rabbits, and sly desert postcards featuring bubble-butted tourists in shorts doing stupid things. Dunc bought a toothbrush and a can of Pepsodent powder, a safety razor, a packet of Gillette Blue Blades, put them all in a cheap yellow gym bag.

In the gas station rest room, two bits got him a shower. A shave, really brush his teeth . . . Worth it, even though his money was going fast. Probably have to find a job manning the clipper in some hash house kitchen, before he could get to California.

His hangover was gone, he was ravenous. On the diner's menu he found something called chicken-fried steak: a huge flat slab of pounded beef, breaded and pan-fried in axle grease, sunk in a pint of gooey pale gravy speckled black with pepper. Served with a mountain of mashed potatoes and watery peas and soggy biscuits heavy as rocks.

Dunc had six glasses of milk while he ate everything except the plate and finished off with cherry pie *à la mode.*

Outside, the night pressed in on this puny oasis of light and warmth. It was clear and totally black, the full moon long gone or not yet up or already set. He walked a quarter mile out into the desert, regretting the windbreaker in his duffel bag. He could see his breath against the lights of the truck stop.

Then he heard the *yip, yip, yip, aroooo* of his first coyote. The hair stood up on his arms and the nape of his neck. He'd heard wolves howling at night along the Alaskan Highway, but somehow this was an even lonelier sound. At least wolves hunted in packs. Coyotes worked alone.

What was he doing out here in the desert in the middle of the night, alone, anonymous? Hey, this'd be too damned civilized for old Harry and Señorita, too soft and easy and crowded. Old Harry wouldn't worry about ID.

He wanted to be a writer, didn't he? Well, how the hell did you do it except like this? You went, you watched, you learned, until you knew, like Hemingway said, that you had something to write about. You had to earn the mighty reckoning in a little room Shakespeare had written about. He'd meant the murder of Marlowe, but somehow it fit. Writing, you faced your own mighty reckoning in your own little room.

Back at the truck stop, nobody wanted him. The truckers said unauthorized riders voided their insurance. And nobody with the wives and kids in the car, at night, would take a beat-up-looking guy without jacket or suitcase. Instead of eating his chicken-fried steak, maybe he should have put it on his puffy eye.

After almost an hour, a long cream-and-red Olds 98 pulled in at the nearest gas pump. A big hard-looking man got out, impeccably groomed and wearing what looked like a silk suit. He told the attendant to fill the Olds with ethyl.

"I used to work at a gas station," Dunc said to the big man, "pumping ethyl. Regular, too."

It earned a chuckle. "Looking for a ride, kid?"

"You bet. Going west."

"Toward El Centro? Dago?"

Dunc didn't know where El Centro was. Didn't know Dago was San Diego. "Sure. Or L.A. Whichever is easier."

The big man handed over a five, pocketed the change. His neck was thick, as wide as his head, his hairline was climbing, his nose was flattened, his ears cauliflowered. He looked like an ex-pug, but most of them were punch-drunk and none of them would have the money for those clothes or a new Olds 98.

"I'm going up through Phoenix, from there you can hitch straight west to San Berdoo and L.A. Got a suitcase? Anything?"

"Just me and the gym bag."

"Atsa boy. Travel light." He jerked his head at the car. "Hop in. I'm Lucius Breen."

"Pierce Duncan. Everybody calls me Dunc."

The car was almost as luxurious as Arnie's Cadillac, and there was no honeybun to get him kicked out into the desert. The big man drove fast and well; his hands had distended knuckles but were carefully manicured. He swung the massive head Dunc's way.

"How long you been on the road?"

"Three, four weeks. Just bumming around."

"Atsa boy—do it while you're young." He kept snuffling and blowing. A thought drew down heavy scar-tissued brows. "Three weeks and just that little bag?"

"I got rolled last night in Juárez."

Black rage creased his features. "Fucking greasers!"

Dunc didn't know who had rolled him, but it sure as hell hadn't been Mexicans who had driven off with his duffel bag.

"Did you used to fight?" he ventured at last.

"Yeah. Twelve years pro. I was my own manager, invested my money in houses and lots." He gave a great roar of laughter. "Whorehouses and lots of whiskey."

He got suddenly serious.

"Actually I didn't booze, I didn't chase skirts, and I didn't pay any taxes. Boxers didn't then. I invested. In land around Dallas. Then I brought in a couple wells on my spread, a couple more . . ." He shrugged. "I pump oil, pump my wife, raise kids and horses. I hate niggers, spics, farmers, and anybody from Houston or San Anton'. Going up to Vegas now to referee a fight. They do two, three a year there, little no-'count things usually, but these boys are ranked heavyweights."

Last year Dunc had listened on the radio while Rocky Marciano KO'd Jersey Joe Walcott for the title.

"Would either of 'em have a chance against Marciano?"

Breen snuffled through his nose. "Five years ago Nitro Ned Davenport might have given Rock a fight. Still might, on a good night. But Ned's a fool, stays loyal to . . ." He paused with a calculating look. "Anyway, lousy judgment, lousy management. Tiger Terlazzo is young, fast—but they say he don't like to take a punch he don't have to take. We'll see."

Dunc had played a little stud poker, but Vegas would be *real* gambling. Gambling and professional boxing and all-night excitement. And a good place to earn traveling money.

"How about I ride straight through with you?"

"Atsa boy! Now you're talking."

Dunc was running from one side of El Paso's switching yard to the other, trying to get across before a train got him. But the yard was half a mile wide, and trains were coming on every track with only a half-inch clearance between the sides of the passing cars. Two rushing trains met just where Dunc cowered. He threw crossed arms up in front of his face and screamed . . .

"*Hey!* You okay, kid?"

Dunc was bolt upright on the seat, eyes staring, arms still crossed in front of his face. The 98 had come down out of the mountains and was starting across a flat arc of concrete highway laid on the top of a vast curved structure. Yellow lights illuminated the roadway. There was water close up on one side, an endless drop into nothing on the other. Twin ghostly towers flanked the upriver side of the road.

"Just a bad dream," Dunc finally got out. "Where are we?"

"Boulder Dam. Greatest dam in the world. Lake Mead on your right. Those castle-looking things are silt towers. They work the way they ought to because of a damned good engineer named Will Corfitzen."

They were across the dam, climbing back into the mountains again. The 98's lights cut a twin swath from the darkness.

"I worked on this dam back in the twenties," said Breen. "It was my first job, I was fifteen looking eighteen. Gov'ment farmed the contracts out to engineering firms that knew how to build dams." He chuckled. "Kaiser and Bechtel got the biggest pieces of the pie. They were bastards to work for, but I learned from them. Learned enough so that after Boulder Dam, I never worked for wages again. And I never will."

The next time Dunc woke up, they were coming down into the desert. Everything was dark except for the broad thin glow of reddish light flat on the horizon, pulsing in the clear air like the northern lights when he and his dad used to go out poaching rabbits on full-moon nights after a new snow.

"Las Vegas," said Lucius Breen in a voice laced with conflicting emotions Dunc could only guess at: love and hate for sure, maybe nostalgia and anger and anticipation. Excitement.

THREE

Whores, Fours, and One-Eyed Jacks

Chapter Nine

The little town of Las Vegas baked in the desert sun. Dunc walked down lower Fremont Street, gaping up at the facades of the gambling halls. The Gladiator had to be somewhere in this five-block area of the Main Stem known as Glitter Gulch, wall-to-wall gaming clubs for high rollers and penny-ante players alike.

He went by the Hotel Apache's ornate sign, the Las Vegas Club, the Pioneer with its huge neon cowboy in jeans and tight shirt and neckerchief, cigarette in his mouth, ten-gallon hat on his head, his cocked thumb pointing toward the casino. Dunc had already passed the Golden Nugget and the Eldorado Club.

At the curb was a gray 1942 Ford four-door sedan like the one he'd driven up to Fairbanks two summers before. He'd loved that little car, and here was its twin parked only half a block from the gold neon boxing glove marking the Gladiator Club.

On the carved wooden door a pair of heavyweight fighters duked it out, one sinking a left hook into the gut of his opponent—who was just landing a roundhouse right on the first fighter's chin. Dunc could almost smell the sweat and rosin, hear the thud of blows, the grunts of effort.

Inside, two women in slacks with bandannas around their big pink hair rollers played the slots as if the lives of their kidnapped children depended on the whirring dials.

Over the bar crowded framed photos of tough-looking men in Everlast trunks and sparring poses. A faded blowup was captioned as the last bare-knuckle world championship fight: on July 8 in 1889, the great John L. Sullivan had beaten Jake Kilrain for the title in seventy-five rounds of boxing at Richburg, Mississippi.

No clocks were visible anywhere. You'd have to check your watch for the time—if you hadn't hocked it for a few bucks to lay down at the tables. In his single afternoon of wandering around town, Dunc had learned that much about Vegas.

He slid onto a stool near a slight, slender man with the most alive eyes Dunc had ever seen, shining darkly in an ascetic olive face as thin and sensitive as a woman's. He wore a tuxedo and black tie at five in the afternoon, and there was nothing feminine about him: strong chin and high cheekbones, dark brown curly hair. Large, even, gleaming white teeth flashed in his dark face when he laughed.

He chuckled and sipped white wine and said to the bartender in musical, unaccented English, "*Everybody* but me says Siegel was nuts, Nicky, putting up the Flamingo on the L.A. highway six, seven years ago when you couldn't get building materials—"

"Hell, Pepe, he *was* nuts—they killed him, didn't they?"

Nicky was beefy of neck, massive of chin, dark heavy brows, getting thick around the waist but with no marks of professional fighting. His pink shirt had a high rolled collar and French cuffs with miniature silver boxing gloves as links.

"Maybe. But look at Vegas today. Population almost twenty-five thousand by the last census, growing by leaps and bounds. It's—"

"In the middle of the fucking desert." Nicky gave a deep rumbling chuckle. "I'll believe that Las Vegas News Bureau crap about beating Reno as the gambling capital of America when—"

"But we have Lake Mead and the Colorado River to give us water. With water and gambling this close to L.A., I say Bugsy was right."

Nicky grunted, turned to Dunc. "What'll it be, chief?"

"I'm looking for Nitro Ned Davenport. The fighter."

"Hey, how about a little service here? A martooni for me, a Scotch Manhattan for the lady. Two olives in the martooni."

The fat man who had crowded up to the bar between Pepe and Dunc wore a light cashmere sweater stretched over big shoulders and heavy arms. Massive hips billowed under his slacks, and the dividing line of his belt rode high up on the mound of belly.

"Aw, serve yourself, asshole," muttered Nicky after the man turned away, then added to Pepe, who was laughing silently, "He brings all his goddamn broads in here, expects them to get free drinks. How in hell do you make a Scotch Manhattan?"

"Put Scotch in a Manhattan," suggested Dunc.

"Ha! Well, by Christ, that's what he's getting."

Dunc checked out the backbar mirror; with the fat man at one of the otherwise deserted tables was a blonde in her low twenties wearing a sleeveless blouse and tight skirt, a Lana Turner look-alike.

Nicky flipped open the hinged part of the bartop and carried the drinks over to the table. No money changed hands; the freeloading part was apparently true.

Pepe stuck out his hand. When he smiled, fine lines calipered his mouth, making him look older than at first glance. He said in a courteous, musical voice, "My name is Pepe."

They shook. "Everybody calls me Dunc."

"Goddamn Scotch Manhattan." But Nicky, grousing, had barely returned when the fat man appeared to slide the Scotch Manhattan across the stick.

"Hey, this isn't right. You didn't use Scotch in this."

Nicky grabbed a bottle off the backbar with his big right hand, held it out for inspection. "*W-h-i-t-e H-o-r-s-e.* White Horse. Scotch." He turned to Pepe as if the fat man weren't there. "Why can't they ask for something I've heard of?"

The fat man slapped the bartop twice with a pudgy hand, pointed at Nicky. "Just make her another one, Nicky, okay?"

He grunted and waddled on his heavy thighs back to the table. Nicky took up the returned drink and tasted it.

"Christ—it's awful. Some people'll drink anything." He poured it down the brushed stainless-steel sink. "We'll try blended—I'll be damned if that puss can taste the difference."

Pepe laughed and said to Dunc, "When I was your age, we'd chew a couple of sticks of Juicy Fruit gum while we drank a shot of whiskey, and, *voilà!* Instant Manhattan."

Nicky took the remixed drink back to the table, set it before Lana Turner with a flourish, came back, and shut the hinged section of bartop. "Now, what's your squawk, chief?"

"No squawk. I was told Ned Davenport would be playing poker here this afternoon, that's all."

"You was told wrong. The poker room's closed 'til seven."

"A man named Lucius Breen gave me a ride into town last night. He said Davenport would be here."

"That Lucius," said Nicky, "he's just an old softy. Like iron underpants. Gave you a nice easy ride, did he, in that big black Connie of his—"

"Maroon-and-cream Olds 98."

"Yeah, sure, I forget. Ride from where?"

"Tucson."

Pepe said softly, suddenly, "Short odds you're a college man, hitchhiking around to see the country."

"That's it," said Dunc almost eagerly. "I graduated from Notre Dame a month ago."

"Nicky, I say the kid's okay."

"Ain't your ass you're wrong."

There was a shriek and the sound of cascading coins from one of the slot machines. *"I won! I won a jackpot!"*

A suddenly genial Nicky raised his voice. "Of course you did, ma'am. Our slots are the most generous in town."

"I heard one spilled its guts just last Christmas Eve."

Ignoring Pepe, the fat man called across to Nicky, "*That* Scotch Manhattan was perfect. Now, how about another round here?"

Nicky mixed the martooni and Scotch Manhattan again using blended. "Told you that puss couldn't tell the difference."

He returned to assemble a boilermaker, two bourbon and branch, and a steaming mug of black coffee from a Silex coffeemaker on the backbar hot plate. He cocked an eyebrow at Dunc.

"Just ginger ale." Too soon after Juárez.

"Didn't know Tucson had that kind of action."

"Juárez. The Red Arrow."

"Notre Dame, huh? The Red Arrow?" He gave a derisive snort of laughter. "Yeah! You're faded."

He put the ginger ale and the other drinks on a tray and jerked his head toward swinging doors in the rear wall beyond a piano nobody was playing.

"Poker room's out back. Tell 'em Pepe the piano player said you was okay. That'll go over big."

Carrying his tray in both hands, Dunc pushed open the swinging doors to the casino with his butt. Four blackjack tables, four craps table, three roulette wheels, a faro setup, a three-card monte layout, and a wheel of fortune. A triple row of slots, all deserted. No poker table, no players—only a lone blackjack dealer and his lone customer. The dealer was late forties, with piercing eyes, a large mouth, strong teeth. His white shirt open to the waist showed a V of muscular, hairless chest. The ends of his untied black bow tie hung down on his shirtfront.

"So, Sabine," he said lazily, "you got hot pants today?"

Sabine was short and dark-haired, with a round laughing face without the laughter reaching dark eyes at once avid and sad. "If I did, I'd go next door and cool 'em off."

"What's next door?"

Sabine slowly revolved on her stool to sweep Dunc from head to toe as if he were for sale by the pound. She created a lot of sexual awareness with a pair of enormous breasts under a skimpy black blouse and a short swirly black-and-white-print skirt that emphasized Mae West hips and waist and shapely calves.

"A bouncer who's hung like a bull." She dropped ten silver dollars from her potbellied black purse on the table. "Deal the cards, Henri my pet."

Dunc stayed to watch. Henri gave Sabine and himself each two cards, one of hers facedown, the other faceup. Both of his were faceup. Both were face cards. Sabine had a queen showing. She tipped up the edge of her bottom card.

"Shit," she said. She scraped her cards on the green felt tabletop twice, said, "Hit me." A five. She gave a shout of laughter and flipped up a hole six. "There *is* a God." Henri slid ten dollar chips across to her. "You the new bar boy?"

"Sure," said Dunc. "Poker room out back?"

"Yeah. But play a hand of blackjack before you go."

He hesitated fractionally, then put his tray of drinks on an unused blackjack table. "Why not?"

He had just two bucks fifty left, but his dad always said, any day you had a place to sleep and food in your belly was a successful day. Well, Dunc had a room for the night he'd paid a buck for, and Lucius Breen had bought him a huge pancake-and-eggs breakfast after they'd hit Vegas that morning.

He put his pair of ones on the baize. Sabine let her ten silver dollars and ten one-dollar chips ride. Henri dealt in a blur of blue bicycles. Dunc's hole card was a nine. Faceup was a five. Henri had 18 showing, by the house rules couldn't hit again; but Dunc had to take another card. Sabine flipped her hole card faceup beside her exposed card. Both were faces.

"Double down," she said.

Henri dealt a card down on each of her face cards. Dunc busted with a 22. Sabine went broke on one hand, won the other. She finger-snapped a silver dollar to Dunc. He smiled and shook his head and slid the chip across the felt to Henri as a tip.

"Well how d'ya like that?" demanded Sabine, offended.

"I like it," said Henri. He tapped the chip twice on the table in ac-knowledgment, pocketed it, squeezed Sabine's hand as she slid her next bet forward. "Kid has class, you must admit."

She pulled the hand back. "Are you coppin' a feel?"

"You come sleep in my room, and you say I'm coppin' a feel? Jesus Christ!"

"Anyone I've met or slept with?"

Henri shook his head as if in pity, said to Dunc, "It's always and only sex with her. Sex with any man comes along."

"Or with a goat. Or a dog. Maybe I'll try a pony one of these nights."

"You got one nasty mouth on you, Sabine."

Dunc turned away from the nearly physical scent of sexual arousal that rose off their bantering like the too-heavy fragrance of massed funeral flowers.

"Just deal the goddamn cards, Henri my pet," said Sabine behind him. "Save the hardnose until you're off-shift, so I can get *something* stiff shoved up me tonight."

Chapter Ten

The Gladiator's poker room was tricked out as an old-time western saloon. Harsh yellow electric light from fake candles set around a fake wagon wheel suspended by real chains above the round deal table gave the players' faces highlights with rich brown shadows. The wallpaper was whorehouse red flock, the ceiling was decorated tin squares.

Nitro Ned Davenport's big left hand held his cards close to his chest as his right hand fanned them cautiously. His hulking shoulders drew taut lines in his black silk shirt. He looked up.

"The question is—who's lyin' an' who's dyin'?"

Davenport's voice rumbled deep from the vast cavern of his chest, fuzzed like bad radio reception by countless blows to the windpipe. Scar tissue shone above his heavy brows. He was thirty-three years old, on the far slope of his career.

"You gotta show 'em to know 'em, Ned," said Carny Largo in a lazy, insolent voice. He was a slender man with a neat, carefully trimmed mustache.

Ned slid chips into the center of the table. "Fifty."

The door across the room was shoved open by a husky black-haired kid backing in with a tray of drinks.

"Private game, Jim," said Largo with an unpleasant smile.

"See," said Gimpy Ernest, pushing in chips. He was a heavy man with graying, wavy hair, full lips, a pouty chin, heavy-lidded eyes.

The kid had kept coming. Largo demanded in astonishment, "Who the fuck is this guy?" and snapped, "Rafe," to a diminutive rat-faced man who was sitting between Gimpy Ernest and the only woman in the game. Rafe started to get up.

Nitro Ned rumbled, "We're playin' a hand of poker here."

Rafe hesitated, looked at Largo, looked at Davenport, then sank resentfully back into his chair. He was barely five feet tall. Beady eyes were close-set on either side of a high-bridged nose too big for his face. His midnight-blue double-breasted suit coat hung open; it had a vertical chalk-mark design.

Dunc brought his tray into the circle of light. Ned offered a huge paw. "You the kid Lucius was tellin' me about?"

"I guess I am. Pierce Duncan? People call me Dunc."

"Dunc's gonna be out to the ranch, helpin' me train."

Everyone looked surprised, Dunc most of all: Lucius Breen had just said to look up Ned Davenport at the Gladiator, that he played poker there most afternoons. Nothing about the kind of job he could never have dreamed about. Excitement, powerful as an adrenaline rush, rose up in him.

Gimpy Ernest began, "Ned, we don't know nothing about this guy. What if—"

"If Lucius sent him, he's okay," said Carny Largo. He chose ten chips from his stack, slid them into the center of the table. The sleeves of his crisp cream-colored cowboy shirt were rolled back two turns. "See you and bump you another fifty."

"I can't beat Ned, I can't beat Ernest, I can't beat Rafe, I can't beat Carny," complained the woman. "Who can I beat?"

She folded her hand and turned sideways to cross long exquisite thighs. They were encased in sheer black hose, displayed halfway to her hips by a one-piece dress of midnight-blue satin, shimmery, clingy. Her opaque nail polish and eye shadow were also midnight-blue. She was stunningly beautiful without being pretty, caught Dunc's stare, winked at him.

"Rafe?" said Carny. "Hundred to you."

Rafe's glittering rodent's eyes were locked on the woman's crossed thighs as if they enfolded paradise. He tossed in his hand without another look at the cards.

Gimpy Ernest picked up a lighted cigarette from the closed folder of paper matches he was using as an ashtray, sucked it greedily. From what he had said, he had to be the big fighter's manager. After studying his hand, he dropped out.

"With Artis already out, that leaves just us, Ned."

Nitro Ned checked the cards tight against his chest again, looked over at Artis. She blew him a silent and ironic kiss. He took the kiss as reassurance; the irony seemed to escape him.

"I see you," he told Carny.

As he was tossing another fifty into the pot, Dunc handed out the drinks. Carny was bourbon and water, as was Artis. Gimpy was the boilermaker. Rafe wasn't drinking. The plain black coffee, not so hot now, went to Ned Davenport; a spilled previous cup had left a dark stain on the felt by his elbow.

Davenport had jacks full, but Carny Largo had a straight flush. Ned sighed and tossed his hand into the discard.

"Chicken feed," he said.

Carny pulled in his winnings. He looked like a casino dealer, but couldn't be: house men never bet the hands.

"Jacks full were good for any hand tonight—until this one. You never allow a margin for error, Ned."

"Back to the ranch, Ned," said Gimpy abruptly. His maroon raglan sport shirt had no shoulder seams and dark moons under the arms. "Tomorrow you gotta look sharp, the press's going to be around to watch you spar with Jantzen. If they knew he'd got a decision on you once—"

"*Nobody* knows that," chuckled Ned complacently. "If it had of happened, we woulda been fightin' a long time ago and a long ways from here under two different names. Who's dealin'?"

"And what's wild?" asked Carny with a grin.

"Whores, fours, and one-eyed jacks," said Artis promptly.

Dark hair was pulled severely back from her face to show small ears with dangly gold and blue-stone earrings. Her complexion and predatory eyes were dark, her nose was bold, her wide mouth unexpectedly sensuous. Dunc was still breathless.

Ned rumbled, "You know damn well there ain't ever gonna be anything wild in any poker game I'm in."

"Really?" she laughed, then added, "Guts," and began dealing with blazing speed.

Ned said, "Dunc, have Nicky give you a drink on my tab. You can ride out to the ranch with me when I go."

As he left, Artis was saying derisively, "Rah-fay-e-lay, quit trying to see up my skirt and put up your ante . . ."

Now the tables in the gaming room were jammed, the slots whirring and clanking, the noise level deafening. Shrieks came from a group of women playing the wheel of fortune. Sabine was nowhere to be seen, but Henri was still dealing blackjack, his bow tie now in place. They exchanged grins.

All the bar tables were taken by couples and foursomes. The fat man and Lana Turner were elsewhere. Cigarette smoke fogged the lights. Three waitresses in short, bright, sexy one-piece costumes flitted around the room like butterflies, bringing drinks from the bar or food from the kitchen.

The stools around the perimeter of Pepe's piano bar were crowded. On a felt doily was a big brandy snifter stuffed with singles, near his elbow a glass of white wine.

Nicky, who had been joined by another bartender, said, "Here comes that fucking ginger ale again." He dropped ice into a glass, swirled it, squirted in ginger ale. "On the cuff."

"Thanks."

Dunc went over to the piano bar. Pepe mopped his face, shook his head. "It gets worse later, when all the divorcées who struck out for the night show up. How did it go with Nitro Ned?"

"God, Pepe, I can't believe it, he's giving me a job out at the ranch, helping him train for the fight."

"Not so dumb at that," Pepe said. "Terlazzo's fast—and ten years younger. Maybe Ned needs you to push him a bit."

Ned Davenport shoved back from the table to stretch his long, thick, almost apelike arms over his head. He intertwined his fingers, pulled to make something pop in his upper back.

"Time for me to get my beauty sleep."

Artis started putting her chips into her purse.

"No," snapped Gimpy Ernest. "In bed, alone, goddammit. We don't need any complications right now. And I don't like you hiring that guy."

"Lucius says he's a good kid, smart."

"Okay, but Artis stays in town for one goddamn night. I'll be along after Carny and me discuss some business."

Ned's deep-set eyes got hot under heavy brows. Any hint of something that might have seemed benign had left his face.

"Not business about Terlazzo."

"Of course about Terlazzo," said Carny. "I'm guaranteeing the gate, for Chrissake, we'd *better* talk about the fight."

"Just so you know I fight my *own* fight." Ned turned to Artis, ignoring Gimpy. "I'll be up front, baby."

Loud voices, the clink of chips and whir of slots came through the door when he opened it, were cut off as it swung shut. Carny Largo sighed as he watched torn cigarette smoke eddy together again behind Ned Davenport's broad departing back.

"If that man had a brain, even a piece of a brain, he'd be fighting Marciano in ten weeks instead of Terlazzo in two."

"Poor Ned," said Artis. "Over the hill without a brain—just like the scarecrow." Contempt lit her face. "Don't you believe it—and he's still got that dynamite right hand."

"So go keep your punchy prince happy," sneered Carny.

She crossed the room with long savage strides, her hip motion holding Rafe spellbound. Gimpy started wheedling again.

"Carny, not tonight, the reporters are like vultures—"

"He's only sparring with Jantzen tomorrow, for Chrissake." Carny leaned across the table, his face suddenly set. "I've kept Terlazzo under wraps for two years, but eventually he's going to need an old-timer like Ned under his belt."

"I hope you're not saying what I think you're saying."

Carny leaned back, bit the end from a lean cigar.

"Whatever happens with Terlazzo, a few more bouts and Ned's hearing bells. Now, we have some serious things to talk over."

Chapter Eleven

A woman with a sad eroded face and a good figure and an expensive dress asked for "Mood Indigo." Pepe sang it in a bluesy voice, segued into "Stardust," finished with "Willow Weep for Me." The woman cried while he played, stuffed a five-dollar bill into his brandy glass, and fled.

"Oldies but goodies," said Dunc.

"Like the lady."

Then he started a seemingly pointless story about a gambler at the Desert Inn, which had opened three years before, the fifth major hotel since 1941 on the extension of South Las Vegas Boulevard now known as the Strip.

"There's a big Joshua tree out in front of it—Vegas was originally settled by Mormons and they gave Joshuas that name because all those angular branches looked like outstretched arms beckoning to them from the wilderness."

"And they went forth and they found Vegas," grinned Dunc.

"And lost it just as quick." Seemingly of its own volition, his left hand started a Fats Waller walking bass as he managed a small shrug. "Mormons and gambling." He tilted his head in the direction of a tall lean player who'd gotten up from his table to stretch. He said, "That's him there—he once held the dice at the Desert

Inn casino for twenty-eight straight passes, but he was a careful bettor and walked away with just $750."

"Sounds pretty good to me," said Dunc.

"Pretty good? It was a million-to-one chance! If he'd let his winnings ride he would have had $289,406,976. Artis in there at the poker game would never miss her big chance by being timid like that."

"What is Artis short for?" asked Dunc.

"Heck, Dunc, who knows? She never says."

"Why do they call Gimpy Ernest Gimpy?"

"He limps—you don't notice it until he stands up. Says he got it in the ring, but I doubt he ever was a fighter."

"And Carny? He looks like a house man, but he was betting on the hands along with everyone else."

"You have a good eye—he owns the place."

"Then he's your boss."

His left hand kept on walking. "For my sins."

"Okay. The little guy. Rafe."

"Rafaele Raffetto. Little, yeah—but watch out." Pepe's right hand made eerie arpeggios far up in the treble keys. "Rumor has it that he's a dangerous little bastard if Carny points him in your direction."

Dangerous, that little rat-faced guy? Well, maybe. Pepe was going on as his fingers roamed the keys.

"Listen, Dunc, a record producer might come out from L.A. in a week, ten days to talk about cutting a demo. That happens, I'm gone like a shot."

"Jesus," said Dunc. "That's great! Good luck with it!"

"Don't tell anybody—especially Carny."

Big, grinning Nitro Ned punched Dunc playfully on the shoulder. Dunc's whole upper arm went dead. Ned exclaimed, "You can always tell a good piano man by his left hand."

Doing arpeggios with his left hand, Pepe said, "And you can always tell a champion by his *right*," and sang:

"One fist of iron,
The other of steel,
If the right one don't get you,
Then the left one will."

The other people around the piano recognized Davenport and started applauding. "Place is full of glad-handers," he said, as if secretly pleased by the recognition.

Artis appeared. Ned put an arm around the tall woman's shoulders. "What kept you, babe?"

"I had to cash in my winnings."

"Way you watch your money, you're gonna end up rich."

"That's the idea, big boy."

"Come on, you suckers, come to Vegas and lose your shirts!" Artis paused outside the Gladiator as she tried to consider Las Vegas through Dunc's eyes. She gave a little self-conscious laugh, added in softer tones, "Glitter Gulch didn't glitter until we got neon a couple of years ago. Now Second and Fremont's the brightest-lit corner in America west of Times Square."

Dunc believed her. Flashing sequential bulbs spelled out CASINO, CAFE, LAS VEGAS, GAMBLING, MONTE CARLO CLUB, and OVERLAND HOTEL in man-high letters.

The three of them turned east; Fremont dead-ended in a little egg-shaped city park beyond which was the Art Deco train station. Opaque glass-cube windows and wide doors opening on a platform for the moment devoid of even redcap porters. But at 2:00 A.M. the Union Pacific's City of Los Angeles would steam in with its trainload of hopes.

Overlooking the park was a big, orange brick building with a soaring T-shaped sign reading HOTEL SAL SAGEV. Its front was ablaze with lights.

"Las Vegas backwards," said Dunc in swift comprehension.

Davenport rumbled with laughter as he stopped at the gray 1942 Ford four-door Dunc had admired that afternoon.

"Took me two weeks to figger that out."

Artis got into the front seat, Dunc slid into the middle of the backseat.

"Two years ago I drove a car just like this up to Alaska. A 1942 Ford four-door sedan. I called it the Grey Ghost."

"Ain't hardly anyone knows Ford sold any '42s. Quit when the fuckin' Japs attacked Pearl Harbor, and when they started civilian production again in '46, they was just jazzed-up '42s."

Pearl Harbor. December 7, 1941. Dunc remembered listening to President Roosevelt's "date which will live in infamy" radio speech and feeling scared and solemn. He'd been eighteen days short of his tenth birthday.

Ned was saying in a flat voice, "Not that I can bitch about my war. I spent my army years in the ring fighting soldiers with my fists 'stead of Japs with a rifle."

He didn't sound happy about it. Only now did Artis realize that her big lumbering fighter, who always bragged about how he'd sat out the war, had actually wanted in on the fighting desperately.

He'd U-turned the car through the lights and crowds of Glitter Gulch, people crossing Fremont without regard for traffic. He turned off into Fifth Street, then into Clark and finally Las Vegas Boulevard, and the city fell away behind them. Seven miles southwest of Glitter Gulch on the wide dusty boulevard was the fabled Strip: a big splash of light marking a hotel or casino, then relative darkness until the next glamorous resort.

Artis said, with a sudden strain in her voice, "Here it comes, the Fabulous Flamingo."

She remembered opening night vividly: December 26, 1946. They had been rained out. She had worked her first party for the mob guys from back east that night. Start of her downhill slide.

"Built by Bugsy Siegel, right?" asked Dunc, feeling a little bit like a native listening to Nicky and Pepe talk about Siegel and the sprawling horseshoe-shaped complex.

"I knew him," said Davenport. "He liked the horses, liked pugs like me. He was a quiet little guy."

"Unless you called him Bugsy to his face—or said something nasty about Virginia Hill," said Artis.

The lush hotel dropped away behind them. Before Bugsy, before the Flamingo, this had been a nice little town. She had met Carny Largo at a party at the Flamingo. Even with Bugsy dead and Virginia run off to Europe, the people who had blasted Bugsy scared her. Cross them you got buried in the desert. And you never knew who they were, watching, waiting . . .

She'd been lucky, maybe the luck of Artemis, the Greek goddess of the hunt and destroyer of men. She shivered. She had the money fever, true enough; but couldn't she get what she wanted without helping destroy someone else?

She stole a glance back at Dunc. Just a few years younger than she was, but it felt . . . *nice* to be here in the car with her hulking fighter and the kid. Felt as if nothing too bad could happen to her while they surrounded her.

Brightly lit letters spelled out the turn to McCarran Airfield. Built just five years ago, but now there were one-arm bandits in the terminal and the sign was flanked by husky towers aflame with glowing neon propellers.

After another couple of miles, Ned turned left into a narrow sandy road. Their lights, jumping and swooping with the dips and twists of the track, cast long shadows of creosote bush and rabbitbrush out across the desert floor, then locked onto a low rambling adobe ranch house that seemed to go on forever.

"Home sweet home," said Artis in her ironic voice.

The Ford squealed to a stop. Dunc was ravenous; he hadn't eaten since Lucius Breen's big pancake breakfast eighteen hours before.

But Nitro Ned said, "I'll show you the bunkhouse, kid. Four A.M. comes mighty early."

Chapter Twelve

Okay, guys, drop your cocks and grab your socks."

It seemed that Dunc's head had hardly hit the lumpy pillow filled with what felt like corn husks. Yawning, he sat up on the edge of the bed. A kerosene pressure lamp was lit, evoking sudden Georgia memories. Thank God no dreams had brought him up yelling in the night. Nothing more embarrassing in a room full of tough guys than crying out like a girl in your sleep.

Some kind soul had neatly stacked sweat clothes and jockstrap on the foot of his bunk. Dunc washed up sketchily and dressed, wearing his own tennis shoes. He walked up to the main house drawing in great lungfuls of air rich with sage, horse manure, and, elusively, food. When was he going to get fed?

A band of predawn light lay against the eastern horizon, so fragile the very pale gold looked off-white. The gray line of cloud above it had a delicate lemon belly. Ned was just coming down the front steps in his own gray sweat suit. He held out a bottle.

"Take a gulp of this." It was hot water with a lemon squeezed into it. "How long since you've done any roadwork?"

"Month, month and a half."

"You'll be okay, then. We're just loosenin' up anyway. Five little miles, then breakfast."

They walked side by side out into the desert. By the dim light,

Dunc could see they were in twin ruts that would make a ninety-degree left when they met a barbed-wire perimeter fence some distance ahead. Ned suddenly started talking, the words tumbling out as if until now he'd had no one to say them to.

"Listen, kid, this is my chance, this fight. My last chance. I take Terlazzo, Marciano's gotta deal with me. I been close to a shot before, but never this close."

"I'll do anything I can to help," Dunc said lamely.

But what could he do? He'd done a bit of Golden Gloves sparring, but his first loves had been football and the weights.

"Just don't let me dog it," said Ned. He started a slow jog. Dunc kept up with him. "We got only about two weeks now."

Dunc felt the sweat starting out on his body, felt his muscles start to loosen up, get limber. He felt good. The track made another ninety-degree angle to the left inside the boundary fence. A startled snort, the brief drumming of nervous hooves, huge hinking shadows throwing heads in near-dark.

"Horse ranch," said Ned. He started tossing punches as he ran, snorting like the horses. "Better'n staying in town and trainin' in a gym—too many distractions, an' anyone can watch, check your moves. Grub's better out here, too."

Dunc's mind drifted to Artis. What a woman. Ned's woman. He started snorting and tossing punches of his own as he ran.

"That's it, kid." A grin was in his voice. "You're a natural."

Ned was throwing combinations, shoulders dipping and weaving as he jogged and jabbed. Dunc kept stumbling while trying to watch those slashing hands in the dim predawn light. He didn't know enough to do Ned any good.

The fence turned again. The horses in the center of the paddock were trotting to keep up with them, dimly seen in the lifting darkness, throwing their heads in delight with the game.

"They run with me every morning I'm out here," said Ned, then suddenly yelled, "Okay, I race you the last hundred yards!"

Dunc was surprised but turned it loose, legs flashing, arms pumping, but Ned skittered around the corner of the ranch house two strides ahead of him. Hadn't seemed like five miles.

"Hah! Got ya!"

They slowed to a walk, still tossing shadow punches as they angled toward the barns past a regulation boxing ring set up under a grove of cottonwoods with rough bleachers arranged for maybe forty, fifty spectators. It was full daylight now.

They had the old converted feed barn to themselves. A sprung hardwood floor, a ring, a trio of heavy bags hanging on chains from one of the ceiling beams, two speed bags screwed to the wall on metal frames. The place smelled like every gym: rosin, stale sweat, unwashed socks and jocks. Over this, faintly, the unfamiliar sweet-sour memory of fermented silage, under it an acrid iodine tang he realized was dried blood.

This was for real! This was professional! Damn, he was glad to be here! Ned handed him a pair of cracked, sweat-stiff gloves and started to pull on a pair of his own.

"We spar a little to cool down before we go eat."

"Oh, uh . . . should you do this before you box with Jantzen?"

"I just wanna show you a couple things." Ned gave him a rubber mouthpiece to protect his teeth. "Hey, how can you tell if a girl's wearing falsies?" Dunc shook his head. "Falsies taste like rubber."

In the ring Ned kept his feet solidly on the canvas, sliding them, slightly crouched. Dunc tried to ape his stance.

Ned said something that sounded like "Throw a few." Dunc started sending out tentative jabs. Ned slipped his rubber to say, "I told you to throw 'em. Put some beef into 'em."

He put his mouthpiece back in and Dunc started putting his arms and shoulders into the punches. None of them hit anything except air or Davenport's gloves. Getting frustrated, he threw harder punches, a real flurry of punches, roundhouse swings off the floor, now heavy-armed. Ned wasn't even breathing hard.

"You got strength but . . . Here, lemme show you something."

Dunc was reeling backward, vision blurred, his nose flowering blood. Ned had eight fists, all hitting him at once, but without real force: quick light jabs. He tried to block them, but each time Ned's glove was tagging him elsewhere. A final one in his gut with some muscle in it curled him over. His eyes were watering. A gentle open hand laid against his face pushed him off balance backward so he bounced off the ropes.

"An' you meet an uppercut comin' off the floor, an' you're kissin' canvas."

Dunc stood with his head hanging, his gloved hands on his knees, nose dripping blood on the canvas as he tried to get his breath back. His ears were ringing.

"You gotta teach me how to do that," he panted. His vision was clearing. "I'd see 'em coming, but I couldn't stop 'em."

The fighter was pulling off his gloves. "C'mon, a little rubdown an' then breakfast."

Gimpy Ernest and Artis were standing on the front veranda watching them come toward the ranch house.

"Joe Louis once said that if you see an opening, it's too late. You gotta already have hit the other guy. Otherwise—"

"I'll be kissing canvas."

They were both laughing as they went up the weathered steps to the veranda. Ned faked a punch at the dour crippled man's belly, making him flinch, then opened his arms to Artis.

She avoided his bear hug. "You're all sweaty, lover."

The showers were in a converted equipment shed: concrete floor, a few tinny lockers, some benches to sit on. The hot sluicing water felt wonderful. Afterward they lay facedown, nude, on a pair of towel-covered tables to be worked on by a brace of masseurs. Dunc had never had a rubdown before. As strong fingers pungent with witch hazel massaged, rotated, delved, soothed, he forgot his nudity and almost fell asleep.

They each ate a pound of steak sizzling in butter, aided by six eggs each and abetted by a mountain of hash browns and about a half a loaf of toast. Dunc got as many glasses of milk as he wanted. He wanted a lot.

"You can ride into town with one of the guys to get your stuff from the rooming house." The big fighter dug in his pocket, came out with a ten-dollar bill. "Here. You're gettin' twenty-five bucks a week an' room and board. Just be back by three o'clock for Jantzen."

A lot of money. He rode in with a man named Max. "The train station at two-thirty," Max said, and drove off, a battered Nevada license plate swinging off the rattly pickup's rear bumper by a lone screw.

Dunc walked six blocks to the rooming house and collected his yellow gym bag. The large-bodied landlady said with instant hostility that he didn't have any refund coming just because he hadn't slept in the room. He said he didn't expect any.

At a smoke shop with a rack of paperbacks, he picked up a two-bit Signet edition of J. D. Salinger's *Catcher in the Rye.* After being seduced by a chocolate malt at a soda fountain, he let the inevitable one-armed bandit hold him up for his change, and ended up on a train station platform bench, reading.

When Max honked the horn, he'd just got to the part where the teenage prostitute had come to Caulfield's hotel room for a five-dollar "throw," and Caulfield had chickened out. Even as Dunc would have done, probably even if Artis was making the offer.

When they got back, cars full of newsmen and hangers-on and avid-eyed women were pulling into the yard. Gimpy Ernest was there, Artis was not. Flashbulbs popped and were ejected onto the ground as fresh ones were snapped into place. Ned wore satin trunks and a light robe with his name embroidered on it. He stood in the outdoor ring, looking out at the well-filled bleachers, nodding to this person, cracking a joke to that.

He saw Dunc standing near the ring, gestured with a gloved hand. Unlike this morning, his fists now were taped to protect them. He kept banging them together.

"Hey, Dunc, c'mon up an' be one of my cornermen."

The fat Negro who'd been Ned's masseur was wearing a T-shirt that had NITRO NED emblazoned on it. He was getting the spit bucket and water bottle arranged. He grinned, stuck out a huge black paw.

"Wesley Harding Jones. Wes."

"Pierce Duncan. Dunc."

"You ever tended a fighter before?"

"Nope."

"No sweat. This ain't but patty-cake anyway."

Jantzen climbed through the ropes on the other side of the ring. He was even bigger than Ned, his body white but his face and neck burned dark by the sun like a farmer's. It wasn't a face, it was a mask: scar tissue massed over the eyes, the nose a broad splodge between the shapeless lumps of ear gristle on the sides of his head. He grinned vacantly across the ring at Ned.

But when the bell was struck, Jantzen seemed to go crazy, leaping from his corner, snorting, arms windmilling. He hit hard, but Ned picked blows out of the air like swatting flies, and every once in a while would work a lightning combination of his own, *thunk thunk THUD*, each blow driving Jantzen back. His famous right was never uncorked.

After the caravan of newspeople and hangers-on had driven back toward Vegas, Jantzen asked anxiously, "Ned, I done all right, huh?"

"You done great," said Ned, putting an arm around the punchy fighter's shoulders.

Later, when Gimpy Ernest had limped away taking his apparently permanent sour expression with him, Dunc saw Ned slipping the big punch-drunk brawler a fistful of folding money.

Chapter Thirteen

The church was empty and so was the confessional. Dunc went back out into the sunlight feeling relief. He'd tried to go to confession and no one was there. He hadn't *done* murder, maybe the only truly mortal sin, but he'd helped, jerking the scattergun from Hent's hand, holding Hent down so the knife could go into his belly. Yet even now he was flooded with confusion about the part he had played. So how could he make confession?

He had to before he could receive communion, that's how; it was going to be the hardest thing he had ever done. Only by making it an offering for Ned's victory could he do it.

In the driveway of the church rectory a husky mid-thirties man with dark curly hair had his head under the raised hood of an old junker. In passing, Dunc heard the man's grunt of satisfaction when the engine coughed into life in the Sunday morning quiet.

The black-haired guy came out from under the hood.

"I'll meet you at the confessional," he said.

How had he known? Dunc returned to kneel in the twilight box. The little window slid open. He could dimly see the priest through the veiled opening.

"Bless me, Father, for I have sinned. It has been eight weeks since my last confession . . ."

The halting whispered phrases took a long time.

"An evil man, son," said the priest when he had finished. "Come to an evil end." He paused. "But you didn't come here to tell me somebody else's sins. What was yours?"

Hent, all meanness burned out of him by imminent death, was more vivid in memory than he had been in reality.

"I didn't try to stop it, because I was afraid if he lived he'd come after me next. Even now I don't know what I should have done."

"So your soul shut its eyes and has been silent?"

"No. I've had dreams. Bad dreams. Nightmares."

The priest grunted with the same satisfaction he'd shown when his old junker of a car had turned over.

"Life isn't a book and the people you meet on the road aren't chapters. It's real, they're real . . ." The priest was silent for a long time, finally sighed. "Say twelve rosaries, son. Don't just rattle them off. Take a couple of weeks, contemplate the Mysteries, think about what sort of light they might shed on what you've experienced. They're not your penance, they're just preparation for it . . ."

He spoke seriously again. It was not like any penance Dunc had ever heard of. He didn't know where to begin.

"I . . . I'll try, Father."

"No. You'll do. You may not recognize the opportunity as it arrives, maybe no one else would, either, but when the time comes you'll say, 'This is it!' and you'll do it."

On Monday it was up at four for ten miles of trotting, fast walking, occasional sprints on the soft sand track that would not give them shinsplints like hard-surface city streets. If not twice around the horse paddock, then a single huge loop through the chilly desert on a narrow Jeep track.

The desert runs were pure magic. Ned's hulking silhouette gaining definition until the risen sun cast their shadows long and thin beyond them. The thud of their shoes, the raucous call of a flicker arrowing above them. Invariably advice.

"Breathe through the nose. Keep your lips pressed tight together. Mouth breathers don't got no real stamina."

Once they saw a roadrunner with the curved beak and crazy tufted head feathers made familiar by the cartoons, beating a foot-long lizard on a rock with swift sideways jerks of its head. It dropped its prey, crowed like a rooster, grabbed up the limp reptile crosswise in its beak, and dashed off into the desert.

They saw a lot of black-tailed jackrabbits, and a couple of times glimpsed coyotes far off on a hillside. It was Ned who spotted a desert tortoise one morning when they were crossing a deep dry wash called a *barranca* in this part of the country.

His high-domed shell was deeply incised in concentric diamond shapes with orange centers. He trundled his slow way across the yielding sand floor, totally ignoring the two men. Deep within his 300 million years of dim genetic memories were dinosaurs and great armored fish and pterodactyls, the rise of mountains, the drying up of vast shallow inland seas . . .

Human beings? What were they?

In the barn they would put on their gloves and spar, working on combinations whose geometry was baffling. Feint with the right, hit with the left. Feint twice with the right . . .

"The old bare-knuckle brawlers could last a hundred, two hundred rounds 'cause when they threw a fist, they had their elbows out and their thumbs down."

Dunc threw fists thumb-down until his arms were lead.

"Hell, kid, you're arm-hitting. Do this." Ned's fists flew, Dunc went backward into the ropes, head ringing, covering up. "Good! Good! When I'm comin' at you, go into your shell."

In teaching the kid, Ned knew he was reinforcing for himself what he already knew. It would take all his skill, all his guile, all his knowledge, to win this one. His blows traveled no more than a foot, some of his hardest only six inches. His whole body threw his uppercuts. Nitro Ned.

"The left hand delivers the mail, the right covers your chin an' explodes when the time comes."

Sometimes he just stood there with his arms at his sides, bobbing and weaving. He slipped most of Dunc's head shots, and those he took, he took going away, so their force was dissipated.

"Don't dance—shuffle. You're a bear, not Fred Astaire."

By telling Dunc his most cherished secret, he told himself.

"When you throw that right at his jaw, you shift your left foot four inches to the side. If he's throwin' a right at *your* jaw, too, you'll connect an' he'll go over your shoulder."

Late in the afternoon Ned would spar between five and ten rounds in the outside ring, never pulling a punch or asking his opponent to do so. There were knockdowns and two broken jaws.

After all that work, play.

Dunc dropped Ned, then parked. He had started calling the little gray Ford Grey Ghost Two, in honor of his original Grey Ghost. Inside, the Gladiator was the same: no Lana Turner, no fat man; but a woman playing the slots, Nicky behind the bar.

"Hey, the fuckin' ginger ale!" and splashed it all over the cuff of his pink shirt. He shook his wet arm, cursing. "Fucking French cuff. Fucking rolled collar." He ran a finger around the inside of his rolled collar. "Goddamn wife bought me nine of these things for my birthday, they cost me $189, tailor-made. So goddamn mad, I said to her, 'I love ya, baby, but you ever do that again I'll break your fucking neck.'"

"The shirt fits you great," said Dunc.

"Like hell. A guy like me with two chins, f'Chrissake, it makes me look like I got no neck."

"You *do* got no neck."

Pepe had appeared, laughing, moving like a dancer, supple and graceful. He shook hands with Dunc.

"Where's the freeloaders?" Dunc asked. Nicky didn't answer. "You know," he persisted, "the fat guy and the blonde."

Nicky didn't answer. Pepe beckoned Dunc back to the piano.

"She pissed him off royally, he slapped her around, made a phone call, and nobody's seen her since." He played a few bars of the *Marche Funèbre.* "It's a big desert out there, Dunc." He immediately slid into "Slaughter on Tenth Avenue" and added, "The record producer's due in town tomorrow."

"You're gonna knock him dead."

Dunc carried the tray of drinks back to the poker players.

"What's with him an' Davenport?" asked Nicky.

"The son Nitro Ned never had," said Pepe.

After delivering the drinks, he wandered, stopping to become Henri's first customer at the blackjack table.

"Where's Sabine?"

"Her divorce came through. She left." Henri shook his head and chuckled. "With the bouncer from next door."

"Hung like a bull?" asked Dunc.

"Shit, kid, don't rub it in!" laughed Henri.

The casino was filling up. A woman in shorts and a T-shirt over pendulous breasts, loose flesh hanging on her legs and a face trashed by excess, turned to her husband with a hand out.

"More nicks for the bandit, baby!"

At the bar a man in a suit was telling a used-up-looking brunette with eyes like distant fires, "Everybody's having a good time, am I not right? The money's going, but it's going slow."

"Just give me the money, I'm happy."

"Baby, it isn't the money, it's having a good time."

"With me it's the money," she said.

Nicky said, "She's got bedroom eyes—pillows under 'em."

Dunc nursed his ginger ale, feeling guilty about not writing more in his notebook. He'd hoped to take Grey Ghost Two out to Lake Mead and just sit there and write, but poker at the Gladiator was Ned's relaxation, and he wanted Dunc there.

He showed up at Dunc's elbow. "Let's go out to the ranch, kid—I wanna turn in early."

Gimpy Ernest had lost heavily again and had gone home also. Carny gestured Rafe out of earshot, asked Artis, "You aren't *falling* for Ned, are you?"

"No, Carny, but I like him. He's a square shooter." That evening she was wearing yellow; on her, it looked like spun gold. Her fingernails flashed as she stubbed her Lucky, lit another. "But the kid has him working like a horse out there at the ranch. Ned's in terrific shape."

"So what? Gimpy owes me six grand."

"What does that mean?"

When he didn't answer, she snuffed out her new cigarette, went around behind Carny's chair, took his head between her two hands, and tilted up his face so their lips were touching.

She whispered, "I've done what you asked me, Carny, but it seems like forever." Her tongue darted between his lips. Her eyes were closed. "I need it tonight, baby. From you."

Carny's open eyes watched her face. He broke the kiss.

"You'd better go keep the big guy company, Artis. If he smelled another man on you, he'd go crazy."

She sighed and nodded and stepped back. Rafe was turning a chip over and over across the backs of his knuckles without looking at it. After she had left, Carny sneered at the little man, "Why don't you go into the men's john and jerk off?" Then he chuckled coarsely. "Patience, *amico,* your turn will come."

At 5:00 A.M. Pepe came out of the Gladiator and turned toward the center of town. Twelve hours straight at the piano, singing and playing in his little monkey suit while no one listened. Play your little tune and rattle your little tin cup, little monkey. He *would* be glad to leave this place.

The sun was reddening the sky above the casinos. Pepe went by the Golden Nugget and turned right again, up Fifth Street, turned in at his rooming house.

It was fun, just for a few moments, to think about just playing the piano, singing, cutting records . . .

Chapter Fourteen

It was Thursday afternoon. Nitro Ned lay facedown on the narrow massage table under the hot yellow light. Wesley Harding Jones skillfully slapped and kneaded his big, smooth, lax muscles. Gimpy Ernest came in to sit down on a wooden bench. The green lockers behind him were rusted from shower steam, the air acrid with witch hazel and the ghosts of cigarette butts dead on the floor.

"They're saying Terlazzo's a heavyweight Sugar Ray Robinson, hard to hit as smoke in a dark room."

Ned's voice was made quavery by the massage. "Then maybe he should wear lace tights an' take dancin' lessons."

Gimpy jerked his head at the door. Wes Jones departed. Ned sat up to reach for his clothes as Gimpy leaned toward him.

"Remember the night the kid showed up, Carny saying you should always figure on having more than you think you'll need? A margin for error? Well, Carny wants his margin for error."

Ned sat in jock and socks on the training table. He had been feeling on top of the world. Now he felt lousy.

"You talkin' fuckin' dive here, Gimp?"

Gimpy made himself sound hurt. "Jesus, Ned, to even *think* I'd suggest that!" He swiped bristly jowls with a sodden handkerchief. "It's just that, uh, Carny needs a round."

"I don't trust Terlazzo an' I don't trust Largo an'—goddamn you, Gimpy—maybe I don't oughta trust you, neither."

"Hear me out, Ned. You . . . ah, carry Terlazzo until the, um, seventh, then take him. He's willing to do it for his price, you know what I mean? You make it look like a tough fight, but you manage to beat him. He demands a rematch—an' you smash him. Then Marciano's people *can't* balk at a title bout."

"I've always tole you, Gimp—no fixed fights, never."

Gimpy Ernest sighed. "I'm into Carny for six K. If you don't do this for me, I'm a dead man. Raffetto . . ."

"It's a terrible thing you're askin' me to do, Ernie."

"It's terrible things they'll do to me if you don't, Ned."

Friday morning. Ned, sitting on the edge of the ring, said suddenly, "Early on, kid, Jantzen ast me to carry him to help boost his career. I got double-crossed, lost the decision. He's never tole nobody about it, ended up punchy, that's why I use the poor bastard to spar with. I tole Gimp then, no more rigged fights, ever. Then yesterday he ast me to shade the fight."

Dunc felt sick to his stomach. "You can't do it, Ned."

"Yeah, I know I can't." He sighed. "C'mon, let's dance."

Thirty seconds after they'd entered the ring, Nitro Ned knocked Dunc cold with a right cross. He came out of it sprawled on the canvas, Ned kneeling over him, face tight with remorse.

"I didn't break nothin', did I?"

Dunc managed a weak, lopsided grin. He was starting to remember what had happened. He'd taken the punch that had been meant for Gimpy Ernest.

Friday, July 3, 6:00 P.M., twenty-four hours before the fight. Through open windows of Carny's suite at the Flamingo, resort sounds: laughter, voices, the splash of swimmers from the pool in the center of the plush hotel. Carny sat with his drink balanced on the soft leather arm of the couch.

"Nick the Greek favors Ned, four-to-one. We'll clean up."

Sprawled on one of the twin beds, handsome lean-faced Tony Ter-lazzo made a derisive sound. He had a beautifully sculpted body, wide in the shoulder and narrow in the hip, was sharp and dressy in a tie-less white dress shirt and tight green pinstripe pants with pegged cuffs.

"I can take that old fart with one hand tied behind me."

"You'll take him when I tell you to take him."

Artis sat beside Carny, her head back and her fine dark eyes shut. Raffetto, lounging in a leather chair across the room, had his eyes on her skirt, ridden high up on her thighs.

"Terlazzo *is* going to dive in the seventh, isn't he?"

"I don't dive, lady," said Terlazzo. "Only on muffs."

"Not interested," she said coldly.

Carny pointed his cigar at Gimpy. "*You* had to dress it up. Couldn't tell Ned he had to take a dive, had to—"

"Ned won't dive even for me, Carny. But this way—"

Terlazzo cut in, "This way, in the fourth Gimpy tells Davenport to let me hit him so people don't think it's a fix. He thinks I'm diving in the seventh, so he opens up—*whammo!*"

Artis stood up, smoothed down her tight green skirt with green-tinted nails. She adjusted one of her jade earrings.

"You're going along with this, Gimp?"

"Hey, what can I do? I owe Carny a lot of money."

Artis nodded, sighed. "Ned, the poor sap, wants to be alone to plan his fight, so he has me doing the town with Dunc."

Artis looked incredibly beautiful in a glittery gown cut on a bias. Her eyes glittered, her teeth glittered, stones set in gold glittered at her throat. She gave a deep, carefree laugh.

"You look . . . Christ, *sensational!*" exclaimed Dunc in awe.

Dunc had bought a dress shirt and a tie and a sport jacket, and had picked Artis up in Grey Ghost Two at the Flamingo, where she had a room until after the fight. Dunc hadn't even entered any of the Strip's plush resort hotels; tonight he was walking into the exclusive, expensive Copa Room of the Sands Hotel with the most beautiful woman in Vegas on his arm.

They ordered drinks, he tore a match out of a book, stuck it between the second and third fingers of his cupped right hand, lit it, held it to the tip of her Lucky. He'd seen an ex-con do that in some movie. He knew he probably looked ridiculous, especially with his bruised, swollen jaw, but he didn't care. He was out with Artis for a night in Vegas.

She blew smoke from the corner of her mouth, put down the cigarette. When she took both his hands in hers, her hands were warm. He felt a stirring in his groin.

"Dunc, I want to ask your advice on something—"

"Welcome, ladies and gentlemen, to the Sands Hotel."

The M.C. wore a tux; he was there to make the audience laugh out loud so he could count their gold fillings.

"Here at New York's Copacabana Gone West we have for you the greatest star in the Las Vegas firmament, the Copa's own Sophisticated Lady, Miss . . . *Lena* . . . *HORNE!*"

Horne sang her special songs. "Paper Doll." "The Birth of the Blues." "The Lady Is a Tramp," to finish with "Stormy Weather." Dunc hardly heard her. Artis needed his advice.

She never got it. A big hard-looking man towered above them. He was impeccably groomed and wore a silk suit, just like the first time Dunc had seen him outside the Tucson truck stop.

Artis's smile dazzled. "Join us, Lucius."

"I'm with another party. Just wanted to say hello." He looked down at Dunc, intelligence shining from those battered features. "Everything's okay? Ned's ready?"

"Better than ready! Dynamite! Nitroglycerin, in fact."

Breen chuckled. "That's swell! Then the best man'll win."

The evening became a kaleidoscope of casinos and lounges and bars and sexual tension and expectation, with no time for questions. They drank and danced and she taught him roulette.

Noise and smoke assaulted the senses. Hatchet-eyed men watched, beautiful women prowled, suckers crowded the tables four-deep. Anything was possible, even the disappearance of a Lana Turner look-alike into the desert's anonymous sands.

Anytime he tried to pay for anything, Artis put him off, saying she'd make out big by betting on Ned tomorrow night. Then suddenly the night was over, in the wee hours he was walking her down the silent corridor of the Flamingo to her room. What did he do? Handshake? Good-night kiss? What?

Artis solved his problem. She ground her crotch against his while thrusting her tongue into his mouth for one searing moment, then stepped back with a throaty laugh.

"A lick and a promise 'cause you're such a sweet kid, Dunc."

Despite the whiskey singing in him, Dunc was ashamed of his instant erection. She was Ned's woman, for Chrissake! Then she gave him a chaste peck on the cheek, keyed the door, and was gone. The walk down the thickly carpeted corridor from her room seemed endless. He couldn't stop thinking about both lick and promise.

Ned was sitting on the front steps by the dark of the moon. Dunc sat down beside him, the guilt at Artis's kiss forgotten. In a few hours Ned faced the biggest bout of his career.

"Thinking about tomorrow night?"

Ned shook his head. "Gimpy."

"Jesus, Ned, I thought that was all settled."

He looked over at Dunc in the near-darkness. "I don't do what he ast me, Raffetto comes after Gimp, an' I'm not sure I can stop him. He's greased lightning with a black-steel Commando knife he carries down the small of his back. But if I do it in the seventh, Gimp'll be safe—an' I'll still win."

"There's winning and there's winning, Ned! You can't just sacrifice your fight for Gimp. What if it's another double cross? He's the one screwing you over, you aren't—"

"Yeah, yeah, kid, I know all that." There was a great sadness in his face. "But dammit, can't you see, I *gotta* do what Gimpy's askin' me. If I don't an' somethin' happens to him, then it's the same thing as if I killed him myself." Then he burst out suddenly, "But Jesus Christ, Dunc, I hate it!"

Chapter Fifteen

Dunc was jerked awake at 6:00 A.M. by the rest of the training crew stirring around. He just wanted to stay in his bunk forever, but only he knew that this fight day wasn't worth getting up for. He rode into town with Max in the pickup.

"Be at the depot at two just like usual, Dunc. Ned wants you to drive him to the fight tonight in his car."

Jesus, what would he and Ned talk about in the car? In Ned's place, Dunc would do the same, but this was Ned's whole life. Yet if he didn't . . . Dunc's thoughts circled endlessly like buzzards over something dying on the desert floor.

He walked down Fremont. The Fourth of July, Vegas, fight night. It should have been almost unbearably exciting, but he felt only secret shame. Ned would beat Terlazzo, but not as they'd planned. It would be as Carny Largo had planned.

Seven celebrities were out in the middle of Fremont and First, clowning around and stopping traffic. He recognized only Milton Berle, Red Skelton, and Spike Jones, but the girl next to him in the sidewalk crowd knew them all. She was his age, tiny, with a mist of soft red curls framing a pixie face.

"That's Gale Storm next to Skelton," she said. "And Anna Maria Alberghetti between Spike Jones and Vic Damone. And of course the tall one on the end in the striped shirt is Herb Shriner.

He does five minutes five days a week on CBS radio. They're doing publicity for the Las Vegas News Bureau."

He tried to get into the spirit of the day, made himself recall how he'd loved Red Skelton's goofy movies . . .

"When I was a kid I thought it was Red *Skeleton*."

The girl giggled. She had freckles and a pert Irish nose.

"Are you going to the parade?"

"No. Are you going to the fights? Nitro Ned Davenport is going to be the next heavyweight champion of the world."

"Boxing?" Her face screwed up in disgust, and she moved away from him. Yawning, Dunc slipped away also. Three hours of silliness and noise until Max would take him back out to the ranch, and he hadn't brought his book. He'd try the Gladiator.

Nitro Ned Davenport usually slept like a baby the night before a fight, but he woke after only a few hours of troubled slumber. Why the hell did he get involved with people? First Dunc, wide-eyed and hurting 'cause Ned was going along with the setup. Then Artis, hurting, too, in her own way.

In his room a warm breeze stirred the gauzy curtains in the wide window looking out on the horse paddock where they had taken so many training runs. He pulled his steamer trunk out from under the bed. Old and battered and iron-bound, it had been with him since he'd scored his first KO in 1937, at age seventeen. He took out the oiled leather pouch that held his personal papers, signed one of them, and put it in a separate envelope.

In the bunkhouse he pulled Dunc's yellow gym bag out from under the bunk, packed it, and locked it in the trunk of his car. The envelope he locked in the glove box. If things went okay, Dunc would never see it.

Dunc paused inside the double doors, letting his eyes adjust to the Gladiator's dimness. Nobody played the slots, nobody was at the tables. Only a relief bartender, taking occasional drags from the cigarette balanced on the edge of the stainless-steel sink. And Pepe at the piano in jeans and tennis shoes and a flowery sport shirt, making "Stardust."

"Play one of your own," said Dunc.

Flushed with pleasure, Pepe did. Then another, this one evoking city streets and cold autumn wind around skyscraper corners. When he was through, Dunc applauded.

"How did it go with the record producer?"

Pepe banged out "How High the Moon." "Number one on *Your Hit Parade*. I cut the demo on Monday in L.A."

"That's fantastic, Pepe. And come back when?"

Like a dirge, "There's No Tomorrow." "I don't. This works out, I'll be playing piano on the Sunset Strip."

Dunc felt a sudden hole in his life. "I'll come and see you there."

"Sure you will, kid. Sure you will."

Rafe was mixing drinks. Gimpy Ernest was fussing with the bouquet of flowers left by a tip-conscious maid. Carny sat on a red leather barstool, his well-manicured hands carefully rotating a thin cigar in the flame of a silver lighter.

"We'd better get over to the field," said Gimpy.

"I'm catching it on TV," Carny said. "He's got the nigger and the kid to hold his hands, he doesn't need me."

Artis was sitting on the couch again, head back and eyes closed. She was wearing a white silk blouse with a gold cross at her throat, dark slacks with high-heeled sandals that had gold straps over the arch of her foot.

Carny removed his cigar. "You give the kid titty last night?" When she didn't respond, he persisted, "He's such a cool cat, I bet you gave him titty *and* stink finger."

"Lucius Breen came around asking questions about Ned."

Carny stiffened. Everyone knew of Breen's power, his love of boxing, his incorruptibility as a referee. He would go to the Boxing Commission, kill the fight if he got proof it was fixed.

"You think Breen's heard something?"

"Not from Dunc, that's a gut. The poor sap said all the right things—because that's what he believes."

"How about you? What did you say to Breen?"

"Ask Lucius," she said with a vindictive smile.

Dunc was driving north on Las Vegas Boulevard from the ranch, Ned beside him, Wes in the backseat with the equipment. Las Vegas fight cards were staged at Cashman's Field, a minor-league baseball diamond a mile and a half north of the Strip. The house would be much greater than the usual two thousand; two ranked heavyweights as headliners, and the Visitors Bureau had gotten *The Gillette Cavalcade of Sports* to make it the first televised Vegas fight card. To hold the spectators after the cameras were turned off, fireworks would follow the boxing matches.

The ring was set up about where home plate usually was, with a portable wooden floor laid down on the infield for rows of ringside folding chairs at twenty-five bucks. Bleacher seats were ten.

"Nick the Greek has me odds-on favorite," said Ned, "so a lot of ham-and-eggers are makin' bets on me. If I lose—"

"You won't lose," said Dunc almost sadly. This wasn't what they had trained for.

The ball field was ablaze with lights, though the sun was hours from setting. The uniformed guard on the gate bent to peer into the car, straightened up with a broad grin.

"You got my money ridin' on you, Nitro!" he exclaimed.

They walked in under the bleachers, Wes carrying Ned's gear in a military-issue olive-green duffel bag. Down a set of steps and along a dimly lit concrete corridor to the dressing rooms, lockers, and showers. Ned paused.

"Listen, Dunc, if I don't show up right after the fight, you an' Artis get out of Vegas. Check the glove box of the car. Your gear is locked in the trunk. This here is just a what-if, okay? Now, why don't you go on out an' look the setup over? You won't get no chance once the crowd starts gettin' here."

Two technicians in greenish coveralls were up ladders in the ring, fussing with a square of lights scaffolded above it. On the second-base side was a sturdy wooden framework to support the TV camera. Heavy cables snaked away into the outfield.

Lucius Breen climbed through the ropes, and a microphone on the end of a cable descended from the metal pipe framework above the ring. One of the technicians caught it, handed it to Lucius.

"Could we do a sound check, Mr. Breen?"

Breen's voice boomed out over the field. "In this corner, wearing red trunks and weighing in at two hundred twenty-one pounds, Nitro Ned—"

"That's great. Thanks."

Breen caught up with Dunc on his way back to the dressing rooms. Dunc's new guilty knowledge about the fixed fight lay like lead in his belly. Lucius was straight and the fight wasn't. Dunc wasn't. They stopped at the head of the ramp.

"Anybody asked Ned to lose the fight?" Breen asked bluntly.

"Ned would never do that, Mr. Breen!"

"To stall, maybe? Maybe pick a round?"

Somehow, Dunc met his eyes. "He doesn't have to."

Dunc finally understood that Lucius Breen knew all about the kind of man Carny Largo was, knew about Gimpy Ernest's gambling problems, had, in fact, gotten Dunc into Ned's training camp just so he could ask him these questions on fight night.

Dunc almost ran after him to tell him the truth about the fix. Maybe this was the act of moral recompense the priest had said he would recognize when the moment come. But it couldn't be. It wasn't his secret to tell. Talk, and he would destroy Ned's only shot at the heavyweight title. Destroy Ned.

He'd had to lie. What else could he have done?

Chapter Sixteen

Nitro Ned hung up the corridor pay phone and returned to the dressing room, ritualistically donned socks, supporter, cup, trunks, and shoes like a knight donning his armor. Usually Ned would have been deep down inside himself by now, everything else excluded, just him and how he would fight his fight. But not tonight. Tonight someone else was going through the ritual of preparation, of dressing, of hand-taping. Oh, sweat tickled his spine and his mouth felt dry and cottony, as before any fight, but it meant nothing. Nothing at all.

Dunc, wearing unlaced gloves, held up his hands palm-out, and Ned slammed blows at them. A light sheen of sweat covered his body now, his feet working combinations Dunc knew by heart, even though the accompanying punches weren't being thrown.

Someone knocked. Wes crossed to the door, opened it to a uniformed guard's face that brought with it a roar from the playing field overhead as from an opened furnace door.

"Last prelim's startin' now."

Dunc took off the unlaced gloves. Gimpy Ernest's heavy-lidded eyes were dark-circled, his face pasty. A wilted white shirt clung to the rounded, meaty shoulders under his loud sport jacket. Pudgy fingers were close to shredding his dime cigar. He got Ned in a corner away from the others.

"You sure you got it straight, Nitro?" he said, low-voiced. "You just carry him 'til the seventh, don't worry about points." Sweat dripped from his sagging jowls. "I'm countin' on you, Ned—me an' Artis."

"Yeah, Gimp. You an' Artis." Ned began slamming his gloved fists together as if Terlazzo's head were between them.

Surrounded by his entourage, Terlazzo pranced up the aisle first, turning his torso from side to side, arms above his head. He wore a purple robe with gold piping, the hood up to cover his sweat-gleaming black curls.

Ned's red robe billowed out around him in regal splendor. The roar was deafening as he went down the aisle: the common guy's choice, the battered club fighter who'd worked his way up through the years with honest bouts against all comers.

He went to the rosin box and scuffed his shoes in it. His bitterness at the fixed fight didn't show. Wes and Gimpy Ernest were his cornermen. Dunc had the closest seat first row ringside; the seat next to his was for Artis.

A tuxedoed announcer strutted around the ring, his amplified voice boomed out over the public address system.

"Ladies and gentlemen, we are very lucky to have with us tonight a legendary figure of the fighting world, former heavyweight champion of the world, Mr. . . . *Jack* . . . *DEMPSEY!*"

Dempsey bounded up into the ring, pushing sixty and a little paunchier than when he had won the title from Jess Willard in 1919 by KO. He shook Ned's gloved hand, then Terlazzo's.

"Ladeez an' gennelmen . . . Ladeez an' gennelmen . . ."

Artis, looking haggard, slid past Dunc. She patted a purse bulging with betting slips. "Out getting my money down."

Dunc hadn't bet. The announcer was introducing the fighters; the din was terrific. Wes pulled the robe off Ned's shoulders. His skin was sun-baked dark as a red Indian's, he wore three days' beard to toughen his face against cuts.

Tony "the Tiger" Terlazzo flicked the robe away with a dramatic gesture, dancing and throwing punches and shadowboxing all over the ring. Ned, solid as a monolith, just stared at him.

Breen gestured both fighters into the center of the ring, instructed them on how he wanted the bout fought, gesturing to show no low blows or rabbit punches. They both nodded, accepting the well-known instructions. The fight was only moments away.

Pepe packed methodically. Carny Largo had been a shitty boss, but that had been a given going in. He'd liked Nicky okay. And Dunc. The kid always asked to hear Pepe's own stuff, and actually seemed to listen. A good kid. But after tonight, Pepe would be out of Vegas. As usual, he wouldn't miss it. He went someplace, did his job, moved on. Then the phone rang.

The opening bell. The fighters came out, Terlazzo dancing, Ned shuffling. They touched gloves in the center of the ring over Breen's outstretched arm, Terlazzo instantly tagged Ned with a strong right hand that reddened his forehead. The crowd gasped. Ned had been slow in covering and had thrown no counter.

"He'll be okay, he'll be okay, he's just feeling his way," Dunc chanted, his upper body jerking slightly to the action in the ring as if he were throwing and taking the punches himself.

"That's what I'm afraid of," Artis said obscurely.

Dunc didn't say anything about the seventh round, although she had to know about it. He couldn't bring himself to speak of it. That's why Ned was so lackadaisical, wasn't it?

In his room at the Flamingo Carny Largo relaxed against the leather couch. On the television a cartoon parrot was hawking Gillette Blue Blades between rounds. Gimpy had played Davenport perfectly, after all. The big stupid bastard was going along with the fix to save Gimpy, well behind on points already.

Terlazzo was trying for a KO. Why not? He didn't have to wait for a certain round. And if Davenport made it to the fourth, Gimpy would tell him to open up and let himself get hit so it looked like a fight—and the Tiger would pounce.

"Open a bottle of champagne," he told Raffetto. "We're both going to score tonight."

Rafe made even Carny a little queasy. But hell, there were no guarantees in this life. Artis was a hell of a woman, dynamite in bed, but she knew too much. Dangerous. After Rafe had her, she'd be harmless. Hell, she'd be wishing she'd become a nun.

Dunc watched the second-round action with stunned eyes. Ned was merely covering up, while the Tiger was coming in with roundhouse lefts and rights now, savaging the big fighter all he could before taking his dive in the seventh. But what if he wasn't going to dive; the fix was in, but what if there was *another* fix in? No. Gimpy would have to be in on it . . .

One of Ned's instructions to him came back.

If your man loops his punches, go inside.

He realized he was shouting it at the top of his voice.

"Go inside! Ned! Go inside!"

Ned just kept backpedaling, covering up. It was Terlazzo who started to go inside, crowding Ned, pumping blows into the heart and the belly. Not even Ned could stop all of them.

If he's a body puncher, keep your elbows in and snap jabs at his jaw as fast as you can pump 'em.

"The jaw! Ned! Jab his jaw! Jab—"

The bell.

Back in his corner, Ned sprawled on his stool, eyes shut. Some of the fight fans had started stamping their feet in unison. He should be giving his followers at least the illusion of a fight, but it didn't matter, except for Dunc seeing it. He had to await Gimp's instructions in the fourth to be sure.

Wes sponged him down, gave him water to spit into the sand bucket. "What you doin' out there? He's whuppin' yo' dumb ass."

Ned asked, "How'm I doin', Gimp?"

"Don't listen to him, you're looking great, kid."

Crowd noises died during the third except for the stamping of feet and a rising crescendo of boos. Ned kept clinching, what he'd told Dunc to never do; each time Breen separated them, Terlazzo got in a solid shot to the kidneys.

Ned slumped on his stool. Wes used the styptic pencil in the open cuts above his eyes, trying to stanch the bleeding. Lucius Breen came over to take a look. Gimpy Ernest hung back.

"Is this fighter okay?" Breen demanded.

Wes didn't look up from his work. "He's fine, ref, he's okay, nothin' wrong, jes a little ding 'bove de eye."

"Then what the fuck you doin', Davenport?"

"Fightin' my fight, Lucius."

"You're fighting *somebody's* fight," said Breen.

Gimpy was beside Ned in an instant. "Even the ref seen it—you been covering up too much. Open up. Fake a few at him, let him tag you a time or two, make it look like a fight . . ."

The warning buzzer sounded. Artis said suddenly to Dunc, "Terlazzo's going to KO Ned this round." Dunc started to his feet, but she said, "I told Ned last night, put all my money on him tonight. But only he and God know what he's going to do."

Wes started to put Ned's mouthpiece in, but Ned stopped him with a gloved hand to say, "Better pray, Gimp."

The bell sounded for round four.

Chapter Seventeen

Ned seemed to be following Gimpy's instructions. He not only opened up, he actually had his arms hanging down at his sides. Terlazzo danced in, throwing punches, Ned bobbed, weaved, moved his head fractionally as the blows came at him—as he'd do with Dunc when they were sparring.

"Jesus!" whispered Dunc.

Each time Tiger Terlazzo missed, Ned struck, *wham wham WHAM!* combinations as fast as a striking snake. Gimpy Ernest was limping up the steps to the ring with a towel in his hand. He would throw it in the ring to stop the fight. But as Gimpy threw, Dunc snatched the towel out of the air.

Nobody even saw it. Tiger Terlazzo and Nitro Ned were toe-to-toe, mid-ring, slugging it out. Blood, snot, sweat flew, both men grunted with the effort of blows thrown, taken. The crowd was on its feet, screaming. Dunc was, too. It was coming, the secret that Ned had never told anybody but Dunc.

When you throw that right at his jaw, shift your left foot four inches to the side. If he's throwin' a right at your jaw, you'll connect an' he'll go over your shoulder.

Both men snapped off cannon-shot right hands. Everybody in the first five rows heard Ned's terrible blow shatter the Tiger's jaw. The back of his head rebounded off the canvas. Lucius Breen started the count, steady as a metronome. At ten he went to the neutral corner and raised Ned's arm in the air.

Dunc laughed out loud. Ned had won it fair and square. But Artis had hold of him, wouldn't let go.

"Carny'll come after us, all of us!" She was wild. "I've gotta cash in. Get Ned, pick me up at my house."

The ring was filled with excited men, Breen and a doctor were shielding Terlazzo from trampling feet. Ned went through the ropes, Gimpy hanging on to his arm like a puppy.

"Ned, you gotta square this with Carny! Gotta tell him it was your idea, not mine . . . An' I . . . I bet all our money on . . ."

Ned's puffy lips drew back in a grin. "We ain't gonna need money where we're goin', Gimp. Not you an' me."

Carny Largo's beautifully manicured right hand switched off the TV set. He kept twisting the knob until it came away in his fingers, then threw it into a corner as he cursed in a low guttural voice. "Nitro Ned. And Gimpy Ernest. And Artis. And even the kid. I want all of those fuckers dead. *Dead.*"

Rafe said, "When I do Artis, can I—"

"Make sure she's dead first. Then do whatever you want."

Carny started pacing. He had to come up with something, quick. Look what the people back east had done to Bugsy when they thought *he* had been holding out on them. And he'd been one of their own. Carny was no made man, just a guy who owned a Glitter Gulch casino and did them favors now and then . . .

Yes! They wanted to become his partners in the Gladiator as Bugsy Siegel had done to that degenerate gambler Wilkinson who had owned the Flamingo. So what if he offered them the Gladiator, free and clear, to prove he hadn't ripped them off?

His hand shook as he reached for the phone to try and reach Meyer Lansky in New York. It would work. It had to work.

*   *   *

Ned pushed by anyone wanting to talk with him. Sweat still gleamed on his face, one of the unbandaged cuts above his eye still oozed blood. "Is Artis in the car?"

"She left right after the fight to cash in her tickets. She said she'd meet us at her place. She said—"

"Artis an' her goddamn money." Ned stopped dead, his face foreboding. "Not good, kid. Not good. If . . ." He trailed off and shook his head. "Okay. Do what I said. Go get her . . ."

Raffetto would want to do them at the ranch, it was too public here, but Gimpy was taking no chances. He switched off the lights, checked the deserted hall before stepping out. Drive straight to Mc-Carran field, catch the first flight out.

He went up the steps. High in the sky above the parking lot was a *thump!* and a flower of twinkling colored lights. The crowd above and behind him went "Oooh!" and "Ahhh!" As he took his car keys from his jacket pocket, a man stepped around the front of his car. Barely five feet tall and wearing a midnight-blue suit and black shirt and white tie.

"Carny told me to give you this."

Rafe's right hand, lengthened by eight inches of black steel, slashed horizontally across Gimpy's throat. Gimpy made a strangled sound. He'd thought Rafe would be waiting at the ranch; should of left a margin for error. Rafe wiped his blade on Gimpy's coat, thrust it back into the sheath between his shoulder blades, faded back into the other shadows. Nitro Ned next. Then the kid. The best for last. Artis.

As he opened his car door, a familiar voice said, "Rafe?"

Carny Largo, phone to his face, was doing the selling job of a lifetime. It had taken him a half hour to track down Meyer Lansky, not in New York but in Miami.

"Yessir, Mr. Lansky, the Gladiator, that's right, your accountants can . . . Thank you, Mr. Lansky. Thank you."

As he hung up he heard Rafe coming back in. He turned, using his wadded handkerchief to wipe the sweat from the hand that had held the phone. He gasped.

Nitro Ned Davenport, battered but whole, said amiably, "I called 'em before the fight, anonymous-like, tole 'em you an' that fighter of yours, Nitro Ned, was workin' a cross against 'em. I should of knowed you'd talk your way out of it."

"You're a dead man, Ned," said Carny. "So's your bitch girlfriend and Gimpy and the kid. I sent Rafe—"

"Yeah, you did, didn't you?" Still grinning amiably, Ned advanced like an earthmover. "So now Rafe ain't here. I am."

Carny emptied all five steel-jacketed slugs from the .25-caliber revolver in his jacket pocket into Ned's lemon-yellow shirtfront. Ned staggered, but kept coming. Still grinning. Carny's lips thinned, panic flickered yellowly in his eyes as he tried to twist away. Too late. Ned's huge hands had him.

"The margin of error you was always bleatin' about, Carny. Five pills would stop 'em all in time—all of 'em 'cept me."

His dying hands folded Carny Largo's head back at a right angle to his body as if it were on a hinge, snapping his neck like a cornstalk.

It was a two-story frame house in a residential area south of Fremont Street. A little run-down, Dunc could see by the streetlights as he slammed to a stop at the curb, but lived-in, inviting. Like the homes on a thousand tree-covered streets back in the Midwest. Lights were on upstairs and behind the front door. Thank God. Artis had made it and he was in time. Without a map, it had taken him twenty minutes to find the place.

Dunc jumped out, ran up the walk. The front door was ajar. She wouldn't have left it that way. He should have brought the tire iron from the car. He could barely breathe for fear, but there was no time to go back for it.

Straight ahead a flight of carpeted stairs led up to the second floor. The stairwell light went out: it was pitch-black except for slight illumination from the streetlight outside.

"Artis!"

A small, quick stairwell shadow came bounding down at him, led by a gleaming blade. Raffetto! Dunc's arm swept it aside, grappled with him. But the little killer was quick as an eel, strong as electricity. He broke free, ran down the stairs. The front door slammed.

Light showed under the closed door of the front bedroom. Dunc smashed it open.

Artis was sprawled on a dressing bench at the foot of the bed, leaning back against the coverlet. Her once-white silk blouse was red. The sweetish smell of blood filled the room. One hand clutched a small gold cross with a thin broken gold chain. One foot still wore a blood-spattered high-heeled sandal with gold straps over the arch. The other sandal lay on its side a yard away. Dunc dropped to his knees beside her.

"I'll get help. Don't move, it'll be okay. I'll . . ."

Those intense black eyes opened to look at him sternly. She had so much to tell him. Had to tell him a whole lifetime of never being a player, just one of the suckers. Had to tell him about her murder.

"Christ, kid," she said, "it hurts."

Then she died.

Four police cars were parked at odd angles in front of the Flamingo, revolving lights spilling blood over the crowd. An ambulance was just pulling away, siren keening.

"Two men dead," somebody said.

"One of 'em was the boxer," said another. "Nitro Ned."

"Other one was some gambler ran a casino in Glitter Gulch."

"Bet the fight was fixed and they fell out over the split."

Dunc went back to the car. Suddenly he was crying, swiping the back of his hand across his face like a little kid. He hadn't cried when his grandpa had died, and he'd really loved that old man. But this . . . Ned . . . Artis . . .

He should go to the cops and . . . And what? Raffetto had killed Artis—but he had no proof. He had nobody to fight for, nothing to hang on to. Ned and Artis were both gone. So was Carny Largo, but Raffetto was still out there looking for Dunc.

Like Pepe, it was time for him to leave this town.

Fifty miles west of Vegas he was stopped at a barricade across the state line. Uniformed men asked him if he was carrying any fresh fruit into California. The question was so bizarre he started to laugh, but it choked into a sob. They waved him on without noticing.

At Baker, a little town in the desert, he stopped at an all-night gas station with a café attached. He wasn't hungry, then wolfed down everything in sight. Back outside, he saw the black desert night was awash with stars, felt the cold desert air. Sage was acrid in his nostrils. Just a few weeks ago he had been going toward Vegas on a night like this, hopes high and excitement surging. Now . . .

God, what would his nightmares be like from now on?

He got his gear out of the trunk of the car and opened the glove box as Ned had told him. In it was the title slip to Grey Ghost Two, signed over to him. Ned must have done it yesterday, before the bout, after Artis had told him about the fix.

Even then the big fighter had known what he was going to do—and had known he wasn't going to make it to California.

FOUR

An Angel in the Smog

Chapter Eighteen

Three weeks had passed. The blond man hulking over Dunc snarled, "Ve haff vays uff makink you talk!"

"Never!" croaked Dunc.

He was chest-deep in the half-dug grave, shirtless, almost black from the pitiless California sun; sweat rolled off his naked torso. When he drove his shovel into the dirt, in his mind Hent slashed the shovel down to cut the turtle in half.

Dunc unobtrusively picked up a dirt clod as big as his head and held it at arm's length. "Alas, poor Yorick! I knew him, Horatio; a fellow of infinite jest, of most excellent fancy . . ."

"Vat nonsense are you tellink me?" roared the blond man.

"It's from *Hamlet*—the gravedigger scene in Act Five."

"But it's not from a movie! You lose!"

"Olivier did a film version four or five years ago."

"Oh yeah! I remember. Jean Simmons in a nightgown."

"Except she killed herself." To his earthen skull, Dunc said, "Now get you to my lady's chamber, and tell her, let her paint an inch thick, to this favour she must come; make her laugh at that . . ." But the clod wore the dead face of Artis. He threw it from him. "You win, Gus. I buy the beer tonight."

Gus Trabert, another Notre Damer, was staying the summer at his uncle's big old sprawling white frame house in Eagle Rock. He'd offered Dunc a place to stay, maybe a job; while waiting for it, at Dunc's suggestion, they dug graves at nearby Forest Lawn.

Dunc struck the shovel in the dirt, upright, put his hands on the edge of the opening, kipped up easily, turning in midair to land sitting on the edge with his legs dangling into the hole.

"Gimme the water and start digging."

Gus handed him the wet-sided canvas water bag, sat down beside him. He was taller than Dunc by half a head, but not as beefy of arms, chest, or shoulders. Blue eyes, blond hair. His people were from northern Italy.

"Friday," he said. "The eagle shits tonight."

Only five minutes to quitting time. They covered the grave with plywood, at a hose bib halfway down the slope sloshed the dust off their arms and chests and cleaned the shovels.

"Uncle Ben heard anything yet?" Gus's uncle had heavy connections with the Los Angeles Catholic Archdiocese.

"I bet he'll have the word tonight."

These six hundred fantasyland acres of death were brilliant green, dazzling with flowers; in the distance, buildings gleamed like the Emerald City of Oz. Tomorrow the place would be full of tourists and people paying their respects; children would romp through Lullaby Land where dead children were buried amid hearts of living flowers and gingerbread castles with stone turrets.

"Why'd you want to work in a place like this?" asked Gus.

"I read a novel about it at Notre Dame. *The Loved One.*"

Uncle Ben was out watering the lawn, a tall leathery man with thin features and dark hair with gray wings swept back over his ears. During the 1936 Berlin Olympics he had taken bronze in the breaststroke. He turned the hose on them.

"You two bums are in luck!" he yelled. "You start work Monday out at the San Fernando Mission's new seminary complex!"

Thoroughly drenched, they fled into the kitchen. Aunt Pearl was mincing onions, tears glinting on her plump cheeks despite a slice of bread between her teeth to stop the fumes.

She made shooing gestures, a housewife driving chickens from her kitchen. "You're soaking wet! Go on, get out of here!"

Grandma Trabert had lived in this house as bride, wife, and widow for fifty years, now spent most of her time in what once had been her sewing room. She was dwarfed by her huge leather armchair in front of the TV with its bunny ears and round eight-inch screen. A gun went off on the TV.

"Just the facts, ma'am," said Gus.

"What day is it today?" asked Grandma in her sweet old lady's voice as stern *dum-de-dum-dum* theme music came up.

"Friday, Grandma Trabert," said Dunc.

"Joe Friday," snickered Gus too softly for Grandma to hear.

A man wearing a cap with a star on it was holding a gas hose in his hand and urging his viewers to use Texaco Sky Chief gasoline with Petrox for maximum power plus engine protection.

"No, no, dear. The date."

"The twenty-fourth. Of July."

"Oh, boys, how exciting! Only two days to St. Anne's Day. My patron saint! We'll have such a good time! Don't oversleep! I want you to hear the music at High Mass, Gus—you too, Dunc. The choir is so wonderful since Mr. Spinelli came to us."

Gus winked at Dunc over her head. "Sure thing, Grandma."

Actually Gus wanted to try and get into the pants of a trailer park gal out at the beach who belonged to a cult called the Seven Priests of Melchizedek. The priest, Gus said, would be great for Dunc's notebook. He hadn't written a word since Vegas.

Grandma Trabert called after them over the television, "I'm going to start praying right now that you boys don't have to work with a bunch of niggers and spics out there at the mission."

A huge Dutch windmill marked Van de Kamps bakery at the corner of Fletcher and San Fernando; if you wanted to eat inside on a

Friday night, you stood in line for an hour. They preferred the drive-in; it had been one of the world's first after the war, and featured young pretty carhops in tight clothes.

A teenage brunette took their orders. As they watched her backside twitch busily away, Gus said, "Paint a 'W' on each cheek, when she bends over—WOW!"

She returned with trays she hooked over the insides of their open windows and braced against the doors below. They munched cheeseburgers and fries and slurped chocolate malts.

Dunc had to talk with Pepe about that last terrible night; he sure couldn't talk to Gus about it. So he said, "I met a piano player in Vegas who said he'd be playing on the Sunset Strip. Let's go try to find him."

"Better than Van de Kamps," said Gus.

Sunset Strip on Friday night was Glitter Gulch without casinos. An unending stream of cars drove each way on the wide boulevard with lights flashing, horns braying, guys hanging out of windows to shout and whistle trying to attract girls. Some of the clubs were big and brightly lit, with marquees and floor shows and valet parking for gleaming expensive cars disgorging men in suits and women in gowns. Others were small and dim.

Pepe could be playing in any of them, alone or in a combo. No wonder he had been so cynical about Dunc finding him. By 1:30 in the morning they were bleary-eyed over draft beer in a little bar with nobody else there except a tough-looking bartender washing glasses and listening to Eddie Fisher's throbbing overamped "I'm Walking Behind You" on the jukebox. Maybe if Dunc had been walking behind Artis that night, or beside Ned when he'd gone up against Carny Largo . . .

"Gimme the goddamn keys," growled Gus in his ear, holding out his hand. "I'm driving home."

"Smooth move, Ex-Lax," agreed the bartender.

Dunc surrendered the keys, realizing with mild surprise that he was a little drunk. The night had been a busted flush. Maybe tomorrow at the beach everything would be different . . .

"I'm going to Mexico for my vacation." Fayme had scraggly blond hair and a white blouse tied up to show her middle; faded loose blue shorts did nothing for her legs. "Look for a little talent." She winked at Angela. "Why don't you come along?"

Angela looked good in her tight swimsuit, but like Fayme was past thirty. In her lap was a little hairy dog named Muffy.

She gestured with her glass. "What about Muffy?"

"Leave him here with Birdie. Or at a kennel."

"It would be no vacation without my Muffy," said Angela.

The trailer court was on a low dusty hill where the rumble of Coast Highway 1 traffic from above merged with the mutter of the sea from below. They were sprawled in deck chairs under a canvas awning, drinking cold beer from beaded bottles.

Birdie leaned forward. "Joyce took her two Chihuahuas to Mexico last year and they both nearly died of the heat."

Birdie was really old, over forty, with a pixie face full of wrinkles, and an amazing body under a clinging light blue one-piece dress. Gus had his deck chair hiked close to hers.

"Isn't Joyce still down there?" asked Angela.

"Mexico City. But she lost her student permit."

Birdie gave a throaty chuckle. "I didn't know you needed a permit for what she's been doing—not in Mexico anyway."

A man came out of a trailer three doors down. He was tall, boxy, about fifty, wide in the body, a sack of stomach pushing out under his blue-and-white-striped sport shirt. Sandy hair straggled across his bulbous forehead.

"This is Hector," said Birdie. She added, "My husband," as if both surprised and distressed by the fact. "Gus you've met. This is Dunc. Are you joining us?"

"Ahhh . . . *no!* I'm going to see my son."

"Will you be back tonight?"

Without answering her, he ambled off along the sandy path that angled up toward the parking lot beside the highway.

Gus put his hand on Birdie's thigh. "I didn't know you had a son." She removed the hand.

"*His* son—from wife number one. I'm wife number three. And he's lying, he never goes to see the smart-ass little brat."

Gus wanted to get laid, but Dunc couldn't listen to any more inanities for a while. "I'm going down to the beach."

"Leave the car keys," Gus called quickly, "and money."

Dunc did. The narrow trail wound about, over, and down between dirt hummocks covered with low wiry vegetation.

He relieved himself against the side of a dune, writing the opening of *Ulysses* in the sand until he ran out of urine on the "g" of "Mulligan." The beach, churned with footprints, was as deserted as if the bomb had fallen. He tried to imagine that searing whiteness against his eyeballs, and thought of Artis.

Two seagulls slipstreamed overhead, each with a tiny drop of red on its beak that looked like blood. A tern sliced the air with razor wings. The water shone like shook foil. When the sun touched the ocean would it hiss? But it sank without a sound.

When he returned, the light over Fayme's trailer door cast a warm golden glow under the awning. Everyone was eating, they hadn't bothered to send anyone down to get him. Gus handed him a can of beer and a church key, Angela gave him two burgers.

Her mouth full, she said, "We were too hungry to wait."

Birdie laughed a slow laugh. "Some surfers wanted to pick us up but Gus defended us. He was sweet."

"I flexed at 'em. Gravedigger muscles."

Dunc drank beer and snapped at a hamburger like a hungry wolf. Fayme finished her second burger and lit a cigarette.

"God, I never eat this kind of crap! Vegetables and fruit and broiled fish—healthy food. This is awful for you. So much grease.

You two think you're big tough musclemen, but inside you're in terrible shape. Your organs—"

"Hey, baby," said Gus, "have I got an organ for you!"

"Men!" hissed Fayme. "You're disgusting!"

Birdie looked up from her nails, said, "Oh, do get off it, Fayme dear. What will you be doing in Mexico for two weeks?"

Fayme jumped to her feet and stormed up the flimsy steps to her trailer and slammed the door. Dunc had finished his burgers. Gus had his hand on Birdie's thigh again when Fayme came clattering back down the steps, a framed picture in one hand, her eyes flashing. She thrust it under Dunc's nose.

"What do you have to say for yourself?" she yelled.

In the picture, she stood posed nude on the beach with her head back, eyes fixed on some distant goal. Her breasts were firm, the nipples erect, her pudenda had been shaved so the dark lips were visible. Dunc felt a stirring in his groin but said nothing.

She yelled, "Why were you looking at it while I was gone?"

"I've never been in your trailer, lady."

Angela said almost lazily, "I was looking at it earlier."

"Oh." Deflated, she sat staring at her photo. The traffic had died, but waves thudded; the surf had risen since Dunc had watched the sunset. "I've had enough. I'm going to bed."

The door to her trailer slammed behind her. Birdie also stood. "Come on, you," she said to Gus, "let's go get sweaty."

Angela looked warily at Dunc. "I'm not going to sleep with you, so don't get your hopes up. We're a bad lot, you can't get mixed up with us. You aren't Gus, you've still got your innocence. Believe me, once it's gone, it's gone."

"How about I sleep on the floor with Muffy?"

"He sleeps on the bed with me."

A half-moon was up, playing tag with clouds scudding in from the ocean. Dunc went up to Grey Ghost for his sweatshirt and Gus's windbreaker; it would be chilly sleeping on the beach.

He was glad Angela had refused the pass he hadn't really made. But going by Birdie's trailer he heard the steady thump of her bed against the thin aluminum shell. Sexual images exploded inside his head. And then pale light from the long narrow open window above the head of Fayme's bed brushed his face as he passed the back of her trailer. He stopped, stared down.

Fayme's nude photo was wedged upright on the cedar chest at the foot of the bed, flanked by lighted candles. Fayme herself was naked on the bed, her head propped up by her pillow so she could look at the photo, her legs splayed so her heels could be hooked over the edges of the bed. Her left hand was rolling her left nipple, her right hand was curved down around her crotch, the hidden fingers working diligently. Her body arched up and a soft cry escaped her lips.

He whirled away, zigzagged down the dirt path between the hummocks, jinking and cutting like a halfback in the open field. On the beach he tore off his clothes, splashed out to let the surf batter him with icy fists, knock him off his feet, kick his ribs, smash him against the bottom upside down. He fought his way out of the moon's lead-foil wake, shivering, his hair full of sand.

Long after moonset, wrapped in sweatshirt and windbreaker, he drifted into uneasy teeth-chattering slumber.

Chapter Nineteen

A few miles north on the Coast Highway I, Fayme and Angela, Muffy on her lap, directed him down a steep blacktop past a weathered sign reading CHURCH OF THE ORDER OF MELCHIZEDEK. He parked behind a bankrupt motel next to a hulking olive-green army-surplus Jimmy six-by-six personnel carrier with slat sides and a canvas top. The cabins were set around a circular gravel drive. There was a cross over the office door. The swimming pool was half filled with foul water, its concrete apron tilted and broken.

The women took the last two of a score of deck chairs set out on the crumbling concrete; Dunc sat on the side of the pool. Rephaim, the Seventh Priest of Melchizedek, a tall man in white robe and leather-strap sandals, stood on the tip of the diving board and gently bobbed up and down as he spoke to his congregation.

" 'Melchizedek king of Salem brought forth bread and wine: and he was the priest of the most high God.' Genesis." Hector appeared behind him wearing an ecstatic look and yesterday's clothes. "Now come we to the 110th Psalm. 'Thou art a priest forever after the order of Melchizedek.' "

Rephaim easily rode the narrow springy plank up and down as it bounced, silver-bearded face crosshatched with wrinkles, lustrous hair gleaming long and silver in the morning sun.

"Paul echoes this, pointing out that the Psalmist was speaking of a Davidic Savior who was also a High Priest."

The sun was making Dunc sleepy . . . He came awake with a start. Rephaim's eyes, dark and hawk-piercing and much younger than the man himself, seemed fixed on his.

"Now, who do the Psalmist and the Epistle writer mean will be a priest forever after the Order of Melchizedek?"

Hector slipped away into the former office. Rephaim, arms spread like an eagle's wings, bounced on his diving board.

"Paul knew, Paul understood, Paul remembered, and Paul gives us the answer in his Epistle to the Hebrews, Chapter Five."

A score of short, silent, hard-bodied Mexicans with dusky faces and straight uncut black hair right out of *Viva Zapata!* had joined the otherwise all-white congregation. They stared at Rephaim with uncomprehending eyes.

"It is Jesus Himself Who is forever a priest after the Order of Melchizedek—and His message is *love.* That is why I am here, I, the Seventh Priest of Melchizedek. Are you stuck in your lives while other people seem to be going somewhere?"

Dunc stole a quick look over his shoulder. Fayme and Angela, and the other women, were leaning forward intently. They were actually buying this tripe! He couldn't believe it.

"That's *all right!* Where you are is where you should be. Your job is to love. Love God and love God's works, nothing else matters. The Kingdom of God is in your own backyard."

Not my backyard, thought Dunc. He asked, "How can there have been only seven priests of Melchizedek since the time of Christ? Do each of you live like three hundred years?"

"You choose to misunderstand. There are always seven of us in the world; when one dies another is chosen to take his place."

Hector reappeared in a dingy white robe with gold trim, cradling a woven wicker basket. Behind Dunc, Fayme said, "I'm glad I'm going to Mexico. There's no one here to love."

"There's Muffy," said Angela. "I have Muffy."

"Hector the Seminarian will now pass among you," said Rephaim, "so that you may tithe to our Order of Melchizedek."

Hector and the loot had departed, the knot of Mexicans had disappeared. The faithful were milling about as if a movie had just let out. Rephaim made his way to Dunc. His eyes burned.

"You do not believe," he said in deep rolling tones.

"Maybe I just don't understand," Dunc told him earnestly. "Who chooses a new priest when one of you dies? The other six?"

"None of us knows the others."

"Then how do you even know one of the priests is dead?"

"One feels the call here." He laid a hand over his heart.

"Will you ever move up to Sixth Priest of Melchizedek?"

"I shall forever remain the Seventh." Then he thundered, "Enough questions! You do not believe!" and Dunc found himself thrust into the outer darkness by eager female devotees. A remarkably pretty girl about Dunc's age fell into step with him.

"You do not believe," she said in a Rephaim voice.

"Nope. Do you?"

Laughter danced in her eyes. "Nope. But even Aunt Goodie takes advice from him. Drives Uncle Carl nuts." She offered her hand. "Penny Linden."

"Pierce Duncan. I'm sure we've met before."

"I'd have remembered," she said gravely. Her chestnut hair was in a sort of bun at the back of her head. Her face was round, with a generous mouth that laughed easily, a short nose, sparkling wide-set hazel eyes under beautifully arched brows.

The army six-by-six came wheeling past, Hector at the wheel, to disappear up the gravel road to the highway with roaring motor and clashing gears. Under the canvas top, tight-packed figures.

"Hector making his getaway with the loot?"

"Hector? Never. He spends every Saturday night here, helping Rephaim with his Sunday sermon."

"And the guys in the back?"

"Fruit pickers from the San Fernando Valley. Hector gets them for the Sunday service and takes them back afterwards."

"You're saying they understand this guy?" She just laughed and shrugged, so he said, "You don't seem to fit in with—"

"With Angela and Fayme and Birdie? The coven? Of course they aren't a *real* coven of witches, but don't you think Rephaim might be some sort of mystic con man?" Her clear hazel eyes flashed sideways at him from beneath luxurious lashes. She took his arm. "Come on. Aunt Goodie and Uncle Carl were in pictures, they can give you *all* the dirt on Rephaim."

Uncle Carl was a short man in white shirt and slacks with crisp blue-black curly hair and bright eyes and a recent layer of fat on his cheeks. Aunt Goodie was a plump cheerful-looking blonde in shorts and red halter. Their arms were entwined.

"Your niece says you used to be in the movies."

She grinned. "Birdie and I were extras at Paramount for a few years after the war." She nudged her husband. "But Carl was a chorus dancer in all those MGM musicals, weren't you, hon?"

Uncle Carl said, "How did you like Rephaim? I keep telling Goodie, the man's selling snake oil. Back in the thirties, before he started dating Christ, he was in a slew of B pictures that—"

"Carl!" Goodie gasped. "What a way to talk!"

Penny said quickly, "Weren't they sort of horror films?"

"Most of them with Bela Lugosi," nodded Carl.

As they started away, Aunt Goodie said to Penny, "See you at the car, love," leaving them alone together.

Dunc ventured, "Uh, Penny, have you heard of Muscle Beach?"

"Isn't that where all those bodybuilders hang out?"

"That's it. I was thinking of going down there to look the place over next Saturday. If you aren't doing anything . . ."

She touched the intricate gold pin on her blouse. "I'm pinned. My fiancé is coming out from Iowa tomorrow for a week."

"Pinned?"

"When a man gives a sorority girl his fraternity pin, they're sort of unofficially engaged. We'll be married after I graduate from the U of Iowa next June."

"Oh." Dunc was forlorn. "Notre Dame doesn't have frats."

She shook his hand. "They're waiting for me, Dunc."

Only after Uncle Carl's car had pulled away did he realize that, feature for feature, she'd been the beautiful twenty-year-old in his Minneapolis dream who'd told him to face the killer.

Now she was gone and he didn't know how to reach her. And even if he did, the girl of his dreams was pinned.

It was Thursday, their fourth day on the job at the San Fernando Mission some twenty-five miles north of Los Angeles, erecting three long two-story seminary buildings in a U-shape around a courtyard out behind the mission plaza. They were hod carriers on a cement crew, doing prefab work before the pours.

The other hod carriers were two Negroes and seven Mexicans. Osvaldo, who spoke English, brought the other Latins each morning in a rusty, rattling pickup, took them away at night.

"Dunc! Gus!" Mike Donovan was the crew supervisor, a red-faced Irishman with a beer drinker's gut and pale bloodshot eyes. "Help Samuel and Joshua with those goddamn forms."

Samuel was about thirty, good-looking, light-skinned, blocky and muscular, with thick, shapely arms shown off by a blue work shirt with the sleeves cut off. He had a habit of smoothing his heavy mustache with the side of his finger.

Those goddamn forms were sheets of plywood that contained and shaped the liquid cement in the monolithic pours—so called because each new layer was bonded to the layer below.

Samuel told Dunc, "We wet down the inside of the forms. Then we grout 'em." Grout was hand-mixed liquid cement liberally splashed into the forms and over the rebar to bond them with the poured cement. "Then the cement crew itself makes the pour."

Joshua was older, maybe thirty-five, India ink to Samuel's milk chocolate, long and lanky and slightly stooped, with huge hands and

long arms banded by stringy muscles of great strength. He wore
Can't-Bust-'Em coveralls, and his normal splayfooted gait was a slow
shuffle.

"Ain't got me but one speed—supreme low. But watch out when I's
coming through."

At lunch break Dunc wolfed down Aunt Pearl's sandwiches, then
cut across the old-style Spanish-mission compound to the small fully
restored red-tiled church. He knelt in a back pew with the rosary he'd
bought for the penance given him by the Las Vegas priest. Thursday.
The Joyful Mysteries. Perfect. He felt pretty much joyful right now,
where he should be, when he should be. Of course Penny was pinned
by somebody else, but . . .

Gus slid into the pew next to him, oblivious to the burning sacristy
light that marked the Sacred Presence in the tabernacle behind the
altar. "Get a look at those walls—seven feet thick at the bottom, five
feet thick at the top. Built to last."

Native designs of bright primary colors covered them. "Who did
the artwork?" whispered a resigned Dunc. "Indians?"

"Originally, yeah. These are just copies."

At quitting time Dunc drove them south through Sepulveda's endless traffic toward Los Angeles, inching them into the smog, eyes
smarting, thinking of Penny. Gus broke in on his thoughts.

"Birdie wants me to spend the whole weekend with her."

"Congratulations," said Dunc. "I'm going to Muscle Beach on Saturday, I'll drop you off."

On Friday morning they were on top of the wall pounding nails
into forms. Dunc paused to wipe the sweat off his face; he noticed
Osvaldo going into the portable latrine just as a blue sedan followed
by a closed van raced up the dirt track to the seminary site. Two men
in suits and two in uniform jumped out.

Mike Donovan cupped his hands to yell up at them.

"Dunc! Gus! Down here on the double."

The Mexican members of the cement crew were being herded into a van by the uniforms. Osvaldo started from the latrine, saw this, stepped back in quickly, and gently closed the door.

A blocky man with lank reddish hair and a jaw like a sledgehammer walked over to Dunc and Gus. He had quick eyes set too close together. His thick neck bulged over his collar.

"Where were you boys born?"

"Rochester, Minnesota, but what business is it—"

"You?"

"Springfield, Illinois," said Gus. "What's this about?"

"Routine." He went back to the sedan, got in beside the driver. The van was pulling out. Donovan raised his voice.

"Okay. Back to work. We're gonna be shorthanded 'til Monday, everybody's gotta pick up some slack."

Back up on the forms, Dunc asked Samuel, "What's going on?"

But it was lanky slow-moving Joshua who answered.

"Immigration and Naturalization. Those guys was illegals, they got busted. They's on their way back to Mexico right now."

Dunc felt outrage. "Why didn't Osvaldo get grabbed?"

"He's got his green card. Happen every two weeks, steady as clockwork."

At the lunch break Dunc tried again at the chapel. Friday. The Sorrowful Mysteries. The Agony in the Garden while the Disciples slept—the bewildered faces of the Mexicans being taken before they got their pay, while he and Gus just watched. It put the day's events under a spotlight. That priest had known what he was doing. *You may not recognize the opportunity, but you'll say, "This is it!" and you'll do it.*

Was this the chance he had meant? And if it was, what could Dunc do about it?.

Half an hour before quitting time Donovan gave them their first week's paychecks: $100 less withholds! A lot of money.

"Remember, you gotta cash 'em with the hod carriers' union."

The union's office was a California-style bungalow in a tract so new half the houses weren't finished yet, some of them not even framed. No landscaping, no lawns, no plantings. A two-by-four sheet of half-inch plywood leaned against the wall beside the open front door with big black letters painted on it: HOD CARRIERS LOCAL #2784.

In the middle of the living room was a battered hardwood table. On the table was a dark green money box, a stamp pad and rubber date stamp, a stack of gray-covered booklets about the size of bank-books, and a pair of meaty elbows.

The elbows belonged to a swag-gutted man with the sleeves of a white dress shirt rolled up over thick forearms. His face, unsoftened by the cigar that graced it, looked as if it had been used for batting practice a long time ago.

The room's only other furnishings were a couch and another straight-back chair, each holding a carbon copy of the deskman, equally blue of chin and flat of eye. The deskman snapped impatient fingers.

"Paychecks." He threw them back, disgusted. "Endorsed." As they endorsed, he wrote each man's name in a booklet off the stack. "Your membership books. We keep 'em here for youse guys so's they won't get lost." He used the rubber stamp on the first page of each booklet. "Fifteen bucks a week dues."

He carefully counted out greenbacks into two equal piles, then extracted two twenties and a ten from each pile.

"We gotta take out your onetime initiation fee for bein' let into the local."

"Fifty bucks?" demanded Dunc, outraged.

"Local's gotta lotta expenses."

"Yeah, a table, a couch, and two chairs."

"Union rules. You don't like 'em, there's plenty of guys want your jobs. You're gettin' top dollar here."

"Your goddamn union's getting all the dollars underneath."

The chair-man gave a grunt of laughter. "All the dollars underneath. That's a good one. All the dollars underneath."

"Under the table, too," insisted Dunc.

"Shut up, wise guy," rumbled the couch-man, half rising.

Gus grabbed Dunc's arm. "C'mon, let's get outta here."

Osvaldo pulled his truck up outside in a cloud of red-brown dust, and Dunc got mad all over again; he could do nothing, the other Mexicans were on their way back to the border, but dammit, they'd been screwed out of their wages.

Gus drove Grey Ghost back down the dirt subdivision street.

"It's better than digging graves," he said, thinking Dunc's anger was still about the hefty union initiation fee.

"At least digging graves nobody got fucked."

"Here we get a hell of a lot more money."

"The Mexicans didn't."

"But I did—enough for the weekend with Birdie."

Chapter Twenty

Since the radio predicted an unseasonably cool evening with fog at the beaches, Penny put on her favorite dress, a warm red wool knit that displayed her full bosom and narrow waist to perfection. She fastened her lustrous wavy hair back behind her ears with silver combs, and examined herself critically in the mirror. Light glinted from her matching silver earrings.

"Penny." Gerald, outside the bathroom. "Are you ready?"

"In just a minute, hon."

The week had not gone well. He had to report to his father in Cedar Rapids on California business conditions, so it had been aircraft factories instead of studio tours, tracts instead of romantic dinners. "Penelope!"

"Coming."

They'd get married next June after he got his master's in biz ad and she got her bachelor's in history. Her mom liked him, and her sister, with two little kids, adored him. And she'd done an admirable job of keeping Pierce Duncan out of her thoughts.

She added subdued red lipstick, blotted it by pressing her full lips together with a tissue between them. On the tissue the O of her mouth looked huge. No time for anything else.

The cozy two-story house was one of many in Highland Park snatched up by returning vets. Uncle Carl was in his easy chair in the living room, watching the Saturday baseball game. Aunt Goodie appeared with iced tea and chocolate-chip cookies. Gerald was by the archway to the front door, impeccably groomed, sandy-haired, compact, his blue eyes impatient.

On impulse Penny twirled around in the middle of the room, her arms out and raised as if she were dancing.

"Hey! Hubba-hubba!" exclaimed Uncle Carl.

Penny was suddenly blushing. Goodie set the tray down on the coffee table to slap her husband's arm.

"Carl, you stop that now, you're embarrassing her."

"Hey, am I blind? Am I dumb? She's a great-looking girl."

"Penny, you know what I think of that dress." Gerald's mouth was prim. "It's too tight, too revealing."

"Not in Tinsel Town," said Carl with a quick grin.

Goodie poured, Carl grabbed cookies. Penny crossed her legs, Gerald reached over and pulled down her hem.

"Let's go watch the sun set over the Pacific," she said.

"The Seaside Hotel has a nice little restaurant called the Anchor Room that looks over the ocean and does good seafood. You kids take the car, and don't worry about getting home late." Aunt Goodie tipped Penny a bawdy wink that Gerald could not see. "And if that fog gets too thick, get rooms at the hotel."

Her aunt had married Carl mainly for sex, and claimed to only occasionally regret it. Sure, save yourself for your wedding night, she told Penny, but there was something wrong with a man who didn't at least *try* to sleep with his fiancée.

"Just south of the Santa Monica sport-fishing pier," said Carl. "At a place they call Muscle Beach."

Muscle Beach! A jolt of electricity ran through Penny's body; she hadn't driven Dunc out of her subconscious, after all.

"You have to wear a coat over that dress," said Gerald.

Muscle Beach was a narrow strip of sand between the Santa Monica pier and a big old shabby hotel a quarter mile to the south. Dunc drifted down the boardwalk in the gray, chilly afternoon, past fried shrimp, ice cream, hamburger, beer, and Pronto Pup stalls decorated with photos of the bodybuilders and lifters who had trained there over the years.

He had started lifting in high school, with a hundred-pound barbell set that had a booklet of exercises modeled by the movie actor Fred MacMurray, had kept on at Notre Dame. But these guys!

In fact, even the gawkers were interesting: faddists, beach bums, physical culturists, high school girls with condoms in their purses getting their jollies from all the exposed male flesh, queers doing the same: a fringe world by the Pacific.

One girl with her back to him stood out from the rest, a diamond among zircons, wearing a red knit dress like the girl in his dream. When she turned to say something to the sandy-haired man at her side, he realized she indeed was Penny Linden.

Forty minutes before, Gerald had said icily, "You just stay here and order me a martini," and went out to get Penny's coat. She had forgotten it in the car and had gone into the Anchor Room brazenly exposed in her red dress.

He never acted this way back in Iowa. A nice start to their romantic night at the beach! "A martini for my fiancé, and . . ." She felt rebellion within. "A . . . third rail."

The bartender had scar-tissued eyes and a flattened nose and wore a starched red knee-length apron.

"When I was fightin' I always trained on good beefsteak an' tomatoes. Lotsa protein, that's what it takes." He set the drinks in front of her, put a foot on the beer cooler, leaned forward confidentially. "Thirty-five fights, light-heavy like Billy Conn. I even got the same first name, but between you an' me, I like tendin' bar a hell of a lot better."

"I bet you were a very good fighter, Billy," Penny said.

"*Billy?* I leave you alone for five minutes and you know the bartender's first name?"

Thinking he was joking, she said, "Oh, hi, honey. Billy was just telling me what it takes to be a prizefighter."

"Years and years of no schooling."

"Gerald!" she exclaimed, astonished. "What a terrible—"

"And you've had too much to drink."

He grabbed the glass from Penny's hand to slam it down on the bar. Penny grabbed it back up and drained it and waved it.

"I'll have another one of these, Billy."

She'd had a third, in fact, before Gerald finally got her out of there to "walk it off." The third rails had bombed her.

"I'm sorry, honey," she said in a little voice she hoped wasn't slurred. "Let's not let it ruin our last night together." On a wooden platform twenty yards from the walk, three gargantuan lifters were taking turns doing three-hundred-pound repetition squats. "Let's go watch those huge men lift those huge weights."

Dunc didn't like the boyfriend's looks, his clothes, his build, anything about him. Especially his prim little mouth. When they moved back to the boardwalk from the lifting platform, Dunc tagged along behind. Muscle Beach was a rough place.

A teenage boy leaned against the edge of one of the stalls and blew into an empty beer bottle to make hollow whistling tones. Another, slightly older, wearing only swim trunks, was behind the counter tapping two Coke bottles together and moving his lean tanned body to the beat. A third squatted on an empty pop case playing the spoons back-to-back.

An older guy in his late twenties was crouched on a three-legged stool in front of the stand, pounding with an almost sexual fervor on the bottom of a five-gallon ice cream container. He wore Levi's, hack boots, a crushed cycle cap, sunglasses, and a two-day growth of beard. The sleeves of his black leather jacket barely contained his massive biceps. *Big* guy.

He brought a bottle of dago red out from under his jacket. A silver skull ring glinted on the ring finger of his left hand.

"Hey, man, anybody got any more of this Sneaky Pete?"

The crowd parted for a pimply teenager wearing khakis and a white sweatshirt with a ketchup stain down the front of it.

"I got money, Johnny!" he said proudly.

"Hey hey hey! Double Bubble, run and get me my bongos."

An overweight blond girl trotted off, her enormous breasts jouncing with each stride. Johnny winked at the crowd as he beat suggestively on his ice cream container. Reluctantly Dunc drifted away. After all, Penny was betrothed, not his to save.

"Isn't it exciting, honey? These kids with no money, no jobs, no security, but with all that music inside. They're—"

"Exciting? They're tramps, beach bums!" Gerald realized that he hated California and everything it stood for. He heard himself blurt out, "That drummer with the greasy hair and the sunglasses, that's what you find exciting. First the bartender and now this animal—"

Her fingers were icy but she managed to unclip his fraternity pin from the bosom of her dress. She dropped it into the pocket of his jacket. "I believe this is yours," she said.

Gerald slapped her very hard across the face. In the same instant he regretted it, but she was already gone, leaving her coat behind on the sand. He returned to the Anchor Room, ordered a martini. She'd show up. He had the car keys.

Penny, wandering around alone! And then Dunc lost her in the crowd. Johnny's bongos had arrived, along with a guitar and a set of maracas. They had moved to boxes set in the sand, had lit a forbidden driftwood fire. Dancing flames made red masks of their youthful faces. The bongo beat was formless, primitive.

"Dance!" someone shouted. Other voices made it a chant. "Jimmy dance! Jimmy dance! Jimmy Jimmy dance dance dance!"

The lithe boy in the swim trunks leaped into the middle of the circle to gyrate frenziedly. He arched back until his hair brushed the sand, came erect with deliberate pulsing movements.

A Negro girl wearing tight black pedal pushers and no bra under a half-open black sweater leaped into the firelight facing him. She and Jimmy whirled, churned together, apart, against one another, on their knees. The sweater came completely open; eyes, cheekbones, ebony breasts shone in the firelight.

Jimmy fell, all through, was dragged away by his ankles like a vanquished gladiator. Johnny, head down and heavy shoulders hunched forward, punished his bongos savagely, thighs straining around the drums as around a woman's body.

The Negro girl spun away, finished, but Penny, barefoot, threw away a wine bottle, drunk, languid, danced in her place without frenzy, undulating, almost dreamy, unutterably sensual. One silver earring was gone. Her hair had come loose, fireglow-lit with fluid highlights. The tight red skirt had slid up, her long legs flashed, richly ivory. She was magnificent.

Johnny was still attacking his bongos, but now his head was up, his eyes behind their sunglasses were fixed on Penny as she moved. Where in *hell* was her fiancé? This guy was huge, six-two, with arms like an ape. Together, maybe, just maybe, the two of them could handle him, but not Dunc alone. Could he?

Gerald was irritated. Perhaps he hadn't been entirely blameless tonight, but after forty-five minutes and no Penny he stormed back out into the night. There was a bonfire on the beach, from the boardwalk he could see some cheap slut with her skirt up . . .

Oh God no! It was Penny!

He tried to elbow through the crowd to the ring of fire, but was shoved this way and that, casually. Flames danced redly as from the entrance to the Pit. Drums throbbed in his skull.

The music stopped, the crowd parted. Penny shambled by him, unseeing, eyes glazed, skirt still halfway rucked-up. Gerald floundered after her through the soft sand. But someone was before him, slipping a thick possessive arm around her waist.

That horrible greasy-haired drummer!

"Hey, *chiquita.*" Minus the sunglasses, Johnny's eyes were blue and expectant. His bongos were slung over one broad shoulder. He sang in a good baritone, "Chiquita banana, and I'm here to say, my banana's gonna get you in a certain way—"

"Stop that!" cried Gerald. "She's *engaged* to me!"

Johnny laughed. One big hand began massaging her breasts. She tried to bite it. The other big hand planted itself in Gerald's face, pushed. Gerald windmilled backward into the sand.

"You can have her back tomorrow, but tonight—"

But another man had materialized from the darkness, six inches shorter than Johnny but equally broad. Johnny let go of Penny and spoke in a soft, pleased voice.

"Hey, great, next to fuckin' I like fightin' best!"

"Dunc?" asked Penny in belated recognition.

Gerald got shakily back on his feet. How many men did . . .

Johnny came in a rush, heavy arms swinging like clubs. Dunc ducked and weaved desperately, but one of the haymakers caught him on the forehead to open a shallow cut with the silver ring. Despairing, panicked, Dunc aped one of Ned's special three-punch combos: a slashing left jab to the nose, a hook to the heart, a right cross to the back edge of the chin.

As if by magic, Johnny went down, nose blossoming blood.

And just for an instant, Penny's soft lips were pressed fiercely on Dunc's as in another dream, then she was gone. Johnny, a surprised look on his face, was sitting on the sand, legs wide, waggling his jaw gingerly with one hand.

"Fuck you hit me with, man? A Mack truck?"

"A Nitro Ned Davenport combination," said Dunc happily.

Chapter Twenty-one

But Penny, after all, had gone home with the wrong guy. Dunc still didn't know how to reach her. After washing the blood off his face in the Anchor Room's john, he had a beer at the bar.

"Get in a brawl down on the beach?" asked Billy.

"Yeah. You look like you've gone a few rounds yourself."

"Thirty-six fights, but to tell the truth I never was much of a boxer." Billy waggled his chin with one hand. "Glass jaw."

Glass jaw. That must have been why Johnny had gone down so easily. Couldn't take a punch. Talk of fighting inevitably led to thoughts of Nitro Ned. As Dunc drove north along the Coast Highway I, in no mood to go home to bed, he thought: for a minute there tonight Ned had been guiding his fists.

At the trailer park everyone's lights were out. Pound on Birdie's door? Gus might not even be there, and the fog made it too cold to sleep on the beach. He would sleep in his car by the Church of the Order of Melchizedek. Maybe Penny would show up in the morning to attend Rephaim's service.

He parked behind the manzanita bushes at the foot of the road, at 6:00 A.M. sat up yawning and shivering. Had the cold awakened him? Or the smell of beans and chili? He got out, shut the car door carefully and quietly, and whizzed in the weeds, shivering in his light windbreaker. Why so stealthy? Why hadn't he parked behind the motel last night?

The grass soaked his shoes and pant legs as he swished through it. The massive old surplus army six-by-six loomed up through the drifting ground mist like a misplaced rhino, so abruptly only an outthrust palm against the wet hood kept him from walking into it.

The smell of Mexican cooking got stronger. Through the thin wall of a boarded-up cabin he heard low male voices speaking in Spanish. The farmworkers. Hector had already picked them up; the food was for them. Except the hood of the six-by-six had been stone-cold. That engine hadn't been fired up in hours.

A Mexican about Dunc's age materialized from the mist, just buttoning his fly. He had a narrow-jawed face and aquiline nose and brown liquid eyes that would have been gentle had one upper lid not been pulled awry by an angry red scar like a knife cut.

"Buenos días," said Dunc.

The Mexican broke for the front of the cabin. Dunc shrugged. He'd go find something to eat, return; the little diners that dotted the ocean side of the Coast Highway 1 would be open for the surfers. The door of Rephaim's church opened and Hector came out. His whole manner was different from their first meeting, and his voice was bellicose.

"Hey, you. What are you doing snooping around here?"

Dunc just nodded, waved an airy hand, and kept on going. At the stand of manzanita, he looked back. Hector had gone back inside, the door with the cross over it was shut.

When he got back from breakfast, Rephaim was on his diving board, arms wide, well into his spiel; Dunc recognized the knife-cut Mexican among the Latins, but none from last week. Neither Penny nor her relatives had showed. Not even any of the coven.

He left. He needed the order, assurance, and peace of Sunday Mass. The phone book gave him noon High Mass in Santa Monica. Back in Eagle Rock he found a singularly unrepentant Gus full of lurid sexual adventures he didn't want to hear about. He went to bed early. They had a pour tomorrow, had to be on-site at 7:30, which meant up at six.

It was after eight when Osvaldo showed up with the back of his old pickup filled with a new complement of workers.

"Where'd he find another crew so quick?" Dunc asked Joshua.

"There's lots of wetbacks looking for work," said Samuel.

"Does the union know they don't have green cards?"

"Course the union knows they's wetbacks, but they keeps their traps shut, they gets fifty dollah a man 'nitiation fees."

Something about this bothered Dunc, he didn't know why—not yet. Another thought hit him. "Does Donovan know?"

"Wa'm bodies, that's all he care 'bout."

As if on cue, Donovan yelled, "Get back up on those forms!"

At the lunch break the Mexicans clustered together in the shade, eating rice and beans and tortillas out of folded pieces of newspaper. One of the brown-skinned men had a narrow jaw, aquiline nose, gentle brown liquid eyes—except the right upper lid had been pulled awry by the scar of a knife cut.

"*Buenos días,*" Dunc said to him.

Again, surprised and scared. But he said, "*Buenos días.*"

Osvaldo sprayed him with rapid-fire Spanish, turned to Dunc with a big grin. "No Eeenglish, no use talking with heem, *señor.*"

How did the slender Mexican get from the boarded-up motel out by the beach to a construction site in the valley in just one day? Being there at Rephaim's Sunday morning service made no sense anyway. The man had no English, he wouldn't know what Rephaim's sermons were about.

Who could Dunc ask about it all? Gus wouldn't know any more than he did. Joshua. He waylaid the lanky Negro.

"Lordy, child!" Joshua slapped his knee with delight. "This here was all in place befo' you show up, gonna be here long after you's gone."

That was that, Dunc thought. The guys were illegals, after all, most of them would try again, a lot of them would make it.

On Wednesday night he was lying on his bed reading a copy of Faulkner's *Sanctuary* he'd borrowed from the Pasadena Public Library when Uncle Ben called up the stairs.

"Dunc! Telephone."

He yelled his thanks and rolled off the bed. Now that they knew where he was, his folks were calling once a week. He picked up the receiver off the table in the downstairs hallway.

"This is Penny."

It was like getting punched in the stomach it was so unexpected. "*Penny!* I thought . . . I didn't . . . Hey, hi, it's great to hear your voice. Listen . . ." He reached over to snag the *L.A. Times* sports section out of the wicker magazine basket beside the table. "I don't have your phone number there."

He wrote it down on the edge of the sports page and blurted out, "How does your boyfriend like California?"

"Gerald? He left Sunday. Actually he's not my boyfriend anymore." She laughed that wonderful laugh. "Aunt Goodie says she'd like you to come over on Friday night so we can all thank you for saving me."

"I tell my mom something like that, she'd have a bird."

"Oh, I can tell Aunt Goodie anything. Can you come? About seven-thirty?" *Could* he? She gave him the street address. "We're in Highland Park two blocks off Figueroa. It's a little white two-story house in the middle of the block with an old-fashioned swing on the front porch."

They were pouring the second-story walls. The grout had to be wheelbarrowed up two flights of plywood ramps, then out across empty space on two-by-twelve planks that bounced and shivered under their weight, to the open forms. At first Dunc had been terrified, but by now he and Gus were nonchalant about it.

Samuel was wetting down the forms so they could splatter in shov-

elfuls of grout to prime the rebar. Joshua was on the ground two stories below, using a garden hoe to mix up more grout in a wooden
trough. He tipped back his head and shaded his eyes.

"Come an' get it!" he yelled up at them.

Samuel pointed the hose straight down the face of the building.
The water blasted Joshua right in his upturned face. He lowered his
head, carefully laid down his hoe, turned and plodded slowly away
from the building. Samuel kept moving the hose outward to keep the
stream on the top of his head.

Out of range of the hose, Joshua stopped and turned and slowly
looked up. And slowly raised one fist and slowly shook it at Samuel.
By that time, Dunc and Gus were laughing so hard they almost fell
off the narrow planks.

At quitting time, still soaking, Joshua pointed a bony forefinger at
Samuel's gut as if the finger were a knife blade.

"Open," he intoned. He made circular motions with the switchblade finger. "That's all-l-l-l gonna be open in there."

Then he started to laugh along with the others.

Chapter Twenty-two

They just stuck 'em in the van and they were gone," Dunc was saying. "What if they had families or—"

"They don't bring their families," said Uncle Carl with vast authority. "They come to make money to send back home."

"That isn't all. They brought a new crew in on Monday—one of them was at Rephaim's Sunday service. I saw him myself."

"Everybody at Rephaim's says they're farmworkers," said Aunt Goodie.

"Farmworkers, construction workers," said Penny. "People see Mexicans and they see illegal aliens."

They walked from the ice cream parlor on Figueroa through the warm flowery August evening back to the house, two abreast on a narrow sidewalk made uneven by tree roots. Aunt Goodie said, "I think it's time us old folks went up to bed."

"I'm not tired," said Carl.

"You are now."

"Good night, Uncle Carl," said Penny with her silvery laugh.

"Why do I get the idea I'm not wanted out here? Dunc, defend me, men against—"

"Good night, Uncle Carl," said Dunc.

Carl followed his wife inside, laughing. Dunc and Penny sat on the old-fashioned front porch swing. He moved them lazily forward and backward with little shoves of his toe. The moment of truth: was Penny the still water that didn't run very deep, or . . .

"Dunc, I've been thinking about those men the Immigration Service picked up. How often do they come out there?"

What had Joshua said? "Every two weeks."

"Can't you do something?"

Her hazel eyes were wide with compassion. Responding synapses seemed to suddenly crackle in his brain.

"Maybe there is a way—I'll tell you in a week."

She said teasingly, "Why do I have to wait so long?"

"So you'll have to go out with me again to find out."

She nudged him with her shoulder. A comfortable silence fell. Dunc found himself edging an arm around her.

"Aunt Goodie didn't suggest asking you over," she said abruptly. "I did. To thank you and apologize for getting—"

"Apologize? You don't—"

"So drunk. Gerald and I had a big fight about what I was wearing and . . ." She was watching her fingers twist together in her lap as if by their own volition. "He was sweet as pie Sunday before he left, he said he was sorry he'd hit me—"

"*Hit* you!" Dunc realized he was on his feet.

"Dunc. Don't. Please." She tugged him gently down beside her again. "It's just so . . . Nobody's ever . . ."

"Nobody ever should."

"He wants to talk it all through when I go back for the fall quarter."

He didn't like anything about that, her going back to Iowa, her talking things over with Gerald. He put his arms around her and kissed her. Her lips responded. It was a long kiss, closed-mouth but tender and passionate. When they finally drew back, he felt dizzy, as if he'd drunk too much.

"I didn't want that to happen," said Penny. "Not yet."

"I've been wanting it to happen since I first saw you." His voice was shaky. Their faces were still only inches apart. "And that was in a dream I had on the road."

"You saw me in a dream?" She was pleased. "When you hadn't met me yet? How can you be sure she was me?"

So he told her about it, though not about the killer being a dead man from a Georgia chain gang with a new face. "She was you, Penny. She was wearing your same red knit dress."

"Maybe your mind supplied the dress after seeing me in it."

"Nope," he said, "that dress, exactly."

She believed him, but almost wished he hadn't told her. It was too strange. She gently disengaged herself to stand up.

"I have to go in, Dunc. It's really late . . ."

"Tomorrow is Saturday. You can sleep in."

"We're going down to Newport Beach for the weekend with some friends of Aunt Goodie's . . ."

He stood up and took her upper arms, drew her close. "Okay. But don't forget we have a date next Friday night for the next dynamic installment of the Saga of the Misplaced Mexicans."

"I wouldn't miss it for anything."

They both laughed, she raised her face to be kissed. For a long moment she melted against him, then stepped back hastily.

"G-good night, Dunc."

He went back to Grey Ghost Two, wondering if she'd stepped back so fast because she'd felt the instant erection he'd got from kissing her. Or maybe he'd been too insistent . . . No matter. Penny was going out with him next weekend!

On the way home he got lost, didn't care, finally got back onto the parkway and drove to Eagle Rock singing "Vaya con Dios" at full voice. Go with God. And God, what a great girl!

When he went down to breakfast on Saturday morning, Gus waylaid him to shove a letter under his nose. It was from the office of architect Frank Lloyd Wright in Chicago. Gus Trabert had been accepted for a two-year all-expense-paid architectural fellowship. He was supposed to show up at Taliesin West in Phoenix by the end of the month.

"Hey, Gus, that's *great!* Tonight I guess we'd better—"

"That's what I wanted to talk to you about." Gus led him out on the porch where the rest of the family couldn't hear them. "I . . . ah . . . want to spend the weekend in the sack with Birdie."

"Sure," said Dunc. "I don't blame you."

"Thing is, I . . . ah, well, I'd like to take her somewhere away from the trailer park. You know, get a motel room, really have a weekend with her."

Dunc dropped the keys to Grey Ghost Two into Gus's palm. "This'll give me time to finally get caught up on my notebook."

He was really just looking forward to some time alone. That was one thing being on the road gave you—time alone.

He walked all the way to downtown Pasadena, in the huge old ornate library returned the Faulkner and checked out *The Long Goodbye.* Two of his favorite movies had been based on Raymond Chandler novels: *The Big Sleep* and *Murder, My Sweet.*

Goodbye hooked him completely. He read it at the library, he read it on the bus home, he read it in bed far into the night and finished it at three in the morning.

The rich beautiful woman who attracted P.I. Philip Marlowe, Linda Loring, was nothing at all like Penny but reminded him of Penny all the same. It took a hell of a good writer to get his characters into your mind that way. How did you get that good?

Dunc was always saying that writing was all he would want out of life, but then was always getting himself sidetracked, neglecting his own dream for Nitro Ned's, letting Penny take over his whole mind. Where would he find the discipline?

"Put your typewriter on a table and your butt on a chair," his creative writing teacher at Notre Dame, Mr. Sullivan, had said, "and start typing. When you stand up ten years later, you'll be a writer."

But Hemingway had implied that if all you did was write, you'd end up with nothing to write about—and here was Dunc with a whole summerful of experiences, and he wasn't even keeping up his notebook.

Sunday morning after church he helped around the house, then sat out under a tree with his notebook and started writing. He had nothing down about Las Vegas, was already forgetting details, and some of the details he remembered were almost too painful to write down.

Nitro Ned, his huge spirit stilled at last, being carried out of the Flamingo Hotel . . . Artis, covered with blood, dying eyes burning fierce into his . . . He wished he had the notebooks Falkoner had driven off with in El Paso. He had to get them back. Sometime . . .

Chapter Twenty-three

Gus would leave for Taliesin before Labor Day; Penny would go back to school right after the holiday. Dunc would move on then, too. Like Shane. The lone gunman, fixing things up before riding off into the sunset. Friday would tell for sure.

He talked to Gus as they wheeled liquid "mud" up the ramps and across the top of the building on the spidery network of two-by-twelves. "Who around here do you think knew that the immigration guys were coming, and knew *when* they'd come?"

"Osvaldo," said Gus promptly. "He's got his green card and he's been around long enough."

"That doesn't mean he's the Judas goat, but he just *happened* to go to the john just before the immigration guys came—right at the morning break, so they were all together."

"So it's safe to assume he's the one. What do we do?"

"You're the architect. Design something—like a sticking door on the crapper so he can't get out and see what I'm doing."

"Gotcha," said Gus. "And what will you be doing?"

"I'm going to *hablar* with Alejandro"—he nodded toward the young, scarred Mexican—"whenever we're working together. I want him to get used to me, so he'll understand and trust me when the time comes."

* * *

At 9:50 Friday morning Donovan headed for the job site office, where he could put his feet up and drink coffee for the fifteen-minute break. Sure enough, Osvaldo headed for the portable toilet. Gus sauntered along behind him.

Dunc gestured to Alejandro.

"Vamos," he said. Alejandro stared at him with uncomprehending eyes. Dunc grabbed his arm, half dragged him to his feet. *"Venir. Rápido."* He swept his arm at the rest. "All of you. Ah . . ." He'd memorized the phrase. *"Todo el mundo. Rápido! Rápido!"*

Alejandro spat Spanish at them, they scrambled to their feet, Dunc started running for the cornfield fifty feet from the edge of the construction site. They ran after him, impelled by fear of unknowns he couldn't even imagine. Thirty yards in, surrounded by head-high stalks, green and rustling, heavy with golden-silked ears, the rows at right angles to the seminary, Dunc stopped. He pointed at each in turn.

"Ustedes," he said. *"Esperar. Yo regresar. Comprender?"*

He lay down in the depression between rows to give them the idea, stood up again, swung his arm around in a big circle, then pointed in turn to each of them.

"Usted . . . usted . . . usted . . . comprender?"

They understood. As they spread out through the corn rows, Dunc ran back to the site. When he heard the car and the van roaring up, he sat down quickly in the shade, lay back with his hands interlaced behind his head, the sweat drying under his blue work shirt.

The vehicles skidded to a stop. The four agents jumped out and began to fan out through the site. Suddenly they stopped and looked around, surprise on their faces. No Mexicans.

"Hey! You!" It was the redheaded immigration agent with the bulging neck who'd braced them two weeks ago.

Dunc sauntered over to them, all innocence. "Yeah?"

They ringed around him in a loose circle.

"Where are the Mexicans?" asked Thick-Neck.

Dunc shook his head in simulated bewilderment. One of the uniformed agents snapped, "The wetbacks."

"The illegal aliens," Thick-Neck amended quickly, his close-set eyes darting about. "We received a report there were illegal Mexican immigrants working on your cement crew."

"You guys took 'em away two weeks ago."

"Bullshit!"

"Gotta talk to Donovan about that. I just wheel cement."

"Where's the Mex honcho?" The other man wearing a suit was lean and stooped, with a big Adam's apple.

Dunc tried to look stupid. "They all look the same to me."

Osvaldo appeared, Gus strolling along a discreet distance behind. The agents surrounded the Mexican for low-voiced discussion and arm-waving. Osvaldo kept shrugging, looking more and more miserable. Finally they got back into their vehicles and spun out of there in an angry cloud of red dust.

"Royally pissed off," said Dunc happily. "How'd you keep Osvaldo in there long enough?"

"Stuck a little wedge in the bottom of the door, he finally had to kick it open. He didn't even notice what it was."

Dunc brought the Mexican crew back from the cornfield. Joshua collared him when he got back up on the forms. "Didn't I tell you leave well 'nough alone?" he scolded.

"Who's going to do anything about it? Osvaldo?"

"Wasn't thinkin' of him," muttered Joshua darkly.

At the union office Joshua and Samuel were ahead of them, just pocketing their greenbacks. The table-man gave a start of ill-concealed surprise when the Mexicans came crowding behind Dunc and Gus, chattering and laughing among themselves.

Dunc would remember it later. But not today. Tonight he had a date with Penny, his workweek fatigue was dropping away.

*   *   *

The front door opened and Penny skipped lightly down the front steps. Dunc ran around the car to open the other door. Her hair was loose around her face, she brought the scent of flowers with her. She was wearing a plaid skirt and a blue blouse and dark blue pumps. He got in under the wheel. She turned to face him on the seat, eyes shining.

"Okay, tell me! What are you going to do?"

"Gee, about what?" he asked blandly.

She lunged toward him, laughing, pretending to strangle him. Her skirt rode up, giving him a glimpse of inner thighs. He instantly looked away. She blushed and pulled the skirt down.

"You know very well what I mean! The Mexicans."

"Oh, *them*. We already did it."

On the parkway he told her about his day. Toward the end her elation turned to concern.

"What did Joshua mean? Why was he worried for you?"

"I'm not sure. I'll ask him on Monday."

They went to see *Strangers on a Train* in Pasadena. Dunc gave a start of surprise at the credits: one of the screenwriters was Raymond Chandler, his new writing hero!

And what a great scary movie to take a girl to! When the old-time carny worker was crawling bug-eyed through the muck and mire under the out-of-control roller coaster near the end of the film, Penny jammed her head up against Dunc's chest with her eyes squeezed tight shut.

They ate in an Italian restaurant called Louise's Trattoria in shabby old Pasadena on East Colorado Boulevard. In a dark-wood booth, in the voluble care of dark-haired waiters, they split an Italian-sausage pizza and drank draft beer and talked about their whole lives.

Penny had never met anyone before who was actually trying to be a writer, and was full of questions. She said she loved Hemingway's romanticism, and Dunc explained at great length that you had to call it doomed romanticism.

"How about you, Penny?" he asked finally. "What do you want when you get out of college? Love, marriage, kids?"

"All of the above—doesn't everyone? But after I broke up with Gerald, I knew that I really want to come back out west."

"California," said Dunc with not a little complacency.

"Not really. The *real* West. I want to work on one of those great ranch estates that have horses and real western food, and people who come to stay, like a hotel."

"A dude ranch," said Dunc.

"Is that what they call them? All right, someday I want to have a dude ranch of my own."

When they had stopped in front of Aunt Goodie's house, Penny brought up the question of the Mexican illegals again.

"If you're right that you saw the one with the knife scar on his face out at Rephaim's church—"

"Alejandro," said Dunc. "He was one of them, all right."

"So you mean that most of the farmworkers at Rephaim's don't have their green cards at all."

"We don't know for sure, of course, but Rephaim could be smuggling them in. Wouldn't the Church of Melchizedek be a good transfer point after they get up here? I don't know much Spanish, but I think Alejandro said that they pay a hundred bucks each, up front, to get smuggled across the border."

"Rephaim is too tied up in his church to—"

"Even Uncle Carl thinks he's a con man."

"That's because he's jealous of the way Aunt Goodie listens to what Rephaim says." She paused. "Oh, Dunc, be careful!"

She was worried about him! Suddenly they were in each other's arms, kissing almost wildly, tongues darting, panting for breath. Her head was back, her arms clinging to him.

Somehow, Dunc's hand was on one of her brassiered breasts through the thin fabric of the blouse. His other hand moved up inside her skirt along the silken length of her inner thigh. He was wild with desire. She wrenched herself away.

"Dunc! No! Please!"

He stopped instantly, panting. "I . . . I'm sorry, I . . ."

She came back into his arms, whispered against his throat, "It's just that . . . so soon . . . not here . . . not now . . ."

He walked her to the door, both of them still a little breathless. She pressed against him again.

"Tomorrow?" he asked.

"I can't." She gestured at the house. "Next Friday?"

"Next Friday," he said, then added quickly, "and Saturday."

She laughed. "And Sunday. Good night, darling." And she kissed him and was gone.

Dunc drove home feeling the agony and the ecstasy—ecstasy over the "darling," agony over his case of lover's nuts.

On Monday Dunc asked Joshua if he'd meant the immigration people might give him a hard time over hiding the Mexicans.

"Trouble I'm talking 'bout come, you be knowin' it for sure."

Which told him nothing. At least being shorthanded meant Dunc had to concentrate on what he was doing instead of spinning emotional and sexual fantasies about Penny all the time.

Driving home from work, Gus was in a foul mood. "I couldn't get *near* Birdie last Saturday. After a whole summer of practically handing her to me on a platter, all of a sudden Hector tells me he never wants me to speak with her again."

"You're lucky he didn't come at you with a shotgun."

"You don't know the half of it. *Last* week he walked into the bedroom when we were humping away."

Dunc was amazed. "What'd he do?"

"Called her the Whore of Babylon and said 'Excuse me' and stalked out again."

"You're making it up."

Gus made the old Boy Scout sign with two raised fingers. "Scout's honor. I tell you, Dunc old son, I'm out of my depth. Where are the honest, virtuous virgins of St. Mary's?"

"Maybe he heard we hid the Mexicans in the cornfield."

"What's this 'we,' white man. And anyway, what difference would it make to him?"

"I'm just saying 'What if?' Alejandro was at Rephaim's on a Sunday morning and at the seminary construction site on the Monday. This weekend Hector tells you to get lost."

Gus nodded. "And he knows we're buddies." Then he shrugged. "Whatever the hell reason, I'm like the guy lost the key to his girl's apartment. Now I get no new-key."

There was no smog, nobody could figure out why it sometimes didn't appear. The traffic on Sepulveda was at a standstill. Somewhere ahead of them flashing lights pinpointed an accident.

Gus leaned back in the seat and crossed his hands behind his head. "I've got a special place I'd like to show to you and Penny, Dunc. How about I take you guys there on Sunday?"

"I'll ask her about it—but if she comes, don't mention Birdie. Birdie is one of her aunt's best friends."

Penny chose the movie on Friday night, a romantic comedy called *Roman Holiday*. They both were wild about it. Audrey Hepburn was like a delicate bird, and Gregory Peck had been one of Dunc's favorite actors since he'd played the writer dying on the African veldt in Hemingway's *The Snows of Kilimanjaro*.

After they had thoroughly discussed everything from *Roman Holiday* to Gregory Peck to Hemingway, Penny brought up Rephaim.

"I've given this a lot of thought, Dunc, and I still don't think he's involved in smuggling illegal aliens. I don't believe in him any more than you do, but *he* believes in himself. Totally. And *he* wouldn't profit by turning them in. Who would?"

"Well, the Immigration Service, for one."

"Do they pay informers?"

"I doubt it, but maybe those guys have a quota to fill."

"All right, who *else* profits in this whole thing?"

"Whoever gets them across the border."

As he said it, Hector popped into his mind. But he didn't say anything to Penny. Neither of them mentioned her impending departure, as if the infinity of time lay before them.

Dunc hadn't ridden a horse since he was ten, when his family'd had a very sly pony named Tricksy. But Senator was a big horse, sedate and good-natured as he plodded along the winding bridle trails through the scrub brush and dusty-leaved live oaks of Griffith Park. Penny rode Yankee. She was a terrific rider. He'd have to practice so he could keep up . . .

Except it all ended in three weeks. Don't think about it.

She spread a tablecloth under a smooth red-boled manzanita and gathered a bunch of wildflowers for a centerpiece. They ate fried chicken and potato salad and drank lemonade out of a thermos. Senator nudged between them to eat the bouquet.

As they returned to the stables on the northern rim of the park, Penny brought Yankee up beside Senator for a fierce saddle-to-saddle hug. "This has been one of the best days of my life!"

"Since you're gonna own a dude ranch, I thought we'd better practice up."

Their unsaddled horses ambled about the enclosure; Dunc mentioned Gus's mystery location the next day.

"It'll be fun," said Penny. "And since he's your friend I want to meet him before he goes off to Frank Lloyd Wright's place in Phoenix. Do you think he could design a dude ranch house?"

"Sure, and the stables. And he specializes in outhouses."

She patted her horse's shoulder. "Sound good, Yankee?"

Dunc almost said it then, what had been growing in his mind. Ask her to stay, skip that last year of college; but he couldn't. It wouldn't be fair to her. Or to him, either.

A lion roared in the nearby zoo, and he thought of Hemingway's African stories. Christ, he wanted to be a writer!

*   *   *

On Sunday Gus drove them down through a broad flat sprawl of little houses in South-Central L.A. east of the airport. "Just a couple of years ago this area was more white than black."

From blocks away, they could see a strange openwork tower thrusting far above its surroundings, glinting in the noonday sun as if studded with jewels.

"What *is* it?" asked Penny in awe.

"A tower a guy named Watts has been building for years."

The base of the tower was heaped with broken glass from bottles of every description—pop bottles, beer bottles, wine bottles. There was also a hand-lettered sign, "Admission, 25 cents." Watts was a short middle-aged man who knew Gus and shook hands with him. Inside the tower, Penny and Dunc gazed up at its spires in amazement. Crazy wooden scaffolding flanked its sides.

"Concrete and broken bottles," said Penny in surprise.

The concrete looked almost liquid, as if still dripping down the sides of the tower like candle wax. But it was totally dry. They spent over an hour there, gawking, touching.

"What a strange thing to spend your life working on," said Penny as they headed home.

"He works alone, it just came to him that he had to do it."

"He's driven to it," said Dunc, and hoped he would be that driven to writing when the time came.

That night, after Goodie and Carl had gone to bed, as they drifted back and forth together on the creaking porch swing, Dunc was surprised to hear Penny chuckle to herself.

"I was just thinking, maybe Gus isn't the right architect for the ranch house. Even less for the stables. Can you imagine how a tower like that would spook the horses?"

"His drawings are nothing like the Watts towers, honest."

Suddenly sober, she hugged him close. "Oh, Dunc, time's getting so short."

Chapter Twenty-four

Dunc was driving over to see Penny every night and getting home at one or two in the morning. Each day he knew he'd have to stay in and sleep that night; but when quitting time rolled around, he could hardly wait to go see her.

They took long rambling walks along darkened neighborhood streets, making up stories about the people behind the lighted windows. They'd see a movie, sit in a soda fountain, watch TV, swing on the old-fashioned porch glider. Always they ended up parked in a little wooded area across the parkway, feverish and excited, going a little further each time in mutual need.

Friday, Gus's last day in L.A., he skipped work to spend time with his relatives, particularly Grandma Trabert; she had aged over the summer. Donovan gave Dunc a big ration of shit about the missing Gus, but labor was plentiful, he'd have no trouble getting a replacement for Monday's pour.

Without Gus, Dunc went to Joshua for help getting the Mexicans hidden away in case Immigration came earlier. The lanky Negro gave his high laugh and clapped Dunc on the shoulder.

"Osvaldo!" he yelled. "Mr. Donovan says you an' me, baby, we gotta go wait for the truck to bring the *ce*ment."

Dunc led the others out to the edge of the field farthest from the building site, in case Osvaldo had learned where they'd been hidden last time. And sure enough the immigration agents arrived at 9:15, an hour early. When they saw no Mexicans, they stormed right over to Dunc. Osvaldo obviously had been talking.

Thick-Neck's close-set eyes were angry slits.

"Okay, wise guy, where are they?"

Again, Dunc was all innocence. "Who?"

This time all four agents ranged around him like the hyenas around the dying writer in *The Snows of Kilimanjaro*. And like the hyenas their jaws were mighty: scavengers, Dunc thought with a touch of alarm, but also government men.

"We know you hid them in the cornfield last time."

"I don't know what you're talking about."

Thick-Neck said, "We can arrest you for obstruction of justice and aiding and abetting federal fugitives."

"I have to get back to work. We're shorthanded today."

Just then Joshua, shaking his head over the cement truck that mysteriously hadn't arrived, returned with Osvaldo. The immigration agents halfheartedly poked around in the cornfield without success, finally drove off in a cloud of dust.

Dunc felt shaky. This had been just a game to him, but the agents' anger had been personal and vindictive. Maybe they did have a quota. What worried him even more was Osvaldo. Dunc had expected open hostility from the Judas goat, but Osvaldo just looked scared. Of what? Of whom?

At the hod carriers' office were just the deskman and the chairman, whom he had learned were Tony and Luigi. He laid down his check. "Take out thirty, I'm paying Trabert's dues, too."

Tony counted out his money, stamped the union books. His eyes shifted, and a heavy shoe slammed into Dunc's kidney. He yelled in pain and arched back at the same time that he was driven forward, half running, into the wall. He fell down.

"Smart little fuck!" exclaimed Tony.

They were advancing on him, coming in from either side. Dunc staggered to his feet and backed up against the wall.

"We're gonna show you what happens when you fuck around in union affairs," said Luigi.

Suddenly, too late, Dunc saw it all with blinding clarity. Who Osvaldo was afraid of. Who had worked out the scam in the first place, who had been profiting from turning in the illegals every two weeks, even why the immigration agents' anger had been so focused and personal. He held up placating hands.

"Wait a minute, wait a minute, I didn't know—"

"Well you're gonna know now, fuckface."

He charged them as he'd done so often in football when double-teamed by blockers protecting the quarterback, hoping to burst out between them and run for his life. He didn't make it.

Luigi smashed an elbow into his jaw. He used his own elbow, felt a satisfying jar. But Tony's arm was around his neck from behind in a chokehold, he was hauled bodily upright; Tony outweighed him by seventy pounds.

Dunc clawed at the tree trunk arms, couldn't get any leverage. The kidney kick had weakened him, the half nelson was cutting off the blood to his brain; Luigi, in front of him, looked blurry.

"Hold him still. Fucker broke my nose."

A pile-driver fist smashed into Dunc's gut. His abdominal muscles were so work-toughened it didn't quite rupture anything.

Tony said behind him, "Shit, you can hit him in the gut all day. He's tough from working, this baby. Go for the face."

Luigi's right cross to the side of his jaw sagged his knees and blurred his vision even more. The next one would put him on the floor, where they could kick him to death if they wanted to.

Then Dunc heard a grunt of effort and Luigi drifted up off the floor in slow motion. He was spun into Samuel's rising boot at the apex of his kick. It put him on the floor flat as a pancake, arms and legs wide, face full of blood.

In his place was Joshua, a surprisingly baleful grin on his ebony face.

"You bes' let go of him," he said to Tony.

But Tony warned, "I'll break his fuckin' neck!"

Joshua made a graceful movement too fast for the eye to follow, and was pointing his switchblade finger at Tony's ample middle, as he had done to Samuel the day he'd been doused with water. Only now his finger was an opened-out straight razor, the gleaming blade making little eager circles in front of him.

"I takes me a swipe with this here razor, Mr. Union Man, an' when you tries to nod your head you be in fo' a big surprise."

Tony stepped back, arms out wide from his sides. Obviously neither he nor Luigi had thought they'd need a gun to beat somebody up. Dunc gulped in great lungfuls of air.

"International's gonna be mighty innersted in whut you been doin' in this local," Joshua said. "I hear they be as tough as you guys pretend you are. Dunc, we be goin' now."

The three of them backed out the door. Samuel's rattletrap was alongside the Grey Ghost with both doors hanging open.

"I thought . . . you guys . . . were already gone," panted Dunc.

"We figured you might need a little help when you went to cash your check." Samuel was thoughtfully rubbing his boot in the dust to rid it of Luigi's blood.

Dunc's kidney burned, but it was not as bad as a kidney shot he'd taken from an opposing lineman's helmet during his high school football days. Then he'd pissed blood for a week.

"You guys . . . knew all along . . . what was going on."

Samuel shrugged. "Near enough."

"Figgered you was havin' a lotta fun workin' it out your own se'f," said Joshua. "But we think maybe you won't wanna work here no mo'. Those guys gonna have long memories."

"But what about you? If you lose your jobs over this—"

"Shit, man," said Samuel, "we can work anywheres we want."

Joshua gave his hee-hee-hee laugh. "We be the dynamic duo!"

"You go on now, Dunc," said Samuel. "Jes in case they got some life in them yet."

They didn't. No one appeared at the open door of the tract house serving as a union office. It was all over. Joshua stuck out his hand; Dunc hugged him instead, the way he hugged his dad when he hadn't seen him for a while. He repeated with Samuel.

"Christ, you guys, you—you saved my life!"

"Jes yo' ass," said Joshua, and all three of them laughed.

Driving away from the hod carriers' office for the last time, in the rearview mirror Dunc could see Samuel's ancient Plymouth bouncing along the dirt track in his dust.

At Sepulveda they went their separate ways.

Chapter Twenty-five

That evening Dunc regaled the family with the story of how his plan to again hide the Mexican laborers in the cornfield, which had gone so perfectly the first time, had gone awry.

Uncle Ben said, "You look pretty beat-up, Dunc. Something ought to be done about that assault at the union office."

"I learned my lesson. I'm just going to let it lie."

He called Penny for some loving commiseration and invited her to see Duke Ellington the next night. After another long hot shower he went to bed; there had been only the faintest pink tinge to his urine, so he knew his kidneys were all right.

Next morning the whole family trooped down to see Gus off on the Phoenix-bound Greyhound. Gus and Dunc shook hands.

"Christ, I wish I'd been there yesterday."

"Then we both would've gotten the shit kicked out of us."

Suddenly they knew it had been a good summer. One that could never be repeated. The women were fussing over Gus, tears on everyone's cheeks; Dunc was suddenly homesick for his folks. Gus got a window seat, he and the family mouthed silent sentences at each other until the driver climbed in and the door hissed shut. The big vehicle was moving, and Gus was gone.

*   *   *

Dunc found a place to park on a side street a block from the Strip, in front of a small dark bungalow with a dried-out lawn but hot-purple bougainvillea rioting up the front porch posts to give the place a spurious festive air. A '36 Chevy pickup was parked halfway up the drive. Dim light glowed against the drawn front room shades; they could hear radio music from inside.

"Good place for Philip Marlowe to discover a murder," said Penny in almost a whisper.

They walked up the inclined street to Sunset holding hands. The air was warm, flower-scented; palm fronds clacked overhead. Dunc was very aware of the swing of Penny's thighs beneath the clinging red dress.

As they strolled past an Art Deco cocktail lounge called the Purple Cockatoo, a posterboard beside the doorway caught Dunc's eye. He stopped dead to stare at the photograph of a dapper black-haired man in a tux framed beneath the lettering:

COME IN AND ENJOY THE
PIANO STYLINGS OF
PEPPER PAGLIA

Pepe, who had conned Nicky into letting Dunc go back to the Gladiator Club's poker room for the fateful meeting with Nitro Ned and Artis in the first place! Pepe, who had sung to his piano riffs as he told Dunc stories as Dunc perched at the piano bar next to the tip glass on its felt coaster.

"That's him!" he exclaimed. "It's his photograph." Penny already knew most of Dunc's Las Vegas adventures, all except watching Artis die. Penny took his hand and drew him toward the door. "You need to talk to him," she said. "You're the only ones still alive."

The Purple Cockatoo was a narrow room full of smoke and a lot of potted plants with spearlike palmetto leaves, but no cockatoos, purple or otherwise. Two barmen sweated behind a stick alive with the din of the alcohol voices of sharp-dressing men and blondes in revealing dresses and too much makeup.

Dunc shouldered a path for Penny toward a piano bar bathed in a purple spotlight. Pepe was singing the Tony Bennett version of "Cold, Cold Heart." He looked up, did a double take, and schmaltzed up a dozen bars of the "Notre Dame Victory March."

"Dunc! And the loveliest lady in the place!"

Penny gave a mock curtsy. "Thank you, kind sir."

Dunc introduced them, then asked Pepe, "Are you the purple cockatoo they named the place after?"

"The purple spot?" Pepe chuckled. "Management insists."

He looked just the same as he had at the Gladiator Club, impeccably groomed, slim and elegant, with the white wine, the cigarette smoldering in an ashtray, the glass bowl of greenback tips. Dunc realized all over again how much he liked this man. Pepe gestured them to stools at the almost empty piano bar.

"Same old story. People come to a place like this to pick up women, not listen to the music." He grinned. "Not like Dunc. Always my biggest fan."

When a harried waitress in a tight black uniform that showed a lot of breast and leg came by to take their orders, Pepe launched into Frankie Laine's "Jezebel."

"Pepper?" asked Dunc at the end of the piece.

"My producer's idea. 'Pepe' sounded too Mexican. Pepper Paglia—possibly Italian, possibly a recording star."

"You got your record deal!" exclaimed Penny.

He raised sad elegant shoulders. "Not quite yet, Penny."

Between numbers they drank and talked about Penny going back to college, about Dunc maybe trying San Francisco, about Pepe playing his piano . . . And finally about Vegas.

Dunc asked, "Did they ever catch Raffetto?"

Pepe's hands momentarily forgot to play. He shook his head.

"Dunc, I don't even know! I got a call about my record deal and had to leave before the fight. A bad business." He raised his glass. "To life!" he said.

"I'll drink to that," said Dunc.

There was an explosion of white light that momentarily blinded them all. Pepe was on his feet, face white and drawn, glaring at the photo girl.

"Hey, this is great! A picture of the three of us together!" Dunc told her, "Three prints, miss."

Pepe said sheepishly to Penny, "I thought it was a bomb. Mickey Cohen used to have his bookie joint in the basement of the haberdashery right next door at 8800 Sunset. Sell you a suit upstairs, take you to the cleaners downstairs. Somebody who wanted to take over his vice empire set off two bombs under his house."

"Did they ever succeed?" asked Penny, wide-eyed.

"The mob, no, but he got five years for tax evasion."

"And his vice empire?" asked Dunc.

Pepe chuckled. "Now *everybody* wants to take it over."

The photo girl in her brief costume came back. It was a good shot, not as somber as the moment had felt to Dunc.

"Ah, we were young then," said Pepe.

"Monday we're going to the American Legion Labor Day picnic at Griffith Park," said Penny. "Could you—"

"I'd love to! How kind of you to ask."

"I'll drop by midweek with directions," volunteered Dunc.

There were still a lot of things he needed to talk to Pepe about that he couldn't say in front of Penny. Arriving just too late to save Artis from Rafe Raffetto, Ned giving him the car, maybe even the priest's weird penance . . .

"I'll be here," said Pepe with mock resignation.

It was too late to catch the Duke, but the Strip was still alive with moving people, honking cars, cruising police vehicles. They walked with their arms around one another; once off Sunset, they stopped every few paces to kiss. The house where Philip Marlowe might have uncovered a corpse was dark. Their eyes met.

Dunc said, "Let's go . . . somewhere."

"Yes," she whispered.

Out beyond the Strip, Sunset Boulevard was wide and dark, traffic light. At Westwood Village Dunc chose a glowing red neon *MOTEL—Vacancy* sign, turned in. His heart was pounding.

He parked, trying to remember warnings from college studs about checking into a motel with a girl. After rehearsing his story in his mind, he rang the night bell.

A yawning woman with a round pleasant sleep-filled face came into the little office to buzz him in. Before Dunc could even fumble out his wallet, she put down a registration card.

"Double with bath is six bucks. Noon checkout."

California! He loved it. Inside, they embraced, kissed. He unzipped the red dress and drew it down her shoulders and arms. She drew it down past her hips and thighs herself, looking like countless French paintings, *Herself Surprised*.

She stepped out of it, leaving the dress a crimson puddle on the floor, and caught his silver belt buckle to draw him close to her. They clung dizzily to each other, with deep, long kisses, then she was opening his buttons as he unfastened her bra and her breasts sprang free, achingly beautiful in the dim light.

In bed together, naked, touching one another, both inexperienced. When he finally began to enter her, Penny arched her back and drew in a sharp breath.

A whisper, "Dunc, please, be . . . It's . . . my first time . . ."

He was wild with passion, nothing had ever been harder than the restraint she needed. Moving slowly, ever so slowly, he had not even fully entered her before he came. He had never known anything as exquisite in his life.

He withdrew, still half engorged. They clung together, entwined. She whispered, "I . . . I love you, Dunc."

"Love you, my lover," he said into her hair.

Her hand found him, he started to get hard again.

"Oh, Dunc . . . yes," she whispered.

This time, no holding back. Her legs locked around him, held him tight as he bucked and thrust. Suddenly she arched with a small astonished cry and he spent, and spent, and spent again.

The Purple Cockatoo was dark except for a bright fan of gold from the open door in the back wall marking the office where the manager tallied the night's receipts. Pepe pulled the fitted cloth cover over the piano; he wouldn't be playing here again.

Dunc had found him, Dunc would be back to talk about the deaths of Artis and Ned, things that Pepe couldn't talk about. This was a smart, observant kid. If he started remembering . . .

Pepe sipped his white wine, considered. He couldn't have Dunc in touch with him, but it would be smart to keep track of where Dunc went, what he did. Yes. Smart. He'd make a phone call. No telling what the kid was thinking about right now.

They slept, woke, found one another, slept, woke again shortly before noon in each other's arms to the sounds of people moving around outside, cars starting. Kissing, shyly, neither of them moving. Then moving, slowly at first, then faster, faster, then wildly to mutual explosion.

When they finally got up for a quick shared shower, there were two fine streaks of blood on the sheet. It awoke in Dunc a strange, exciting meld of emotions he had never known before: possession, an intense desire to protect, commitment to her.

Chapter Twenty-six

Penny reassured romance-loving Aunt Goodie from a pay phone, then Dunc drove them out along winding Sunset Boulevard toward the Palisades. It was a warm and sparkling day full of music, he had a hard time keeping his eyes off Penny. She was wearing dark glasses, the windows were open and her hair was blowing around her face. Her legs were tucked under her, tracing the taut line of her thigh against the red skirt. A scant hour ago he had been between those thighs. He couldn't believe it.

"Where are you taking me, mystery man?"

"I was thinking of lunch," he said.

She slid over beside him to rest her head on his shoulder. "I knew there was something about you that I found attractive."

Dunc stopped at a seafood place on the ocean side of the Coast Highway, at a window table they ate fisherman's platters and watched swimmers splashing in the languid surf.

"I wish . . ." Penny left the thought unfinished.

"Me too," said Dunc.

Farther north they saw the turnoff to Rephaim's church and said in tandem, "Yeah, let's," and laughed in delight at the shared thought. Here they had first met, just over a month ago. They wanted to remember it. They would. A tan '52 Ford and a police black-and-white were parked outside the open door with the cross over it. Three men emerged.

The first was tall and athletic with a hard-bitten face and frown lines on his forehead. The second was a uniformed bull with a revolver on his hip. The third was Rephaim in his flowing robes, his magnificent head of silver hair wild, his eyes even wilder. He raised both manacled arms to point at Dunc.

"Thy heart is deceitful above all things, and desperately wicked: who can know it?" He advanced toward them, quivering with righteous rage. He cried, "Let the wicked forsake his way, and the unrighteous man his thoughts!"

"I haven't done anything to you," said Dunc, taken aback.

Rephaim thundered, "I will feed thee with wormwood, and give thee water of gall to drink."

"What is happening here?" demanded a bewildered Penny.

The cop led Rephaim away to the prowl car. The hard-bitten detective said, "We're not too sure ourselves. We got a memo about the San Fernando police cracking a big illegal-alien smuggling ring out in the Valley."

"But what does that have to do with Rephaim?" she asked.

"Well, this morning we get a call from somebody belongs to this Church of the Order of Melchizedek, complaining about greasy Mexicans, so we attend the reverend's service unannounced, we find a couple dozen wetbacks. The reverend says they're members of his congregation, but none of 'em has a word of English. No papers, no home addresses, no money. So we called Immigration."

The prowl car with Rephaim in back accelerated up the road.

"The reverend just keeps saying they were farmworkers from the Valley, he has no idea they were illegals. But—"

Penny said forcefully, "I think he was telling the truth." She turned to Dunc. "Honey, what's going on?"

"I told Gus's uncle about getting beat up. He must have passed it on to his friends in the archbishop's office, and they may have gone to the police. But this I don't understand, the aliens getting busted here . . ."

The detective said, "Anyway, we really wanta talk with his acolyte or deacon or whatever the hell he calls himself."

"Hector?" asked Dunc.

"Yeah." The three of them walked over to the edge of the pool. The detective added, "The reverend seemed pissed at you."

"Maybe he thought I was the one who called you."

"Maybe. Anyway, this guy Hector's got a lot of explaining to do. I really want to talk to him."

There was a roar like an enraged bull elephant. They whirled—the six-by-six was roaring down the road at them, Hector hunched over the steering wheel, shrieking, face distorted.

"I'll kill you! I'll kill you!"

The detective dodged one way, Dunc dragged Penny the other, the massive truck's nose and front wheels missed them all and hit the surface with a great splash, sending an inverted waterfall of filthy water out over the concrete skirting at the far end of the pool. Its rear wheels rested on the broken concrete apron, its engine drowning to silence.

"Here's Hector now," said Dunc to the detective.

It made the Metro section of the Monday *L.A. Times,* with a picture of Hector's truck nose-down in the swimming pool at the church of a zany cult calling itself the Seven Priests of Melchizedek. Smart police work by the LAPD, said the paper, had broken up an illegal-alien smuggling ring involving the cult, three officials of a hod carriers' union, and four immigration agents, who had been suspended pending an internal investigation. Six mentions of policemen, one of the archdiocese, none of Dunc.

They read it lying side by side on their stomachs on a big gaudy towel at Malibu beach, Dunc in dark blue boxer-style swim trunks, Penny looking like a movie star in her dark glasses and a shiny light blue one-piece swimsuit.

"So it was the union men all the time," she said.

Dunc nodded. "They collected the first week's dues and the fifty-buck initiation fee from each batch of Mexicans Hector and Rephaim brought up across the border at a hundred bucks each. They were making a mint."

"I still don't think Rephaim was involved."

They rolled over onto their backs. "Okay, every two weeks *Hector* would deliver another crew. Immigration would show up every two weeks, steady as clockwork. They'd get a rake-off and great efficiency reports."

"What about Donovan?" she persisted. "Was he involved?"

"Maybe he knew in a general way, but I don't think so—he got too big a kick out of me hiding them away in the cornfield."

He wanted to spend every minute with Penny until she went back east, but she needed her temp job for next term's tuition. Dunc wanted to give her what he'd saved from his summer's labors, just to have the time with her, but she wouldn't take it.

After he picked her up from work, they'd go to a movie, or to eat dinner, or both; before he took her home they'd find a place to park and make love. No motels: Penny staying out all night would stretch her Aunt Goodie's romantic nature too far.

One night when Penny had to work late, Dunc went to the Purple Cockatoo. But Pepe's picture had been replaced by that of an impossibly blond woman calling herself Skylark Nightingale.

"When did Pepe leave?" Dunc asked the square-headed Germanic bartender. He had meaty hands and thick wrists but a surprisingly delicate touch mixing drinks.

The blue eyes looked blank. "Who?"

"Oh—uh . . . Pepper Paglia. The piano player."

"Never heard of him."

"He was playing here just last weekend," said Dunc, fuming.

"I was off." He turned away toward another customer.

Dunc nursed his beer. Would Pepe show up at the picnic on Monday? Or had he moved on again, abruptly, as he'd left Vegas? He always expressed himself better with music than with words; maybe he didn't want to talk about that bloody night. Trying to hold him was like trying to hold quicksilver in your hand.

They were standing with a score of others in a line stretched out across the field, a wall of people on either side. Dunc wore Frisko jeans and a sport shirt; Penny, shorts and a sleeveless blouse. She had her hair pulled back behind her ears.

"May the best man win," said Dunc with a manly grin.

Penny gave her marvelous laugh. "Or woman."

A whistle blew. They began hopping frantically down the field in their potato sacks. Dunc tripped over his own feet and sprawled in the dirt. Penny won. Goodie and Carl were with Dunc; Carl sadly laid a dollar on his wife's hot little hand, said to Dunc with a sneer, "Some great athlete!"

"I didn't play football in a potato sack."

Penny was aghast. "You bet against your own niece?"

A brass band was playing John Philip Sousa, the blare of horns carrying even over the cries and laughter of children. Cooking meat wafted its smell over from the picnic tables. At Griffith Park the great American Legion Labor Day picnic was in full swing. Pepe hadn't showed.

"The turkey shoot starts in a few minutes," said Carl. "I will single-handedly bring dignity back to the males."

"Every year he enters the turkey shoot, every year we have to buy our Thanksgiving turkey," Aunt Goodie said sadly. To Penny she added, "Let's go reserve a picnic table."

Penny said solemnly to Dunc, "Shoot one for the Gipper."

Not that it was a literal turkey shoot. The contestants shot at suits of playing cards printed on paper. The one who got the best poker hand with five shots won a frozen turkey.

A large red-faced man was telling a joke about a sailor up from San Diego to pick up girls in L.A. A bartender had told him to go way out Sepulveda, find a shopping center, and carry the groceries of a pretty woman wearing a wedding ring to her car.

" 'Married broads are horny, she'll take you home to bed.' "

" 'What if we're in bed and her husband comes home?' asks the sailor. The bartender says, 'You run into the shower, and she tells her husband you're her cousin in the navy up from San Diego. Then you get dressed and leave.' "

The big man was at least forty, at least an inch over six feet, with a round rubicund face and silvery receding hair swept straight back from his forehead. His nose was small, almost pug; his surface impression of beaming good nature was somewhat belied by small, quick blue eyes, watchful in repose.

"So they're going at it when the husband drives up. The sailor runs into the shower and the wife tells her husband her cousin is up from San Diego. The husband takes one look at him and says, 'You son of a bitch, I said *way* out Sepulveda!' "

They shot with .22 rifles with open sights; almost everyone was older than Dunc and nearly all of them had been in the service during the war. Uncle Carl was indeed a deplorable shot: only one of his five bullets even hit a card. The big jokester tried for a full house and got two pair, the best shooting yet.

"I can taste that bird now," he grinned.

Dunc tried for a full house, too, and got it. Aces over eights. The big man came over to congratulate him.

"The dead man's hand," he said. "That's fancy shooting."

"Thanks," said Dunc. Carl handed them both icy cold bottles of beer. The ladies appeared. Dunc said to Goodie, "You don't have to buy your Thanksgiving turkey, after all."

"How about a rematch?" The big guy was deceptively soft-looking; under his flowered sport shirt were thick arms and a wide chest.

"You're on!" exclaimed Dunc. Penny hadn't been there to see him win, but she was smiling confidently, serenely now. He really wanted to beat this guy in front of her.

His opponent tried for a full house again, this time got it. He turned to Dunc. "Beat that one, kid."

Dunc put four consecutive bullets into the ace card.

"And Christmas, too," he said to Goodie.

Penny hugged him, laughing in delight. "My hero."

The big man drew him aside, stuck out his hand. "Eddie Drinker Cope. Everybody calls me Drinker."

"Pierce Duncan. Everybody calls me Dunc."

"Where in hell'd you learn to shoot like that?"

"Going out plinking gophers and blackbirds with a .22 back in Minnesota. Bluejays, sparrows, squirrels, chipmunks, feral cats—just about anything that moved and wasn't a songbird."

"None of the above for me," said Drinker Cope. "I learned mine in the Marines." He paused, frowning. "Duncan. Pierce Duncan. Yeah!" He snapped his fingers. "The alien-smuggling case—goofy religious cult, hod carriers' union, some racketed-up immigration guys. You did some great detective work there."

"Are you a cop?" asked Dunc.

"Used to be. Believe me, you got the knack, you could develop into a top-notch investigator." He gave Dunc a card.

Edward Cope Investigations
Commercial and Domestic

1610 Bush Street
San Francisco 9, Calif.

Telephone ORdway 3-4831

"Ever up my way . . ." said Drinker Cope.

On Tuesday morning Dunc packed and carried everything out to the Grey Ghost. Uncle Ben shook his hand and Aunt Pearl cried again. Even Grandma Trabert gave him a careful hug.

"You have a good life, Dunc. I'll pray for you."

"I'll pray for you, too, Grandma."

Before he got in the car and drove off, he promised them that he'd keep in touch, knowing that he wouldn't. He was already starting to feel like a balloon slipping its tether.

At the nicest motel he could find close to Aunt Goodie's house he got a room, picked Penny up at seven and promised to have her home by midnight. Her train left at ten the next morning.

For the first hour they just lay in one another's arms and talked. Then Penny started sobbing quietly.

"Oh, Dunc, what are we going to do? I'll have to spend Christmas with my mom and my sister's family in Dubuque."

"I know." He was lying on his back with her head in the crook of his neck. "How about semester break? When is it?"

"End of February. But we only get a week."

"Use both weekends, you can stretch it to nine or ten days." He kissed the dimple at the side of her mouth. "Smile." He did it again, she giggled and dodged and caught him in a long kiss on the mouth that ended in frantic loving, then laughing, then Dunc holding her and stroking her head while she cried again.

Aunt Goodie and Uncle Carl, with their usual understanding, asked Dunc if he could drive Penny to Union Station. They clung to each other, hardly noticing the stucco-colored Art Deco station walls, not getting a chance to finish their coffee and tea and Danish before Penny's train was called.

"I feel like I'm in *Casablanca*," she said sadly.

Once inside, she opened her compartment window and leaned out. By stretching up, Dunc could just reach her hand.

"Write to me," she said.

She was crying again, but he couldn't hold her and stroke her head this time. Far down the track the conductor called *"Board!"* and the train gave a sudden lurch, was slowly moving.

"You too." He was walking along beside her, holding her hand. "You forgot to give me your sorority house number."

The train was moving faster. Dunc was now trotting to keep up, holding on to her fingers as long as he could.

She called despairingly, "Where can I mail it to you?"

Their hands parted. Almost running now, he was still falling behind. He yelled, "General Delivery, San Francisco!"

The train had rumbled away from him, its metal wheels going *ca-chunk ca-chunk* on the joins where two sections of rail came together. He stood, watching until it was out of sight; Penny's sweet small arm never stopped waving out of her window.

FIVE

South of Market

Chapter Twenty-seven

Dunc drove north on Highway 99. That way he had started through familiar territory, going across the San Fernando Valley past Eagle Rock, out past the mission and half-completed seminary buildings. Then up and over the San Gabriel Mountains on the Grapevine and down into California's great central valley. This was a three-hundred-mile oval bowl with the Sierra on one side, the Coastal Range on the other.

When he got to Chowchilla, the sun was near the tops of the Coast Range, silhouette after receding silhouette of hills the most intense purple he had ever seen. From here California 152 meandered west some one hundred miles to Highway 101, which would take him up through the Peninsula into San Francisco itself.

At Gilroy he turned north on 101. It was dark and he was tired and hungry, so he ate steak and eggs and cherry pie and drank three glasses of milk at the diner attached to the all-night station where he gassed up. He felt lonely and depressed; where was Penny right now?

The way north became endless: endless lights of oncoming cars, endless light-festooned trucks to pass when the opportunity offered, then, after San Jose, endless stoplights where important Peninsula arteries joined 101.

So he almost missed it: stopped by a red light for University Av-

enue, he was already moving before he saw a city limits sign: PALO
ALTO. Palo Alto, where Jack Falkoner lived, the man with his duffel
bag and precious notebooks in the boot of a little red MG.

He jerked the wheel over for a right turn, wandered around until
he found a narrow raised earthen road that went out across a vast mud
flat stretching too far for his high beams to reach. No houses, no traffic. Perfect place to find a wide place in the track and go to sleep.

At morning light he stretched, yawning, and stepped out to take a
whiz and look around. He was so startled that he yelled "Hey!" out
loud. He was surrounded by water a bare two feet below the road.
Last night it had been five mud feet below the track.

He started to laugh. He'd obviously parked on a tidal mud flat and
the tide had come in. What did a Minnesota kid know about tides?
Good thing nobody had seen his momentary panic. Something to
write Penny about. Penny . . .

Jack Falkoner was in the phone book. Dunc parked the Grey Ghost
in front of a brown-shingled bungalow on the corner of Melville and
Bryant off a wide through street called Middlefield Road. A sparkling
neighborhood with overarching trees.

A curving walk led up between two carefully trimmed pine trees to
the front door. The woman who answered the bell came to his shoulder, a vest-pocket Venus with an oval face and full sensuous lips. A
tight halter and skimpy shorts barely contained rounded breasts and
molded hips. She had it all: easy to imagine her handling a couple of
lovers and a husband besides.

Except she had a beauty of a shiner, the flesh almost purple around
her right eye. She must have reconsidered divorce.

Dunc managed to ask, "Mrs. Falkoner?" in a normal voice.

"Yes, I'm Ginny Falkoner."

"Does Jack, uh, still live here?"

"Of course he does, why . . ."

She had a quick, almost strident voice. Dunc explained who he was and why he was there.

"Oh, that guy. Well, Jack's at the gym, working out."

Floyd Page's Gym was over the Western Union office, with ceiling-to-waist windows overlooking High Street. Falkoner was the only person on the floor, doing seated dumbbell incline presses with one hundred pounds in each hand. Dunc waited until the set was finished, then spoke Falkoner's name.

Falkoner whirled to look at him, feral-fast, stared for a moment, then grinned. "What the fuck're you doing here?"

"My duffel bag," said Dunc.

He slammed himself in the head with the heel of his hand.

"Shit! In the boot of the MG! Shit! That night in El Paso, I sort of forgot all about your stuff. It's probably sprouting mushrooms by this time, the way that fucking car leaks. Gimme another half hour, forty-five minutes. Grab yourself a workout if you'd like. Floyd isn't here but he won't care."

Dunc had never seen a professional layout like this before. He got his workout stuff from the car, went through a full workout using maximum poundage for each exercise, three sets of ten each. He was pouring sweat when he finished. He'd waited three months for his duffel bag, Jack Falkoner could wait an extra thirty minutes for him.

When he came out of the shower, Falkoner had already brought the duffel bag up from his MG, had left it at the desk, and had departed. So much for Auld Lang Syne.

Dunc went off the Bayshore Highway, as 101 was called, on San Francisco's Third Street. It was a tough-looking industrial area, mostly colored, with Hunter's Point Naval Shipyard and government housing projects covering the low hills.

Downtown was totally confusing, bursting with life and traffic, trolleys running up and down Market Street. One-way streets, honking cars, gesturing cops. He finally found Bush, but it was one-way the wrong way. One block up, Pine was going the right way. At Powell he had to wait while a boxy little open-sided cable car passed, clanging its bell cheerfully.

It was after four o'clock when he finally parked in front of a Chinese grocery store to walk down the steeply slanting street to 1610 Bush, upstairs over a beauty salon on the corner of Franklin. On 1610's street door was:

EDWARD COPE—INVESTIGATIONS
Commercial and Domestic
Licensed and Bonded

The narrow interior stairway went straight up from the street. He climbed it to the tune of a rapid-fire typewriter. When his eyes were level with the floor, he glanced to his right and was staring at the high-heeled shoes and shapely calves of a woman behind a desk beside the stairs. Her thighs were hidden in the desk's cubbyhole.

The office was made into an L by a supply storeroom at the head of the stairs. Windows with venetian blinds ran the length of the long wall overlooking Franklin Street. More windows over Bush Street. There was a partitioned private office with windows on both streets and the door closed.

On the desk were two telephones, a typewriter, an intercom box, In and Out baskets stuffed with letters, papers, and file folders. The woman herself was in her mid-thirties, blond, tall and slender but well formed. Her shirt was white, man-tailored, with a gold stickpin holding it together at the throat. What he could see of her skirt was dark blue.

"You come to repossess the furniture?"

Dunc started. "I beg your pardon?"

Her narrow sharp-featured face had good cheekbones, a thin wide lipsticked mouth, and smart brown eyes under pale brows. "You were looking the place over pretty good. Or did you just come up to try and see my legs from the stairwell?" Dunc felt himself coloring up.

He had been, without realizing it. "Don't worry—better men than you have tried and failed."

Dunc cleared his throat. "I . . . I'd like to see Mr. Cope."

She pushed a button on a box on the top of her desk. There was no answer, but she seemed to expect none. Drinker Cope came out of the private office in his shirtsleeves. He looked solid and somehow very tough despite his benign pink features.

"My fucking sins catch up with me." He turned to the woman. "Sherry, this is the one I was telling you about."

"Your bastard son from Toledo," she said without levity.

Dunc felt like someone who'd come into the film at the start of the second reel. "I . . . Down in L.A. at the Labor Day picnic you said—"

"I was drunk at the Labor Day picnic."

"Your bastard son from Los Angeles?" asked Sherry.

"You said I'd make a good detective," Dunc blurted out.

"Oh Jesus Christ," said Sherry, and threw up her hands.

"I said you might develop into a good investigator. Might. With hard work and experience I ain't gonna pay you to get."

"You told me to look you up," said Dunc stubbornly.

"You've looked me up," said Drinker Cope. "G'bye."

"Try me out for a week. If you don't like my work, you don't owe me anything." Cope turned on his heel. Dunc said to his back, "And I can outshoot you any fucking day of the week."

Sherry laughed out loud. Cope's hard eyes were unreadable in that rubicund face. "One week, be here at eight tomorrow."

The blonde stuck out her hand. "Sherry Taft. Charmed."

"Pierce Duncan. Dunc."

"The sign says investigations, commercial and domestic. We take any case that walks in the door," said Drinker. "Good guy, bad guy, legal, borderline, we go all the way. That bother you?"

"No."

Sherry said, "Where are you staying?"

"Nowhere yet. But I—"

"Ma Booger's. We stash witnesses there sometimes." She was writing on her memo pad. "Mrs. Adelaide Boger. Three blocks down Franklin and a half-block to the left, 1117 Geary just up from Tommy's Joynt. Seven bucks a week." She handed him the memo slip. "Welcome aboard."

Chapter Twenty-eight

The room was big, with twelve-foot ceilings and two eight-foot windows with frayed lace curtains and pull-down shades. Two single beds, made up, and a small round table with a floor lamp and a sagging easy chair under the window. An open closet was in the left wall, half taken up by a narrow chest of drawers.

"It's got a nice little kitchen counter and its own sink and a two-burner gas hot plate," said Mrs. Adelaide Boger. "But I'll only charge you seven a week 'cause Sherry recommended you."

He didn't much care what the room looked like as long as it was clean. He wouldn't be spending a lot of time there.

"There's a shower and a bathroom at each end of the hall, very convenient."

The chest-high kitchen counter had two tall straight-back stools beside it. Inside the cubbyhole beyond were a sink and a counter with the gas hot plate beside it. Cabinets overhead.

"This is great," said Dunc, wreathing her face in smiles.

"You just stop by the office and sign the register when you're unpacked," she said.

He hung things in the closet, stuck his underwear and shirts in the chest of drawers, bounced on the bed a couple of times, put his notebooks on the round table, then went down to his landlady's office at the head of the street stairs.

Adelaide Boger was in her late sixties, a fleshy German lady with a kindly face and concerned eyes behind thick glasses; her big nose, red from allergies, made Ma Booger a natural.

Confident Cope would hire him, Dunc paid a month's rent up front. Ma Booger gave him a front door key and a room key on a ring with a tab that had 1117 Geary stamped into it. She also told him Tommy's Joynt on the corner was a San Francisco tradition.

It was jammed. Along the left wall was the bar with a hundred different kinds of beer. At a hot-food counter on the right wall under the Geary Street windows, beefy chefs with tall white hats and long carving knives cut sandwiches to order—"carved before your eyes!" A house special was buffalo stew. Dunc had to have that; it tasted pretty much like stringy beef.

He was up at six and beat another guy to the shower. Foster's all-night cafeteria, catty-corner across the Van Ness/Geary intersection from Tommy's Joynt, had something called toasted English muffins: an order was two of them, hot and crispy and drenched in butter. Wonderful!

He opened the agency street door at 7:45 to the rapid-fire staccato of Sherry's typewriter.

"You're early. I like that. Coffee?"

"No thanks. I . . . don't like it much."

Today she wore a navy-blue dress and white trim at throat and wrists. Her desk was covered with case folders—one opened—and a yellow legal pad with scrawled notes on it, some underlined, others with exclamation points beside them.

"Skip-tracing," she said. "When a subject—the person the case is about—takes off and doesn't want to be found, he's called a skip. He's skipped out. We try to track him down, trace him—skip-trace. You're a field agent. You talk to people, follow people, find people, window-peep, serve subpoenas, go undercover to stop employee theft, check government records—everything that can't be done by phone from the office."

"Okay. Sure."

"Only Drinker deals with the clients. The client doesn't want to hear that Drinker's working a slew of other cases at the same time, he doesn't want to hear that some field agent is working his case instead of Drinker. Got it?"

"Got it," said Dunc.

"Not yet, but you will, believe me. Drinker is going to assign you just one single case, because you're new to the game. But it's a tough nut we haven't been able to crack. Subject, Chauncey Jones, who was a municipal bus driver in Dayton, Ohio. Walked out on his wife and kids three years ago, left 'em without a bean. Nine months ago he came into a sizable inheritance."

She flipped open a case folder. Inside was a single printed form with scanty typed information on it.

"Only he doesn't know he's got an inheritance, and they can't collect without him. He was traced as far as San Francisco from their end. We found he was driving a bus again, and developed a residence address. He's gone from both places. Drinker expects written reports every seventy-two hours."

She handed him the case file, took him to a desk in the back of the office, near the mimeograph machine. There was a swivel chair, phone and phone book, letterhead and work sheets, multiple report forms, and a typewriter.

"Familiarize yourself with it, then go knock on doors."

The form had *in re* with the subject's name typed in, CHAUNCEY JONES. *Last known address:* 1144 Eddy St., Apt. 4. There were two further lines for *Previous addresses:* one had Toledo, Ohio, typed in, the other was blank.

Last known employment was Municipal Railroad, San Francisco. *Personal references* was blank. *Relatives* had only Mrs. Jones, Dayton, Ohio. No given name, no address. He guessed Drinker thought he didn't need to know them, at least not now.

Enough time in the office; he was dying to get out into the City. He headed for the door with his file, stopped at Sherry's desk. "What do I tell this guy when I find him?"

" 'When'? I like that. *When* you find him, say you're employed by an attorney in Dayton with an inheritance for him."

"Check." Dunc clattered down the stairs to the Grey Ghost.

*   *   *

Drinker Cope came out of the private office where he had been silently waiting and listening. He stopped at Sherry's desk, stood behind her massaging her neck with small delicate fingers. "So, what do you think?"

"I like him."

"That's the hell of it, so do I."

"What if he finds our Mr. Jones and talks with him?"

"That would put Sam Spade to shame. And in his own city, yet." Drinker gave a snort of laughter. He went back into his own office and this time left the door open.

Eddy was three streets below Geary, but 1144 was three blocks farther out than Dunc's 1117 Geary, between Octavia and Laguna, across the street from a small green city park called Jefferson Square. It was in a row of converted gingerbread Victorians, with no tenant's name in the slot for apartment 4. But when Dunc pushed the bell he was buzzed in.

A young Negro woman answered the door with cool eyes and a wary manner. Dunc asked for Chauncey Jones.

"Ain't no Chauncey around here, ain't been no Chauncey, ain't gonna be no Chauncey. We moved in three months ago."

Dunc thanked her, went back out into the sunshine and paused. Landlady. She might have a forwarding address. He rang the MGR bell. She was short and hunched, with streaky blond hair and nicotine-stained fingers and bags under her eyes.

"Son of a bitch moved out on me three months ago."

"Did he leave you any forwarding address?"

She glared at him. "Bastard left owing two months' rent, you think I got a forwarding? G'wan, get outta here!"

Gone three months. He sat in his car and watched kids playing in the park while he tried to figure out what to do next. The kids were mostly colored. Chauncey Jones was white. A mixed neighborhood. Okay, San Francisco Municipal Railroad. He should have looked up the address while he was still in the office—or brought the phone book with him.

The corner grocery store would have a phone book.

The Up To Date Market was narrow and cluttered and smelled of onions and garlic. A husky guy in a white apron was stocking the shelves down its single narrow aisle.

Dunc asked him, "You have a phone book I can use?" He did. Muni Railroad, 949 Presidio Avenue, phone FIllmore 6-5656. On an impulse he asked, "Do you know a man named Chauncey Jones? He lived up the block, drives a bus for the Municipal Railroad, maybe bought his groceries here?"

The clerk was frowning. He had a wide open Irish face, pale hair. Then he gave a chuckle.

"Yeah, Chauncey—the streetcar driver. More like he bought his booze here, not groceries. He drank, he didn't cook."

Dunc could get no leads to girlfriends or associates, so he thanked him and left. He had brought no notepad, either; he had to write down everything he had learned on the back of the case assignment sheet. He looked up Presidio Street on the map.

It intersected—indeed, dead-ended at—Geary Street.

The yard of the hulking brick Muni Railroad building was half filled with idle streetcars and buses. Inside the door marked OFFICE a hardbitten man in his fifties strolled up to the counter where Dunc waited. He had a gray cardigan sweater and steel-wool hair and a cigarette dangling from a corner of his mouth. He squinted at Dunc through the smoke.

"I'm trying to reach one of your drivers, Chauncey Jones."

"All employee records are private."

Dunc found himself back on the street. He wandered around the cavernous yard until he found a high window labeled DISPATCH OFFICE. A thickset balding dispatcher in a lumberjack shirt slid open the window to look down at Dunc in the yard below.

"I'm looking for one of your drivers—Chauncey Jones."

"Sec." His head disappeared for a moment. "Don't show him on the dispatch sheet. You sure he's working outta this barn?"

"All I had was Muni Railroad."

"They can tell you at the office."

"Guy in there told me to go to hell."

"That asshole," he muttered under his breath. "Sec." He left, came back. "The Potrero Barn out at 2500 Mariposa."

Mariposa ran west from the Bay to end at Harrison, but it didn't go all the way through. It took Dunc thirty minutes to find his way to the Muni's Potrero Barn off Hampshire. Jones had quit six months before. The dispatcher's records didn't show why.

The shift was changing, so Dunc talked to some of the off-duty drivers. A Negro with shifty eyes and nervous hands said he thought Jones had taken a job with Yellow Cab.

"Why leave a steady job like this for pushing a hack?"

He looked around unhappily. "Some guys come around . . ."

Dunc looked up Yellow Cab. His map said he could backtrack to Potrero, go to Division, which intersected Townsend, which . . .

The Yellow Cab dispatcher had a round face and Shirley Temple ringlets. She was smoking and drinking coffee and eating a doughnut and talking into her radio all at the same time.

"A woman in red'll be outside. She needs to get to the airport pronto." She released the transmit button, looked at Dunc. "Tell me something'll make me wet, cutie."

"One of your drivers? Chauncey Jones?"

"That don't make me wet." She snapped her fingers and held out a palm. "A buck." Dunc put a crumpled dollar bill on it. "A month back he got let go, as the feller says."

"Feller say why?"

She tipped back her head. "Glug, glug, glug."

"Know where he's living now?"

She flopped a ledger open on top of her other paperwork. "Yeah— 1563 Revere Avenue."

Chapter Twenty-nine

Revere intersected Third at Bayview, in that tough industrial area Dunc had driven through the day before. The door at 1563 had been split in half from top to bottom, then clumsily patched with a sheet of plywood. A woman opened the maimed door a crack.

"He just roomed here," she said in quick alarm. "Been gone two months, honest. He just went out one day, never came back." Memory emboldened her. "He still owes two weeks' rent . . ."

Dunc shook his head. She slammed the door in his face. He heard the dead bolt being shot home. The nearest liquor store was a narrow storefront on Bayview.

He asked the colored clerk bluntly, "Did Chauncey Jones get his booze here?"

"Who's askin'?"

"Mr. Green."

Dunc's dollar disappeared with dazzling speed.

"Jes 'fore he quit comin' in here, he bought him a jug of Wild Turkey. That stuff *costs*, man. Said the ponies was gonna make him well. Had him a lady ovah in the East Bay. Near to Golden Gate Fields." He squinted his eyes. "Amanda. Brought her in here once, she shook my hand."

"You don't remember her last name, do you?"

"No, I . . . Wait a sec! Amanda . . . Harris. That was it! Amanda Harris. I 'member 'cause I got me a Uncle Harris."

Dunc wasn't even sure what—or where—the East Bay was. He drove back to the office. Since it was his first day, he felt he ought to write a report. Sherry said, "Even your shoes sound tired. Did you hit the wall?"

"I've got a lead, I just don't know what to do with it."

Dunc told her about his day. She said, "Nice. Meaty. You go type your report, I'll see what I can do about Miss Harris."

The report forms were white, green, pink, and yellow snap-out sheets interlarded with thin carbons. White to the client, green into the file, yellow for memos to other field operatives or skip-tracers, pink to be stapled face-out to the back of the operative's assignment sheet.

Standing beside Sherry's desk, Drinker read the original of Dunc's report. He dropped it with a grunt, went into his office, and closed the door.

"Does that mean he likes it or he doesn't like it?"

"Drinker's grunts enlighten no man. Or woman." She handed him some scribbled notes. "Amanda Harris was a junior at UC-Berkeley, dropped out last year. She has—or had—an apartment in the Berkeley flats and works—or worked—as an admission ticket taker at Golden Gate Race Track in Richmond."

"How did you get all that?" demanded Dunc, amazed.

"Cross-directories, a few lies on the phone. Tomorrow cross the Bay on the Oakland car ferry. It's really fun."

At eight the next morning Dunc drove Grey Ghost into the wooden belly of the beast by the Ferry Building at the foot of Market. He could see Alcatraz and beyond it the green mound of Angel Island, nearer at hand wooded Yerba Buena and the flat man-made pancake of the navy's Treasure Island.

Bright sun, no fog, crisp air, the gulls whirling and crying as they looked for handouts behind the boat, occasionally dipping to grab something out of the white, churning wake. Passing under the Bay Bridge, he looked up, saw a passenger train on the lower deck going west toward the City. The noise of the bridge traffic was like muted thunder beyond the horizon.

When he figured out how to get to Berkeley from the Oakland Ferry Terminal, he sought out Amanda Harris's address on Prince Street off Shattuck. She was long gone—of course—but he knocked on the apartment door anyway, and a stocky, bright-eyed girl answered. She had been one of Amanda's roommates.

"She'd be graduating this year if she hadn't met *him*." She twirled a dark curl around a forefinger, twisted it. "He was . . . She just . . . fell for him. Like that. I couldn't stand him."

"She got the job at the racetrack after she met Jones?"

"Yes. He talked her into it."

She didn't know if Amanda was still working there. Dunc used his map, drove up the sweeping blacktop road to the parking lot behind the grandstands, tried to find someone who would tell him more than terminated "for cause." He was in luck; a former coworker was delighted to have lunch bought for her.

Amanda had been fired for dipping into the till, and soon after had moved down the Peninsula. Near Tanforan Race Track.

The last solid information he got on Jones himself was from an exercise boy—the boy was older than Dunc—walking a horse at Tanforan. Jones had been working for a horse owner named Al Eisner as a trainer, had been fired for an undisclosed cause.

"I think he was trying to dope one of the old man's horses. Mr. Eisner just gave him the boot. Myself, I'd of liked to of put the boot into the bastard's face."

Dunc abandoned Jones, for the rest of the week crisscrossed the City in his search for Amanda Harris. He learned how to set up a "swing" for the day's investigations in geographical sequence. From Sherry he learned how to work the phone for information, how to lie and dissimulate and make promises he couldn't keep. In those brief days he drove two thousand miles without ever leaving the Bay Area. He loved every minute of it.

On that Friday evening he knocked at the door of an apartment in a brown wood four-unit building on Worden, a half-block alley below Telegraph Hill. The fog was in, swathing the City in a clean wet gray blanket.

Amanda Harris was a slight brown-haired girl with the first genuinely green eyes he had ever seen. She still dressed like a college coed, sweater and plaid skirt and penny loafers, and was calm, sad, resigned to something Dunc had come to already suspect.

"He was no good, I knew that from the very start." She had served tea, their cups were cooling on the coffee table. "But somehow, whatever he asked me to do . . ."

He'd wanted her to steal from the admission office at Golden Gate Fields. She had. He'd wanted her to do the same thing at Tanforan. She had. She said he had been ruined by a big killing at the track he'd made while still a Muni driver.

"He became obsessed with it, and then he got in with some men who doped horses, and then he tried to steal from *them* . . ."

The next day, a Saturday, Dunc drove down to Colma to finally find Chauncey Jones. Even with Amanda's directions, it took him the better part of two hours.

On Monday morning he trotted up the steps to Drinker Cope's office with his bulging case file on Chauncey Jones. Sherry was at her desk, Drinker by the coffeemaker.

"So, Dunc, how goes the great Chauncey Jones trackdown?"

It had been ten days since Drinker had handed him the file. He had been to fifty-seven addresses, had talked with 122 people. He hadn't filed a report since the first one.

"Over the weekend I stood over his grave and told him what a rotten son of a bitch he was. The bastard's dead—as both of you very well knew when you sent me out after him."

Sherry sat up straight behind her desk. "You *what?*"

"I crossed your tracks a dozen times, Drinker. It was a hit-and-run, but the gamblers he crossed killed him. Tell me straight—is Amanda Harris in any danger?"

Drinker Cope was still for a moment, then shook his head.

"Was there ever a wife back in Dayton?"

"No. Different client, different assignment, but it seemed a nice file to dummy up for you to cut your teeth on."

"You know what pisses me off the most?" asked Dunc. "I never even saw the guy. It feels unfinished somehow."

"They often do," said Sherry.

Drinker straightened up, set down his coffee cup.

"Just ten fucking days," he said. "Okay, three hundred a month, retroactive to the day you started. You can charge your gas and oil at Emil's 76 station around the corner on Pine and Franklin. Keep receipts of your expenses. And kid, go out and get drunk tonight—you earned it. A hell of a job."

He picked up his coffee, retreated to his private office.

Sherry said, "Since you don't like coffee, Dunc, I bought a box of tea for you."

Penny met Gerald at the student union after her Monday afternoon class. He had been calling the sorority every few days since school had opened, asking her to meet him, and she'd been putting it off. Not that she was afraid of her own feelings. She knew her own feelings. But he had dominated her life for over a year, he might assume he still could . . .

He sat down at her table. "Hello, Penny."

She nodded coolly. "Gerald."

He looked the same as ever, a lean and hungry man with pale eyes—what had she ever seen in him? "I . . . Look, Penny, I . . . owe you a great apology for the way I acted that night . . ."

"You apologized the next day, Gerald. There's no need—"

"I . . . Nothing like that will ever happen again." He reached for her hand, took her unresponsive fingers in his own. "I want things to be the way they used to be. I *need*—"

"They never will be, Gerald. You have to know that."

"All right. Of course." His blue eyes were very earnest. "I know that. But I can make you happy, I . . ."

And his other hand came out of his pocket and he tried to slide a diamond engagement ring onto her finger. Penny jerked her hand back as if the tabletop were hot. She was glad he had done this. It made her remember, really remember, who he was.

"Gerald," she said low-voiced, intensely, "don't call me again. Don't write. Don't drop around." She was on her feet, looking down at him. "I don't want to see you again."

She walked away from the table. Gerald started to cry.

Chapter Thirty

Dunc let the Monday night crowds carry him down Market. Instead of getting drunk, he'd gone to the movies, a triple feature, any seat in the house thirty-five cents. One of them had been *The Asphalt Jungle*, Marilyn Monroe baby-faced and luscious, kissing suave corrupt Louis Calhern. There had been a drawing for a set of dishes, and a washed-out blonde with big knuckles and veiny hands had almost cried when Dunc's stub held the winning number. She *did* cry when he gave her the dishes.

The night was clear, without a hint of fog. This was *his* city. Already he loved it. On impulse he turned in at the Fog Horn, a dark narrow bar just off Seventh. It was a typical Market Street watering hole, full of sad men sucking on draft beers, their pockets full of nickels and their heads full of ghosts. The bartender swished a damp rag around in front of him.

"What'll it be?"

"Draft."

Behind the bar, painted on black velvet, was a huge mural of the San Francisco/Oakland car ferry passing under the silver Erector Set arch of the Bay Bridge, a bone of white water in its teeth. It made him nostalgic for this city he still barely knew. He and Grey Ghost had used that ferry during his dead-man hunt; soon it would be no more. The lower deck of the bridge would be converted from trains to autos, and the ferries would die.

He finished his beer, wandered down Market Street. There was always something astounding—and instructive—for a rookie private eye to see on the City's midnight streets.

At the foot of Powell, a man and woman stood arguing on the cable-car turnaround. He was young, blond, well dressed, she was blond, dark-eyed, good-looking. He was crying, tearing bills from his wallet and throwing them down on the gleaming rails.

"Go ahead, take it, take the money! That's all you're after, isn't it? Isn't it? That's all you're after!"

The girl didn't answer. She was on her hands and knees like a scrubwoman, scrabbling after the greenbacks.

When Dunc came out of a Third Street greasy spoon after a piece of tired cherry pie and a glass of milk, a gray-haired man wearing rumpled clothing and tired whiskey eyes was arguing with a short dapper Mexican. One of the Mexican's hands waved a nearly empty Tokay bottle while the other tried to fit his new white Stetson on the old bird's head. Thrust away, he spread his arms wide and ran into a parking meter. Then he grabbed the other man's arm and tried to drag him down Third Street.

"No! You already sank me in a sea of troubles down there."

The Mexican wandered off singing to himself. The gray-haired man said to Dunc with an almost sheepish grin, "I spent my last dollar on a good bottle of Tokay, and then I gave it to that Mexican. Then I found out he already had plenty of glue—folding glue. A fool and his money, et cetera." His faded blue eyes stared worriedly after the Mexican. "And down there where he's going he'll lose it all."

"Where's down there?" asked Dunc.

"South of Market. Like going north of the bridge on Clark Street in Chicago, or down Washington Ave to Second in Minneapolis. I've seen them all. Pawnshops outnumber everything but liquor stores and at night only the bars are bright. Cops work in pairs, winos like me sleep on street corners until the wagon takes them to the drunk tank at Kearny and Washington."

South of Market. Dunc had never heard the term before. He said to the gray-haired man, "You're very poetic."

"Cowper said that poetry is mere mechanic art. I used to teach it. Poetry."

"I used to be an English major." Dunc stuck two dollar bills in the jacket pocket. "For a new bottle of Tokay."

"A decent man." He chuckled. "I think I'll fool you. I think I'll get something to eat with this. I have a room at the Wessler Hotel, Third and Twenty-second. Ajax Kiely. If you ever find yourself way to hell out Third Street . . ."

Way out Sepulveda, thought Dunc. "Maybe I'll drop by."

He watched the old man slouch off. At first glance he had seemed just another grifter among the Third Street juiceheads and happy girls and silent drifting Negroes, but he reminded Dunc of Frank O'Malley, the fabled Notre Dame prof who was also a fabled martini drinker. Last St. Paddy's Day, O'Malley had held his Modern Catholic Authors class in the Oliver Hotel bar.

South of Market, Kiely had told Dunc. When you'd quit shaving every day and your hand shook reaching for that first quick one in the morning, you were said to have gone south of Market. As much a state of mind as a location. Dunc liked it.

In a dark deserted stretch of Folsom between puddles of street light, a lean black 1951 Lincoln slid to the curb, its exhaust murmuring *poh-poh-poh* in night air now turned cold. A heavy blue-chinned face with a cigar screwed in the middle of it was poked out of the open window.

"Hey, give ya a lift, boyfriend?"

Dunc kept walking. The car shot ahead, rocked to a stop as the short fat man who belonged to the cigar bounced out and gouged Dunc's belt-buckle with a switchblade knife. The blue chin joggled the spitty cigar up and down like a frayed brown finger waggling in his face.

"In, boyfriend."

Twist away from the knife, smash an elbow into that cigar—nonsense. Despite forty extra pounds of rich Italian cooking stuffed under his topcoat, the knife gave the fat man the edge.

His partner had the build of a fast light-heavy, wavy blond hair, and cold blue eyes that seemed to focus on something a foot behind Dunc's head. He took the Lincoln out Eighth with the lights to Bryant, then cut left toward the waterfront. The stubby Italian worked the car lighter.

"Call me Emmy," he suggested.

"Listen," said Dunc in a voice wobbling with earnestness, "you have the wrong guy. You made a mistake."

Emmy leaned forward to speak around him. "He says we make a mistake, Earl." He shook his head. "We ain't made any mistake. Right, Earl?"

Earl swung the Lincoln into the dead end on First Street across from the squat gray mass of the Seaman's Union, and parked facing out toward Harrison with dimmed lights.

He had a soft burring voice. "What's the handle, kid?"

Dunc, drenched with sweat, realized he was terrified.

"Pierce Duncan. Everybody calls me Dunc. But you got—"

"Make it easy on yourself, Dunc. Tell us about Kiely."

"I don't know anybody named Kiely."

On the corner was a dive with a red neon sign above the door. Two men came out, glanced incuriously at the Lincoln, and angled across Harrison. Yell for help? Try to shove Emmy out and dive out after him, run like hell? Emmy waggled the switchblade; light shimmered off the gleaming steel.

The dark figure came hurtling down at Dunc, led by gleaming steel. In her bedroom upstairs was Artis, dying.

"We tracked him here from L.A., so we knew he was in town," Earl said reasonably. "Tonight we spotted him talking with you outside that slophouse on Third—but there was a prowlie behind us, so we had to go around the block. When we got back, he was gone. You weren't. We followed you."

"That's the guy you're looking for? That old wino? Hell, he was just a juicehead, bummed me for a buck."

"Did he say where he lived?"

"No. Nothing. Not even thanks for the handout."

Earl was tapping his fingers on the steering wheel. He said abruptly, "Emmy, let him out."

"Hey, listen, Earl, how do we know—"

"Let him out."

Emmy clambered out and Dunc slid over. He felt he was visibly shaking, but knew it was internal. When he was standing beside the car, Emmy shoved a face wreathed with garlic fumes into his. "Go down Harrison without trying to look-see the license plates, boyfriend."

"Can the musical comedy act and get in here," snapped Earl.

After walking a block on Harrison without looking back, Dunc leaned against a wall and held out his hand. It was steady. He was glad. It seemed important that the hand be steady.

What did he do now? Call the cops? Forget the whole thing and start the long trudge back to Ma Booger's?

A hot Las Vegas wind seemed to blow through him, raising sweat in the cold San Francisco night. It left him no choice.

Chapter Thirty-one

The bus dropped Dunc in front of the Third Street precinct house, and he walked two and a half blocks to the Wessler. It was a flophouse over a saloon. Apart from a car sliding into a parking place in the next block, he had the street to himself. He could see his breath.

Twenty minutes before the 2:00 A.M. bar-close. The downstairs saloon was an old-fashioned place with high ceilings; plain heavy glass bowls filled with hard-boiled eggs were set out on the bar. Two Italian laborers were drinking draft beer, one shaking salt into his glass to raise the head.

A balding heavyset barkeep who probably had a blackjack on his hip and a .38 under the bar said, "What's yours, Jack?"

"I need to talk with a guy named Ajax Kiely." He pointed at the ceiling. "He lives upstairs. He wants to see me."

The barkeep's wet dirty towel moved around on the top of mahogany as if by its own volition. "Go ask at the kitchen."

Dingy yellow light shone from the connecting doorway. Dunc could smell garlic and frying steak. The kitchen barely held a fat black iron stove and a fat red-faced Italian lady with a fine assortment of chins and her hair pulled back in a wispy bun.

"I ain't doing anything but steak sandwiches tonight."

"Ajax Kiely told me to meet him here."

She flipped over the sizzling steak, cut it enough to peek in, took down a heavy platter, and reached for a loaf of French bread as she made up her mind about him. She cut the bread with a broad serrated knife, added the steak, shoved silverware and the platter with the sandwich on it into Dunc's hands.

"He's out back. Tell him he owes me a buck."

Beyond a washed-out green curtain was a big barren room with long tables pushed back against the walls to open the hardwood floor for Saturday night dancing. Kiely was in the second of the dark-wood booths along the left wall, staring into a glass of dark amber liquid he held in both hands like a chalice. He looked up, startled, when Dunc slid the platter across the table and himself into the other side of the booth.

"The lady in the kitchen says you owe her a buck."

Kiely grinned. "Hey, sport! I bet you're here to ask me about the New Criticism." Dunc shook his head. "Then 'why meet we on the bridge of Time, to 'change one greeting and to part?' "

"Who said—" He stopped. "Yeah, I know, you said it."

"No, Sir Richard Burton said it. Guy who translated *The Arabian Nights.*"

"Listen, there's really something I have to tell you—"

But Kiely kept talking as he chewed and hot beef juice ran down over his fingers, his drink temporarily abandoned.

"It was in the service during the war that I developed my fondness for strong drink. I'd enlisted in the air force and captained a flying squad in Australia, never've liked a limey since. One of 'em sold me a jug of juice for ten bucks American, when I opened it, I found out it was tea."

"Maybe he was trying to save your life," said Dunc.

Kiely laughed, picked up his glass. " 'I wonder often what the Vintners buy one-half so precious as the stuff they sell.' "

That one Dunc knew. *The Rubaiyat.* "Two guys," he said. "They're looking for you."

The change was remarkable. Kiely's fork hit the plate and spanged off onto the floor. In the bar the jukebox was blaring "Goodnight, Irene" as a reminder to all that it was closing time.

"Earl and Emmy, is it? 'Machinations, treachery, and all ruinous disorders.' How'd they slice it for you, sport?"

Dunc was on his feet. "To hell with you, Mr. Kiely."

Kiely pointed at a scratch on Dunc's silver belt buckle. "From Emmy's knife, ain't it? Oh, I know those guys! Spend three years on the lam from Philly to New York and Chicago and Kansas City and L.A., with amiable lovely death looking over your shoulder, and your nerves get galvanized like a frog's. How d'you think they knew I was here?"

"Probably an L.A. skip-tracer. Why are they after you?"

"Teaching seemed tame after the war and besides alcohol I'd become addicted to high-stakes poker. Three years ago I got in very deep to very bad people, there was a heavy-money game . . ."

"You knocked it over."

"Helped to. I was inside man, Earl and Emmy pulled the actual robbery. It went swell—except Earl shot the dealer dead, tried to kill me, too. I ran—with all the money."

He clawed open the top buttons of his shirt. A small leather pouch was slung around his neck on a leather cord. From it he took a flat metal toothed key with "181" stamped on it. He laid it reverently on the table between them.

"There it is, sport, wealth arithmetic cannot number. Eighty grand. Safe-deposit box, but only Kiely knows the bank and the city and the name it's under. Fact is, I'd give it all to Earl, but he'd just kill me anyway."

Dunc said, "Pickwick Stage Depot at Fifth and Mission—I'll front you a Trailways ticket out of here, right now."

A forefinger pushed the key across the table. "Hold this for me, will you, kid? I just got a feeling. Give it back when I get on the bus, and we'll laugh about it. Okay?"

Dunc said, "Okay," and stuck the key down inside one sock.

They went in the adjacent door with a single light over it and up a flight of creaky stairs. The small, stuffy office at the top was empty. A strip of faded maroon carpet led them down a narrow hall and around two right angles to Kiely's door. It was narrow as a pauper's grave, sour with recent cigar smoke.

Kiely chuckled as he switched on the light. "They'd give a lot to know what they want is right here." Dunc turned back to set the night chain when Kiely used a sudden breathless voice.

"I was playing poker with a fellow in K.C. named Moran—"

He drew in a sharp breath. Dunc tried to turn. Was gone.

Obscenely gay flowers were painted around the cheap tin waste-basket, and the brown carpet tickled Dunc's nose. A middle-aged man regarded him thoughtfully from a broken-down easy chair across the narrow room. He looked slightly familiar.

"What the hell?" said Dunc.

Kiely? Yeah. Ajax Kiely. Memory trickled back. Former poetry teacher, high-stakes poker player. Always quoting.

"What the hell?" Dunc asked him again, thickly.

He got to his hands and knees, got himself erect. His pockets had been turned out. He bent to gather up his money and wallet, straightened quickly. Jesus! Pain had shot through his head. Bent again with exaggerated care for his belongings. His keys were gone. His shoe skittered something metallic across the rug to rattle against the base-board. A knife. He picked it up to peer at it as if he needed reading glasses.

Switchblade. Smell of cigar smoke in the room. Emmy. Kiely's shirt wore a new red necktie. The end of it lengthened to drip twice in his lap. In Dunc's memory a car slid to the curb in the next block. Christ! He'd fingered Kiely, after all. And Kiely'd been halfway afraid of it.

The room had been torn apart, Kiely's meager belongings scattered about, his pockets turned out as Dunc's had been.

Outside, a lightly touched siren growled. Precinct station a couple of blocks away. Anonymous phone call . . .

Hide the knife. Blood on it. Blood on his jacket, smeared on. His head throbbed, he was still woozy. He closed the knife, dropped it into his jacket pocket, thought, I can't hide Kiely.

Heavy shoes were pounding up the stairs. He wrapped his jacket around his arm, slammed it against the window. The glass burst outward, taking the shade with it. Fresh air stung his sluggish brain awake. An equally heavy fist made the door quake.

"Police! Open up in there!"

Dunc cannonballed into darkness. His heels crunched a pail and flipped it over, landing him in a shower of garbage. He dodged through a junk-littered yard to the back fence, made the top on first try. A flashlight beam probed the yard and voices shouted from Kiely's window. Dunc went over without pause.

At the foot of a shallow muddy embankment he trotted along railroad tracks to Twenty-fifth Street, turned uphill, away from Third, climbing toward the Potrero Terrace housing projects where he had interviewed a witness just last week.

Closed-up little grocery store. Pay phone. He leaned against the side of the booth with his eyes shut, ringing Drinker Cope's home phone, belatedly standing on one foot to check on the safe-deposit box key. Yes. Still in his shoe. Drinker answered on the third ring, voice thick with sleep.

"It's Dunc. I'm in real trouble."

Voice bright and clear now. "Tell me what I need to know."

"Two guys killed a third guy tonight in a Third Street flop. I was there. The law is looking, but not for me specifically."

"The bad guys looking for you?"

"They got my keys, so they'll know where I'm staying."

"Where are you now?"

"Potrero Terrace."

"Walk down to the foot of Connecticut, have a Yellow pick you up by that big green warehouse on the southeast corner . . ."

*   *   *

Dunc's shoes echoed hollowly on the concrete ramp down to the all-night auto park in the basement of the Bellingham Hotel on Sixth and Mission. A husky Negro about his own age was dozing on a cot in the bright cramped office. The name of the garage was stitched in neat red script across his blue coveralls.

Dunc said, "Nat?"

The Negro's brown eyes opened, focused, sharpened.

"You're Dunc? Little cool to be running around outside without a jacket." He jerked open a desk drawer, took out a bottle. Dunc shook his head, instantly regretted it.

"Wow! You got any aspirin?"

He washed four of them down with a paper cup of water. Nat dropped a key onto Dunc's open palm.

"Geary and Octavia, third house from the corner, yellow with lots of gingerbread. Front room on the first floor. Ground floor's the garage. I got a shackrat'll put me up for a couple days. Don't let the landlady see you—she's death on whites bein' in her house." He reached an army field jacket down off a hook in the wall. "Be sunup when I leave, I won't need this."

Dunc laid his rolled-up jacket down on the desk to shrug into the field jacket. When the warmth it fostered hit him, he shivered. Nat had picked up the jacket.

"You look all used up, man. I'll get rid of this for you after I call a cab."

Chapter Thirty-two

At noon Dunc sat on the edge of the bed looking out between lace curtains at a slanting street drenched in golden light. No town was lovelier than San Francisco when the sun was shining. A little colored girl was skipping down the sidewalk in a bright red cloth coat, her hair sticking straight out from the sides of her head in two tight black braids. Behind her came three Negro boys and one Chinese boy, all dressed in gaudy windbreakers and brown corduroy trousers. Two of them carried schoolbooks.

Down at the corner by the bus stop, Drinker Cope was just getting out of his powder-blue '51 Plymouth. Five minutes later he was sitting in Nat's easy chair gulping black, steaming coffee fresh from the hot plate. Dunc told Drinker everything, starting with the movies and ending with Kiely's key in his hand.

"You're good at finding trouble, ain't you, kid? Gimme." Dunc tossed him the key, he stuck it in his watch pocket. He chuckled. "But you're lucky at winning things, too, ain't you?"

"You call a dead man in my lap lucky?"

"I call a key to eighty grand in your hand lucky."

He started to prowl the room, deceptively soft-seeming but moving like a much smaller, quicker man. He dropped back into the easy chair, shook his head, gave an exasperated chuckle.

"Jesus, you're green, kid. Any way I look at it, I gotta think you're trouble. You get mixed up with a guy gets dead, then you give your jacket with the blood on the sleeve and the murder weapon in the pocket to Nat because he says he'll get rid of it."

"I figured he was one of your field agents. What was wrong with that?"

"It was the fucking *murder weapon,* for God's sake. With your fingerprints in the victim's blood all over it."

"Nat said he'd—"

"*Fuck* what Nat said. *Never* put yourself in another man's hands that way. You can trust Nat, don't get me wrong, he gave them to me and *I* got rid of 'em for you. But if you're gonna work for me, you can't be stupid."

"I'm sorry," said Dunc.

"Don't be sorry. Be smart. What was this Kiely to you, you go warn him? You didn't know about the eighty grand yet."

Emmy with his gleaming knife evoking Raffetto, coming at him after murdering Artis, that's why he'd done it. But he hadn't told Drinker anything about Las Vegas, wasn't about to.

"It seemed like the right thing to do."

"The right thing to do." Drinker shook his head again in disbelief. "I assume they followed you to Kiely's place."

"Yeah," said Dunc bitterly. "It was their Lincoln I noticed pulling in down the street just after I got there."

Instead of the justifiable scorn he expected, he saw interest light up Drinker's round red face. "And then?"

"They see me go into the bar downstairs, one of 'em stays outside—" God, how could he have been so stupid? "and the other goes upstairs and checks the hotel register, jimmies Kiely's lock, when we come in he takes out Kiely and saps me down and it's all over."

"Why d'ya think one downstairs and one upstairs? Why didn't they make sure of the money before they killed their man?"

Dunc thought about it, finally sighed. "Because Kiely went in saying what they wanted was right there in the room. He was stabbed, Emmy likes the knife." He caught Drinker's glance at his gouged belt buckle. Guy didn't miss a trick. "Earl would have made sure of the money before he killed Kiely. Emmy, no."

"Why didn't this Emmy character do you, too?"

"Wanted a fall guy?" He made it a question.

"He smart enough for that? If he was too dumb to—"

"The fall guy would have been Earl's idea."

Cope chuckled. "Maybe so, kid, but I doubt it. He'd wanta turn you upside down and shake you for what'd fall out—only now he's gonna have to turn *me* upside down and shake me instead." He opened his briefcase, tossed the morning *Chronicle* on the bed. "Educate yourself. You can go out to eat, they won't be looking for you here in boogietown, but stay close."

"Don't you want me to go out and try to track 'em down?"

Drinker looked at him like he was nuts. "I don't keep heroes on my payroll. I'll put people on the street and get word to you when I want you to move."

"What are you going to do with the key?"

"I'll talk to the chief of detectives in the Kansas City P.D. We've tipped a jar or two together. He'll check for a bank box under the name of Moran. If there is one, he gets a court order, if the money's there, we all split the reward."

Dunc merely nodded. He doubted the box would be found.

After dark, he walked four blocks out Geary to Fillmore and ate at the counter of a rib joint, the only white face to be seen. Back at Nat's place, a teenager was pleading outside an open hallway door with a woman in her thirties. She smelled of strange sins. They stopped talking as Dunc passed, staring at him across the racial gulf.

A little before ten, there was a light tapping on the door. Dunc crossed the room on silent stocking feet, stood by the closed door, sweat sheening his forehead. "Y-yeah?"

"Got a message fo' you."

It was the woman of the exotic perfume. She had clear brown eyes slightly slanted, a beautiful brown oval face, black hair lustrous and coiling. Her house robe showed enough cleavage to cause a stirring in Dunc's groin.

"Yes, ma'am?"

" 'Ma'am'?" She gave a throaty chuckle. "Drinker say, jes parade 'round Market Street where you was last night, you be met."

Dunc thanked her and started to shut the door, but she put out a detaining brown hand. "Scared, ain't you, white boy?"

"No, I'm just . . . Yeah."

"Don't gotta be 'shamed 'bout bein' scared. You got the time, honey, *I* got the time, too. Don't cost you nothin'. But you ain't got the time, has you?" Again, the big belly-shaking laugh. "Too bad, shugah. I's the bes' you'll nevah have."

"Hey, buddy, got a light?"

Dunc stooped to light a cigarette for the legless man who peddled pencils on Market Street. The man rested on his square castored board, cataloging every person who passed without even turning his heavy handsome head. He spoke around his cigarette.

"The fat one's been using Yellow Cab 238."

"Thanks," said Dunc, "can I—"

"No. The Drinker asked me to keep an eye out."

Half an hour later Yellow 238 drove up to the cabstand by the Greyhound Depot on Seventh Street. The driver was a tall stooped number with brown hair and brown teeth.

"Fat guy I picked up? Sure, if . . ." He rubbed thumb and forefinger together. Dunc dealt him an ace. "He barhopped down around Third and Folsom for an hour, kept me on the meter. Then to Jones and Eddy. Cheap bastard. No tip."

The driver buried his nose in a movie magazine as if it were a schooner of beer. Dunc started away. The fat man running the nearby newspaper stand called out to him.

"Stan, newsstand on Market and Kearny, he's got something to tell you, said it was important."

"Hey, thanks."

"Thank the Drinker."

The downtown streetcar passed Powell, Dunc remembered the young guy throwing money in the street. Just twenty-four hours ago!

Stan was huddled up in the corner of his square green booth wrapped in a bulky blue sweater against the cold. He came up to the counter when Dunc showed. "You'll be Dunc." His heavy bohunk accent was that of the line workers at Studebaker's South Bend plant. He had a square, honest face. "Tall one, hard eyes, he go down Third Street maybe two hours ago. Looking."

"For me," said Dunc.

"Other one, fat one . . ." He blew out his cheeks like a squirrel's and patted his belly above his gold watch chain. "Barbary Coast Hotel bar. Eddy between Leavenworth and Jones."

"Many thanks, Stan." Dunc offered to shake hands. Stan shook. Dunc offered him money. Stan shook his head.

"On the Drinker. Listen, they got a big Lincoln in the lot on Eddy between Larkin and Leavenworth. They the bad guys?"

"They're the bad guys."

"Then you and Drinker, you get 'em, hokay?"

"Hokay," said Dunc, with a certainty he didn't feel.

Chapter Thirty-three

Fog-shrouded midnight streets threw his footsteps back at him. The Golden Gate Bridge's foghorn bellowed desolately about being out in the Bay on such a night, the Alcatraz foghorn agreed. He thought fleetingly of lifers tossing on iron cots, insomniac in dank cells, then of Kiely, permanently somniac.

Swirled pearl hazed the streetlights. Passing cars were muted moving shadows, were gone. Men of chilled smoke hurried by in search of warm rooms and good drinks and maybe soft women to make them human again.

And somewhere in the muck was Earl, moving as a hungry tiger moves, his fist full of bills to buy Dunc's whereabouts. What was Dunc searching for? The answer to a question posed in Las Vegas, with only a shadow to go on?

He shivered in Nat's army jacket and wished for a topcoat. He'd check out the Lincoln, then at least confirm that Emmy was drinking at the Barbary Coast Hotel. That would suggest they were staying there and Emmy was waiting for Earl to return.

The Lincoln was parked nose-out amid a dozen other cars in a narrow unlighted gravel lot sandwiched between two red brick office buildings put up just after the '06 quake. No attendant, maybe he could even the odds before he called for help.

No doorman at the Barbary Coast Hotel, either. He went in—

gingerly. Dim lighting, stuffed chairs with nobody in them, dusty potted palms, a desk with a half-dozing clerk. In one sidewall unlit red neon, *Coffee Shop*, in the other a doorway screened by a beaded curtain with *Shanghai Lil's* in red neon above it.

Dunc stuck a quick head through the curtain, withdrew instantly. The beads made a muted tinking sound. It was a dim place with indirect lighting and a nautical motif, fishnets draped from the ceiling, potted palms to suggest the tropics, big glass floats a foot in diameter from the nets of the Japanese fishing fleet. Chinese fans above the bar, atmospheric oriental screens to give privacy to the couples at the tables. Half a dozen drinkers studding the stick, Emmy among them.

At a phone booth by the parking lot, Dunc used street light to look up Shanghai Lil's in the directory, dropped his dime, gave the heavy-voiced bartender a nasal, whiny voice borrowed from a pecker-wood chain-gang guard in Georgia.

"Fat guy at the bar. Name of Emmy. I wanna talk to him."

Emmy couldn't refuse a call. He didn't. "Yeah?"

"You lookin' for a joker name of Dunc?"

"As a matter of fact, yeah, I, uh . . . wanna talk to him."

"Talk! You think I'm crazy, boy? Talk's fer Church. Meet me at the 76 station on Franklin and Pine in ten minutes. Bring plenny green an' be ready to travel. He's got his mitts on heavy money, he's checkin' out tonight. Ten minutes, dickhead."

Emmy waddled up to the Lincoln panting, sweat gleaming on his forehead. Dunc, remembering the labor union goon in L.A., hit him in the kidney with the hardest right hook he'd ever thrown. Emmy shrieked and hurled himself backward against the Olds next to his car, his back arched like a bow.

But when Dunc went in swinging to finish him off, a fat hand flicked a deadly steel finger at him. Dunc's left hand locked around Emmy's wrist, his right hand broke Emmy's left thumb as it tried to gouge his eye. Emmy yelled again, but for thirty seconds they hung there between the two cars, veins cording their necks and sweat burning their eyes. Holding that right wrist was like trying to hold the greased pig at the fair.

His right hand covered Emmy's face, slammed the back of the head against the car window. It starred. Again. Shattered glass spattered them. Dunc snarled through his teeth.

He used a knee between Emmy's fat thighs. Emmy's foot growled on the gravel, he tried to fold down on himself. Dunc slammed the head against the door of the Olds. Emmy's head left dark vertical smears on the metal. He was making wheezing noises.

The switchblade hit the gravel, Emmy sat down suddenly, like a fat man at a picnic, fell over sideways and stayed there. From the entrance of the lot came a whiskey-burred male voice.

"Yeah, this is the one."

Dunc groped for the switchblade, found it. He felt sick.

"This goddamn fog!" exclaimed a woman's loose voice. "Which goddamn car is it?"

"Down at the end. By the Lincoln."

He made himself grope in Emmy's pockets, find a tabbed hotel key with a room number stamped into it. He found his own keys, too. As long shadows came jerkily up the gravel, he edged around the back of the Lincoln away from the Oldsmobile.

Sloppy kissing noises. The woman's drunken giggle. They would find Emmy, call for help . . . A sudden scream.

"What the hell's the matter with . . ." The male voice trailed off. "Jesus Christ! Let's get to hell outta here!"

Doors slammed, a motor grumbled to life, wipers snicked at the haze, tires scrunched gravel as they backed out. Dunc was already three cars away, his adrenaline rush gone, throwing up against the side of someone's new Ford.

He felt groggy, punch-drunk; he'd come this far, he'd do it alone. No Drinker Cope. No ambulance call, either. If Earl learned his partner was down and out, he'd be wary, on guard. Dunc wanted to be waiting, lamp in hand like in his dream, when Earl entered their hotel room, all unsuspecting.

He did his quick check through Shanghai Lil's beaded curtain. No Earl. Used the men's room to wash out his mouth, splash his face, then used the house phone to dial their room. No answer. He rode the elevator up to seven, went down the fire stairs to six, found the room, knocked on the door.

"Room service."

Nothing. He eased the key into the lock, palmed the knob, drifted the door open. Ambient city light through lace curtains showed him an empty bathroom, empty closet alcove except for a suitcase on the floor, dimly seen, a spare suit on a hanger.

The brass lamp on the dresser would make a passable club. The adrenaline was pumping again, his throat was almost closed off as he waited against the wall beside the door, holding the lamp at his side. Where was Earl now? Did he know about Emmy?

Clang of elevator doors, muffled chirrup of operator.

"Good night, sir."

He could smell his own fear. Would Earl? He could taste it, too, as if he held a brass cartridge case between his teeth.

A key in the lock. Then nothing. A minute, nothing.

The room was flooded with light. Dunc whirled. Earl stood just inside the open connecting door to the next room, grinning, a Colt .22 Woodsman target pistol dangling from his right hand.

Stick the key in the lock to keep Dunc focused on the door, slip around to his adjoining room. This had been Emmy's room—a single suitcase in the closet. Stupid, stupid, stupid!

Earl waggled the automatic. "Drop the lamp." Dunc dropped it. "I always figured Kiely stashed my money in a safe-deposit box, gave you the key to hold last night. I checked your room—no key. So, turn around—hands on the wall."

Dunc didn't move.

"I catch a prowler in my room, I shoot him dead. Turn around so I can search you."

"And then shoot me in the back."

Earl stared at him for a long moment, then gave a slight shrug. "You want it in the face or the back of the head?"

Dunc threw himself bodily at him, as if tackling a fullback coming through the line. A gun roared, Earl leaped to meet him, they fell to the rug in a bloody tangle.

"The back of the head," said Drinker Cope conversationally.

He stood inside the door Earl had used, in his right fist a huge old Army Colt .45 faintly wisping black-powder smoke.

Dunc rolled free. The blood was Earl's, most of his face was gone. Little chips of skull bone stuck to Dunc's face. He would have vomited again except he had nothing left to throw up.

"When did you . . . how did you . . ."

"I've been behind you all night. You okay?" Dunc reached for the cloth doily off the dressertop to wipe his face. Drinker said, "Don't touch that. You're gonna be gone before the cops get here, you weren't here tonight. Just me and . . ." He gestured with his gun barrel. "The boyfriend here."

"But why . . ." Dunc began, then broke off. "Emmy! He's —"

"—dead in the parking lot. Somebody ran over his head. G'wan, get to hell out of here, quick."

"But why are you—"

"It's simpler this way. I was tailing Kiely for the agency, these two killed him, wanted to kill me, too."

"For the agency? But we don't have a client to—"

"Sure we do. The chief of detectives in Kansas City asked me to look for Kiely. Hell, I used to be a cop in this burg, the police and the hotel'll want this buried on the obituary page."

Dunc said belatedly, still dazed, "You saved my life."

Drinker straightened from leaning over the corpse. He gave an ironic snort.

"The safety was on. He wouldn't have shot you before he got that safe-deposit key. He wanted that fucking eighty grand just too much.

I got your marker on this one, kid. Now get to hell outta here before the cops arrive."

Dunc was going down the fire stairs as the police were going up in the elevator. He sloshed water on his face in the men's room off the lobby, asked the deskman what had happened upstairs, got a non-committal grunt, and walked free and clear out into the San Francisco fog.

<u>SIX</u>

A Death Before Dying

Chapter Thirty-four

Pinned to the large woman's robe was a carnation set in a spray of greenery. She beamed with warm crinkly eyes but a rather dreadful smile on the two people standing in front of her.

"By the authority vested in me by the State of California, I now pronounce you man and wife. You may kiss the bride."

The groom did, voraciously, as if devouring raw oysters.

Standing back against the rear wall of the San Mateo County office used for civil ceremonies, Dunc thought he wouldn't mind kissing the bride himself. She was a pretty woman in her mid-twenties with brown hair and a cute little rabbit nose. He hated to do it to her new husband at their wedding, but Sherry had said this was the first time the guy had surfaced in six months.

He plucked a single yellow rose from one of the vases of flowers banking the corner of the room behind the justice of the peace, bowed slightly, and handed it to the new Mrs. McGowan.

"For the happy bride." She beamed. To her husband, he handed a three-folded Summons and Complaint backed with heavy blue paper. "For the happy groom. Alex McGowan, you have now been legally served in the matter of *Rossiter versus McGowan*. Congratulations on your marriage."

"You son of a bitch!" the groom yelled at him.

His beloved spat in Dunc's face and screamed, "I hope your wife dies of syphilis."

As Dunc walked out wiping the spittle from his nose with one of the spare handkerchiefs he had learned to carry for such occasions, he decided the new bride wasn't so pretty after all.

He couldn't see Penny until February, but the Kiely case had disappeared just as Drinker had predicted, and he was learning the detective trade. Even process-serving had its funny moments. At a birthday party for the live-in girlfriend of a San Francisco shipping tycoon, Dunc had shown up in a clown suit. Instead of a singing telegram, the girlfriend had gotten alienation of affection papers from the tycoon's estranged wife.

They worked any kind of case for any kind of client. Dunc quickly learned to have no emotional investment in these cases, but to act as though he did. One week might be background checks on an insurance company's clients; the next, collecting facts for someone suing that same insurance company.

Sherry was teaching him how to skip-trace as Drinker gradually introduced him to a vast army of informants: waiters, bartenders, newsies, hotel clerks, bike messengers, car parkers, even cops picking up a few off-duty bucks. He was learning fast, loving the City at night.

It was a week before Christmas, and Dunc had just come in off a two-night stakeout in the Sunset District. An address on a postcard to her sister had convinced a Dallas, Texas, husband his missing wife was shacking up with a lover in San Francisco.

Sherry asked, "So, is the wandering wife there?"

"Not unless she's got a goatee and is going bald."

"Give me the report when you finish. Meanwhile . . ." She tossed a case file on his desk, stood up to brush invisible lint from her skirt. "Wellman Industrial Design in Burlingame. See Drinker. The client wants action on it."

Drinker was tipped back in his swivel chair with his feet crossed on the corner of his desk. An empty glass and a half-empty bottle of bourbon were resting on his desk blotter. Dunc sat in the client chair across the desk from him.

"What kind of a camera is worth ten thousand bucks?"

"An industrial layout design camera." Drinker poured himself another modest shot. "A father-in-law slash son-in-law beef. The old man sets the kid up in some kind of design business that depends on this camera, the marriage goes sour, now the daughter wants hubby's nuts in a paper bag."

"Short of that, what do we do?"

"Without the camera the kid's out of business. Daddy's got the sales slip on it, Daddy wants us to steal it."

"We're working for the wrong guy," said Dunc.

"What else is new? A technical expert from the camera's manufacturing company is coming in on the one A.M. flight from Chicago. You and Nat pick him up at the airport—it's such a delicate piece of equipment it's gotta get dismantled just so."

"We'll need a truck," said Dunc.

"Nat's getting one. Haul it up to the client's warehouse here in the City." He slid an envelope across his desk. "Two keys. Alarm system, warehouse."

"Where's the Wellman Industrial Design key?"

"That's why Nat's the one I called to go with you. He's handy with a set of lockpicks."

Nat's chocolate face wore a wide grin as Dunc climbed into the truck. "Hey, Dunc, remember Delia, working girl in my rooming house, wears perfume'd make a monk hike up his habit? Well, she's been asking after you, lady thinks you're cute."

"Lady has impeccable taste."

Gregory Stout didn't live up to his name. He was a Jack Sprat kind of guy with horn-rims and quick, nervous movements and a mop of gleaming black hair he had to continually brush back. As they walked three abreast through SFO's echoing, almost empty terminal, Dunc asked, "You need tools or anything like that?"

Stout patted his carryall with a sort of prim precision. "All I need is a screwdriver. I'll fly straight back after I've dismantled the camera. I'll sleep on the plane."

The enclosed back of the three-year-old Dodge moving van was stacked with ropes and padded furniture blankets. Nat had slipped an airport cop a buck to leave it at the curb in front of the baggage area with the blinkers flashing. They left the Bayshore at the Broadway-Burlingame light. Dunc eyed his watch.

"We've got time, let's check it out."

Wellman Design was in a light industrial area between the Southern Pacific tracks and El Camino Real. Big shutters were down over the glass storefront windows.

"Looks like there's a loading area in back that can't be seen from the street," said Nat, turning his head as they passed.

Gregory Stout said nervously, "Ah . . . what time will the person we're meeting be here to let us in?"

"After the bars close," lied Dunc.

Nat drove back to Broadway and a bright splash of bar light. They killed time until last call playing shuffleboard and eating pretzels and sipping draft beer. Outside, it was a cold, clear night; Dunc could see his breath. They got into the truck, Nat started the engine so the heater could cut the chill.

"We'd better keep moving around," said Dunc. "Cops see three guys in a panel truck parked with the motor running . . ."

After half a block a cruising police car passed them going the other way on Broadway. Dunc kept his eye on the rearview.

"They're turning into El Camino."

"How long d'you figure their loop takes?"

"At least an hour."

Stout said, "Why are you men so jumpy about the police?"

Nobody answered. Nat stopped in front of Wellman Design with his turn blinkers on. Dunc got out. He could feel his adrenaline kick in. Stout was looking around nervously. Nat was backing the truck into the narrow alley between the building and a chain-link fence with ivy on it.

"C'mon," Dunc said to Stout, "we just walk down to the corner and back, talking, while Nat checks it out."

Nat came hotfooting out of the alley, grinning. "Hell, they got a loading dock." He took a small leather case off his hip, added appreciatively, "Plenty of street light."

Dunc took out the alarm box key. "The alarm box is supposed to be on a post to the right of the door. I'll have sixty seconds to deactivate once you've—"

"Hey, wait a minute, wait a minute." They both turned to look at Stout. "Wha . . . what are you guys doing?"

"Breaking and entering," said Dunc.

"But . . . what if the cops come?"

"They'll shoot us."

He grinned, and Nat, bent over the door lock, snickered. But Stout was backing away, holding up a hand to ward off demons.

"Uh-uh. No! I'm not . . . I didn't know you were . . ."

He turned, almost stumbling, and walked briskly away up the street toward Broadway without looking back. Dunc and Nat looked at one another, then both burst out laughing.

"I think maybe I handled that guy wrong," said Dunc.

"Yeah. He's takin' all his screwdrivers back to Chicago."

"That toddling town," said Dunc, which was enough to break them up all over again.

Just over a minute later, Nat said, "We're in."

Dunc's pencil flash showed the post with the red alarm box mounted on it. He keyed it, turning the red light to green.

Fluorescents flickered and then glared whitely. "Lights on, we look legit," said Nat. "A flash bouncing around the walls will bring the cops knocking at our door."

"Christ," said Dunc.

The camera was a great black box mounted on a floor-to-ceiling steel pipe framework with a massive bellow lens pointed straight down at a four-foot-square metal-framed sheet of opaque glass.

"Wish that guy hadn't run," said Ned. "How much of this shit we supposed to steal?"

"Everything we can unfasten."

"We can wheel the stuff right onto the truck with a hand dolly," said Nat.

They found screwdrivers, started in. Nothing seemed delicate or too intricate to understand. Who needed an expert? When they had the four-foot sheet of framed glass loosed from the brackets that held it, Nat opened the loading dock door and they hand-carried it into the truck because of its fragility.

Nat wheeled and padded and roped while Dunc dismantled the camera and its metal pipe framework. They put the camera on its back in the truck with its lens pointing straight up at the roof.

"It'll be safe unless somebody dive-bombs us," said Nat.

The whole operation took just under an hour and a half. Dunc reset the alarms and they left.

The client's warehouse was tucked up against the almost perpendicular base of the hill on the Chestnut Street stub just off Montgomery on the far side of Telegraph Hill. In just over another hour they had unloaded the camera and its accessories.

"I'll pop for breakfast," said Nat with a stifled yawn. "The Greek around the corner from the office'll be open."

"And I'll leave Drinker a note after we eat."

In Chicago, that broad-shouldered town, a disheveled technical expert walked into his supervisor's office smelling of pretzels, beer, and stale bar smoke.

"Don't ever send me to San Francisco again," he said in his prim, angry voice. "It's just a nest of thieves out there."

Chapter Thirty-five

At 7:55 Dunc clumped up the interior stairs to the office. Drinker was waiting for him. "Good—I got a hot skip-trace and I gotta be out of the office and Sherry's off sick. You got contacts in Vegas, don't you?"

Dunc didn't even remember telling Drinker of his weeks there. He still had a hard time thinking about Vegas, about Ned, about Artis. "Not really. I was friendly with a bartender and a blackjack dealer at the Gladiator Club, that's about it."

"Broad you're gonna be looking for disappeared from the Fabulous Flamingo—isn't that what they call it?"

"Have a heart, Drinker. I've been up all night, I just came in to type my field report before going home to bed."

Cope's sleepy eyes gleamed. "You got the camera? Good. Make your report meaty. The client's good for a lot of dough."

"I'll make it meaty, all right. Your expert from Chicago crapped out on me. Don't pay the bastard his fee."

"You're learning, kid." Drinker pointed at the unlisted phone on Sherry's desk that was always answered with *Hello*, never with *Cope Investigations.* "Use the skip-tracing phone. Read my notes on the file before you start in."

As he went down the stairs in his topcoat, fitting his fedora on his head, Dunc leaned over the railing.

"Who's the client on this?"

Drinker paused. "Don't worry about long-distance phone charges, the client's good for it." Then he was gone.

Another of Drinker's unnamed-client cases. Dunc opened the file. Kata A. Koltai. What kind of name was that? Something central European? Age twenty-five, listed address on Glover—a one-block street on Russian Hill above the Broadway Tunnel. No listed employment, no listed references. A sister in Portland, Oregon, with a different last name. Pride. Polly Pride.

Koltai had driven to Las Vegas a month ago in a new 1953 Mercury Monterey station wagon, then had disappeared. Drinker had called the SFPD for wants or warrants. None. He had also called around the western states to sheriffs and highway patrol offices. She had been arrested in Arizona two years before for running a "mitt camp" at a county fair midway. Mitt camp; palm reading, right? Anyway, she'd gotten off with a fine.

The motor vehicle departments of Georgia and Mississippi, where cars could sometimes be licensed with just a driver affidavit of ownership, had no record for her. Louisiana DMV, where fraudulently registered cars could often get a clear title that bypassed the original lien-holders, also had no record.

Was the car in her name in California? Did she hold the pink slip? Maybe Drinker knew there wasn't any lien-holder who might have further leads to her, but Dunc didn't. He had to find out. The Searching Registration Service in Sacramento would check DMV records for two bits and mail you the result. For a buck they'd do it in an hour. Dunc asked for the hurry-up service.

While waiting for their callback, he tried the TUxedo exchange number. No answer. The Polk cross-directory gave him phone numbers for the other five apartments in her building. Only a Marta Gold was at home, six drinks and a deck of Luckies into her day.

"Kata Koltai?" Sudden wariness. "Who wants to know?"

"California Savings on Geary Street. She's three months delinquent on her Mercury Monterey and—"

"She ain't had it three months."

Oops. He tried to sound confused. "That doesn't square with our records . . ." He took a flier. "Is her rent current?"

"Course it is. Ain't her who . . ." Dunc waited through a coughing fit and a heavy-duty throat-clearing. "You got too damn many questions, buster."

Dial tone. So. Somebody was paying Kata's rent. He called Portland information and got the sister's phone number. Polly Pride. After four rings a woman's voice answered.

"Kata?" asked Dunc brightly.

"Polly. Haven't seen Kata in months. Piss off."

She slammed down the receiver. Hell, a long shot anyway.

SRS called back collect on the regular agency phone. The Mercury was in Kata's name, she owned it, free and clear.

Owned it, drove it to Vegas, disappeared. Their client had to be the man keeping her. She had run out on him and he wanted her back. Dunc had to bite the bullet and call Vegas. Though Carny Largo was gone, the Gladiator Club's new owners wouldn't have dumped Nicky; good bartenders were too hard to come by. Dunc got put through to the lounge.

"Gladiator Club, hottest slots in town."

"Gimme a Scotch Manhattan, Nicky."

"Shit, Dunc!" exclaimed Nicky. "Howzit, kid? Ain't seen you around, figured you left town after Ned and all. Terrible thing. Not that I miss fuckin' Carny Largo, y'understand, or that little bastard that followed him around."

"Rafe. Did they ever catch him for—"

"Hell, poetic justice got done for the little fucker. Somebody stuck a knife in him."

A surprising wave of relief went through Dunc. Rafe had paid for Artis, and Dunc was safe—if he'd ever been in danger.

"Listen, Nicky, who's running the place now?"

Nicky got his mouth closer to the phone. "Would you believe, the fat guy with the Scotch Manhattan?"

And the Lana Turner look-alike buried in the desert. He said, "Listen, Nicky, you know anybody out at the Flamingo?"

"Couple bartenders. And Henri of course."

"Henri the blackjack dealer?"

"Yeah, he's a pit boss there now."

Henri seemed genuinely glad to hear from him. He demanded, "Remember Sabine? Left with the bouncer with the seventeen pounds of dangling meat?"

"I don't remember her putting it just that way, but—"

"Anyway, I guess it was so heavy he couldn't get it up, so, *zut! alors!* she's back wiz Henri, ze *fantastique* lover."

They laughed, Dunc congratulated him, told him the story.

"A missing lady? Sure, give me the dope on her and I'll run it past the registration desk. Ten minutes."

Kata had checked in under her own name a month earlier, had checked out the next day. "That quick? Any phone calls?"

"Not to her room. And she didn't make any calls out."

"Anybody else asking about her?"

"Funny thing, I asked that, everybody got glassy-eyed."

That explained why the client had taken a month to hire Drinker Cope. He had Vegas connections, had been looking for her himself, had struck out. Where to look next? Why wasn't Sherry there to tell him? What was Drinker doing that was so damn important?

"I plan to die in the saddle, babe," gasped Drinker Cope.

He withdrew, rolled onto his back, blew out a big breath. Sherry Taft reached for the tissues on the bedside table.

"Better not do it in *my* saddle, buster," she grinned.

He sat up against the headboard, flushed from sexual exertion. His muscles were smooth under almost hairless skin. Sherry sat beside him, knees drawn up. Afternoon sunlight, muted by lace curtains, gave her racehorse body a seductive golden glow.

He put two cigarettes in his mouth, lit them, stuck one between Sherry's lips. There were whisker burns on her chin.

"I'm going to look a sight tomorrow, Drinker."

"What's the diff? I've got you out sick today."

She feathered smoke, looked over at him. "Why'd you want to put Dunc on this woman? He's learning to skip-trace, but—"

"Wants to be a detective, he's gotta learn sometime. And it's as good a way as any to find out about his Vegas contacts."

She shook her head fondly. "Drinker, you like living danger-ously. What do you care about his Vegas contacts? If Mr. David knew you had him skip-tracing on this . . ." She paused. "Why do you? Really?"

"You know I hate skip-tracing and we were overdue for a day in the sack."

"I'll work on her tomorrow," she promised.

He sucked hungrily on his cigarette, looked at the glowing tip, sucked again, and reached over to mash it out in the ashtray.

"How about you work on me right now?" he asked.

Dunc worked on Koltai for the rest of the afternoon, but the first break came from one of Drinker's highway patrol calls.

"Is Inspector Cope there?"

Dunc put a cop's boredom into his voice. "Eddie? He's down in records checkin' a file. I'm coverin' his phone."

"Tell him his suspect got a speeding ticket outside Rancho Mirage nine days ago. Driving a 1953 Mercury Monterey."

Rancho Mirage. Dunc checked the California map. Near Palm Springs. Long-distance information had no new listings for Koltai in the area. Was she living there? Just passing through? With some new guy? If not, what was she doing for money?

Hey! Busted for palm reading in Arizona two years before! Ran off from Las Vegas. Nine days ago, a speeding ticket near Palm Springs. *Deserts.* Always deserts. This was thin. Really thin. Still, a lot of deserts. Deserts and palm reading. Palm reading under what name? Madam Kata? Madam Koltai?

If the sister up in Portland knew, could she be tricked into telling?

He studied approaches to her like a coin dealer examining Spanish doubloons, picked one, called her again.

When she picked up, he asked, "Polly Koltai?"

"Polly Pride." She gave a half-belch. "Pride for short but not for long." Some drinking had been going on. Loud music in the background. "Gonna d'vorce him. Bastard got sent to the state pen for five-to-ten on an ADW beef 'n' left me hangin'."

"You're doing the right thing," said Dunc solemnly.

"Damn right."

"Your sister mentioned your name and where you lived, and, well, I took the liberty of getting your phone number and—"

"Damn right you took the liberty. Well?"

"I met her in a . . . well, in a bar here in Palm Springs, to tell you the truth, a week, ten days ago."

"Palm Springs? Hell she's doin' there?"

"She told my fortune, and . . . I gotta talk with her again."

"Hey, mister, 'm shorry I can't help you, but I din' even know she was in Palm Springs. Her an' her goddamn deserts! Me, gimme rain an' pine trees an' . . ." A bottle tinked against glass. "Why'd you say you wanted to see her again?"

He put desperation in his voice. "Okay, look, I'll level with you. She's . . . We, ah, spent an evening together and . . . and I fell for her. Okay? I called around to a bunch of bars for a Madam Kata or a Madam Koltai, reading palms, but—"

"Hell, she never uses her own name! Madam Pollyanna." She giggled. "Get it? My name's Polly an' her middle name's Anna."

"That's really clever!" exclaimed Dunc. "She must think a lot of her little sister, use your name that way."

"How'd you know I was younger?"

"You *sound* so much younger."

"Damn right." Another pull at her drink. "Prettier too. You tell her that when you see her, okay?"

"Sure. If you could tell me where she—"

"Hey, wait a minnit, I'm talkin' too damn much . . ."

And she hung up, as if suddenly regretting her gabbiness. Dunc kissed a finger and laid it on the phone. Yes! Kata had to be somewhere around Palm Springs, reading palms under the name of Madam Pollyanna. Had to be. Now, a lot of phone work . . .

He settled lower in Sherry's now-comfortable chair. Madam Pollyanna, always gave a rosy-futured reading. If she was Madam Pandora, she could foretell only dire events for her . . .

"Wake the hell up." Drinker Cope loomed above him in topcoat and fedora, wide as a house, shaking him by the shoulder. "Hell of a way to cover the phones."

Dunc sat up, stretched. "Just resting my eyes."

"Then your eyes snore. Whadda ya got on Koltai?"

Dunc recounted everything he had done on the file. It sounded thin to him now. He didn't *know* she was in Palm Springs . . .

"I, uh, haven't had time to start calling around for—"

"I saw how busy you were, sacked out in Sherry's chair." Then he punched Dunc in the shoulder and gave a triumphant laugh. "I'll be a son of a bitch, that's great work—connecting up deserts and that old mitt-camp charge. We got her, kid."

Energized, Dunc said eagerly, "Can I go look for her?"

"Hell no. We're out of it from here on . . . Close and bill. The client's got business interests in Palm Springs, they'll ask around, when they find her he'll send one of his own people down to get her."

Chapter Thirty-six

The stewardess was checking reservations. "Name, please."

"Simmons," said Falkoner.

During the thirty-five-minute flight from Los Angeles his startling blue eyes, slightly askew in a sun-tawny face, studied the woman huddled across the aisle with melancholy contempt. She wore a cheap brown hat and clutched an old straw purse. Updrafts over the rim of the desert made her fists whiten with strain and her eyes burn with fear. He found her disgusting. Death was swift, casually given.

A slight sandy-haired man in a short-sleeved sport shirt, khaki pants, and open sandals of crisscrossed brown leather took his arm when he left the plane at Palm Springs. Falkoner's only luggage was a briefcase that held his shaving gear and a change of underwear, just in case. Not that he thought he'd need it.

"I bet Mr. David sent you down," said the sandy-haired man in too-intimate tones. "I'm Langly. My car's here in the lot."

It was a blue-and-white 1952 Chrysler. On the two-lane blacktop beyond the airport the sun was hot but the air dry and fresh. Scraggly clumps of dusty green vegetation of no interest to Falkoner spotted the flat tan desert.

"It's so *dry* around here they all have these just huge root systems to suck up whatever moisture they can and—"

"Shut the fuck up and drive," said Falkoner.

Langly lapsed into hurt silence. They passed a man and woman on horseback, wearing riding breeches, who waved gaily. Langly waved back. "He's a director at RKO. They—"

"Shut the fuck up and drive."

An Eldorado roared by like an escaped rocket, piloted by a pair of bleached blondes goggled with bright-rimmed sunglasses.

"Who're they, the Bobbsey Twins?" Before Langly could respond, he demanded, "Where's the woman, goddamn you?"

"She's got just a horrible shack in a date grove near Rancho Mirage—it's a new section this side of Palm Desert—and reads palms at a Mex place in Palm Desert. The Caliente Club. She goes in at five in the afternoon, she'll be home now."

"She'd better be."

But Langly could not be silent. His voice tingled ripely.

"Mr. David must want her *terribly* badly, I just notified Los Angeles last night, today here you are from Frisco to—"

"Just take me out to her place."

This guy was not only a pain in the ass; he might be dangerous. Beyond the plush Thunderbird Club and before the Shadow Mountain Club, they turned left on a dirt road. Dust swirled behind them.

"When word came she'd been telling fortunes in Scottsdale a few years ago, and had disappeared from Vegas, well, I just put my thinking cap on. It just seemed to me that she might try it here—I mean, the country's just almost the same. Then I—"

"A San Francisco skip-tracer told you she liked the desert. Told you she was picking up traffic tickets here. Told you she was readings mitts as Madam Pollyanna."

"But that was all so vague, so *tentative. I* spotted her at the Mex place from her name and photo, and—"

"And megaphoned Mr. David's name all over. Are we close?"

Beyond an old wash, the date groves started. Langly said snidely, "Next road to the right, if you must know, first house on the left." Almost grudgingly, "*Only* house."

"Drive past the mouth of the road, not past the house."

"I'm not stupid, you know, Mr. High-and-Mighty."

"You sound stupid," said Falkoner. "You act stupid."

Twenty yards in on the narrow dusty track through the date grove, the tail of a black '53 Mercury Monterey station wagon with wood paneling protruded from behind a palm. The shack itself was hidden by the date trees.

"Turn around and let me off and go back to town."

Langly was a spoiled child. "But you'll need me to—"

"I need you to shut your face."

He walked around the car to drop an envelope in through the open window onto Langly's lap. The envelope crinkled.

"Your thirty pieces of silver." He smiled his not-nice smile. "What sort of work do you do, nance?"

"I . . . I've been parking cars at one of the clubs." His voice got almost shrill with malice. "But I did good work on this and I'm going to make sure Mr. Dannelson in Los Angeles knows all about it and about how you've treated me."

Falkoner leaned into the Chrysler. "You ought to write mystery novels, you got that kind of pansy imagination. Mr. David wants her back, he's fond of her, he asked me to drive her back up in her car. *Capisce?*"

"I . . ." Langly was looking straight ahead. "I—yes."

"You don't call Dannelson, you don't call anyone, you never heard of me. *Capisce?*" Langly jerked his head stiffly in acquiescence. Falkoner nodded dismissal, said, "Go park cars."

He removed the Mercury's distributor cap, eased the hood back down. Something, probably a palm rat, gnawed with cautious haste in the palm fronds clicking drily on the roof of the shack. His shoes made the noise of cats' feet on glass as he crossed the sagging porch. He cupped his eyes to peer into the living room.

A beaten-down green couch, a red easy chair that looked almost new. One leg of the wooden table in the middle of the room had been cracked and stapled. A plaque that read GOD BLESS OUR HAPPY HOME with embossed flowers around the frame. Foot traffic had worn certain areas of the linoleum almost white.

He knocked on the door frame with his knuckles. A woman's voice called from somewhere, "I'm not doing any readings today."

Falkoner kept on knocking. Kata came through the inner doorway. An intricately colored silk scarf was twisted twice around her neck; her striking figure was displayed by a tight black dress. She was nearly as tall as Falkoner's six-one. Her arms were raised and her hands were fooling with her hair; three hairpins were between her thin hungry lips.

"I told you I'm not doing any readings until tonight at the club." Her face was fine-featured: straight nose, high cheekbones. Her usually husky, seductive voice was thick with anger. "Now, get to hell away from here or I'll call Pablo . . ."

The screen door was unlocked. Falkoner stepped in.

"You don't have a phone," he said.

Her face went stark white. Her mouth dropped the hairpins. She tried to push him back out the door, slanted dark eyes smoky with terror.

His almost gentle hands on her shoulders pushed her off. "Pablo, huh? Quite a comedown for you, Kata."

"Goddamn you, he's the bouncer at the club."

"The Caliente Club," he said with indifference.

Through the archway was a bedroom with a double bed that looked as if two large animals had been fighting on it. Stiff yellowish stains on the sheets testified to Pablo's virility. The whole setup was perfect—except for the nance, Langly.

Drawing on a pair of thin gray gloves, Falkoner sauntered back to the living room. Kata was standing stiffly in the middle of the floor like a songbird mesmerized by a snake.

"What does he want from me? The Mercury? I earned it."

"On your back," he said in brutal indifference.

"Under *you* a couple of times when he was out of town," she said shrilly. Her anger died. "I got tired of men like him and men like you. Money and power and women, that's all you—"

"The men at the Mex place are different?"

"I have to eat. I didn't steal anything from him, did I?"

"How about his peace of mind?" suggested Falkoner.

Her hands crawled like broad white spiders up the black dress to her breasts, squeezed them brutally, unconsciously.

"I, look, I don't know anything, I didn't see anything, I didn't hear anything. I'm no threat, I . . ." In a low, almost throaty whisper, she asked, "Why can't he let me live in peace?"

"He can't let you live at all, Kata."

She tried to twist away, but his quick hands were already closing about her scarfed throat like an act of love. She scrabbled wildly at the iron-hard forearms, tried to claw his eyes, tried to knee his crotch with the strength of desperation.

But his hands had the strength of death. He spun her about, shoved her facedown on the couch, got a knee in the middle of her back as his hands found the ends of the scarf. He dragged it tight around her throat.

Her black skirt was up around her waist, opaque black panties molded the ripe globes of her buttocks. Her thrashing body under his, her smell of sweat and perfume and fear made his erection immense; but the M.E. would find his semen in her, there would be questions. If he took her away with him, he wouldn't put it past Mr. David's minions to check her body cavities.

He couldn't chance it. Her movements became erratic, lost volition, ceased. He stepped back and blew out a long breath. He was drenched in sweat as from a heavy workout.

When he rolled her over, her face was almost black and her tongue, pink as a baby's thumb, was sticking out of one corner of her mouth. She sprawled in a lewd doll-pose of surrender, but there was nothing seductive about voided bowels and loosened kidneys. Her eyes stared beyond him into death with a sort of infinite horror. His lip curled with contempt. Dying was easy.

And Kata was just a disposal problem, just cooling meat.

Chapter Thirty-seven

As the bleating sheep swung past him, strung up by a leg on the conveyor loop, the big Negro jabbed his gleaming needlepoint spike into its ear. The animal gave a convulsive jerk and was carried away, dripping blood from its nose, to be skinned and eviscerated. The big slaughterer reached for the next one.

Out on the loading dock, Dunc transferred the sheep's carcass from his shoulder to the last empty hook in the Niarchos Meats van. A burly man in a blood-splattered white smock chomped his cheap cigar and made a check mark on his clipboard.

"That's the one we been looking for," he said.

Dunc made ritual reply. "Too bad they saved it 'til last."

He inserted his time card, the clock punched out 6:13—almost forty-five minutes past quitting time. Maybe tonight would be the night. He added his card to the others already in the rack.

The locker room was filled with tall rows of double-stacked metal lockers with wooden benches in between. A few stragglers still pulled on street clothes after their showers. As Dunc entered, a redheaded Irishman with freckles and overmeaty earlobes paused in the doorway to raise a fine tenor in song:

> *"He has a brown ring around his nose,*
> *And every day it grows and grows!"*

There was sudden silence in the locker room. Dunc had been working there only three days, he knew Flaherty didn't like him, but this was the Irishman's first direct challenge.

"I guess you know the color of your own nose," he said.

And pushed past into a locker room now noisy with laughter. He kept going, down between a row of lockers, cursing himself for saying anything. He wasn't here to get into a brawl; that could spoil everything. But as he stripped off the bloodstained white smock and stuffed it into an already bulging canvas laundry bag, he breathed a silent sigh of relief: Flaherty's voice, bragging as if he had won the confrontation, was retreating down the hall.

When Dunc came back with wet hair and a towel wrapped around his middle, the big colored man was at the next locker.

"You ever get into a fight with that guy, watch out," he said in a rumbling bass voice, "he's good at kicking kneecaps."

"Hey, thanks."

The Negro flashed a big grin and was gone. Dunc dressed slowly. By the time he was tying his shoes, he was alone. He'd jimmied the storage closet's lock the first night, so he went in, pulled some boxes out from the back wall just far enough to slip behind them, and sat down with his legs stretched out in front of him. He leaned back against the sidewall to wait.

Falkoner leaned against the window of the gas station pay phone on South Palm Drive, smoking a cigarette and waiting for his connection to a SUtter exchange number in San Francisco.

The operator said, "I have a collect call for anyone from a Mr. Simmons in Palm Springs. Will you accept the charges?"

A flat voice answered, "Put him on."

"Go ahead, sir. Your party is ready."

Falkoner ground out his cigarette against the window, said "Yes" into the phone, and hung up without waiting for a reply.

After paying for his gas, he drove the Mercury out of Palm Springs and westward across the desert. He'd strangled Kata with the scarf to avoid finger marks on her throat: he'd intended to leave her strung up as a suicide. Even without a note, suicide would have been accepted. A woman used to the good life, reduced to telling fortunes in a Mexican bar and sleeping with the Mexican bouncer, takes a hard look at her future, the scarf is already around her neck, the ridge beam is convenient . . . He would have left the car and walked back to town.

But he'd decided he just couldn't risk it. Langly had a leaky face. So he'd packed the clothes and personal items she would take when moving on, had put them in her suitcase that was beside him on the Mercury's front seat. Kata herself he had wrapped in a blanket and stuffed in the trunk's spare-tire well.

Dunc listened to the cleaning crew leave the locker room, went down the corridor and out across the slaughtering floor. He had twenty minutes until the 8:00 P.M. arrival of the night watchman. The blood had been washed down the drains, and the conveyor belt was silent, but the smell of death lingered; the very walls were impregnated with it.

On the mezzanine was a walkway in front of glass-fronted offices. Dunc let the tight little O of his pencil flash lead him to the personnel file cabinets. In the drawer marked "F–J" he found FLAHERTY, DENNIS MICHAEL. Pulled it out.

Yes! The Social Security numbers matched!

He'd nailed the bastard. Six months ago a certain Shamus Herron had been working as a butcher at McSorley's Meats in East Orange, New Jersey, when he had lifted $25,000 in cash from the safe. Since McSorley made book on the side, the cash was unreported and he couldn't go to the police.

But last week Herron had given the pay-phone number of a San Francisco bar to his former girlfriend, Margie McConnell, back in East Orange. McSorley had offered a rather extravagant cash reward for information about him; Margie had cashed in.

Dunc had snooped around and had learned enough to get a job at the slaughterhouse on Evans Avenue in the Hunter's Point district.

Tonight he'd confirmed that Dennis Flaherty's Social Security number was also Shamus Herron's. Social Security withholds were recorded primarily by account number, not name.

He drove in on Third Street past the Wessler—poor old Kiely was already retreating into memory—and parked across from Ma Booger's. At Tommy's Joynt he had a ninety-nine cent roast turkey leg with mashed potatoes and stuffing, and went up to bed.

At U.S. 99, Falkoner went north to Colton, then cut across to U.S. 66 on a dirt road, once again pointed the nose of the Mercury at the far thin glow of Los Angeles. He counted bugs as they squashed against the windshield, and at nine o'clock ate Mexican food in a small adobe diner. The bright serapes decorating the walls reminded him of the Red Arrow.

Tomorrow night back in Palo Alto he would use each of his wife's orifices in turn. It had begun after his first two kills, the personal ones, had continued and intensified after each of his three professional assignments from Mr. David. She had chosen to whore around, what did she expect? Red roses?

At midnight some unease made him pull in at a motel near Glendora, two hours from the city. It was a single row of neat, freshly painted white cottages that had covered carports and doors leading directly inside. The cabin closest to the road had a red neon sign, *MOTEL*, with *vacancy* smaller underneath.

After he rang the bell twice, a light went on and an old man in an old-fashioned nightshirt that covered him from neck to midthigh came out rubbing his eyes.

"I have trouble sleeping if I can hear traffic passing," said Falkoner. "Is your last unit in the line empty?"

Clicking his false teeth together, he leaned past Falkoner as if to make sure there was a last unit. Up close like this he had an old man's incontinent smell of urine. "Yep."

"How much?"

"Five bucks."

"Commercial rates. Three-fifty. It's after midnight."

After a long moment, he gave a defeated nod. "Okay."

Established as a commercial traveler on a budget, Falkoner wrote "Simmons" on the registration card in a slanting backhand script not his own; mixed up the license number in a way that could have been accidental; and took Kata's suitcase with him before locking the car.

Kata herself he left in the spare-tire well: the cold night air would keep her fresh.

Chapter Thirty-eight

In the morning Dunc did two hours with the weights at the downtown YMCA on Golden Gate Avenue, then ran a mile on the oval track on the mezzanine above the basketball court. A half hour under a hot shower couldn't wash away the slaughterhouse stink, because it was in his mind, not on his skin.

Tonight he would say the seventh of the dozen rosaries given him as pre-penance by the priest in Las Vegas five months ago. It was Tuesday, which meant the Sorrowful Mysteries.

"Let me talk to Danny," said Falkoner into the service station/garage pay phone. He rubbed his eyes and cursed the gray fingers of smog reaching even out here from Los Angeles.

"Yeah, who's calling?"

Morning traffic made it difficult to hear. "Falkoner."

"Falkoner? I'm sorry, Mr. Dannelson is out."

Falkoner squeezed the receiver with a hand gone suddenly sweaty. There were muttered angry words, a click, and Danny Dannelson's jovial voice came over the line.

"Hello, Jack? That damn fool didn't get your name right. We expected you last night, boyo. Where in hell are you?"

Falkoner hung up, thought for a moment, then went around behind the repair garage. With his Swiss Army knife he removed the license plates from a parked car, walked back to the motel with them under his jacket, and changed the Mercury's plates.

The maid had made up the room. He turned on the radio, used one of the fresh towels to wipe everything he'd touched. Dannelson's clumsiness had prepared him for the 10:00 A.M. news.

Police were investigating the disappearance and possible murder of a woman who had been telling fortunes at the Caliente Club outside Palm Desert under the name of Madam Pollyanna.

At the Olympus Cafe on Franklin Street between Bush and Sutter, Elias Stavropolous, a short wide swarthy Greek with a brigand's mustache, put two English muffins into the toaster and brought Dunc a pot of tea without being asked.

The 10:00 A.M. news was saying that two boys playing near the woman's house had seen a man carrying a blanket-wrapped body to her black station wagon just at dusk. They had told their parents, who had alerted the cops.

Dunc opened the *Call-Bulletin* and started reading what the Board of Supervisors had to say about Herb Caen's proposal in the *Chronicle* to string a wire in the Broadway Tunnel so car radios wouldn't die on the way through.

The police had found no sign of a struggle, no blood, said the newsman; the woman's clothes and personal items and car had been gone. But under the paper lining of a kitchen shelf they had found over $700 in small bills.

"Who's gonna run off on her own an' leave that kinda money lying around?" demanded Elias as he returned with Dunc's food.

Dunc nodded indifferently, crunched muffin, slurped tea.

Chester Langly, a parking attendant at the Blue Owl, had given the description of a hitchhiker he'd left off at the mouth of the road where the woman's house was located.

Damn him, Falkoner thought as he sopped up the last of his egg yolk with his toast. Mr. David had given him the contract on Kata

Koltai personally, so now Falkoner—because of Langly—was too compromised to be left alive.

Los Angeles and Las Vegas and San Diego—probably Tucson and El Paso, too. Seattle. Airports, bus and train depots, seaports like San Pedro to prevent him trying it by boat.

Where in Christ's name *wouldn't* they be looking for him?

He grinned to himself. Of course. It was what they should expect of Jack Falkoner. At the motel office he paid cash for three more days and told the indifferent clerk he wouldn't need maid service. Kata went into the bathtub. Leaving the air conditioner on high might add a day before the smell got noticed.

Sherry was explaining over the phone, in clipped businesslike tones, that she had an application for employment from a Mr. Charles DeWitt and needed his current residence address. She tipped Dunc a wink, wrote things on her pad, hung up.

"Where have you been? Drinker's having a fit."

"Gee, Dunc, great job on Flaherty," he said.

Her eyes widened theatrically. "So he's our man! Good work, Dunc! I'll tell Drinker to close and bill—"

"*Dunc, goddammit,* get in here!"

Drinker had the blinds turned halfway up to keep bands of sunlight from hitting the top of his littered desk. He pointed at the hardback chair. Dunc sat.

"You nailed Flaherty? Great. I got a hot one for you." He put his elbows on the desk. "Old pal of yours skipped with a quarter million bucks worth of bearer bonds and our client don't wanna move against his surety bond. So I want you to—"

"I don't have any old pals that smart," said Dunc.

"The client's covering all the usual places himself—buses, trains, planes, airports, seaports. All they've come up with is a big fat zero." He fixed his eyes on Dunc's face. "I want you to tell 'em where to look."

"What's the joke? I don't know anybody who—"

"Jack Falkoner. Guy you told me you was with at Juárez."

"Hell, Drinker, I also told you I had a day on the road with him, a night in Juárez, and an hour in Palo Alto when I picked up my stuff."

Drinker Cope adjusted the blinds again to keep the sun out, said almost vaguely, "Yeah, you did. But at least you know him. I'm grabbing at straws here, kid, but this's a hell of an important client and you got the instinct."

Dunc felt a little strange, trying to find someone he'd gotten drunk with and fought beside. But he didn't owe Jack Falkoner anything; the man had stranded him in El Paso. And it was satisfying that Drinker was starting to think of him as a real private eye, after all.

He went back to his own desk in the rear of the office, put his feet up, and let Jack Falkoner stride through his mind.

Running around on me . . . I'll deal with them . . .

Army surgeons wanted to cut my arm off . . . Fuck 'em . . .

In Mexico we can do more than we're big enough to do . . .

Suddenly he knew what he had to do. He went into Drinker's office without knocking. "I'm going down to Palo Alto."

"For Chrissake, Jack Falkoner isn't in Palo Alto."

"His wife is."

Dunc put his finger on the buzzer and kept it there. The brown-shingle bungalow at Melville and Bryant hadn't changed in the three months since he'd last seen it. Ginny Falkoner finally opened the door to peer out fearfully.

No tight halter and skimpy shorts to show her tempting figure: now a shapeless housedress. No black eye, but a drawn look and pasty skin almost jaundiced in color. And she'd lost weight. Her shoulders were hunched as if she feared a blow.

"Pierce Duncan," he said. "I was here in Septem—"

"I remember. About your duffel bag. Jack isn't here. I don't know where he is. Jack never calls when he's on the road."

"They've been here, haven't they?"

In almost a whisper she said, "Yes." Dunc went in past her, she shut the door immediately. Somehow, they both knew he didn't mean the cops even though he wasn't sure who he did mean. "I told them what I just told you."

"Did they believe you?"

"They left."

They were standing just inside the door. The polished oak floor gleamed. "Did they tell you he stole a lot of money?"

"Jack? Jack wouldn't steal."

Something, maybe even fear, turned over in his gut like a striking bass. "Why didn't you go through with the divorce?"

Her voice was just a whisper. "He said he'd . . ."

She stopped. This was the strangest conversation he'd ever had with anyone in his life, yet both of them understood it.

"And you believed him?"

"I . . . There were . . . I had two friends . . ."

"Lovers," pronounced Dunc. "He told me about them."

"It wasn't like that!" she cried. Her momentary animation died. "Friends. Nothing more. I . . . They're both . . . dead."

Dunc couldn't keep looking at her. Why had he ever wanted to be a detective? A brace of suitcases stood just inside the living room archway. He finally asked her, "How?"

"Jerry was found dead in an alley in San Mateo during a race meet at Tanforan. The police said it was a mugging." Her eyes and voice faltered. "The other one, Tommy . . ."

"If he was in danger, where would Jack run to?"

Clear blue eyes met his. Her voice was suddenly strong. "Jack would never run. Jack is an *implacable* man."

He almost didn't call in. Something was awry about the stolen bearer bonds, but he knew he wouldn't get any answers out of Drinker Cope. In the end he dropped coins into the same pay phone he'd used to look up Falkoner's address three months ago.

"What?" said Drinker's impatient voice.

"He'll double back on them."

There was a long pause. "Shit, he'd be nuts to do that."

"You say he's nuts, his wife says he's implacable. I say I'll see you in the morning."

"Wait a minute, it's the middle of the goddamn afternoon."

Dunc had hung up. He deliberately hadn't said anything about Ginny Falkoner being all packed up to leave.

Drinker would think she was maybe going to join Jack, would want her shadowed. But Dunc knew that she believed she had to flee for her life, either from her husband or from his pursuers, and that she felt there was little to choose between them.

Chapter Thirty-nine

A light blue Ford pulled out behind Jack Falkoner on the traffic circle at Bakersfield. He cursed silently to himself; the tail job was clumsy, but why was the pursuer there at all?

North of Delano he squealed off old U.S. 99 near Earlimart to pull up in front of a little run-down country crossroads sort of store still occasionally surviving in the San Joaquin Valley.

A short man wearing a defeated face and dirty overalls came out chewing an outsize cud of tobacco.

"Fill it up—regular," said Falkoner. The man unhooked the nozzle. The pump was old-fashioned, an overhead glass cylinder full of yellowish gas that gravity-flowed into the car's tank. "You got a pay phone here?"

"Our own phone, out back—cost you a dollar to use it."

Good. His follower couldn't call anyone. "I can wait."

How had this guy gotten onto him so quick? Mr. David? He didn't have the kind of mind to foresee Falkoner's strategy. Ginny? She knew him that well, but she'd be too scared to tell.

Three noisy barefoot children slammed through the screen door to clamor at the candy counter like puppies worrying a bone. A tall faded woman in a washed-out housedress came from the bowels of the store to scream harsh threats at them.

The blue Ford rounded the corner, braked sharply when the dri-

ver saw Falkoner walking around behind the building toward the outdoor rest rooms. The lean-to was flanked by latticeworks into which
thick vines had grown. Falkoner slammed the door sharply, then slid
out of sight behind the greenery.

Cautious feet scuffed the dust. Foliage rustled. Falkoner could see
part of the man's face through the leaves. Young, big, redheaded,
homely, deceptively like a farm kid from Hicksville.

The redhead jerked open the door with a squeal of hinges.
Falkoner slammed the knife edge of his hand on the kid's wrist. The
.357 Magnum fell to the dirt. The redhead made the mistake of going
down to scrabble for it. Falkoner lifted a knee into his face, scooped
up the Magnum, dragged him around behind the lean-to, and killed
him with the gun butt. He removed the man's identification and took
the Magnum's shoulder holster.

The surly man in the dirty overalls was still cleaning bugs from the
Mercury's windshield when the blue Ford, Falkoner behind the wheel,
dug out to speed past the gas pumps.

Dunc was lying on the bed thinking about Ginny Falkoner when
Ma Booger slid two phone slips under his door. He got up to look at
them. Both from Drinker Cope. Call him at the office. Call him at
home. Dunc lay back down. Ginny said Jack wouldn't steal. Ginny
said Jack was implacable. Drinker had lied to him.

They weren't looking for Falkoner because he was a thief, they were
looking for him because he was dangerous. Ginny's bags had been
packed. Maybe to escape Jack's pursuers, but more likely Jack. She believed he had killed her two men friends. Dunc was pretty sure she
was right.

So what did he do to stop Jack Falkoner before he maybe killed
again? He'd already done it with his phone call saying Falkoner would
double back; all that was left was his report. Reports seemed to be as
close to writing as he got these days, so he worked hard at them.

But he just didn't want to run into Drinker when he went into the
office to write them.

He stepped over the phone slips and out the door. Half an hour later he paused outside a narrow joint on Bush between Taylor and Jones, the Say When club, from which jazz poured generously into the night. The sandwich board beside the door said BIG JAY McNEELY in big letters. A woman with ash-colored hair and wearing a man's pea-coat and striped sailor's jersey tapped her feet to the beat as she studied the placard.

"Is he any good?" Dunc asked her.

"What do your ears think?" she asked him tartly without breaking her rhythm. "Chet Baker got his start here at Say When. He was stationed at the Presidio during the war, and Charlie Parker needed a trumpeter. They're all good here."

Dunc edged through the doorway for a look inside. At that moment the long drink of water on the piano stool stood, grabbed a saxophone off its stand, and started blowing it sweet and rich.

"That's Harry the Hipster, he's no sax man," she exclaimed, looking around Dunc's shoulder.

He had to step back as the Hipster, wearing a rumpled suit and a day's growth of beard on sallow cheeks, stalked out still blowing wild on his saxophone. The rest of the band kept right on playing. Harry got on board a passing bus without lowering his horn. They watched it pull away from the curb.

Patrons flowed out into the street, openmouthed, but were drawn back by Big Jay's still-jamming combo. The girl went with them. Dunc looked at his watch. Pushing midnight. He could go type reports now without fear of running into Drinker.

As he started walking back out Bush Street, a taxi pulled up and Harry the Hipster got out still blowing his sax, crossed the sidewalk back into Say When. He hadn't dropped a note while he'd been gone. God, Dunc loved this town!

It was pushing midnight when Jack Falkoner parked the blue Ford. He checked the redhead's Magnum carefully; he was going up against Mr. David himself. In Bible school as a kid he'd read about that other

David, the one in the Old Testament, who had a falling-out with *his* God. Now it was Falkoner's turn.

He walked downhill on the right-hand side of narrow, one-block Glover, crossed over, came up the other side, breathing heavier from the incline. No cars he knew, no dark shapes in any of the vehicles along the curb, no people at all.

Mr. David being here was a long shot, but he'd paid Kata's rent and on Sundays had liked to watch *Ed Sullivan* with her. Even when she wasn't here he'd come to think and plan, usually with only Jack for security. If he was here, an easy hit.

Falkoner climbed the stone steps. No lights. He used Kata's keys to open the heavy oak door. After switching off the alarm, he went aprowling through the lush, five-room apartment, cocked Magnum in hand, rubber soles silent on the polished floors and thick carpets. The place was empty.

The hit was going to be a lot harder at Mr. David's Seacliff home, but Jack knew a way in without tripping the alarm. And since he had kept the redhead from getting to a phone, nobody would be expecting him.

As he slid in behind the wheel, a gun muzzle was poked into the back of his neck. A hand came over his shoulder to lift the Magnum from its shoulder holster. A smooth voice spoke.

"Hands on the head, sweets, and slide over slow."

He did. A dark figure crossed the street, opened the driver's door, got in under the wheel. The interior light did not go on. Falkoner was oddly breathless.

He remembered his fucking wife's second lover, that goddamn Tommy Exeter. "I'm not afraid of you," Tommy had said.

A long black Cadillac drifted around the corner and crawled up behind them. It looked remarkably like an undertaker's car. The Ford pulled out. The Cadillac followed them out Pine all the way to Presidio; they cut over to Balboa, drove decorously, like a midnight funeral procession, out through the dark still avenues flanking Golden

Gate Park. His head ached; he felt a little sick to his stomach. *Jack Falkoner is not afraid.*

The driver was hunched over the wheel. His face was unfamiliar. Maybe Falkoner could . . . The unknown man in the backseat said, "Don't try it, sweets."

"How about a cigarette?"

He laughed. Later Tommy Exeter had cried and babbled and even prayed. Falkoner had laughed before shooting him in the face to spoil the pretty-boy good looks that had seduced Ginny.

Surf grumbled against the concrete breakwaters as the Ford turned left onto the Great Highway at Playland at the Beach, its rides and stalls closed against the chill December rain starting to blow in off the Pacific.

Just short of Sloat Boulevard, they swung in facing the ocean on a deserted dirt lot where neckers parked on moonlit nights. A hedge of dark cypress, bent and twisted by the wind, screened them from the houses on the other side of the highway.

Their lights illuminated wet sand dunes and windblown California bunchgrass; they were doused. The Caddy drew up behind them parallel to the Great Highway, lights dimmed.

Jack Falkoner is not afraid. Jack Falkoner is not afraid.

He shoved the cold, slippery door handle violently down to throw himself out into the night. Behind him something plopped twice and two bees stung him. He fell dizzily out of the half-open door to crash down on his shoulder on the hard-packed dirt.

Just another month, a week, a minute, *a second . . .*

Orange flame spurted. Lead ripped his throat. The man with the gun went over to the Cadillac and got in beside the driver. The Ford backed around to follow them away from there.

Mr. David chuckled and took a hundred-dollar bill from a slim leather folder in the inner breast pocket of his camel's-hair coat. He had crisp wavy hair receding from a high brainy forehead, a generous nose, sensuous lips above a narrow chin.

He proffered the bill to the man beside him on the backseat of the Cadillac. This man was bulky, wore an indifferent suit, had a red face and graying hair combed straight back.

"Jack feared neither man nor devil," said Mr. David. "He was a bad one, that's for sure."

"I like 'em bad," said the man beside the driver, removing the perforated steel cylinder from the muzzle of his .32. "But Sweets was scared—I saw his face when he went under."

"I'd be disappointed if that were the case."

The killer realized he was, too. Fear was what he was here for, but he found it disgusting in Jack Falkoner. Hell, Falkoner of all people should have known how swift death was, how casually given.

Dunc stood at the office window. Below, the light turned green, late night traffic burst up Franklin Street like uncaged animals. Would Jack Falkoner double back to San Francisco as he'd suggested to Drinker Cope? If he did, what would . . .

Galvanized by a voice on Drinker's police-band radio, he grabbed his jacket off the top of the desk and ran for the door.

Dunc pulled Grey Ghost Two into the dirt lot off the Great Highway, walked over to the rain-soaked huddle of people. Moaning wind tore his breath away. Water darkened the shoulders of his sport jacket and soaked his short-cut black hair. He could smell salt sea, wet sand, and, faintly, loosened bowels. A car whipped past, tires hissing on the wet pavement.

By the white glare of their prowl car spotlight, two cops in wet tunics lifted the corpse by a shoulder to see if it bore any life. Dunc stared for a moment, then turned away.

Frozen on Falkoner's features, almost ferocious in its intensity, was an expression of pure terror.

Drinker Cope's office door was thrown open with such force that it rebounded off the sidewall. Dunc slammed that morning's folded-open *Chronicle* down on the desk, jabbing a forefinger hard at the headlines.

"You bastard, you set me up to get two people killed! Kata Koltai! I pinpoint her in Palm Springs, the client'll send a man down to pick her up, you said. He sure as fuck did. Then—"

"A friend of yours, if I ain't mistaken."

"A goddamn killer. Working for one of your goddamn unnamed clients. Then you stuck me on *him* so I could—"

"Shut up!" roared Drinker. *"What'd I tell you the first day you walked in the goddamn door bellyachin' for a goddamn job?"*

Dunc could get hot, Drinker thought, but he couldn't hang on to it. Not a good hater, the Irish would say.

"You said you'd take any case from anybody."

"That's right. Anybody. Any case. And you said . . ."

"I said okay, but I wasn't thinking about people I knew. Kata and Jack are dead because I figured out how to find 'em."

"That's what we do in this office—whatever the client hires us to do. Sure, we get lied to all the time, an' sometimes we end up in a mess like this. But we ain't in the morals business. If you got a problem with that, get out of the fucking detective trade. So what's it gonna be?"

Sherry's face appeared in the open doorway of the cubicle.

"Coffee's made and there's hot water for tea. What's it going to be?"

Dunc had the suddenly almost paralyzing realization that he actually *didn't* have a problem with what Drinker had said. What did that say about who he was becoming?

"Oh, what the hell? Tea."

SEVEN

Spanish Gold

Chapter Forty

Christmas Eve. Dunc was lying on his bed, drinking canned beer and eating pretzel sticks and pretending he was going to catch up on his notebook, or walk up to the office to start a short story. Instead, he sat up.

"Mickey, how about some poetry?" Mickey eyed the pretzels. Dunc began mashing two of them in one palm with the other thumb.

> *"I bought my girl some garters,*
> *At the local five-and-ten,*
> *She gave them to her mother,*
> *That's the last I'll see of them."*

He got silently to his feet, holding the crumbs and his beer can.

"That's from a Red Skelton movie, and my gal ain't here to give any garters to."

Mickey sat up, nose wiggling, when Dunc crossed to the kitchen counter. Mouse-gray—his native color—and less than two inches long if you didn't count his tail. He lived in the kitchen walls and occasionally emerged for these one-way chats.

"She's holding high wassail with her mom and her sister's family in Dubuque, so for Christmas I mailed her a half month's pay.

And my mom can't understand why *I* didn't go home for the holidays." He stretched out his hand, very slowly, to dribble a little salt-glinting mound of crunched-up pretzel sticks onto the aged linoleum countertop. "I also have four rosaries to finish."

Mickey gave two sudden hops to snatch up pretzel morsels with delicate busy front paws and nibbled at them with tiny incisors. He seemed to especially favor the salt crystals.

"How can I do penance when everybody I know gets killed? Is it me? Is that what the priest was trying to tell me?"

Mickey nibbled. Dunc looked at his watch: 12:03 A.M. He toasted Mickey and drained his beer.

"I am now twenty-two years old, mouse," he said.

Heavy knuckles hit the door. Mickey vanished. Drinker Cope strolled in as if things were not still strained between them. He stopped at the foot of the bed to take it all in.

"Great place you got here, spacious, elegant—but where's your ten-foot spruce? Eggnog? Hot buttered rum? Mistletoe? Get your fucking shoes on, I'm taking you out to dinner for your birthday. Afterwards we'll listen to some jazz."

Cypress-shaded St. Francis Yacht Club was expensively ablaze, hordes of people visible behind big bay windows. Sleek sports cars and luxury sedans big enough to live in jammed its parking lots. The rigging of the snailboats was hung with colored Christmas lights; the stinkpots were similarly festooned.

Two men came up a private landing quay on synapse-silent deck shoes. The quay was unlighted, the moon in its first quarter. The larger man checked his luminous wristwatch.

"Twelve-fifteen, Lee. Home for the holidays."

Lee Fong was diminutive, not over five-three, 130 pounds. "I leave the car in left-hand lot, Mr. Wham."

Harry Wham was six-six, wide as a barge. He went past a De Soto parked facing the water in a spot favored by lovers on moonlit nights. This was not such a night. A man wearing a hat and brown overcoat came erect from behind the fender to swing a rubber truncheon at the back of Wham's head.

But Wham had spun down and away, landing on his hands, scissoring with his legs. His assailant's head struck the blacktop to rebound into a fist as hard as a thrown rock.

The blackjack of the other man, coming very fast around the front of the car, also missed, even as Lee Fong's right foot sank sideways into his gut nearly to the ankle. He bounced off the De Soto making a noise like a car with a faulty starter.

"Pigeons," Wham said. "I'm pretty sure who sent them."

Their attackers' car keys made a little splash far out in the channel. Also, in the spirit of Christmas, their shoes.

It was 2:00 A.M. Drinker Cope was eating waffles with a double side of sausage at the counter of Jimbo's Waffleshop on the corner of Post and Buchanan. Dunc ate chicken in a basket because the marquee read *Chicken Hot or Cold, Good as Gold.*

"I thought you said we were going to a jazz club?"

"What can I tell you? There's Club Alabam, Wally's Soulville, Elsie's Breakfast Club—but we're staying right here at Jimbo's Bop City. When the clubs close in the Tenderloin and North Beach and Nob Hill, half the musicians come here to jam."

At the cash register was a slim cool fortyish Negro with a porkpie hat and a cigarette sticking straight out from the middle of his mouth. "Drinker my man! How's the sleuthin' business?"

"Everybody's sinnin', nobody's winnin', Jimbo."

The walls of Bop City's back room were crowded with bigger-than-life photographs of some of the greats who had performed or sat in there—Duke Ellington, teenaged Johnny Coltrane, Sammy Davis Jr., Ella Fitzgerald, Johnny Mathis, and of course the Bird. Drinker grabbed them a table and ordered setups.

"Jimbo Edwards got this place when Slim Gaillard tried to stiff the police." He poured a pitiful dribble of Coke into each glass, added ice and booze. "The cops somehow found a pint of liquor on the premises so they closed him down. Slim gave Jimbo the keys, took a cab to L.A., and nobody's seen him since."

By the Art Deco foyer's indirect lighting, Harry Wham was too hawk-nosed to be handsome, with thick blond hair dissheveled from the roughhouse outside the St. Francis Yacht Club. Beyond the Moorish archway into the living room, his wife was swizzling two cocktails at the marble-topped wet bar.

He began, "I see I caught you and Ferris . . ." and when she whirled, alarmed, added, "just getting back from midnight Mass."

April was five-nine and elegant as crystal in a Christmas-red I. Magnin original. Coiling black hair shot with rich bluish highlights danced around a flawless oval face. A jade pendant glowed sullenly at her throat. Her long-lashed gray eyes had turned merry.

"Mass? Hardly, darling. There's a new comic at the Purple Onion, she's very funny, she calls her husband Fang. A Gibson?"

"Sure. Three onions. Pearl, not purple."

"Find your galleon this time?"

Crossing to the hallway, Harry chuckled. "You think I'm nuts but I'll fool you yet."

Ferris Besner drifted out of the kitchen. He called himself an art dealer, was ferret-slim in a $300 hand-tailored suit and $20 silk foulard she had bought him with Harry's money.

She handed him a Gibson, said in a low vicious voice, "I thought you told me he'd be laid up for hours while they went through the boat. Even Harry isn't entirely stupid, you know!"

Wham reappeared in a white sport coat that would have fit a Shetland pony. He downed the proffered Gibson like a spoonful of cough syrup, set the glass on an inlaid hardwood sideboard.

"Ferris, could you keep April company for an hour or so? When I get back, we'll mull wine and the meaning of Christmas."

He kissed April on the forehead and was gone. Ferris was already at the pink telephone dialing a GRaystone number. He stared bleakly out the bay window at the lights of the International Settlement and Chinatown while he talked, listened, swore, and hung up.

"Harry and the Chink used them for batting practice and threw their car keys and their shoes into the harbor."

"That's Harry's weird sense of humor, all right." April tapped her cocktail glass absently against her small dazzling teeth. "Ferris, I *must* find out what sort of game he's playing."

"Why not just divorce him? This is California, with your looks any judge would give you—"

"In that wall safe are the keys to three safe-deposit boxes of undeclared currency *no* judge would give me."

Besner fingered his mustache. "We grab the money and—"

"—and look over our shoulders some dreamy afternoon in Rio and see Harry coming down the beach after us."

Besner shuddered. "What do we do, April?"

She crossed the room with long, sensuous strides. Her gray eyes were level with his blue ones. "Neutralize him. Find your little April a shrewd, tough, unethical P.I. who's a sucker for brunettes." She took his right hand and cupped it around one of her breasts. "Meanwhile, he won't be back for another hour . . ."

Charlie Parker's alto sax was doing things to "Sweet Georgia Brown" no man had ever done before, flying her out to the edge of the solar system on a flurry of diminished fifths. Drinker Cope said, "Bird must of gotten his saxophone out of hock again."

The placed was jammed with colored and white. As they all went wild at the end of the set, a huge craggy-faced man sat down uninvited at their table. His formidable belly was out over his belt, his suit coat was strained around a massive torso.

"This place taken?" he growled.

"Fuck off, asshole," snapped Drinker.

The man grabbed up Drinker's glass to sniff it. "There's booze in this drink!" he roared, and plopped a heavy gold SFPD inspector's shield down on the table. Bottles began disappearing as if by magic. "Show me some ID, mister, and damned quick!"

"How about I show you the back of my lap?"

Both men started to laugh, wrung one another's hand. The bottles were reappearing at adjacent tables.

"Dunc, this is my old SFPD partner, Wee Jimmy Haggerty. Jimmy, my associate, Pierce Duncan." It was like shaking hands with a two-by-six oak plank. Drinker was paying the waitress for more setups from a large roll of bills. He said to Wee Jimmy, "I'm surprised Colleen would let you out on this holy night."

"Jesus Mary and Joseph, first it was midnight Mass at the cathedral, and then it was to be trimming the tree, so I told herself I had to check on a couple of suspects." He drank spiked Coke and roared with laughter. "And be jaysus, here ye both be!"

Lee Fong stopped the Cadillac directly across from a narrow alley called Old Chinatown Lane. The few pedestrians were all Chinese, the parked cars were beaded with night mist that had settled in the last hour. Harry Wham opened his door, paused.

"You go on home, Lee," he said.

"I park on Stockton, wait for you, boss."

"I'll be at least an hour, maybe two."

"I wait for you, boss."

Harry got out, disappeared into the shadows of Chinatown.

Five-thirty Christmas morning and Dunc had to go to the bathroom, really bad, but didn't want to miss Bird, who had landed on "Scrapple from the Apple" and wouldn't leave. Wee Jimmy Haggerty and Drinker Cope were reminiscing about their police department days, and Dunc didn't want to miss that, either.

"That elevator at the Hall of Justice still get stuck between floors?" Drinker turned to Dunc in explanation. "The felony tank is down on the ground floor, but three, four cops and one felon, they take the elevator up to the court floor."

"Only it stalls between floors," explained Wee Jimmy.

"The felon leaves the first floor pleading innocent, by the time he gets to court, he's beggin' them to plead him guilty."

"Rolled newspapers across the kidneys," chortled Wee Jimmy.

The set was finished; Dunc got unsteadily to his feet.

"Gotta tap a kidney of my own," he told them solemnly.

He had just unzipped in front of one of the urinals when a woman six-three in her three-inch silver heels sashayed in. Jet-black hair danced around her broad *café au lait* face in saucy shimmering ringlets. A skintight silver-sequined dress showed cantaloupe breasts, ripe race-horse buttocks. Her eyelashes were an inch long, her mouth, impossibly juicy, impossibly red, was half a foot wide, her fingernails three inches long and even shinier red than the outrageous mouth.

Dunc scuttled to the door, jerked it open, craned around to see what was written on the outside. MEN. He pulled back in.

"You all right, honey," the woman exclaimed in a rumbling basso voice. "You in the right place."

Dunc *had* to relieve his aching bladder; he returned to the farther of the two urinals. The Amazon hunkered up to the adjoining urinal and flipped up her skirt, pulled down the front of her white lace panties, and from a massive set of masculine equipment directed her own stallion-like stream into her urinal. As she did, she looked over at Dunc and winked.

"Jes our little secret 'twixt us girls."

When Dunc staggered back to the table, Drinker and Wee Jimmy were laughing even harder than the transvestite. "Jesus, the look on your face when you stuck your head out of the door to check which crapper you were in . . ."

"I need a drink," croaked Dunc.

Chapter Forty-one

Desk work today. Dunc was trying to track down a man who lived on a Chinese junk moored out in the middle of the Sausalito harbor and might or might not have been involved in a drunken hit-and-run accident on Christmas Eve.

Drink and the Devil had done for the rest . . .

Dunc was still queasy from his own Christmas Eve. Better ask Sherry how to find the guy and get him to admit liability.

As he walked up to Sherry's desk, a woman came up the stairs. She wore a gray tailored suit to match her eyes, white gloves, high-heeled gray shoes, and a flat little ecru hat.

She told Dunc, "Surely you're not Edward Cope."

"Surely not," he agreed.

She turned to Sherry. "April Wham for Mr. Cope."

Sherry headed for Drinker's office. No intercom for this baby, thought Dunc. Wham, bam, thank you ma'am. Drinker appeared in his doorway. April Wham drifted that way.

Drinker bowed slightly. "Mrs. Wham."

He closed the door, April was already seated and crossing her legs. Instant lust warmed Drinker Cope's cold heart. From her silver-clasped gray purse she took a silver cigarette case and a silver lighter, extracted a Herbert Tarryton. Drinker almost lunged across the desk to light it for her.

Back at her desk, Sherry was looking daggers at the door.

"She's trouble," she said. Dunc was going to make a crack about trouble being their business, but Sherry went on, "I know her type. I. Magnin originals, Joy at a hundred bucks an ounce..." She sat down, gave an angry toss of her head, and lit a cigarette. "Okay, what did you want to ask me about, kid?"

In Drinker's office April was looking at him through her drifting cigarette smoke. Her eyes were very limpid and direct.

"Would it shock you if I said I loathe my husband?"

Drinker waved a dismissive hand. She nodded.

"I want you to find out all about Harry—Harry Wham, my husband. He had what you men call a good war—marine captain in the Pacific island-hopping campaign, a chestful of medals."

She ground out her cigarette very carefully, every spark.

"We've been married for three years. After the war he lived in China, came to San Francisco four years ago with that ridiculous name, money, and many oriental friends. He says he's an engineer but doesn't work at it. No office, no clients, his only employee a Chinese boy named Lee Fong. They spend a lot of time on Harry's motor yacht looking for sunken Spanish galleons."

"I thought Spain's galleons sank in the Caribbean."

"Harry says there was a vast trade from the Orient across the Pacific—gold, jade, immensely valuable vases and pottery. Across the Isthmus of Panama by Indian slaves, transshipped from the Gulf of Mexico to Spain."

Drinker felt stirrings of something other than lust.

"I think he takes a woman with him. I'll pay you five thousand to find out who she is, what she does, where he goes."

Drinker said, "Five hundred, not five thousand, would do it. I think you're more intelligent than that, Mrs. Wham."

She said without hesitation, "There isn't any other woman. Harry's past is completely hidden except for his war stories, and I can't even find out if *they're* true or not."

"I did a little island-hopping myself with the Marines," Drinker said in an almost dreamy voice. "Demolitions man, I blew a lot of Japs to hell and gone out of their little caves. I even knew a few captains with their chests full of medals. One of them saved my life once."

"If you're saying you don't want to—"

"I'm saying I'll know where to look for his war record."

"*Harry Wham!*" she exclaimed. "Where did he get that—Marvel Comics? The gold hunting must be a front for something illegal. I want to know what it is."

"Not the whole story but better," said Drinker. "I'll need a thousand now and a picture of Harry. In this town the Chinese complicate everything."

"I don't have a picture." She was counting out hundreds. "But you won't need one. He's an enormous man with shaggy blond hair. The Chinese boy looks like any other Chinese boy. Harry berths his cruiser at the St. Francis Yacht Club. The *Doubloon.*" Her clear gray eyes met his. He felt their impact in his groin. "I want you to work this personally, full-time, you alone."

"Me alone," he lied.

He walked her to the door. Her perfume still lingered. Someone had told her he would do most things for a quick buck, and that he had a weakness for smart sultry brunettes with the kind of legs that would turn him stupid at just the right time.

Unless April Wham had figured that one out for herself.

He shook his head and said "Whew!" under his breath.

Lying in the sunshine along the dock in Gas House Cove at the blunt end of the Marina Green, the broad-beamed ketch *Marie* reminded Dunc of a battered club fighter who still had a good right hook. The old salt filling the kitchen chair by the wheel had his feet on the after-gunnel and a can of beer in one hand.

So far, seven interviews, seven big fat zeros. Overhead a brown and white gull dipped and cried raucously. The slatted quay sank under

Dunc's weight, sloshing water up between the boards. It was warm for
San Francisco in December.

The old salt had gray-shot whiskers and the far-sighed blue eyes of
a deep-water sailor. The black briar pipe clenched between his strong
yellow teeth was upside down.

Dunc squatted on the dock. "Why upside down?" he asked.

"Won't get put out in a squall. Shove that dottle down in there
with your thumb real good afore you light her, she'll do."

"Nice boat."

"Hell she is. Wouldn't make it from here to the breakwater with a
following wind. I'm MacDougal. Mac'll do."

"Dunc. Do you live aboard?"

The old man guzzled beer. "You from a quiz show?"

"*Call-Bulletin,* working on a story. I thought you'd probably know
all the interesting yachtsmen around here."

"Interesting yachtsmen like who?"

"I heard a guy at the St. Francis hunts for Spanish gold with his
motor launch. Harry Wham, his boat's the *Doubloon.*"

Mac gave a single burst of laughter like the bark of a seal. "What'd
an old man like me know about them rich folks?"

"Everything," said Dunc.

He rolled a ten-dollar bill into a cylinder, leaned forward to poke
it halfway down a punch hole in the top of the beer can.

"Y're a cutie. What d'ya want, son?"

"Whatever you've got worth ten bucks."

Mac drank beer out of the punch hole without a greenback in it.
"He goes out with the Chink six days exactly. Maybe three times every
two months. The *Doubloon's* forty-two foot, draws four and a half,
looks slow but ain't. Shortwave radio, ship-to-shore phone, even a
phonograph, f'God's sake! Has two British Spitfire engines in her.
She'll take anything on this coast."

Dunc asked, "That include cutters?"

"Includes anything, gov'ment or otherwise. Also he's got a Chicago
typewriter and grenades behind a false bulkhead for'ard." He shut one

eye and tipped his head back as if commenting on the weather. "She could make Mexico and back in six days, easy."

"Did you say Mexico?"

"Come around when you ain't working, son, I'll tell you some lies you don't have to pay for."

Dunc had just finished the day's report when the phone rang. He picked up, answered, "Edward Cope Investigations."

Penny's voice, full of laughter and delight, said, "Your Christmas present arrives tomorrow afternoon on the two-thirty plane from Chicago. I told Mom I had to go back to school early, aren't I an awful person?"

"A wonderful person. I'll pick you up at the airport."

"I'll have to fly back to school on Sunday, but we get New Year's Eve together. What should I bring to wear?"

"Anything—sexy underwear. Nothing." He laughed into the phone in sheer delight. "Yeah, that's it—nothing!"

He sat with the phone in his hand and a goofy grin on his face. *Tomorrow* he would hold her in his arms. *Tomorrow* . . .

Finished report in hand, he resolutely strode to Drinker's private office. Couldn't be helped. He knocked, went in.

Drinker shut his file folder and glared up at him. "Yeah?"

"The yacht is designed to outrun anything on the West Coast, including the Coast Guard, and Harry Wham and Lee Fong go to Mexico once a month, six days round trip . . ." He paused; Drinker had almost leaped to his feet to jerk the completed report from Dunc's hand. "And I need five days off."

Drinker looked up from his reading. "Five . . . No fucking way! You've worked here maybe three months. If you think—"

"My girl's flying in tomorrow from back east."

Subtly Drinker's expression lightened. "The girl at the picnic, what was her name, Peggy?"

"Penny. Penny Linden."

"Nice-looking kid. You stuck on her?"

Dunc felt himself coloring up. "Well, you know—"

"You're stuck on her. Back in here Monday morning, early. And call in, tell Sherry where we can reach you in an emergency."

The Richelieu Hotel was on the corner of Geary across Van Ness from Tommy's Joynt. Just the sound of Penny's voice on the phone, the knowledge that she would be in his arms tomorrow—*tomorrow!*— giving him twinges of excitement as he asked at the registration desk for a double for five days.

"Make it something . . . nice," he said. "Something special."

Chapter Forty-two

The room at the Richelieu really wasn't anything special, but, bathed in the warm diffuse late afternoon light, it was made to seem so by the dozen red roses on the round writing table under the window. Their fragrance filled the room.

"Oh, Dunc! They're so beautiful and they smell wonderful!"

She threw herself into his arms there in the middle of the room beside her suitcase and cosmetic case. The embrace warmed to kisses then leaped to fire. Beneath her skirt she wore a black lace garter belt to hold up her stockings, nothing else.

He picked her up and carried her over to the bed with her legs locked around his hips. He didn't put her down that first time, neither of them even undressed.

It was nearly midnight when Dunc went over to Tommy's Joynt to bring back buffalo stew. When he returned he thought the small snuggled shape had fallen asleep. He undressed by the bathroom's dim golden light, and lifted the covers to slide his naked body in beside hers. She gave her marvelous laugh and rolled to meet him, fully awake, her eyes great joyous wells in the semidarkness, her legs opening to receive him.

At midnight Drinker Cope got out of Sherry's bed, careful not to wake her. She made a little mewing sound and snuggled deeper into the covers. Drinker went to the window, nude, smoked a cigarette looking out over the semisleeping city.

Thinking of April, he had gone off like a skyrocket. April obsessed him, even though he saw through her to some grand design of her own. He didn't even have to learn what it was, she would put it in motion soon enough.

"Drinker?" In the dim light Sherry was up on one elbow, watching him. "You're thinking about Wham-Bam, aren't you?"

"Oh, for Chrissake! I'm thinking about her husband." He sat down on the edge of the bed, put his hand on the swell of her hip. "How to get our hands on some of the guy's money . . ."

"We don't need it, Drinker. Dunc's working out great—"

"Go back to sleep, Sherry."

He kept his hand on her hip until her breathing evened, then went back to the window. Damn right, Dunc was working out great. He felt bad about screwing the kid out of his share of the loot from Kiely's safe-deposit box back there in Kansas City, but the K.C. cop had been greedy. Besides, Drinker had given the kid a job, paid him good wages.

His mind returned to April. He was going to possess her, get his pound of flesh, and go after her husband. Meanwhile . . .

He woke Sherry, used her again, savagely, punishing her because she wasn't the woman who obsessed him. Then he slept.

Since it was New Year's Eve, Drinker got to the Customs House at 555 Battery early to catch Gar Cheevers behind his desk. Gar was career civil service, dry and precise and incorruptible, horn-rim glasses set low on his nose, his desk half covered with framed photos of his wife, his dog, his five kids in various stages of growth at their modest summer cabin up on the Russian River.

Incorruptible, sure, but there was corruption and there was corruption. Drinker had pulled one of Gar's daughters out of that same river one summer before she could drown, so the man owed him. Drinker took it out in information.

"What's new in the antismuggling trade, Gar?"

"Just the usual, Drinker—drugs and people."

"Much of it done by boat these days?"

"*Boat?* Wetbacks wouldn't be worth the trouble, and the border's so leaky you can just walk the drugs across. We get 'em at the checkpoints if they're amateurs or get nervous, but—"

"Private yachts don't have to go through checkpoints."

"We leave them to the Coast Guard," he said with a chuckle.

"Anything *else* coming across besides wetbacks and dope?"

Gar mentioned gold. Drinker wished him a Happy New Year, went to the huge gray stone main library across the plaza from City Hall to spend three hours in the reference room, then to Western Union to send a long night letter to a man in Ensenada.

Dunc and Penny spent that morning in bed with the faint perfume of the roses lying over them like a new snowfall, talking, talking, voracious for each other's lives.

For Dunc, deer hunting in northern Minnesota with his dad, one year he had gotten two bucks with two shots. Football. Fishing. Duck hunting at the shack on the Mississippi.

Penny's dad had been killed in an industrial accident three months before she was born; her mom used his union insurance to open a coffee shop in a downtown Dubuque hotel and, working fourteen-hour days, had eventually sent Penny to college.

"We're from the same kind of people, middle-class, Midwest, hardworking, Dunc. We'll have to meet each other's mom soon."

"Soon—but not now."

Oh no, not now. Now the sudden sharp stab of passion . . .

In the afternoon they bought fried chicken and climbed down the bluffs on Land's End for a picnic on a minuscule beach of bright sand. Back at the motel to change for a New Year's Eve celebration, they made love in the shower, and ended up seeing in 1954 without leaving their bed.

New Year's Day, Dunc showed her his sorry little room and intro-

duced her to Ma Booger, then up to the office to show her that, like
a proud parent showing off his kids.

"What about your writing, Dunc?"

"I'm getting lots of material for the notebooks . . ."

"And not writing it down in them."

"I'm keeping copies of my reports for the right time . . ."

On Saturday they went into the great glass Victorian conservatory
in Golden Gate Park, and found themselves alone in the high-domed
main room that was like a small, intense, steaming jungle; they played
Tarzan and Jane in the dripping tropical foliage. Then went back to
the Richelieu to play it for real.

Their last dinner together was at Alfred's Steakhouse up beside the
Broadway Tunnel, huge rare T-bones with garlic toast and baked potatoes and green salads and beer, since Dunc didn't know anything
about wine.

And so to bed. But not, for a long time, to sleep.

It was a blustery day at San Francisco International Airport, with
isolated rain squalls running across the blacktop runways. Winter had
returned to San Francisco.

They kissed a last time. "Keep up the notebook!" Penny whispered,
then with a squeeze she was gone.

On the drive back from the airport, memories came crowding in on
Dunc, surprisingly few of them sexual. He had showed her his city.
Before too many months he knew she would return.

And then? Then . . . they would just be together. That was all they
needed. He would write and try to sell his stories, she would work.
They'd eaten at the Fleur de Lis in Sutter Street, where she had talked
with the French chef about cooking. He'd never had an apprentice,
but *peut-être* . . .

Meanwhile, going through the now-driving rain on the Bayshore,
he felt the first stirrings of renewed excitement about the Wham case.
Look out, Harry, he thought, here I come.

Since it was paid for, he slept a last night in their room at the

Richelieu. He could still smell Penny's scent on the sheets, her perfume and soap in the bathroom. The roses still bloomed bravely by the window, their fragrance a benison. He took them back to Ma Booger's and kept them until they were dried and withered.

Chapter Forty-three

It was not until two weeks later that Drinker Cope brought him back into the Harry Wham chess game. While Dunc interviewed potential witnesses for an upcoming trial, and tailed an errant wife three times to her meetings with her lover at a Geneva Street motel, Drinker was working Harry Wham hard, including an international wireless and a long detailed letter to Hong Kong.

Dunc was glad that operatives who specialized in divorce work burst in to flash-photo the cheaters naked in bed, not he. What if someone had come smashing in like that on him and Penny at the Richelieu?

Then Drinker finally put him back on Wham. "My man in Ensenada says Harry and the Chink are coming in from Mexico tomorrow on his yacht. Talk to that old sailor pal of yours—I want you to eyeball Wham coming in, then I want you to stick to Harry like glue."

"I haven't done much tailing—what if he spots me?"

"Just make sure he doesn't."

"Jesus, thanks, Drinker—great advice."

Dunc, in navy watch cap and heavy blue wool pea jacket, secretly afraid of getting seasick, stood on deck as the *Marie* sailed out under the Golden Gate Bridge, and kept his eyes on the horizon as

Mac had suggested. His queasiness soon passed. He used Drinker's binoculars to pick out the place beneath the bluffs where he and Penny had picnicked. It would be green and full of wildflowers by Easter. Their long letters had crossed in the mail, and they had talked on the phone twice.

"Them're damn good glasses, them coated lenses don't reflect the light." Mac grinned slyly. "You'll be able to watch Mr. Harry Wham whamming in the nude."

"Erg," said Dunc, and made a face, and they both laughed.

They hove-to in the lee of the Farallones, stark black shapes alive with restless squawking seabirds rising like ghostly frigates from the frothing water. In the cramped, tidy cabin Mac poured two thick white mugs full of tea as black as sin.

"The *Marie* is named after my wife. She's dead now, God love her, but we sailed the seven seas, we two together, in this old boat . . ."

An hour before sunset the *Doubloon* met with an innocuous-seeming fishing boat. They watched with the glasses from the shelter of the Farallones half a mile away as Wham handed over two heavy boxes. Mac passed the glasses to Dunc. "*Flying Fish*, ties up at Pier 45 near Fisherman's Wharf. They'll move them boxes late tonight after all the tourists have gone home, probably in fish crates."

"How do you know so much about smuggling, Mac?"

His only response was a wink. It was after dark when he maneuvered battered old *Marie* back into her berth at Gas House Cove. Dunc paid him in cash, dashed to a pay phone to call Drinker Cope and tell him, two boxes, *Flying Fish*, Pier 45.

"I'll cover the boxes, you catch up with Wham and see where he goes. Stick close to him after you make contact."

Dunc left Grey Ghost Two near Portsmouth Square to follow the tall Caucasian by foot through teeming Chinatown streets. Wham ducked into one-block Waverly Place, a narrow alley full of dark shadows. Dunc went down five steps to knock on a door with a faint penumbra of light showing under it. When a short dumpy middle-aged Chinese man in a dark suit and ornate vest answered, the light sent their shadows jumping crookedly up the stairs.

"Sorry," he said. His eyes were almost lost in his moon face. "Is Chinese American Club, is members only permitted."

"Harry Wham. He just came in here."

"Sorry. No Wham here." He started to close the door.

Dunc's foot was in it. "Big blond white guy. Wham."

He suddenly kicked Dunc's foot away, exclaimed "Wham!" in gold-toothed merriment, and slammed the door.

Disgruntled, Dunc went up the steps. He caught movement and got his guard up in time to block a slashing knife hand that numbed his forearm. He blindly fired a left jab where the attacker's jaw ought to be, hit only air.

They shuffled cautiously, able to see only shadows. A foot came flying sideways toward his gut. He turned to take it on the hip, spun back with a good right cross to send Lee Fong crashing into the garbage pails with a clatter and surprised grunt.

Bearlike arms encircled Dunc from behind, pinning his arms to his sides and driving his breath out in one massive *whoosh!* He whimpered, thrashed erratically, let himself go dead-weight. The arms loosened, he tore free, but a fist like a foot knocked him sprawling against the rough brick wall. He ran.

At Grant and California he bent over the mist-wet black iron railing at Old St. Mary's Church, panting, trying to get his breath back. His coat was ripped and his hands skinned; grease blotched one trouser leg. A cable car disgorged a brace of Chinese girls wearing tight skirts slit halfway up their thighs. They passed Dunc giggling to turn in at the Pink Pagoda.

He followed unsteadily, seeking a pay phone. Drinker picked up on the first ring, heard him out. "I didn't tell you to climb in the guy's hip pocket, for Chrissake. Anything broken?"

"Only my spirit."

"Okay, go stake out the alley."

*   *   *

Drinker hung up and the phone rang. It was April Wham.

"Harry just called from Half Moon Bay, he said he'd had trouble with the *Doubloon* and wouldn't be home tonight. He—"

"Harry's here in the City, not down the coast. I was out by the Farallones today to watch him come back from Mexico and tailed him to an alley in Chinatown. Waverly Place, something calls itself the Chinese American Club. Do you know it?"

"No, of course not. What—"

"We can't talk over the phone. I'll come up there—"

"*No!*" Very emphatic. "We'll have to meet somewhere else."

So she had someone there with her. Probably Ferris Besner.

"The Bocce Ball Cafe," he told her. "Twenty minutes."

Operatic arias sung full-voice by some of the City's best professionals pulled people into the Bocce Ball off upper Broadway. Bartenders, waitresses, waiters, busboys—all had been hired because they had operatic aspirations; many of them sang in the chorus of the San Francisco Opera. Several times a night they would serenade the customers with arias, duets, trios.

April came through the door in a slinky skintight green silk sheath, just as, outside, a halted diesel Grey Lines Nightlife Tour bus had its doors levered open fore and aft. She slid onto a stool next to Drinker's.

In a low voice, she said, "Tell me, quickly, what's he up to?"

Half a hundred giggling tourists rushed toward the little round tables to fulfill their one-drink minimums. Few would ever see fifty again. The din was atrocious. The waiters began sobbing out "O Sole Mio" to accompanying accordions.

Drinker grunted as if he had been kicked in the stomach, grabbed his beer bottle with one hand, April's arm with the other, and headed for a heavy hardwood door in the back wall.

Beyond it and down two steps was a long dim quiet room housing two bocce ball courts of hard-packed clay. During the day, North Beach's old Italian men sat on the benches lining the walls to gossip and evaluate, with great solemnity, the quality of the play. Now, at one in the morning, the courts were deserted, the benches bare. Only the slightest shadows of song and clatter made it through the heavy oak door.

April sat down on one of the benches. "Why were you out by the Farallones?" she demanded with an impatience meant to dominate the situation. "What was Harry doing in Mexico?"

"Your hubby makes regular six-day trips to Baja." Drinker stood over her with one foot cocked on the worn oak beside her thigh in symbolic imprisonment. "His Spanish-gold routine struck me as a perfect smuggling cover. After a while the Coast Guard chalks him up as a harmless nut and quits checking him out."

"Harry's too smart to get involved in anything like that."

He gave her his big insincere grin. "Wetbacks or drugs, sure. But why is his cruiser outfitted for trouble and fast enough to outrun anything around, even cutters?"

"He likes expensive toys, he always wants the best."

"Maybe so, but this afternoon he transferred two heavy cartons to a fishing boat outside the three-mile limit so the *Doubloon* could come in clean."

"What was in those boxes, Drinker? Where are they now?"

He looked at his watch. "I might have more for you in a couple of hours, April." He detached a key from his ring. "This is for my flat. Go there and wait for me."

"Why your flat? Tell me what you know right now, and confirm it later." Drinker just shook his head. Her lip curled cynically. "You want it all, don't you, darling?"

He remained silent, a monolith towering above her. She stood. Smiled. Drew a fingernail along the line of his jaw. It burned like dry ice against his skin.

"I have to go home and get my overnight case first."

"Just so you're there when I get there."

*   *   *

A battle-scarred tomcat groomed itself on the lid of one of the garbage pails behind which Dunc had stashed himself to watch the Waverly Place doorway. Half an hour after bar-close, headlights swung across the rough brick wall opposite him. A panel truck stopped with its motor running. Two Chinese males started pulling an obviously heavy FRESH FISH crate out of the back. One lost his grip; the crate landed corner-first to spill out one of the boxes Dunc had seen transferred from the *Doubloon*.

Muttering in Chinese, they lugged the box down the steps to the door which the portly Oriental held open. After the second crate was moved without mishap, they drove off.

Dunc rose creaking from his awkward crouch. The cat hissed away into the shadow. He went in search of a pay phone, but Drinker Cope was waiting outside a darkened chophouse across Clay Street from the alley mouth.

He told Dunc, "I followed the truck from Pier 45."

"Which just delivered to the Chinese American Club the same boxes I saw off-loaded out by the Farallones this afternoon."

"Perfect. Go home and lick your wounds."

"If it's all the same to you, I'll take a shower first."

Just after three in the morning Drinker Cope keyed his apartment door. He smelled coffee. A pulse beat heavily in his throat. April, curled up on the couch in a filmy dressing gown and puffy slippers, had come to her feet at his entry.

"The coffee's strong and hot," she said. "You can tell me what's in those boxes in the kitchen . . ."

"I can tell you all about them in the morning."

Her eyes flashed as if she were about to strike him; then the tension left her. She leaned against him like a stuffed toy.

"Aren't you going to leave the lady with any illusions?"

"The lady doesn't need any."

Drinker Cope put his arms around her, his eyes burning hungrily as he bent his face to hers.

Chapter Forty-four

Dunc grabbed a quick workout in the Y's weight room, took some steam to iron out the kinks from last night's dustup, and got to the office just after 8:00 A.M. Sherry handed him a memo.

"Your lucky Penny called twice, she's at this number."

It was Penny's sorority house pay phone. Dunc mumbled his thanks, from his desk asked the operator for time and charges.

When Penny answered, he said, "Hi, this is Dunc, I got—"

"Oh, darling! I've been hanging around here in the hall, going crazy." She got her lips closer to the phone. "Dunc, I . . . I missed my period. I'm almost three weeks overdue."

He sat in stunned silence, unable for a moment to breathe.

"Dunc, are you there?"

"Yes, I . . . I . . . What do . . . I mean, maybe you're not. Maybe it's just . . ."

"I . . . I made a doctor's appointment, I'll let you know what he says." She turned away for a moment, came back with her voice even lower, very rapid. "There are girls waiting to use the phone, I've got to go." In a lighter voice she said, "I'm sure you're right," in a whisper added, "Bye. Love you, darling."

Somehow he got out "Love you, too" before the dial tone.

He sat behind his desk, too shocked to really think about what she had told him, just running fervid phrases through his mind: Please God, oh please please please, dear God . . .

You may not recognize the opportunity when it arrives, but when the time comes you'll say, "This is it!" and you'll do it.

He went into the Greek's, ordered tea, sat at a rear table facing the wall. He took out the rosary, fingered the beads. That was another thing about rosaries. They eliminated certain alternatives from the equation . . .

Bright slanting morning sunlight woke Drinker Cope. April slept on her side, one creamy shoulder uncovered, face angelic in its relaxed beauty. He pulled on a robe, carried her purse into the living room and rummaged through it. A snapshot stopped him cold: April and a man with a broad good-natured face dominated by a strong nose, set under a mop of bright unruly hair.

A long shudder ran through Drinker's smooth, thick hide. He put the photo in the pocket of the robe, replaced the purse.

He bought breakfast things and a quart of milk at the little mom-and-pop down on the corner of Union. Back up at his second-floor flat, April was in the kitchen in her dressing gown, just brewing coffee. They ate in the old-fashioned breakfast nook; across Gough Street, the Octagon House basked in winter sunlight. April put unexpected perkiness in her voice.

"You promised that this morning you would unlock the riddle of my sphinx of a husband."

He rebuffed her coyness with cold brevity.

"If you weren't such a lousy wife, you might have realized sooner or later that what was in those two heavy cartons you were so steamed up about last night was just what Harry's always telling anybody who will listen."

Now her coldness matched his own. "You're buying that? Spanish doubloons and sunken treasure?"

"No. Gold." He spread opened hands on the table. "Just remember that he stayed on in China after the war, where to millions of Chinese gold means life itself—gold and nothing else."

"Spare me, *puhlees!* Gold is frozen at thirty-five dollars an ounce, small potatoes for a guy like Harry."

"In this country, yeah."

All animation left her face. "He's found out about you," she said with conviction. "Now he's conning you in some way, or . . ." She was on her feet, striding, fiery. "Or you've . . ."

"Yeah, I've sold you out. Get serious. Now, for Chrissake, siddown and listen. We're not talking about this country, we're talking about China—and Mexico."

She glared at him for a moment, then dropped back into her chair. She lit another cigarette. Drinker marked off points.

"One. There's plenty of gold in Baja, and plenty of old prospectors to bring it out to the coast for American dollars. Two. On mainland China the Commies need gold in lieu of hard currency. Three. Wealthy Chinese are smuggling gold to Hong Kong. Four. From there, it gets smuggled again to their relatives back in the old country who need it to bribe their way out if they can, or to keep on living if they can't."

"So why would they need Harry?"

"The Chinese can't go to Mexico themselves for the gold, but Harry can. Handsome, Caucasian, good war record—I bet he's got maps of sunken galleons he shows all over the place."

"Yes, as a matter of fact, he can be very boring at parties. But why would the Chinese trust him? Or he them?"

"I think he does it for old friends from after the war."

Her eyes got flat and vicious as if the concept offended her. "Nobody takes that sort of risk just for friendship."

"Maybe not you or me, but . . ." He chuckled. "I have a feeling Harry Wham would. You can't turn him in as a smuggler for the reward. If you report him, everything he owns—everything *you* own under community property laws—gets impounded along with the gold. So I can't see what else I can do for you, April dearest."

She went around behind his chair, put her arms around his neck, pressed her cheek to his. She used the same phrase she had with Besner. "I want him neutralized."

He gave a bark of laughter.

"Neutralized? You want him dead."

The word hung between them in the air like smoke from her cigarette, almost palpable, almost visible. He went right on.

"What makes you think I'm available for that kind of work? Ferris telling you I'll do damn near anything for money? How do I know you're not just looking for a fall guy?"

She slapped his face, hard, turned on her heel, and stalked out of the room. A very dangerous woman, April, but she had read him right. Eddie Cope always got his pound of flesh. He followed her into the bedroom and shut the door.

Dunc knew what he couldn't do, but what *should* he do if Penny was pregnant? He tried to concentrate on his witness interviews. The instant he lost his concentration, his thoughts deteriorated into panicked babbling in his mind.

Please, dear sweet loving Jesus, let her not be pregnant . . .

Drinker would say: tell her to get an abortion. He'd even know someone who would do it. Or he would say, dump her. How do you know she hasn't been sleeping around back there at Iowa State? No way to be sure the kid is yours.

But this was one problem he'd never take to Drinker. Penny loved him, they were faithful to one another. He was thinking only of himself here; what must she be going through right now?

Back at his room, sitting on the edge of his bed, he thought of his writing. Even now, that had to come first. Ultimately there was nothing he wanted to be except a writer. With a baby, that dream would be gone. He'd end up like those college professors who "someday" would write the great American novel. On the other hand, he wasn't alone. There was Hemingway in Paris with a wife and baby, back in the twenties.

His thoughts kept colliding, he kept grappling with them, ignoring Mickey, crouched farther away from him on the counter than usual. As if everything roiling through Dunc's mind was a betrayal of all that was small and vulnerable.

On the desk was the green blotter, on the blotter were Drinker's elbows. Within easy reach was a bottle of Jim Beam.

Drinker asked the empty office, "Optimist or pessimist? Is the bottle half-full or half-empty?"

The office answered not. He poured Beam, fired it down. He just wanted the dilemma to go away. It wasn't going to.

On one side was April. When he'd entered the bedroom after she'd slapped his face, she was nude, caught between negligee and underwear in the middle of getting dressed, and swung around to face him, eyes blazing. But then she simply fell back on the bed, arms and legs wide, totally open to him. Taking her had been the most erotic experience of a long sinful life. His back still burned where her claws had raked him when she'd come.

Beautiful, insatiable, immoral, greedy April.

On the other side, her husband.

No contest. Except . . .

He gulped from the neck of the bottle, wiped his mouth with the back of his hand. On his blotter he laid two photos side by side. The one he'd found in her wallet. And an old, faded, tattered black-and-white snapshot of a very large man in marine fatigues with a captain's double bars on his shoulders. Dark unruly hair and a big nose, the face half masked by light and shadow laid across it from jungle foliage overhead.

"Too goddamn close to call," he said at last as if he were studying the photo finish of a horse race.

This faded snap was all he had of the marine who had saved his life on Iwo Jima eight years before. What kind of odds would make him Harry Wham? Even if he was Harry, did it make any difference? Marines were trained to carry their dead and wounded off the battleground with them. You could say that Drinker's life had been saved not by a man, but by a conditioned reflex.

"Goddammit," he said aloud.

The phone rang. "Drinker," April's voice purred in his ear, "guess who's waiting all naked in your bed?"

He hung up without speaking, put the bottle back in its drawer, picked up the photos—and crumpled them in his fist. On the way to his car he dropped them in a corner trash can.

Chapter Forty-five

Dunc served subpoenas and worked himself closer and closer to a self-righteous decision about what he would do if Penny turned out to be pregnant. When he trudged up the office stairs two mornings after her call, Sherry was waiting to pounce, her normally cynical eyes hot and angry.

"Dunc, you got a minute?"

Sitting beside her desk was a slight woman in a summer blouse and peasant skirt too light for winter. Her mousy-brown hair was streaked with blond and her narrow face had a delicate pointed chin that was bruised and swollen on one side. The skin around her left eye was a faded mustard color. Another bruise was visible above the collar of her high-necked blouse.

"Dunc, this is Julia Demchuk—Mrs. Stanley Demchuk. Her husband is a journeyman machinist at Kleist Tool and Die down in the Mission. As you can see, he's good with his hands."

"Glad to meet you, ma'am," Dunc said awkwardly.

Julia Demchuk bobbed her head at him, quickly.

"Mrs. Demchuk's pastor has advised her to move out of their apartment. She can stay with two girlfriends from work who have a big flat out in the Avenues near the V.A. Hospital."

Julia raised her head. "I'm afraid what he'll do if he comes home when I'm . . . when I'm packing up my . . . my things."

Sherry said, "Julia, hon, why don't you go down and wait in

Dunc's car?" Julia left with Dunc's keys. Sherry said, "Her hubby keeps a collection of porn under the bed. Grab it, okay?"

He didn't know why she wanted it, but he said, "Okay."

It was a third-floor walkup at Hyde and Jones, with a liquor store underneath. Dunc parked two doors down. Julia insisted on taking only her clothes and personal items; he carried them downstairs and locked them in the trunk of the car.

Julia came out of the bathroom with a shoe box full of cosmetics when Dunc came out of the bedroom with the cardboard box of porn. Nothing erotic or artistic about them, just people pumping away. She dropped the shoe box, flushing bright scarlet.

"No! No, oh please . . . You mustn't . . ."

Dunc was blushing by this time, too, but he said, "He's the one to be ashamed, Julia, not you. Let's get out of here."

A key turned in the lock. Dunc thrust Julia behind him. Stanley Demchuk was like another Stanley—Kowalski in *A Streetcar Named Desire*. Marlon Brando in a torn T-shirt. This guy was in a leather jacket and jeans and metal-toed work boots. He reeked of booze and his eyes were red and a bit unfocused.

"Hey, who the fuck're . . ." Then he saw his white-faced wife behind Dunc. He roared, "*Julia!* What're you an' him—"

"She's moving out," said Dunc.

"The fuck she is."

He put an unexpected hand in Dunc's face, shoved him aside, starting for his wife. Dunc swung him around, put a foot in the small of his back—and shoved with all his might.

Demchuk crashed face-first into the couch. Dunc squeezed his keys into Julia's free hand, pushed her toward the door.

"Go! Lock yourself in the car."

Demchuk bellowed and scrambled to his feet. But Dunc was between him and the door and was a lot bigger than his wife. He skidded to a stop. Cunning entered his bloated red face.

"I'm swearing out a warrant against you, wise guy. Come in here, take my wife, attack me . . ."

"I'm a licensed private investigator, protecting her while she exercises her constitutional rights."

"Shit, you think I won't find her? And when I do—"

"We'll take photos of you following her around," said Dunc. "We'll put a listening device on her phone so we'll have you on wire. We'll get court orders, we'll haul your ass up before a judge and"— he showed Demchuk the box of smut—"introduce all this shit into evidence with your fingerprints all over it."

"Hey, listen, you can't—"

Dunc simulated masturbating with his right fist. "The guys at the machine shop'll get a kick out of going through it. Unless . . ." He paused. "We understand each other?"

Demchuk choked out a strangled "Yeah."

Driving Julia to her new home, Dunc realized how smart Sherry was. He shuddered. Was this where marriages ended up? He gestured at the carton of porn on the backseat, said to Julia, "When you file for divorce, use that stuff in court."

"Oh, I could never do that!"

But there was a new speculative gleam in her eye. Who was it had said that getting even was the best revenge?

He had been back in the office for five minutes, regaling Sherry with his exploits and feeling almost human again, when the phone rang and it was Penny. He went back to his desk, sat down, heart pounding. Made himself breathe deeply and easily to keep all tremors out of his voice, then picked up.

Her voice was small, frightened. "I . . . had the rabbit test and . . . it was positive."

Dunc just sat there, unable to speak, move, think, breathe.

"Dunc?" An edge of terror in her voice. "Dunc? Are you there? Say something, honey, I . . ."

He'd rehearsed it in his mind often enough. Just do it. Quickly.

Brutally. Five utterly horrible minutes and he was home free. But the dam burst, she was pouring it all out, low intense words, getting them out before they stuck in her throat.

"Dunc, I . . . we . . . have to get married real quick—so when our baby's born it'll just seem like it's a month early. It would kill my mom to know I was pregnant before . . . out of wedlock. I've got three days of finals, then . . ."

Dunc plunged into his rehearsed speech, instead heard himself saying, "Penny, sweetie, we'll . . . get married as soon as you can get out here. I . . . I'll send you the money for a one-way ticket through Western Union. Okay? Just don't cry, baby."

She got out, "I'm crying 'cause I'm so happy, my darling!"

When they had hung up, he sat there with the phone in his hand, stunned. How had that happened? What had he done?

He straightened up slightly. What he'd had to do.

A great weight shifted from his shoulders—and another settled there. The one that said in a dry, biting voice that he'd never be a writer. His life as a free spirit had just begun, to be ended by a little wiggly sperm, swimming upstream.

Sean set out a glass of hot clam juice as Drinker Cope came through the door of the Old Clam House. Drinker lifted the four-ounce glass in salute, fired down the hot salty liquid. The very air was awash with the briny smell of fresh shellfish.

The walls were crowded with darkened oil paintings, the hardwood floor was worn, hard drinkers studded the bar. The jukebox was sobbing out Eddie Fisher's "Oh My Papa." A woman's glossy jet-black hair just showing above the back of the farthest booth. The stirring in his groin told Drinker who she was.

April was wearing chocolate slacks and a fawn-colored ribbed fisherman's sweater that would have come halfway down her thighs if she were standing up. She got right down to the reason for her call.

"Harry told me he's going out on the *Doubloon* again in just two weeks. March tenth. He said they have a galleon called the *Cinco Lla-*

gas pinpointed somewhere up the coast around Point Arena. It was supposed to be carrying gold and vases and jade."

"D'you have anything on under that getup?"

Her grin was wicked. "For me to know and you to find out. But only if you do something about Harry."

"Oh My Papa" ended. They stayed silent until Rosemary Clooney started inviting them over to her house.

"Neutralize him?" Drinker said then derisively.

"Neutralize him," April agreed. She deepened her voice to a credible mimickry of Drinker's. " 'I was a demolitions man, I blew a lot of Japs to hell and gone out of their little caves.' "

Drinker stood up abruptly, filled with lust.

"Come onna my house," he said, thick-voiced.

Dunc met him at the head of the office stairs, so tense he was almost hostile. "Penny's flying out, we're getting married this weekend up in Reno."

Drinker gave him a long slow smile, thinking, poor bastard, knocked her up and he's doing the right thing. That's why Dunc would never be dangerous to any man. Too much humanity in him. Pity they got tagged so soon—usually the guy at least got a few months of worry-free humping before the nickel dropped.

"Congratulations, kid. Me and Sherry, we'll go up with you as best man and best woman, or whatever they call it. Okay? But meanwhile, I gotta make a phone call and I want you to go out and track down Harry Wham. Start at the yacht club. Call me here if you connect with him."

An hour after leaving Drinker's bed, April was sitting on her living room couch with her legs drawn up, head back as she blew Tarryton smoke luxuriously at the ceiling. Besner was in the pastel-green lounge chair across the room.

"Do you think we're putting too much faith in Cope?"

"As much as a woman can put in any man. He wants me, bad."

"He's smart and he's tricky and he's mean," warned Besner.

"That's what we need, darling. I gave Cope a deadline of sorts—the next time Harry and Fong take a trip to Mexico, I told Cope they mustn't come back."

Besner blurted out, "Are you sleeping with him?"

"Ferris!" Her sparkling laughter contained only outraged delight. "He's like a . . . a *sausage!*" She was on her feet. "Come on, darling, let Mama show you how much she loves you."

Harry Wham slid onto a stool at the Buena Vista Cafe. "An Irish coffee, John. Lots of Irish, lots of whipped cream."

Reversed in the backbar mirror, the Hyde Street pier reached a finger out toward the bulbous tip of the Municipal Pier to form Aquatic Park. Side-lit gulls flew low against the far dark mass of Angel Island, pink-stranded by a dying sunset.

A big man in a dark overcoat slid onto the next stool. He had a beaming rubicund face and blue twinkling eyes. Gray-shot hair was brushed straight back from a high forehead.

He pointed at Harry's Irish coffee.

"I'll have what he's having." He rubbed his hands together as if cold, then jerked a thumb at two swimmers just climbing out onto the pier. "How can those guys from the Polar Bear Club go swimming around out there all year 'round?"

"A hardy bunch. An hour a day in that water, you'll live forever," said Harry.

"You think so? Fish fuck in that stuff."

They got to talking, as men do, ended up moving over to one of the tables looking out over Bay Street. Eventually they drifted to the war. It turned out they both had served in the Pacific theater. In the Marines. Had even hopped those same islands while driving the Japs back toward their Imperial homeland, had sunk their Land of the Rising Sun in defeat.

Chapter Forty-six

Penny was due in on Friday night. The four of them would drive to Reno on Saturday in two cars; Drinker got carsick in the backseat on mountain roads. Meanwhile, he was a slave driver, in a foul mood, something on his mind for sure, which meant one surveillance job after another for Dunc.

When Dunc stopped off at the office on Wednesday to type up the latest batch of surveillance reports, Drinker spun a case assignment sheet across his desk.

"Go up to Point Arena chop-chop for a witness interview." Dunc had a vague idea that Point Arena was somewhere up the north coast. "Seven months ago this guy maybe witnessed a hit-and-run that left our client in a wheelchair for life. I need his statement." His tone got almost tentative. "Also, find out if the *Doubloon*'s been up there in the past month or so."

"I thought all of Harry Wham's trips were to Mexico."

The snap was back in his voice. "You ain't paid to think."

By the map, Point Arena was about seventy-five miles north of the Golden Gate on narrow, winding coast-hugging Highway 1. The hills above the sea were turning rainy-season green, a light steady rain was falling. Every vista retreated in lacy pastel washes like Japanese prints, every range of hills was a series of dolphin backs, ever more distant, breaking the surface of gray endless seas of fog. The ocean off to his left was obliterated by a drifting water-color wash of mist.

His reaction to Penny's pregnancy had just been panic. Hemingway'd been married when he'd quit being a reporter to try and be a fiction writer in Paris, had just kept on writing, even when they had a kid. Dunc could do the same. It was just that a baby right now made everything so damned *complicated* . . .

The only thing wider than Craven's yellow streak was his mean streak. He looked like his name, jockey-sized, with greasy black hair parted in the middle so it hung down on either side of his thin face like an upside-down horseshoe. His small, nasty, close-set eyes, always on the move, flanked a nose that twitched often, like a rabbit's smelling out danger. Or an illicit buck.

He was sitting on a stack of two-by-sixes in a corrugated tin shed where Giotti Construction was putting in endless row houses overlooking Skyline Boulevard in Daly City. As he bit into his sandwich, a small, surprisingly powerful hand closed around his shoulder. Craven jerked free indignantly.

"You ain't with the cops no more, you got no right comin' around hasslin' me."

Drinker Cope said with his big red-faced insincere grin, "Who got you this cushy job here with Giotti Construction?"

"Yeah, well, you had your reasons," said Craven darkly.

"I'm glad you brought that up. Dynamite. Four sticks. The usual accessories to go with it—you know what I need. Electrical blasting cap, insulated wire, a crimper—just short inventory a bit, you've done it before. There's even a few bucks in it for you."

Greed made Craven's nose twitch. "It's my job if I get caught. I oughta get at least—"

The hand was macerating the shoulder again. "Remember that Ivory soap slogan? 'It floats'? You say anything to anybody, *anybody*, y'understand, *ever*, and you're Ivory soap." Drinker got to his feet.

"Floating facedown in the Bay in among all those assholes from the Polar Club, as in a corpse. You got a week."

Craven watched the big, deceptively graceful man go across the raw earth toward his car. Could he profit from the knowledge that Drinker Cope wanted dynamite and detonators? No. If Cope was a diamond, he'd be the diamond used to cut other diamonds.

In Daly City Drinker had a beer and beat himself at shuffleboard. After two hours at the Buena Vista last night with Harry Wham, he still didn't know if Harry was the marine captain who had saved his life.

He'd have to make up his mind soon—the dynamite was on its way and April was a dangerous obsession, becoming daily more compelling. But he had a pretty good hunch she wouldn't dump him afterward. Besner was a lightweight, couldn't go the distance. But Drinker wanted to be sure. One easy way to find out.

If Dunc found that Harry was innocent enough to actually be looking for a galleon up at Point Arena, it might make a difference in Drinker's decision.

The assignment sheet read: BEN MCKINNEY, 26, married. The only address was P.O. Box 174A, Point Arena.

Point Arena, in the fading light, was a small fishing community clinging to a broad sweep of hillside going down to the sea. Dunc got there at 5:12 P.M. The post office had officially closed at five, but there were lights on inside, a radio was playing, the American flag hung wetly from the flagpole. But nobody would answer his pounding on the door. Un-civil servants.

At his third gas station a teenager with big red knobby hands and a Uriah Heep Adam's apple pointed through the rain.

"You drive down there a mile or so, you'll find a wharf. Take the road leads off between two for them warehouses to the Standard Oil Bulk Plant. Mr. McKinney lives off to the right of the bulk plant, there, up on the hillside. Second house up."

Dunc pulled into the driveway of the second house on a steep gravel road going up the hillside across from the bulk plant. The smell of crude filled the wet air. There were lights in the windows. He went up on the wooden porch and knocked. The rain was slacking off. The opened door spilled out yellow light.

A slight, bent, snuff-chewing man peered up at Dunc from beneath shaggy white eyebrows. He was bald as a boiled egg.

"Ben McKinney?" asked Dunc.

A head shake. "Nope. Father. Ain't it a shame?"

"Sure is. Is your son home?"

"Nope." Head shake. "Left for Santa Rosa five hours ago. Him and his wife. Ain't it a shame?"

"Sure is," said Dunc. "Will he be back tonight?"

"Can't say for sure. Ain't it a shame? Young Willem he drank some diesel oil, he's in the hospital there. Seven months old." A nod. "Yep. Musta thought it was milk."

"Is the boy okay?" asked Dunc.

A nod. "Must be—hospital's lettin' him come home."

Come back later. But as he was turning back into the street past the bulk plant, a 1949 brown De Soto Club Coupe was turning in. A man and woman in the front seat, a kid of maybe five or six in the back. The driver was a lean open-faced man with worried eyes. Dunc stopped and rolled down his window.

"Mr. McKinney? How's your boy?"

The woman put her face in her hands.

McKinney said, "They thought he was all right, but then he got pneumonia and the whooping cough, thanks for asking."

"Gosh, this is a terrible time, but do you think you could give me five or ten minutes for some questions?"

McKinney looked over at his wife, then shrugged.

"Come up to the house. We gotta pack a few things anyway."

Ben McKinney's wife, Marilyn, had been in the hospital at Santa Rosa having their little boy Willem, now on the edge of death, on the very night that Drinker's client had been run down in a Petaluma street after bar-close by the man he was suing. McKinney's car? He had lent it to his brother, now lived in Texas, he had the address around here somewheres . . .

Dunc handwrote a statement for him to sign, which he did with the father signing as a witness, got the brother's address in Houston, and left them to their sorrow.

He found himself pulling for the little kid as he went systematically through Point Arena with a new set of questions: Did anyone know a yachtsman named Harry Wham? Well, then maybe a power cruiser called the *Doubloon*? How about a big blond guy who was followed around by a small quick Chinese kid?

He talked with fishermen, grocery clerks, gas-pumpers, a used-car salesman, two old women at the five-and-dime, the hotel clerk, the town's only motel owner, bartenders, store clerks, the town librarian, a sheriff's deputy, and two volunteer firemen.

If Harry had left footprints—or keel marks—in Point Arena, Dunc couldn't find them. On the long drive home he had things to think about other than his own impending marriage.

A maybe dying baby. How a private eye seldom got the whole story on anything. Would Julia Demchuk get a divorce? Who had put Chauncey Jones in a Colma cemetery plot? What wasn't Drinker telling him about the Harry Wham investigation? Who was their client in the search for Kata Koltai that ended in two murders?

Stories without climaxes. Now, if he were writing these cases as fiction . . . Maybe he should try some private-eye tales. He sure had enough background material . . .

Penny, emotionally and physically exhausted, woke to the voice of the stewardess over the cabin's loudspeaker system. " . . . beginning our descent into San Francisco. Please extinguish all smoking materials and bring your seat backs and tray tables to their upright and locked positions . . ."

There was a shuddering rumble as the wheels were lowered. Penny shivered. She was scared. Did Dunc still love her now that she was . . .

with child? The grandmotherly woman beside her leaned over to ask if she lived in San Francisco.

"I'm coming out to get married," she said, suddenly proud.

But what if Dunc had changed his mind? When she had been out here for New Year's, she had noticed changes in him. He was harder, not so naive, not so open. Detective work seemed to be making him cynical and tough.

Look at Drinker Cope. Look at Sherry. Hard and flip on the surface, but hopelessly in love with Drinker—who wasn't in love with her. Both women had known it without ever speaking of it. Dunc hadn't. Men did not understand.

Oh God, would he be good to her? Would he love her always? Panic washed over her. So often in shotgun weddings there were other women, anger, raised fists . . . She and her baby, alone . . .

No, Dunc would be waiting at the gate with open arms. She'd work at temp jobs as she'd done in L.A. until the baby came, and then maybe she could work at that Fleur de Lis place, or at an inn, any-place she could learn while she worked. A few years down the road, she and Dunc would have the dude ranch she dreamed of. The three of them together. She would run the ranch, Dunc would write and become famous. Like Hemingway. And their baby would ride bare-back like a wild Indian.

Twenty minutes later she came out of the accordion ramp from the plane and there he was, right in front of the gate, solid as a rock, not even aware of the deplaning passengers parting around him.

His arms were around her, tight, they were kissing, she kept her eyes shut, dizzy, feeling him start to harden against her just from this brief embrace, and she knew it was going to be all right.

Everything was going to be all right forever.

EIGHT

Eye for Eye

Chapter Forty-seven

Dunc could remember going to only three weddings; the best had been when he'd served a Summons and Complaint on the groom in San Mateo. Reno's Little Chapel of Eternal Love ("No Waiting, No Delay") reminded him of that occasion, in fact: a single room with fake stained-glass windows and cupid figures and big red plush hearts. "Here Comes the Bride" from a record player while he and Penny were motionless in front of the justice of the peace.

Penny was wearing a rose suit with a fitted jacket that emphasized her waist, and a longish black skirt that followed the lines of her body. Just dressy enough for the occasion, but suitable for an office job if being assistant chef in training for a dude ranch didn't pay enough.

"Dearly beloved, we are gathered here together . . ."

The J.P. was a tall thin man wearing an embroidered western suit and a cord tie with a silver bull's-head clasp. High-heeled boots chased with silver. Spurs. Even a fake six-gun. Penny avoided Dunc's glance not because she sensed his hidden reservations, but because she was fighting back laughter as hard as he was. Suddenly he loved her very much.

" . . . authority vested in me by the State of Nevada . . ."

Penny squeezed his fingers gently after he had slipped the

plain gold band onto her finger. She lifted smiling eyes to his. The dimples at the edges of her mouth—the girl of his dream.

"You may kiss the bride . . ."

He did. With all his heart.

"Champagne!" yelled Drinker, bigger than life and redder of face than usual, wearing a western suit of his own. The J.P. set out four plastic champagne glasses, went out to the next couple in the anteroom. He stuck his head back in a moment later.

"Y'all mind staying a few minutes extra to witness these here lovely folks' wedding?"

Sherry and Drinker went out to warm up the car. While they waited, Dunc and Penny witnessed the other wedding, then bundled up in their coats and went out into the cold to get into the backseat.

"Now the four of us are gonna go out to a new steakhouse and casino I heard about a couple miles outta town." Drinker drove them through the icy Nevada evening; there was banked dirty snow along the sides of the road. "You know, if you put a marble into a glass jar every time you do the deed during your first two years of marriage, then take one out for each time after that, it's a scientific fact that you'll never get 'em all out again."

"My Uncle Carl and Aunt Goodie actually did that," said Penny, "just to see if it was really true."

Sherry turned to look at them. "Well? Was it?"

"They have to keep buying more marbles," said Dunc.

Penny gave him a little shove on the arm, but her look was warm and grateful. The anxiety he'd noticed before was gone from her face. The heater was finally warming up the car.

The Roundup was a long low flat deliberately rustic building built to resemble a big old Southwest cattle ranch, but the blaze of lights prevented any confusion with the real thing.

"Here's the place I should work," said Penny as they entered.

"They just opened it a month ago because their gaming license came through," said Drinker. "The grand opening won't be until the better weather comes."

"Think I could buy it?"

"I imagine the big boys'll move in on them if they make a go of it."

The big boys. Reno brought back memories of Las Vegas. Artis's story about Bugsy Siegel moving in on the owner of the Flamingo; the fat man who buried Lana Turner in the desert and took over the Gladiator after Carny died.

The greeter wore a ten-gallon hat and blond cowhide chaps that swished when he moved; there were longhorns over the dining room entrance. A maroon velvet rope across the doorway kept you from stampeding in and grabbing your own table.

Sherry said, "I put our names in, Drinker, but there's almost an hour wait to get a table."

A folded bill changed hands. Drinker came back to them.

"We'll wait in the piano lounge."

There were no empty stools at the long bar under the windows, and the perimeter stools of the block-long Steinway grand against the far wall were all taken, too. But a table between the fireplace and the window had four conspicuously vacant chairs waiting around it.

"Well, what do you know about that?" marveled Drinker.

"Thanks, big guy," said Dunc.

"Hell, kid, it's your night."

A waiter brought a silver bucket holding two bottles of Cordon Rouge. Dunc was caught by the music; "Moonlight in Vermont" had been followed by an evocative, somehow familiar one he couldn't name that then segued into "Old Cape Cod."

They drank and toasted until their table was called. The steaks were huge and bloody and the baked potatoes smothered in butter and crumbled bacon and sour cream. Garlic toast on the side. The windows were steamed over, snow was piled on the sills outside like in Minnesota, like a Christmas card, the voices and laughter in the room were hearty and exuberant like coming home from duck hunting with your limit of mallards.

For a moment he wished his folks, his uncles and cousins, everybody he had hunted and fished with over the years, were all here to celebrate with them.

They went back into the piano bar for a nightcap, the crowd had thinned, they got their same table back. A waiter appeared.

"Order anything you want, champ," urged Drinker.

The piano was still playing. On an impulse Dunc said, "Ask the piano player for 'Desert Moon.'"

Penny looked at him with slight misgivings, as though she might have forgotten their favorite song, then looked puzzled when she didn't recognize the song at all. A few minutes later Pepe pulled up a chair from an adjacent table with effervescent energy and sat down.

"Pepe!" said Penny. "How did you even know we were here?"

"'Desert Moon,'" he said with a grin. "Nobody but Dunc asks for my own stuff. What brings you two to Reno?"

"They got married this afternoon!" said Sherry.

After hugs and congratulations and introductions, Pepe looked at Dunc with a grin. "Apart from snagging the prettiest girl in Reno, what are you up to these days?" He read Dunc's business card and chuckled. "A genuine private eye? How did you get into that?"

"Remember that Labor Day picnic we were going to at Griffith Park in L.A.? I met Drinker there, he's my boss now—and my best man."

Pepe told Drinker, "You got a pretty damn good man right here." Then, looking embarrassed, said to Dunc, "Sorry about that picnic. An hour after you left that joint on the Strip I got a good gig in Monterey, be there immediately. After that, a couple of cruise ships. Chile, Argentina, and back."

"Did you make your record?" asked Penny.

"Not yet, but thanks for remembering."

She shook a finger at him in mock severity. "If you stayed in one place—maybe L.A.—you'd get a contract for sure."

He laughed. "You got me, Penny—I *can't* stay in one place." He turned to Dunc and Drinker with twinkling eyes. "Private eyes! Maybe you guys can find me a record contract."

They chatted, drank more bubbly. Finally Pepe looked at his watch and sighed and stood up from the table.

"I'd better get back. After the grand opening in May, the piano lounge becomes a show lounge; they're bringing in Vegas headliners, and then where will I be?" He bent and kissed Penny on the cheek. "Long life and every happiness, beautiful bride."

They were staying at a downtown hotel with a garage next door because Drinker had insisted on indoor parking. The two couples rode up to their respective rooms together.

"Where'd you meet the piano player?" asked Drinker.

"Las Vegas," said Dunc.

"Then again on the Sunset Strip," said Penny.

"Now here." Drinker was thoughtful. "Lad gets around."

Sherry's head was on Drinker's shoulder, she was almost asleep, but Penny looked more alive and sparkling than she had all day. Dunc realized all over again how much he loved her, how her vitality energized him. They parted outside the elevator.

Lad gets around, Dunc thought. The guy was a musician, musicians had to go where they got the best offer. Or maybe, the way his mind worked, Drinker thought Pepe was connected with the big boys. But anyone who lived around gambling at least brushed up against mob guys, that didn't mean they were connected.

Despite the champagne, both he and Penny were ready. He entered her tentatively at first, awed at the expanded context of their lovemaking since they'd last been together.

"It's okay, darling," she said. "We can't hurt anything."

He was a piston driving their love, then Penny was bucking under him, her incoherent cries of climax bringing on his own. He gasped, "Move . . . over little . . . man. Make room for . . . Daddy."

Daddy. He was going to be a father. Of a boy, of course.

Pepe closed down his piano at 2:00 A.M., went to the bar to sip cold white wine and stare sightlessly at the backbar mirror.

Dammit, the man had to know. Or suspect. He was a natural-born observer, made even sharper by months as a private investigator. Running into Dunc twice *could* be accidental, but at some point the kid would figure it out. Unless . . .

Could Dunc be that sly? Hiding what he knew behind that open midwestern face, biding his time for the moment to act?

Maybe, maybe not, but Pepe couldn't take the chance anymore. For his own peace of mind he had to act first.

Sometime into Dunc's head would pop the sequence of events during that last night in Vegas. Some night he would sit bolt upright in bed, beside that new bride of his—*she* had known there was significance in Pepe's sudden disappearance from the Strip, he had seen it in her eyes tonight—and Dunc would *remember*. And, remembering, he would go back to read the Las Vegas newspapers for last July 5, and then he would *know* . . .

The hell of it was, Pepe really liked the kid. He wasn't small-minded or mean-hearted, and he was a genuine fan of Pepe's music. Pepe could count his fans on the fingers of one hand.

But survival came first. He didn't want to have to move on as he had in L.A. Keep ducking out before the job was done, and word would go out he'd lost his nerve. Guys like Mr. David had people like Pepe, who had not only fronted for the mob but carried out hits on face-to-face orders from the bosses, retired with flowers the minute it looked like they were losing their nerve. That was the only way someone in his line of work was ever retired. With flowers.

Look what had happened to Jack Falkoner just because a couple of kids *maybe* had seen a body being carried away.

Uh-uh. Not for Pepe that little stutter-step to the coffin. Time to make another phone call about Dunc; not, as it had been in L.A., just to have someone check him out. A careful voice answered the phone in San Francisco.

"Give me Mr. David," Pepe told it. "Right now."

Chapter Forty-eight

On Sunday they didn't even pry their eyes open until noon; it never occurred to Dunc to go to Mass. What with one thing and another, they were lucky to join Drinker and Sherry in the hotel casino at three in the afternoon.

Drinker looked them over critically. "Married life agrees with you," he said to Penny, then to Dunc, "You look like hell."

Penny did look ravishing, her hair full and soft around her face, her eyes sparkling as she laughed at Drinker.

"I love my husband."

Sherry took Penny's hand. "And he loves you, sweetie, make no mistake about that. Come on, let's win a lot of money."

"I'm a killer at blackjack," said Penny.

She had a system, right pocket/left pocket. You bought chips with the stake in your right-hand jacket pocket, played at a dollar table. Winnings went back into that pocket until the original stake was replaced. After that, winnings went into the left-hand pocket. If you lost your original stake, you quit for the night. Penny didn't have to quit, except, finally, to eat.

They'd just started their salad when a bellhop came to their table and said Drinker had a phone call.

"Must be Sherry, calling me from the office."

"Very funny," said Sherry.

They were on dessert and coffee when he finally came back with a troubled face. "That was Wee Jimmy Haggerty," he said.

"He's a cop, Drinker's ex-partner," Dunc told Penny.

"There's been a break-in at the office, I have to go back."

"We'll go with you," said Dunc, half rising.

Drinker shoved him back down again. "It's your goddamn honeymoon," he growled. "Sherry and I can handle it."

Dunc had his hands resting lightly on Penny's shoulders from behind as she played blackjack, aware of her body heat the way you were aware of the heat from the fire on a cold night out in the woods. The same kind of comfort, the same kind of warmth. But his thoughts followed Drinker back to San Francisco. Had the files been rifled? Was it something to do with one of Drinker's private clients whose names were never spoken? Had he left some loose end in one of his own files?

Penny looked back to turn that brilliant smile on him.

"I'm going to pay for our honeymoon, sweetheart."

She was his lucky Penny. When her luck turned at midnight, she cashed in and gaily stuffed the neat fold of her winnings into Dunc's inner jacket pocket. Up in their room, neither of them seemed able to stop making love. Finally they fell asleep from sheer exhaustion, tumbled together on the bed like puppies.

The front desk woke them at 9:00 A.M.: Dunc was needed in San Francisco. He didn't really mind. They were now man and wife, they could do their loving wherever fate might take them.

When he went down to settle their account, he was told their bill had been paid. "Compliments of Mr. Cope," said the clerk. His face was wreathed in smiles. "A wedding gift."

That Drinker, he could always surprise you. What did they call it? A real *beau geste*.

It took him twenty minutes to find the Grey Ghost—he hadn't been drinking when he parked it originally, so why . . . Then he saw it about ten spaces up on the other side of the garage. Well, he'd had other things on his mind. A wedding, for instance.

It was a sparkling day, bright blue sky and temperatures up into the forties. He got the car warmed up and the heater working, he didn't want his pregnant Penny facing the cold.

They gassed up, then went south out of Reno on Nevada 395 to Carson City, then took Highway 50 southwest toward California. They would go up and over Echo Summit, over seven thousand feet high, then eventually down to Sacramento, where the palm trees started.

When they went back to the car after stopping for lunch at sleepy little South Lake Tahoe, Penny wanted to drive.

"I have to learn how to handle the Grey Ghost now that he's part mine, too." Dunc started to object because the road up over the summit might be icy, but she laughed him to silence. "Hey, big boy! I'm from the snow country, too, remember?"

He surrendered, closed her door, slid into the passenger's side, and quickly relaxed against the seat. They sang songs together and miles flew. First camp songs like "Comin' Round the Mountain" and "Little Brown Jug," then on into "Down Among the Sheltering Palms" and "Sentimental Journey." Dunc did a sonorous "Old Man River" with lyrics changes he'd learned in the Glee Club:

> "Tote that barge,
> Lift that bale,
> Get a little drunk,
> And you get no tail . . ."

Penny, both hands on the wheel, shot a quick look over at him and said, "Seems to me that on our wedding night, big boy, you got a *lot* drunk and you got a *lot* of tail."

"And I'm gonna get even more tonight."

"You promise?"

At Echo Summit they pulled off into the vista point. Below them were sparkling, snowcapped peaks with dark armies of pine forests marching up their flanks. Penny plunged them down into the sunlight and shadow on the winding, narrow, two-lane blacktop. Snow was piled two feet deep on the verge of the road, but lay only in patches under the shelter of the trees.

Penny said, "Dunc honey, this is hard to say after Drinker and Sherry have been so nice, but don't you think maybe you should start looking for a new job?"

"A new . . . but I love detective work! It's fun and exciting and I'm getting a lot of material for my writing."

"But you're not writing, and it's changing you, Dunc. When we're together you're sweet and loving, but when you're talking about work you . . . you're harder, colder, it's like you're losing all your finer perceptions. You just see the bold strokes—"

"Jesus!" he burst out. "First I lose my chance to be a writer, now you want me to quit detective work. Why?"

"So you can get *back* to your writing."

"You're saying it's *detective* work that keeps me from writing? Here I thought having a wife and baby to support might have a little something to do with it."

She looked over at him angrily. "You haven't had a wife and you don't have a baby yet, but I don't think you've written a single story since you came to San Francisco. Why are you trying to blame me for that, Dunc? Are you *sorry* we got married?"

"Quit trying to twist around what I'm saying. Of course I'm not sorry, but the baby's timing could have been better."

She wailed in utter misery.

He said, "Oh Christ, honey, I didn't mean—*Penny!*"

Ahead the road had narrowed and steepened, made a sharp left-hand turn. Penny rammed the brake pedal right to the floor and kept twisting and twisting the wheel, the car wasn't turning, wasn't slowing, she screamed, Dunc saw the trunk of the tree coming at him with appalling speed . . .

*   *   *

He was standing on the edge of a curving blacktop road with the reek of raw gasoline all around him. Three or four cars were parked at goofy angles off the road. A half dozen people he'd never seen before were milling around aimlessly. Almost all the way off the road was a gray Ford with the open hood crumpled against the scarred trunk of a pine tree and its ass end up in the air with both back wheels three feet off the ground.

Some asshole was holding his arm. Dunc said, "There's been an accident here, I don't want anything to do with it."

Lying on the ground was a log or anyway something long and cylindrical with a couple of blankets laid over it. Just looking at it somehow made him queasy and reminded him of how much his head ached. He reached up with his left hand; his forehead over his eye felt slippery to the touch, as if he'd been rained on.

That irritating guy was still gently tugging at his sleeve.

"Why don't you come over here and sit down for a minute?"

"Hell with you," said Dunc, feebly pushing him. "There's been an accident and there's plenty of people to help out. I gotta find Penny, we're on our way to Reno to get married."

"But if you'd just sit down and rest for a few minutes . . ."

Dunc shook off the persistent Samaritan, started to stride away up the hill. He heard the far-approaching keen of sirens. He'd known it! An accident for sure. They'd wanta ask a lot of questions without answers, he had to go find Penny . . .

On the other hand it was a long way up that hill. Maybe . . .

He sat down suddenly in the road, then tipped over sideways and lay still.

"You *made it up?*" demanded Sherry, an enraged hornet immobilizing an astounded Drinker with her appalled anger. "How could you *be* so goddamn stupid?"

"For Chrissake, Sherry, I wanted them to have some time alone, okay?" He made placating movements of hands and face. "You know

Dunc. I just thought that when they get back he'll get all caught up in his cases again, and—"

"You're lying," she said abruptly. "You didn't make up that phone call you got in Reno." Fury, fear, sorrow, fought in her face. "It was from her, wasn't it? That woman. April-fucking-Wham. You told her where you'd be, and she called, so you made up your lies and came running down here to—"

He snatched up the ringing phone, snapped "Drinker Cope" into it, glad for the interruption. Listening, he sank down into Sherry's chair like an old man not sure of his balance.

"Yeah," he said tiredly. "Where is . . . I see. Yeah. Okay. I'll be there tomorrow midday for sure."

He hung up the phone. Stared up at her.

"Christ, Sherry, they were in the mountains, they went off the road a few miles this side of Echo Summit."

All color had left her face. "How . . . how bad is—"

"Penny's dead. They called her family, the mother's prostrated, the sister wants her body shipped back to Dubuque, pronto. They're talking as if they blamed Dunc for—"

"Dunc!" she cried. Her voice was fearful. "Is he . . ."

"He's still alive but he's in a coma. They . . . don't know if he'll make it."

"Oh, Drinker!" she wailed, crushing his big graying head to her bosom and crying like her heart would break.

Chapter Forty-nine

Dunc jerked and opened his eyes and looked at the ceiling's white foot-square tiles with rows of little holes in them. He licked his lips. Bad dream. Whew. "Penny?" he said cautiously.

"He's awake," a voice said. Penny leaned over the bed to look anxiously down into his face. He tried to smile. "Could you tell me your name, sir?"

Not Penny. Some of it rushed back, all in an instant.

She wailed in utter misery . . .

"Jesus Christ," he said softly. It was not a curse.

"Try again," said the woman in white bending over the bed.

"Pierce Duncan," he said impatiently.

"And do you know where you are, Mr. Duncan?"

He sat up in the bed. Or at least that's what his brain said he did, but he still just lay there looking at the ceiling.

"Hospital." He thought he pointed at her. "Nurse."

There was a log or anyway something long and cylindrical with a couple of blankets laid over it. Oh dear God.

"Where is Penny? How is she? Please, let me see her . . ."

The eyes looking down at him suddenly filled with tears. He curled into a tight ball of anguish and howled like a wolf. Except he just lay there, unmoving. He shut his eyes again.

*   *   *

Pepe hung up and threw the chair across the room. Still alive. *Still alive.* How could that be? He regretted missing his chance in Vegas and in L.A.

Who was the guy, fucking Lazarus?

In a coma, maybe he'd just die like the nice guy Pepe had figured him for. Or wake up with mush for brains. Put a collar on him and lead him around like a pet chimp. Send the hitter in with a pillow? No. Not yet. The accident scenario could still work.

Drinker's voice said, "I know how you feel, Dunc, but . . ."

Dunc didn't move. Didn't open his eyes. Thought, no, you don't know how I feel, Drinker. I murdered my wife and baby.

"You said he was awake," complained Drinker.

"He was. His vital signs are normal. We've told him his wife is dead and maybe he just can't handle it." Her voice was fading; they were leaving. "He'll come out of it eventually . . ."

You don't understand, Dunc thought. Maybe, by blaming her, he'd robbed Penny of hope, left her only despair. Maybe she had *deliberately* driven off the road.

Not to be borne. Not to be thought about. He felt his bandage. Surprisingly small, neat, tidy. That navy watch cap in his roommate's closet would cover it nicely. His own clothes were in his open closet. Wait in feigned coma until dark . . .

And then start running away. Forever.

Out in the hallway bulky, red-faced Drinker Cope abruptly thrust the flowers in one hand and the candy in the other at the petite black-haired nurse. "You take 'em, he don't need 'em. Tell him I was here. And if there's any change—"

"We will surely let you know, Mr. Cope."

Drinker went away down the corridor. Goddamn, what a mess! Dunc in there, him here, Sherry trying to run the office. Harry Wham to deal with, April too. Craven to check on . . .

✻   ✻   ✻

Standing under the wind-danced streetlight, Peter Collinson watched the Buick's disappearing taillights. Son of Nobody. He blew into his bare hands; the chill had already crept through the garage attendant's shoes a man named Dunc had always worn. After midnight. Six hours to get 250 miles east of Reno. This time of year, only local traffic would be moving until about 6:00 A.M.

A bulky man in a brown sheep-lined coat came by, overshoes squeaking on the hard-packed snow, his fur cap's earmuffs giving him the head of a bear. Dunc asked, "Where's the bus depot?"

"Two blocks back, see the red sign says Casino?" He was pointing. "Go through the gaming room, the depot's out back."

Inside the plate-glass door, a blast of welcome heat greeted him. A few tired tourists and even more tired shift workers sipped coffee and dunked doughnuts at the all-night café. Through the open door at the far end he could see a man in tan work clothes vacuuming the maroon wall-to-wall carpet.

In the casino a bartender polished glasses and yawned. Roulette, craps, wheel of fortune, everything covered with white canvas dust-cloths except one blackjack table. The cardman was dealing to a black-haired woman in a slit black sheath dress that emphasized her hips and haunches. She was dwarfed by a balding man in a loud size 50 suit who seemed to be backing her play.

Dunc crossed to an archway that led to a spacious hotel lobby with potted palms and deep red leather chairs. Behind the check-in desk a stringy-haired man dozed with his chin braced on one hand. His knuckles had pushed his mouth open so a gold tooth caught the light. He could have used more chin and a shave.

"When's the next bus?" Dunc asked him.

He came awake with a start. "Bus to Reno arrives at three-fifty-two A.M. Twenty-minute rest stop, then—"

"East."

"Five-oh-four A.M."

Dunc started, "I'll take . . ." but his hand had brought out only a five and two crumpled ones from his pocket. "Forget it."

He flopped down in a red leather chair. What was he doing, where did he think he was going? Mexico? The South Seas?

"No sleeping in the lobby unless you're waiting for a bus."

"So I'm waiting for a bus."

"Company don't pay the hotel good money so any bum stumbles in here off the street can use it as a flophouse."

The man had a point. With the knit wool cap pulled down over his ears he looked the part. He stuck it in his pocket.

He almost dreaded watching the woman play blackjack. *He stood behind Penny as she played, aware of her body heat the way you were aware of the heat from the fire on a cold night.* But he had at least five hours before there was enough through traffic to give him a decent chance of thumbing a ride before he froze to death.

The dealer had a thin sad face and a pearl stickpin in his lavender necktie. Hands quick as Henri's scooped up her chips.

"Dealer takes all pushes."

She had a smooth aloof face, great cheekbones, and an insolent mouth, but said to the big man in a cloying little-girl voice, "Petie Sweetie, I'm out of gas."

"You cost more to run than my Caddy."

"I want to beat this bastard at his own crooked game."

A paw made to crush beer bottles tossed a heavy leather wallet on the table. A granite jaw and thick neck suggested a ruthless power slightly belied by surprisingly mild blue eyes. She methodically lost a quarter inch of bills, cursing the dealer obscenely for every hand he took. They departed to the bar.

Dunc said to the dealer, "Sweet lady."

"She was explaining my parentage to me." Two red spots burned on his cheeks. "She's a guest at the hotel."

"And the customer's always right. Right?"

The spots faded from his cheeks. He grinned wryly. Dunc said, "A blackjack dealer I knew in Vegas had hands like yours."

He put the cards through an intricate Scarne shuffle, a false cut, dealt himself seconds. "There's one rotten town, Vegas." He finished with that most difficult of card maneuvers, the waterfall, said almost ruefully, "That's my real name. Hands. What could I be except a dealer, hands like these, name like that? Like the kid in *Treasure Island*, he's up the mast with a pistol, he says, 'One more step and I'll fire, Mr. Hands.' "

"Jim Hawkins," said Dunc.

"That's him. Most everybody just calls me Hands."

Dunc hesitated a moment. "Peter Collinson," he said.

His already expressionless face emptied entirely. "Big guy over there calls himself Peter Collins."

"Good old dad," said Dunc. "Mr. Nobody himself."

"Comes in 'cause of Imogene. You just passing through?"

Dunc nodded. "Drifting with the wind."

"A sad wind, maybe? Good luck."

Dunc sat in a red leather chair out of the clerk's sight, under a potted palm near the mezzanine's broad marble stairway. Three A.M. Two hours before he could stick out his thumb. Physically, except for his headache, okay. Penny and their child were dead, but he was okay. He crossed his arms, felt a bulge in his jacket pocket. A folded sheaf of bills, $400. Where . . .

The blackest of despairs shot through him. *Penny cashed in and gaily stuffed the neat fold of her winnings into Dunc's inside sport jacket's pocket.* Penny, loving him, trusting him, and he'd made her want to be dead . . .

A man came in from the side street without seeing Dunc. Cold radiated from his midnight-blue overcoat; a black rakish hat with a narrow brim was pulled low over his eyes. He had thin features and an olive complexion. Dunc thought, Pepe, realized, of course not: Pepe was 250 miles away. But the same type.

Where'd you meet the piano player? Lad gets around. Something quizzical moved in Dunc, was gone.

Imogene came slinking out of the casino. The man in the blue topcoat purred at her. "He in there?"

"I said he would be, didn't I?" Her voice was polished steel, nothing at all like her simpering tones for Petie Sweetie.

"We only pay on delivery."

"I only deliver on payment."

A faint rustling, Dunc imagined an envelope changing hands.

"Our play isn't in here. Get him out to his car and—"

"You gotta be crazy. Up in my bed, asleep."

"Just tell him to wait for you. At his car."

Mollified, she went away. The man in the blue topcoat disappeared into the men's room like a prowling black cat.

Dunc slumped lower in his chair. So what if Collins was hit? He was already Mr. Nobody. Penny was dead, and Dunc . . .

He sat up, frowning. Just as Penny had said, he was different. Eight months ago he'd charged into Raffetto's gleaming blade to try and save Artis's life. But Penny was . . .

Collins and Imogene came out of the casino. His mohair overcoat made him look too wide to fit through doors.

"Go warm up the car so I won't get a chill, Petie Sweetie," she crooned in her pubescent voice. She stood on tiptoe to give him a quick Judas kiss. "I'll be down in ten minutes."

She went upstairs, long legs flashing. Collins crossed the lobby toward the main door as a herd of noisy bus customers crowded in, eager to feed the bandits during their twenty-minute rest stop. The killer prowled out of the men's room after Collins.

"Aw, *shit!*" muttered Dunc, and pulled his silly goddamn watch cap back down over his ears.

Out in the street, icy wind snatched the air from his lungs. Collins was already too far away to call to without alerting the man in the midnight-blue overcoat sauntering along behind. Dunc went padding after them on silent rubber soles.

A wind-danced streetlight cast confusing shadows as Pete Collins entered the parking lot where he'd left his long gleaming Cadillac. Whistling, he bent to unlock the door. A piece of the night leaped at him to drive a long-bladed glittering knife at the unprotected back of his prey. Knife. Glittering.

Glittering as Raffetto charged down the stairwell.

Dunc slammed his clasped hands, clublike, against the killer's head, dropping him where he stood like the sheep in the Hunter's Point slaughterhouse. His knife clattered away without having touched even the cloth of Mr. Nobody's coat.

Collins spun around, shock on his face. He recovered quickly. "I know who he is—who the fuck are you?"

"The guy who just saved your life." But Penny was still just as dead, Dunc was still just as responsible.

"How'd they . . . Imogene!"

He stormed past Dunc, face dark with rage. Dunc said, "She's just spit on the sidewalk. Is she worth dying for?"

Collins whirled, staring at him almost stupidly. He looked down at the fallen warrior, he looked at his car keys, he looked at his Cadillac.

"That's two I owe you. How do I square up? Money?"

And Dunc was thinking again like the private eye Drinker's months of tutelage had made him. Raffetto's blade had been a black Commando knife designed to never reflect light. But there had been another man in Vegas, slight, quick, muscular, who might have wielded a knife.

"A ride to South Lake Tahoe," he said. He gestured down toward the killer slumbering at their feet. "What about him?"

"He wakes up or he freezes, he lives or he dies—who gives a shit?"

Dunc got into the Cadillac.

Chapter Fifty

It was three the next afternoon before Drinker got back to the office. Sherry was at her desk. She started to her feet when his head appeared above the floor level. "Anything?"

"Not a trace." He opened a clenched fist as if freeing a trapped starling. "Like that. Dressed himself and walked out."

Sherry slowly sat down again. "Then why hasn't he called? He could be lying in a ditch somewhere—"

"When did you become his mother, for Chrissake?"

She was suddenly embarrassed. "Yeah, God, listen to me."

"Go on home and get some rest." He had gone around her desk to massage her shoulders. "I'll handle things here."

"Thanks, Drinker. I feel like I haven't slept in a week."

She put on her coat, went up on tiptoe to kiss him on the mouth like a sleepy child, then went down the stairs with a wave of her hand. Jesus, more trouble. How did you tell a woman you needed to help run your office that you didn't want her sexually anymore? But after having just spent two hours with April, he knew in his heart that he wouldn't want Sherry, not ever again.

What was left of Grey Ghost Two was up on the hydraulic lift. The mechanic, a kid barely nineteen, gave a low whistle as he shone his flashlight at the sprung undercarriage of the car.

"Not just the brake line, the steering mechanism, too."

They had known Penny would be with him, Dunc thought. Wouldn't have known about the baby, but that wouldn't have stopped them. *Their* baby. Dead. The child he hadn't wanted had become almost as devastating a loss as Penny herself.

"Why wasn't the tampering found?" he asked at last.

"Nobody looked," said the kid. "What made you want to?"

"When I went to pick up the car on Monday morning, it had been moved. But I didn't do anything. I just let it go."

"They must have cut the line almost through, then taped it to hold until it got a real good pump. A lot of brake fluid must of spilled out on the floor. Funny you didn't see it."

"I wasn't looking," said Dunc, sorrowful to his very soul.

The kid was shining his light again, talking about the steering linkage. Dunc couldn't stand to hear any more.

The car wasn't turning, wasn't slowing, Penny screamed . . .

"Sell it for salvage," he said. "Keep the money."

At the bus depot he bought a ticket for L.A. Dark as his thoughts were, a great weight had been lifted from him. Someone else had killed Penny, not him.

The bus came, Dunc found a window seat, leaned back and shut his eyes. He was pretty sure it had been Pepe, but Pepe wasn't the only one who might have wanted to kill him. Rephaim, Seventh Priest of Mechizedek, thundering biblical curses at him. Hector, acolyte to Rephaim, trying to run him down. Probably in jail, both of them, but he had to eliminate them as suspects.

The bus from L.A. dropped him at Sepulveda and Mission Road. He walked from there. It felt strange to be back in San Fernando. Like returning to a nest he'd helped build and finding it full of fledglings. The seminary was completed; young men in black gowns moved between the buildings, plantings were in, the raw earth was covered with grass.

Dunc waited until the slightly stooped, silver-maned man in the mission's gift shop had sold a tourist couple some holy medals and a rosary. Then he said, "Hello, Rephaim."

The man whirled. Recognition dawned. Some erstwhile fire flashed in those eyes. "You!" Rephaim said in half-whisper.

"I didn't turn you in." Dunc stepped closer, suddenly needing this man's absolution. "I didn't turn anyone in. I was just trying . . . trying to . . ."

"To do good," said Rephaim, so low Dunc could hardly hear him. "I too. I got probation, some kind soul gave me a job here because I am a man of God and because they felt guilty about . . ." A pause. "So I sell rosaries, here, where it all started . . ."

"And Hector?"

"No probation for Hector. My church is gone, my people are scattered, my acolyte is imprisoned . . ."

"But you are still the Seventh Priest of Melchizedek," said Dunc in sudden fierceness. "No man can take that from you."

"Yes," said the old man, wonder in his voice, more light coming into his eyes. "Yes! And God works in mysterious ways."

That evening a different L.A. bus dropped Dunc on Figueroa in Highland Park, pulled away in a swirl of diesel fumes. He walked through the gathering dusk. Together he and Penny had prowled every inch of these nighttime streets arm-in-arm, laughing, whispering, stopping for long giddy kisses . . .

And now he didn't even know where she was buried. Dubuque, Iowa. What was that? Were there flowers on her grave? A headstone? He'd been her husband, but when he'd called her sister Betsy about the funeral, she had cursed him and hung up.

He paused in front of the little white two-story house. The lights were on, he could hear faint television. What would his reception be? More curses? He rang the bell. Aunt Goodie opened the door, stared for a moment, then cried, "Dunc!" and threw her arms wide to receive him.

*　　*　　*

"It was a beautiful service," said Goodie. "And the cemetery is on a wooded knoll near Loras College, overlooking the Mississippi." The three of them were at the kitchen table, iced tea untouched beside them. "We so wished you were there, Dunc."

"Not her sister," he said quietly.

"She even went after Goodie for letting Penny go out with you," added Carl. "As if we could have stopped her."

Goodie said defensively, "It was just too much for them, losing her that way. Penny was everybody's favorite, a ray of sunshine. Her father was killed before she was born."

"By convicts," said Carl.

"Wait a minute," said Dunc. "Her dad was killed in an accident and her mom raised the two girls on the union life-insurance money."

Goodie waved him silent with a small dismissive hand.

"That's just what we told the girls at the time. Penny's daddy was a guard at Iowa State Prison, in charge of a flood-control work gang on the river." Her voice was low. "The prisoners broke loose and killed him."

"And mutilated his body," said Carl.

Dunc felt all the blood drain from his face. He gripped the edges of the table fiercely. Of course that was years before Hent, but . . .

"The girls never knew any of that," said Goodie almost briskly. "Betsy was bitter, she remembered her dad. She must have felt bad when we all made such a fuss over the new baby. Penny was born early, just a week after her daddy died. She was just a lovely, loving child who grew up into a loving woman. A woman who loved you, Dunc, with her whole soul."

His emotions were churning, it was like he was helping murder Hent all over again, and here was retribution, so neat, so clean. Black anger welled up in him at the comic vindictiveness of it. The sport of the gods.

"Dunc?" Goodie was staring at him.

"I'm okay," he said reassuringly. "It's just so soon . . ."

Tomorrow, Las Vegas. Confirm what had happened that July

fourth night that in some twisted way had led to Penny's death. And then . . . Then, by God, do something about it. Henri had said the man was expected at the Flamingo midweek . . .

A week had gone by. Ten days. No word from Dunc. No body in a ditch. The routine of the office had resumed, with Drinker fighting to keep all the balls in the air at once. Just now it was April, striding up and down his living room, cigarette in hand, pouring out words half in rage, half in fear.

"Harry came to my room last night. He hasn't done that in months. Months! And he wanted to sleep with me."

"What else could you do but oblige him?" sneered Drinker.

"He *is* my husband, for Chrissake." She glared at him. "Anyway, this morning we did it again . . ." Drinker was suddenly, perversely, almost dizzily excited by the fact that Harry had been inside her just scant hours earlier. "And then he said that after this trip on Saturday he is going to sell the boat, stay home, and get me to fall in love with him all over again."

She had dropped into his easy chair, blowing smoke through her nostrils, legs planted apart so he could see up her skirt. His groin was almost instantly heavy with arousal. Following his gaze, she savagely slammed her knees tight together.

"No more for you, damn you, until you *do* it."

"Do what?" he asked mildly.

"Kill him, goddamn you! Blow the son of a bitch to hell!" Her eyes were blazing. "For money—or for me."

"For you, lady." Drinker's voice was thick, heavy. He was unbuckling his belt. "Take off your panties. Show it to me."

She slid lower in the chair, smiling wickedly. "I'm not wearing any panties." She opened her legs wide. "See?"

Dunc spread the *Las Vegas Pioneer* for July 5, 1953, open on the library reading table. The headline was three inches high:

LAS VEGAS MURDER SPREE

Ned was there, and Carny Largo. And Artis. And . . . And yes, Gimpy Ernest, throat slit in the parking lot at the ballpark where the fights had been held. Ten feet from him, car keys in hand, Rafe Raffetto, dead from repeated stab wounds to the heart. A Commando knife still in its sheath between his shoulder blades, but with traces of blood on the blade.

It couldn't have been Rafe on the darkened stairwell of Artis's house. He'd been dead for half an hour by that time.

It had been Pepe. Pepe, front man for the mob, the Mafia, put into places like the Gladiator to play his piano and learn everything his bosses had to know for a takeover. Put on the Sunset Strip to oversee grabbing off the jailed Mickey Cohen's vice empire. Put into the Roundup for the same purpose—Drinker had speculated that the mob would soon grab it off.

But wherever he went, here was Dunc showing up. What would he have thought? That Dunc was there to spook him, or to confirm a suspicion aroused there on Artis's stairs? Because Pepe could never be sure Dunc hadn't recognized him, or someday might.

Dunc returned the newspaper to the research desk, went up a floor to the rental typewriters, and wrote what he thought of as his first professional piece of writing. Call it a story, call it fiction because of some guesswork, but he would be paid for it. Not in money, not in revenge, but in justice. Or in blood. Roll the dice.

He even figured he knew who his dream killer had been.

He finished the last page, separated the originals from their two carbons, and started his cover letter:

"Dear Lucius Breen, I need another favor . . ."

That finished, he went out into the soft Las Vegas night.

*   *   *

An hour later Henri, pit boss at the Flamingo, jerked his head across the restaurant and said, low-voiced, "There he is, Mr. David in the lean and hungry flesh."

Dunc looked, casually. A long-boned, rather elegant man in a blue blazer. Wavy hair above a high forehead, assessing eyes, a sensuous mouth.

Henri said, "The only time you can get near him is at seven in the morning when he's doing his laps in the hotel's outdoor pool. There's nobody else around at that hour."

"How do I get by hotel security?"

"I'll find you a bellhop's jacket. After that, kiddo, you're on your own." He turned on his wide grin. "Dunc who?"

In the office behind a carefully locked and bolted street door, Drinker put on thin rubber gloves. From the satchel he took a shoe box holding Craven's four sticks of dynamite. They were bright red and looked exactly like dynamite in the movies.

Drinker used his plierslike crimper to carefully angle a small hole into the side of one dynamite stick. Into this he inserted an electrical blasting cap, a small metal cylinder with a pair of insulated wires sticking out of one end. They were the ends of an *un*insulated loop, called a noninsulated bridge wire, that was embedded in the cap's flash charge. From this loop all good explosions flowed.

Drinker wound electrical tape around the four sticks of dynamite to form a compact bundle, then put it aside for a cheap twelve-hour alarm clock from Woolworth's. He set the clock but did not wind it, then removed the back to expose the alarm bell and clapper. Around the alarm bell he wound the stripped end of one blasting cap wire; around the alarm clapper he wound the stripped end of a free length of insulated wire.

To arm his bomb, Drinker needed only to fasten the free end of the wire from the clapper to one of the two terminals of an ordinary dry-cell battery, and attach to the other terminal the remaining wire from the blasting cap. Wind the alarm clock and leave. When the alarm went off, the clapper would hit the bell and close the electrical power circuit.

Mr. David finished his twentieth lap in the Flamingo's outdoor pool at 7:30 A.M. and whooshed up out of the water sleek as a seal. In a profession where many died young, often violently, he intended to live forever. Dripping water, he lay back on his lounge chair and shut his eyes. He came down from San Francisco often to enjoy this perfect time of the year in Vegas, winter's chill gone and summer's intense heat not yet arrived.

"Mr. David?"

He opened his eyes. A Flamingo Hotel bellhop stood there holding a tray with a letter on it. Mr. David sat up, furious.

"Get out of here! I'm not to be disturbed for any reason."

The bellhop just looked at him. A husky kid with close-cropped black hair, a wide neck, shoulders and arms too thick for his jacket. A new angry red scar above his left eyebrow ran up into his hairline. Jesus Christ, this was no bellhop!

And he without his bodyguards! But this was the *Flamingo*, for Chrissake, neutral ground. Who would have the balls to . . .

The kid sat down on the adjacent chair, still holding his tray. The fear drained out of Mr. David but left him too shaky for renewed rage. Dunc was shaky, too, but he had ice inside.

"I'm Pierce Duncan. I found two people for you. Kata Koltai and Jack Falkoner. Jack murdered Kata, you had Jack murdered in turn."

Mr. David struggled for sangfroid. "You're Cope's man."

"Two Saturdays ago, my girlfriend, Penny, and I got married."

He found himself getting intrigued. This was the damnedest pitch he'd ever heard. He said, "Congratulations."

"On that Monday, Penny was murdered. One of your men wanted me dead, and she happened to be in the way."

Mr. David was actually shocked. "You think that I—"

"No." He extended the tray with its envelope. "I've always wanted to be a writer, so I wrote a story. You're in it, and Kata, and Jack Falkoner, and Pepe the piano player . . ."

Mr. David read the pages. When he had finished, he sat with them in his hand for almost a minute, looking at the blue water and green grass and waving palm trees blooming here in the desert—and not really seeing any of it.

"Instead of Pepe, what's to keep me from—"

"That's a carbon," Dunc pointed out.

"And the original—"

"Is in the hands of a man even you can't touch."

"I see." Mr. David met his gaze. "I think I know what you want. No problem of course, but if you could spell it out . . ."

The cold inside Dunc was now glacial. "You said it yourself. You know who and you know why. Eye for eye."

Mr. David nearly smiled. "You're a careful, clever man."

Chapter Fifty-one

They leaned back against the headboard of Drinker's bed, naked, sated, sharing a cigarette. April giggled.

"On Friday evening we dine *à la chinoise* with Lee Fong, then go to the Alcazar Theater. Eight P.M. curtain. They plan to sleep on board the *Doubloon*, but it will be unguarded from six P.M. Friday until midnight at least."

"Does murder always make you so happy?" Drinker growled.

"Only Harry's. When will you go in? When will it go off?"

"Go in, nine-thirty. Go off, ten sharp Saturday morning."

"Then I'll have him call me on the ship-to-shore phone at nine-fifty-five for a big surprise. Harry loves surprises." She sobered. "But you won't love this very much, darling. This is the last time we can see each other until we open those lockboxes and get all that lovely money a week from Monday."

"No, goddammit!" said Drinker in an angry voice.

"You of all people should understand. Your military record shows you're a demolitions man, I may have been seen going in and out of this apartment. If someone sees Harry's boat blow up . . ."

"Good answer," he agreed reluctantly. "It makes sense."

"For that," she said, sliding down in the bed while Drinker remained where he was, "you deserve a special treat."

*   *   *

It was after 3:00 A.M. Saturday when Pepe finished his gig at the Roundup and drove back to his luxury hotel in downtown Reno. The snow was gone, spring was on its way.

He let himself into his room, clicked the light switch. Nothing happened. Light filtering through the curtains showed him two shadowy waiting figures.

"You're late, sweets," said a soft voice Falkoner would have known. Pepe just had time to make the sign of the cross.

Ferris Besner had spent the night with April in Harry Wham's outsize bed, but was still worried about Drinker.

"April, don't forget—mean and tricky and smart . . ."

"Sweetheart, when the banks open Monday morning you will do your exquisite forgeries of Harry's signature, we will empty the boxes, and we will be gone. Free, free, free!"

"But Drinker Cope *is* a detective, darling."

"He's been well paid. Also, he's a murderer, or soon will be. We just make an anonymous call to the police once we're out of their reach."

At 9:55 they were waiting at the special wireless phone Harry had installed for direct connections with the *Doubloon*. The Piper-Heidsieck was in the silver bucket with two paper-thin crystal champagne flutes waiting beside it.

The phone rang at 9:58.

"Hi, darling! What's this big surprise I'm going to love?"

Sixty seconds. Fifty-five. His life was passing before her eyes. "I know all about your Spanish gold, Harry. Only it's Mexican and it doesn't come from any galleons."

Harry's voice carried respect. "So you found out."

Fifteen. Fourteen. Thirteen . . .

"On Monday Ferris and I are clearing out all your safe-deposit boxes and going away together. I *hate* you. I hope—" The receiver erupted with a brutal, massive noise that made her hold it away from her ear. "I hope you're in hell, darling."

Ferris was twisting the wire off the champagne's cork.

"Exit Harry Wham," she said to him, hanging up the phone.

*   *   *

"Exit Harry Wham," said the big tousle-haired man. "Not a bad last line. Harry Wham will certainly have to be dead."

Lee Fong was at the wheel; the *Doubloon* was in blue water. Harry scaled the phonograph record labeled *Side I* EXPLOSIONS AND DETO-NATIONS (*Exterior Reverberations*) over the side into the blue-gray chop. It sank instantly.

"Where'd you get it?" he asked.

Drinker Cope said, "That little theatrical supply house near the Curran Theater. What happens now?"

He nudged Drinker's large canvas bag with his toe. "A fishing boat will carry you and your twenty-five percent of the loot to Monterey. A car will bring you back up here."

"And you?"

He swung an arm to indicate the breadth of the world.

"No bullshit now, Drinker. Why'd you tell me about it?"

When Cope moved the canvas bag with the toe of his shoe in turn, Wham shook his head.

"No, it had to have been more than just money. You couldn't have been getting tired of April, and don't tell me any crap about lives getting saved on Iwo Jima. Just for the record, I never was a marine captain on Iwo. Not anywhere, not ever."

For once in his life, Drinker was almost speechless.

"But . . . but . . . the photos, the medals . . ."

"Fakes. During the war I flew supplies into China over the hump from Burma. A lot of us got moderately rich on that run. Jewels, jade, carved ivory—once all the struts and aileron wires of my plane were made of almost pure gold."

"Some detective," said Drinker sheepishly. The two big men were silent for a time, each with his own thoughts. Then Drinker said, "I put a mike in your bedroom and a listening post in the basement. April and Besner talked a lot, made a lot of plans."

Harry nodded in acknowledgment. Drinker gestured.

"We'd better throw the bomb overboard. It isn't connected to the dry-cell, but dynamite is dynamite, after all."

"It's not on board, it's under my bed, or it was." Harry looked at his watch. "It was set to go off twenty seconds ago."

Drinker jerked upright, his eyes shocked, even frightened. "Jesus Christ! April and Besner would have been just . . ."

"Exit *April* Wham," said Harry, stone-faced. "Besner is just a bonus. I didn't mind her trying to blow me away, Drinker—there was money involved. But"—he motioned toward the slight, silent man at the wheel—"she hardly knew Lee Fong."

Drinker retrieved his car from the St. Francis Yacht Club lot where he'd left it at nine that morning, after listening to April's final bedroom session with Besner. Compared to April, Sherry would be Cream of Wheat to the rarest, bloodiest steak imaginable, but she had one huge advantage: she was still alive.

Then he laughed aloud. He had *real money*. He'd never have to kiss a client's ass again, never have to sleep with Sherry again. He'd thought what he'd gotten from Kiely's safe-deposit box in Kansas City had been a lot of money, and he'd killed two men to get it—Earl with his .45, Emmy with his Plymouth when he'd found the man comatose in the parking lot near the Barbary Coast Hotel. But this was a hell of a lot more money, and he hadn't had to kill anyone at all to get it.

He found parking around the corner on Green, walked down Gough to his apartment with a satchel in each hand. He didn't want to leave the bomb-making stuff in the trunk overnight.

Dunc was sitting on the front steps in a tan-colored overcoat, a dark blue navy watch cap pulled down over his ears.

Drinker unlocked the door. "You look like a fucking bum."

"I've been on the road, I sort of ran out of money."

Drinker started up the stairs, Dunc tagging along behind. Opening his apartment door, he'd half expected April's perfume to waft out at him, but the place was cold and dreary. He tossed the satchels in a corner, turned on lights, lit the wall heater. Dunc stood looking around; it was his first time there.

"I'm making coffee, you want some? I ain't got any tea."

A head shake. Drinker busied himself in the kitchen; there was a strange look in the kid's eyes, half-mad, half-sad. The scar from the crash was very vivid above his left eye.

"You okay after the concussion and all?"

"Yeah, sure, fine."

Drinker leaned back against the counter, his arms folded.

"Are you coming back to work for me again? You're a damned good investigator and—"

"That's what you told me in L.A. at the Labor Day picnic, wasn't it? If we hadn't gotten into the shooting contest you'd have hooked me some other way." Drinker felt a stab of unease. "Pepe the piano player hired you to keep an eye on me."

"Pepe . . . Jesus Christ, kid, I met him for the first time at that Reno steakhouse. I think you ought to—"

"I'd told him I was coming up here. I'd also told him about busting up a wetback smuggling ring. You praised me for that at the picnic, but my name hadn't turned up anywhere, not once."

Drinker poured himself coffee. "Sure you don't want—"

"No, I'm fine."

He carried his steaming mug into the living room and sat in the leather easy chair, had a momentary vivid image of April in this same chair, opening her legs . . . He made a decision.

"All right, yeah, I was down in L.A. on other business and I got hired by the piano player to get a line on you. But . . ."

Dunc was sitting on the straight-back chair across the room. He took off the navy watch cap.

"You played me like a fisherman plays a trout, played me up here, gave me a job so you could keep an eye on me for Pepe." His face tightened. "Pepe got Penny killed, Drinker."

"What are you talking about? She ran off the road—"

"I saw the cut line and sawed steering linkage myself."

"Aw, Jesus Christ, Dunc! I'm so fucking sorry . . ." He took a gulp of coffee. "Listen, we can go after him! We—"

"I've already gone after him—through Mr. David." Dunc was on his feet, striding up and down the room, ignoring Drinker's reaction to what he had said. "When I told you we were getting married in Reno, you called Pepe to alert him. He told you to steer me his way, he'd decided I was dangerous because of Las Vegas, so—"

Drinker had to ask it. "You never suspected him at all?"

"Not until Penny was dead—and then it was too late." He shook his head. "Just a fucking dumb naive punk kid, Drinker."

Drinker sighed and slumped lower in his chair, knees apart, hands hanging down between them. Dunc kept on pacing.

"But Pepe didn't fuck up the Grey Ghost's brakes and steering. He hired the man on the scene to do that for him."

"Hey, just a minute! You're not saying that I—"

"Of course I am, Drinker. Who else could have done it? That was the call you got—there was no office break-in."

Drinker slumped lower so his right hand was now touching the inside of his left calf. Dunc had stopped pacing.

"You're dead wrong," Drinker said in a weary voice.

Now he was touching the butt of the little .25-caliber backup piece he always carried strapped inside his left ankle.

Dunc went right on. "And then on Monday morning you called to send us flying down the mountain as fast as we could . . ."

Drinker said abruptly, "Did you come here to kill me, kid?"

"I don't know, Drinker. I just—"

Drinker jerked the six-inch .25-caliber revolver from its ankle holster and shot Dunc from six feet away.

The little slug tugged the sleeve of Dunc's overcoat, but by then he was spinning to his left, moving fast, his gloved left hand jerking out Drinker's office gun, a Colt .38 revolver, firing it while on the move.

The slug entered Drinker's right temple from nine inches away, bulging his eyes and slapping his head to one side as its force drove him over against the left arm of the leather chair.

Dunc stared wide-eyed, shocked, at the corpse he had made. If he hadn't meant to kill Drinker, why had he brought Drinker's office gun with him?

Larkie straightened up, holding his bloody prize above his head; then he threw it far out into the swamp.

Suddenly Dunc knew, with a blinding clarity, that this was what the Las Vegas priest had been talking about. Not what he *thought* he had been talking about, but what he had been. Because the weight of guilt over Penny's death had shifted, just a little, inside Dunc. Not the feeling of loss, but the guilt. What had Penny said in the dream? *Now you can go on.*

What said the Old Testament? Eye for eye. Simple justice.

He said to the corpse, "I'm still a better fucking shot than you are, Drinker."

No one was ringing the bell, no one was pounding on the door. The killing could have happened in a vacuum. So go on. Think it through. Blow-back particles on Drinker's right hand. Powder-scorching around the bullet hole in his temple—a bullet from his own gun . . . Suicide.

Dunc picked up the ankle gun, pocketed it. Wrapped Drinker's right hand around the Colt .38, then let hand and revolver fall naturally. What else? *Bullet hole!*

He found Drinker's slug lodged in the wall six inches from a framed picture. Dig it out, or leave it there? But on the far wall was a larger picture, a Maxfield Parrish print, blue ladies in diaphanous gowns with blue mountains behind them. He switched the prints. Maxfield Parrish covered the bullet hole.

He was halfway out the door when he remembered the ankle holster. *Empty* ankle holster. He went back and got it.

At 7:58 Monday morning Dunc trudged up the inner stairs at ED-WARD COPE—INVESTIGATIONS. The newspapers had carried the explosion at the Whams' flat, two dead. April—identified from the teeth in the half of her lower jaw they'd found—and an unidentified male too lightly built to be her husband.

In an allied story a private investigator who had been a marine demolitions expert in the war had been found dead in his apartment, an apparent suicide, with a large amount of unexplained cash and the remnants of a bomb-making kit . . .

Sherry was at her desk, her eyes red with weeping.

"I don't believe it," she said to Dunc.

"That Drinker would set a—"

"He'd kill anybody for money. But kill himself? Never!"

"He kept bad company," Dunc said in a soft voice.

Her gaze faltered. "Dunc, I'm so sorry about Penny . . ."

"Yeah. Me too."

There were volumes in the exchange. She ducked her head, ran for the stairs, ran down them, went out. He stood as if listening for something, then walked over to Drinker's private office. He stood in the open doorway, looking in, overwhelmed with rage, anguish, love, regret, nostalgia, hatred.

All gone. Everything. His beloved Penny. His child. Drinker. Even Sherry. His dreams of being a writer. His joy at being a private eye. He'd clean out his desk, get his stuff from Ma Booger's, say goodbye to Mickey, and hit the road again.

To go where? To do what?

There were tentative female steps on the stairs. He felt an upsurging in his chest. Sherry, coming back. They would sit down, talk it through, hash it out, get everything out in the open.

But it was a middle-aged woman, well dressed, her face crumpled with loss and indecision. She paused at the top of the stairs. "Mr. Cope?"

"Mr. Cope . . . died suddenly over the weekend. The office is no longer—"

"Oh. I'm so sorry." She made a vague gesture of regret, but she might not have heard him. "I had hoped to hire him . . . My daughter . . . she's only sixteen, and I'm afraid she's run away with a man . . .

much older than herself . . ." She wrung her hands with the over the-
atricality of true emotion. "What am I to do?"

Dunc felt an inner stirring. He was surprised to realize he was
standing aside as if to usher her into Drinker's private office, and she
obediently went past him. But Drinker was dead.

"Please sit down," he heard himself saying. He sat down himself in the
swivel chair, drew over a memo pad, and picked up a ballpoint pen from
the blotter. He began, "Maybe you'd better give me the particulars . . ."